RESCUING EVE

ELLIE MASTERS

JEM Publishing

Image/art disclaimer: Licensed material is being used for illustrative purposes only. Any person depicted in the licensed material is a model.

Editor: Erin Toland

Proofreader: Rox LeBlanc

Interior Design/Formatting: Ellie Masters

Published in the United States of America

JEM Publishing

Paperback ISBN: 978-1-952625-24-4

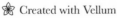 Created with Vellum

Dedication

This book is dedicated to my one and only—my amazing and wonderful husband.

Also by Ellie Masters

The LIGHTER SIDE

Ellie Masters is the lighter side of the Jet & Ellie Masters writing duo! You will find Contemporary Romance, Military Romance, Romantic Suspense, Billionaire Romance, and Rock Star Romance in Ellie's Works.

YOU CAN FIND ELLIE'S BOOKS HERE:
ELLIEMASTERS.COM/BOOKS

Military Romance
Guardian Hostage Rescue Specialists

Rescuing Melissa

(Get a FREE copy of Rescuing Melissa

when you join Ellie's Newsletter)

Alpha Team

Rescuing Zoe

Rescuing Moira

Rescuing Eve

Rescuing Lily

Rescuing Jinx

Rescuing Maria

Bravo Team

Rescuing Angie

Rescuing Isabelle

Rescuing Carmen

Rescuing Rosalie

Military Romance

Guardian Personal Protection Specialists

Sybil's Protector

Lyra's Protector

The One I Want Series

(Small Town, Military Heroes)

By Jet & Ellie Masters

EACH BOOK IN THIS SERIES CAN BE READ AS A STANDALONE AND IS ABOUT A DIFFERENT COUPLE WITH AN HEA.

Saving Abby

Saving Ariel

Saving Brie

Saving Cate

Saving Dani

Saving Jen

Rockstar Romance

The Angel Fire Rock Romance Series

EACH BOOK IN THIS SERIES CAN BE READ AS A STANDALONE AND IS ABOUT A DIFFERENT COUPLE WITH AN HEA. IT IS RECOMMENDED THEY ARE READ IN ORDER.

Ashes to New (prequel)

Heart's Insanity (book 1)

Heart's Desire (book 2)

Heart's Collide (book 3)

Hearts Divided (book 4)

Hearts Entwined (book5)

Forest's FALL (book 6)

Hearts The Last Beat (book7)

ONE

Eve

2 MONTHS AGO

~

HELPLESSNESS IS MY NEW NORMAL.

If not for the protection of my Deverough name, nothing would separate me from the others trapped in this living hell. I walk around free, the *honored* guest of Tomas Benefield, a man who makes his living ruining human lives while they endure horror upon horror. It's been five weeks of living hell, and I don't think I can survive much more.

"Miss Deverough..." One of the guards pokes his head inside my room.

"Yes?"

"Mr. Benefield requests your presence."

Orders are given and I obey. I'm but one step from a slave. The other girls are slaves. I'm going to say that again because I can't believe something like this exists.

They are slaves.

Those girls are trained and sold like chattel. They're nothing more than a commodity moving through the despicable industry of sex trafficking. There's no humanity in this godforsaken place. There's no escape.

I tap my foot and my knee bounces with nervousness. Sitting in front of the makeup mirror, I make myself beautiful for a monster.

I make myself beautiful... I give a sharp shake of my head, but it doesn't help. This isn't a dream. It's all too real.

This is my new life, a living horror show. Unlike the girls, however, I'm treated as a guest. Although an uncomfortable shift hangs in the air. It's been five weeks. Five long weeks waiting for the ransom demand to be met.

"I'm just finishing up."

The guard kicks his heel against the doorjamb. "Now, Miss Deverough."

"Of course." I deliberately set down my makeup brush, making it look like my compliance is my wish rather than Benefield's demand. "Where will I find him?"

"His office."

"Thank you." I glance into the mirror, catching the guard's eye in the reflective glass.

He holds my eye for a moment, then turns with a derisive snort. None of the guards are allowed to touch me, and it irritates them. It's a very small freedom, and I cling desperately to it.

For weeks, Tomas Benefield tells me he will let me go, yet here I remain, his *special guest.*

It's all an act, me getting dressed like I'm going out for a night on the town.

While the guard waits, I take one last look in the mirror and put on my game face. Turning with a false smile, I rise gracefully and walk out of my room as if it's my choice to do so.

The guard follows. He'll trail discreetly behind me, ensuring I don't make a break for it. Like there's anywhere to go.

Ignoring him, I begin the long trek to Benefield's office.

We pass a multitude of girls, all in training, performing their domestic chores: cleaning, polishing, vacuuming, and more. They do it without clothes. Clothing is a reward, which must be earned.

They look at me, or rather through me, with heart-wrenching

vacancy in their eyes. Their innocence fled, along with any hope or any dreams they may have had for a life they will never get to lead.

Trafficked for their beauty, they're among the taken. I am too, but I was kidnapped and am being held for ransom. Those girls come from homes without the resources to buy their freedom. I, on the other hand, come from wealth.

The Deverough name is well known in the shipping industry, and my father commands the resources needed to break me free of this madness.

But something's not right.

The Retreat, which is now my prison, is beyond extravagant. It's a massive display of one man's wealth and the power he wields.

Luscious vegetation spills out of manicured flower beds set in interior courtyards. Fountains spray water in complex designs. Colorful birds squawk in their lavish cages. Three tiny monkeys grasp the bars of their enclosure. They're prisoners just like me.

Stone archways sit atop intricate columns and line the exterior of the courtyard. Between the columns, frescos of impressive artistic talent draw the eye. There's even a butterfly and hummingbird enclosure for the guests to enjoy.

So much money.

I thought the Deverough's commanded wealth, but this is beyond comprehension.

Outside Benefield's office, I take in a deep breath and brace myself. A knock on the door is initially met with silence, but then his gruff voice calls out.

"Come."

I push on the door, but the guard behind me places his palm on the rough wood and forces it open. I step under his arm and into Benefield's domain.

A sigh of relief escapes me. It's just him. No naked slaves with vacant stares.

"You wanted to see me?"

"Yes, my dear. Come over here, where the light is brightest." He points to a window. My stomach sinks when he grabs a newspaper.

I move woodenly to where he instructs and wait.

"Take this." He hands me the local paper. Everything's in Spanish. I don't know the language, but I can see the date. "Hold it up, just under your chin."

May 7th.

This marks the third time he's made me hold up a newspaper while he snaps a photo of me.

"Smile, luv." He holds up his phone. "You can do better. Your father will want to know I'm treating his little girl well."

I'm not a little girl. I'm twenty. I smile for the photograph while my hands shake and make the newspaper rustle.

"Ah, now that is a good shot. You have the most amazing eyes." He takes a step toward me while I force myself not to take a step back. Benefield thrives on fear and I won't give him any more than absolutely necessary. "Let's get a close-up of that date. Hold the paper next to your eyes and smile."

I do as Benefield commands.

"One. Two. Three. Say cheese!" He snaps more than one photograph, then takes a moment to look at them on his phone. "Yes, yes, this will do nicely." He holds his hand out, palm up, and I give him the newspaper.

I want to ask why my father isn't paying the ransom, but I keep my lips pressed into the best false smile I can manage. The first photograph was taken one week after my abduction. The second, I think they call it a *proof of life* photo on the television shows I watch, was taken after spending three weeks in this hellish place. It's been a little over a month now and I can't help but wonder.

Why aren't you paying the ransom?

I don't understand what's going on. My father might be many things. Our relationship is beyond strained, but he would never intentionally leave me in a place like this.

Icy tendrils creep down my spine. Is my father not meeting Benefield's ransom demands?

Is Benefield holding out for a larger payday?

I don't know what's happening, and it's driving me insane.

Five weeks.

Too many days come, and too many days go. Days turn to

weeks, and weeks turn to months. I'm the captive of a silver-tongued madman speaking a mouthful of lies.

Five weeks is one week longer than the span of time a girl suffers beneath this roof. They spend one month being trained, sexually abused, and physically beaten, until any fight within them dies. Misery unites them, and maybe that gives them strength? Or maybe it steals their hope?

I wouldn't know. I'm not one of them.

Yet. I'm not one of them—yet.

Nevertheless, each day is a living nightmare, and I wonder when my status will change. When will I become one of them?

The longer I'm here, the more I believe I'm never escaping this nightmare. But if I do, I'll make it my life's work to bring men like this down. Whatever it takes, I'll learn how to fight. I'll learn how to win. Justice will be served.

But first, I need to survive. I need to find a way out of here. If I don't, my future is written in the leering stares of the guards I pass and in the frank admiration from the guests when I'm near.

The guests.

How to describe those lecherous bastards? Too rich and too bored, they'd rather destroy a life than find a woman willing to stand by their side. They're rotten people. Rotten men inside and out.

Reality is slowly settling in and I don't like my options. My heart rattles around inside my ribcage. Spurred to restless agitation by yet another ransom demand.

"You may go." With a flick of his wrist, I'm dismissed. Before I reach the doorway, he calls out, "Do not be late for dinner, my love. I expect you to be on time."

"Yes, of course." I take great care to be early to those hideous meals, but I was a minute late last night.

"My guests enjoy your company."

I'm sure they *do not.* His guests make my stomach churn.

"You should relax in the spa this afternoon. You look stressed." His brows pinch together, and if I didn't know better, I'd say he really was concerned about my mental state of mind.

He's not. Benefield is a monster.

As for me, tension swirls on every breath and surges with chaotic energy in my veins. It knots between my shoulder blades and climbs up the back of my neck where it settles, making my head pound with the beginning of a migraine.

"That sounds wonderful. Thank you."

I hate the spa. It's only ever used by the girls who are being put up for auction. Benefield wants them looking their best as he sells them to the highest bidder.

I'd refuse, but I know better than to upset my monstrous host.

As I make my way to the spa, I walk on pins and needles, doing everything in my power not to be noticed, which is silly.

Everybody notices me.

I've been singled out for special treatment, deference extended to me where it's not for any of the other girls.

Unable to get over the feeling my fortune is shifting from bad to worse, I'm on edge, and the fear I battle, each and every day, takes on a sharper edge.

It digs in and takes root.

I feel it in the air—a change coming—it swirls around me, infesting the cloying humidity that thickens each breath. It lingers in the muggy tropical heat and saps my strength.

I cross an extravagant courtyard, guard in tow. Landscaped to perfection, my surroundings display the opulence and power of the owner.

I'm a captive within a secret compound, hidden somewhere in the forests of a tropical paradise. I believe I'm in Colombia. At least that's where the shipping container arrived.

The shipping container.

Thirteen of us endured a tortuous journey locked inside a cargo container. Opened once a day to provide meager rations of food and water and to remove a foul bucket of waste; we survived only to endure what came next.

After making port in Colombia, half were loaded onto the back of one truck, and the rest were loaded onto the back of another. I have no idea what happened to the seven girls in that other truck, but I know what happened to the five who went with me.

We came here.

Over the next three weeks, those girls were tortured, trained, and forced to serve. They learned how to serve the needs of monstrous men and how to turn their anger, fear, and hatred into docile obedience. One month later, they were sold and a new set of girls arrived.

This is how I measure the passing of time; each month, a new shipment arrives, and a little piece inside of me dies.

The lingering effects of my summons throw my body into chaos. Adrenaline races around my body. My heart picks up its frantic pace, galloping around the inside of my chest as it feeds off my adrenaline-fueled fear. But while I may be shaking inside, outwardly, I display the calm, cool demeanor of the socialite I was born and raised to become.

I hurry along, trying to ignore the beauty and elegance all around me. It's all a lie.

Breezeways break up the thick walls and pull the eye away from the multi-leveled turrets, manned day and night by diligent guards. Designed to keep slaves inside and outsiders where they belong, it serves one purpose.

I'm locked inside a fortress. Wrought iron gates give the illusion of decoration, but they are the bars of my prison.

Men with depraved tastes are entertained here. Tonight, they'll congregate in the banquet hall for the finale of their weeklong depravity.

It's Auction Night.

The last week of every month, men descend on this lush paradise to sample the merchandise and ultimately purchase the greatest indulgence: a broken woman formed into a docile slave.

I continue over the courtyard's travertine stone, making my way around the fountains and weaving between the locked cages holding parrots, macaws, and cute little spider monkeys.

I pass by the Oasis, a room designed to look like the inside of a sultan's harem, and hold my head high. The deep rumble of men's voices carries in the air. The lightness of feminine sounds layer on top, light titters that are fake but sound real. The girls are well-trained to please. Failure isn't an option.

To the uninitiated, it looks like a sensual paradise, but all I see are ugly men, rotten to the core, touching girls too fearful to pull away.

I endure the stares of our most recent guests. Their interest heightened only because I am untouchable.

Mr. H, in particular, can't keep his oily gaze off of me. An oil tycoon from Texas, he's absent morals and lacks basic human decency.

A shiver works its way down my spine as his hungry gaze sweeps over me. His slow blink churns my gut, and the way he makes a point to lick his lips brings bile rising to the back of my throat. His desire is quickly turning into obsession.

The guards never touch me. They're not allowed that privilege, and they're paid handsomely in the brothels outside these walls. I know because they speak of nothing else when they're around me.

Tomas Benefield is the man I fear. Master of this place, he holds supreme power over his domain. On his whim, I can be given to any of these men: guest or guard.

He's waiting on my ransom, and I wonder again what could be taking my father so long to meet this monster's demands. When does my time run out?

TWO

Max

PRESENT DAY

∽

DESPITE CONCERTED EFFORT ON OUR PART, JULIAN TOWNSEND remains tight-lipped, tenaciously holding onto the information Alpha team is determined to extract from the putrid excuse of a human.

"Bastard's stubborn." I lean against the metal bulkhead with my second, Knox, while the rest of Alpha team interrogates our prisoner. The low drone of the trawler's engines vibrates through the steel.

"You don't say." Knox kicks a foot against the wall, bracing himself. He's bored and fidgety. We've been going at this for well over two hours. He glances at his watch. "You owe me." He sticks out his hand, palm up, and gives a little flick of his fingers. "Pay up."

"I really thought he would cave by now." Digging into the right breast pocket of my shirt, I pull out a raggedy button and slap it in Knox's hand. "How long did you say?"

"Two days." Knox's cheeky grin is in full force as he takes the worn button and shoves it into the front pocket of his pants. "I think he'll crack sooner, though. Look at him. Bastard pissed his pants."

Alpha team likes to bet. Like, how long it'll take before a prisoner cracks. Townsend is a rich, entitled prick. I thought for sure he would crack easily. The bastard's way more tenacious than I gave him credit for.

Griff's boots ring out on the metal deck plating as he moves in a slow circle around Townsend. Alpha team is out to sea, on a trawler in international waters. The air reeks of diesel fuel and steel. Then there's the stench of piss, sweat, and fear layered on top. Our prisoner is holding out longer than I thought, but he will crack.

"God, I hope it doesn't take that long."

"Griff bet five days," Knox says.

"I bet he did." And I wouldn't be surprised if Griff finds a way to extend Townsend's agony to hit that mark. His anger toward Townsend is as personal as shit gets.

"Well, the shithead is tougher than I thought." I blow out a breath.

Like Knox, I'm not a fan of hard interrogations. Not that I don't enjoy the finer art of forcing-people-to-tell-me-shit. It's just not my jam.

Unlike Griff.

Axel prowls in a circle around Townsend, looking intimidating as fuck, while Liam and Wolfe restrain Townsend in the metal chair. They don't need to hold him in place. That's what the duct tape is for. They're simply there to intimidate, a task for which they're well suited.

Griff, our interrogation expert, rears his arm back. As someone who's been on the receiving end of Griff's punches, I wince in anticipation.

His arm shoots forward. His fist connects with a solid thwack on Townsend's jaw. Our prisoner's head whips violently to the side. He sputters and coughs while Griff pulls back for another strike. Townsend's face looks like it's been put through a meat grinder: swollen, bruised, and cut from Griff's warm-up.

Yes, this is only the warm-up.

The real pain comes later, depending on how much self-preservation Townsend has.

Townsend is a buyer, part of a despicable trade peddling unwilling female flesh. His heinous obsession ruins the lives of so many. If it weren't for men like him, there wouldn't be a thriving human sex-trafficking trade at all.

He's not a key player within the organization, but according to Griff's woman, Moira, who the Guardians rescued not once, but three times, Townsend knows who to call to place an order for a slave. We need that information.

Once we have a way in, we'll take them down from the inside out. The Guardian HRS tech team is currently working on that, setting me up as a disgraced Guardian looking to make a quick buck selling slaves. But first, we need the information inside Townsend's head.

Townsend's body jerks as Griff strikes again. We're only at the beginning of the interrogation. Griff's focus is on softening Townsend, wearing him down, before the true interrogation begins. As he pummels Townsend, Axel fires question after question, not interested in answers just yet.

He and Griff work well together. They're messing with Townsend, making him believe answers are his path out of this.

As far as Moira goes, Townsend's interest in her began well over a year ago, back when she'd been a slave to the monstrous John Snowden, a man who no longer walks the earth, but whose business in trading slaves appears to be going strong despite his demise.

"Why do they all do the same damn thing?" Knox vents a sigh and leans his head against the wall.

My second doesn't appreciate the fine art of getting-people-to-tell-us-shit. He'd rather send Townsend six feet under and be done with this.

"What do you mean?"

"They all have to resist. Pretend they're a big man when we all know it's only a matter of time before they break. Seriously, he's wasting our time and making things ten times worse for himself."

"Stubbornness?" I press my lips together and debate sitting on the cold metal floor. Doesn't look like any of us are going anywhere anytime soon.

"It's not like he doesn't know how this is going to end." Knox closes his eyes. "It's torture watching this."

A heavy steel hatch to my left opens a crack. My boss, CJ, pokes his head in and scans the room. When he sees me, he gestures for me to join him outside. I kick off the wall and head to the door.

"Alpha-Two, I need you too." CJ steps back from the door. He joined us on the trawler for Townsend's interrogation. He leads Alpha, Bravo, Charlie, and Delta teams, and is my boss. The chain of command goes through him, to Sam who oversees all of Guardian Hostage Rescue Specialists, our unique company aimed at rescuing those who've been taken.

Knox joins us in the narrow passage while the rest of my team continues tenderizing Townsend and getting him ready to spill all his secrets.

"What's up?" The hatch closes behind us with a solid thud, leaving Townsend to his fate.

"We've got a new case," CJ says.

"We're working a case right now." I hitch a thumb over my shoulder. "He's inside that room." There's zero reason for CJ to pull us away from this interrogation.

"You'll understand in a moment." CJ leads us toward the galley of the trawler we currently call home. Interrogations like ours aren't exactly legal, breaking a slew of laws that could lead to lifelong incarceration if they happened on American soil.

We captured Townsend in California. Technically, we kidnapped him, but Townsend would be a fool to report us. He was in the middle of committing his own crime: kidnapping Moira. As for interrogations, those are complicated. We try not to do them on US soil. International waters, on the other hand, afford us the freedom to be brutally creative. Which is why we're bobbing like a cork in the deep blue sea. Our trawler drifts somewhere off the coast of California.

The three of us cram ourselves inside the trawler's small galley. Designed to hold eight, we're big men, and the room feels small with the three of us in it. Propped on the only table, a laptop streams a video feed. The table, like all the chairs, is bolted to the floor. That way, things don't move around in high seas.

We're currently blessed with nearly mirror-smooth waters, which is nice. I'm not much of a boat fan, which is funny considering I trained in the Navy to become a SEAL.

"Hi guys." Sam's brusque face stares out of the screen. He surveys the room, taking us all in, and gives a nod of approval.

"What's this about a mission?" I want to know why they're pulling us away from the interrogation.

"We secure?" Sam scans the room again, not that he can see anything outside the view of the camera.

"We're secure." CJ shifts in his seat and repositions the laptop to better fit us all within view of the camera.

"Good." Sam leans back. "I have a case for you."

"We're working a case right now." I can't help but respond abruptly. My place is with my team, extracting information from Townsend.

"You're going to find this one interesting," Sam pushes through.

"Getting information from Townsend is critical." My words come out argumentative. Can't help it, that's how I feel.

"Not arguing that, but this is a time-sensitive mission."

"Can't Charlie team take it? Or Delta?" I don't mention Bravo team. They're still two men down. Technically, we're a man down as well. The injury to Griff's leg isn't fully healed, and he doesn't have medical clearance to operate.

"They're tied up. Not to mention this is right up your alley."

No way am I arguing with the head of Guardian HRS, but this goes against standard protocol.

"What's the mission?" Technically, as Alpha team leader, taking on a mission is my call. Refusal is an option. Sam and CJ would never force an operation on a team if the leader didn't agree.

"Evelyn Deverough," Sam says.

A picture of a breathtaking brunette fills the screen. Sam's image shifts to a tiny box in the upper right-hand corner. Not that I pay any attention to him. I can't take my eyes off the striking woman filling the screen.

College-aged, she looks out from the photo with mesmerizing eyes the color of turquoise seas. A radiant smile lifts her entire expression into a glowing display of jaw-dropping beauty.

"She's a looker." Knox shifts in his seat.

A looker?

She's far more than that. The girl is touched by angels. The hand of the divine had a part in sculpting her exquisite features.

"She's been taken." Sam waits for our response, but I'm not sure what kind of reaction he's looking for.

Evelyn Deverough's bewitching beauty mesmerizes me, but there's more. My protective instincts rage against the injustice. Anger pulses in my veins, kicked into a frenzy by the beating of my heart. A strange feeling overcomes me, a possessiveness I've never felt before. I don't understand it. I've never felt like this with any of our other rescues, but I feel as if I just got struck by lightning.

There's no doubt I'll accept this mission. However, I still need details.

"What's the story?"

"It's an interesting one." Sam's image enlarges as Evelyn's shrinks. He stares out of the screen with a fixed expression.

"Why does it feel like I should know her?" There's something about her face tickling my memory bank. I've seen her before. I'm sure of it. There's no way I'd forget that face.

Sam introduces another photo. It covers Evelyn's captivating face. Only, in this image, there's no radiant smile. No stunning beauty. The only thing breathtaking about it is the way fear distorts her otherwise striking features.

Wide eyes. Furrowed brow. Her smile is gone. Her radiance extinguished. Her brilliant eyes dimmed.

"Holy shit." I've seen that photo before.

"Is that…" Knox leans forward. His brows push together and deep furrows crease his forehead. "That was taken months ago." He looks expectantly to Sam. "Why are we only now getting involved?"

"Indeed, it was," Sam affirms with a sharp nod. "Three months ago."

Several months ago, human traffickers snatched Zoe Lancaster, Axel's woman, off the streets of Cancun during spring break. She and twelve other women were loaded into a cargo container and shipped to Colombia where six of those women were brutally murdered. Zoe would've been the seventh if the Guardians hadn't rescued her in time.

Evelyn's picture, along with the other girls, was taken as a trophy by one of the men who held the girls in Cancun.

"Who's the client?" I can't tear my gaze off Evelyn's photograph. "And why now?"

"Her father." Sam leans back.

"Why is he only now looking for her?" We're Guardians, men who'll do anything to rescue those who've been taken, but Evelyn's case is cold, like dead cold. "What has he been waiting on all these months?" Something doesn't add up, but I can't put my finger on it.

"Carson Deverough has been paying escalating ransom demands."

"Come again?"

"You heard me."

"That doesn't make sense." I tap the table. The image on the screen shakes as the laptop bounces. "This isn't the kind of operation that demands ransom, and they sure as shit would never relinquish merchandise once they have it."

"Exactly," Knox agrees. "Miss Deverough is much more valuable as a commodity than…"

"Thirty million." Sam rubs at his jaw. "Mr. Deverough took out kidnapping insurance on his daughter."

"Thirty?" I tap the side of my head, sure I heard that wrong. "Million?"

"Yes." Sam nods.

"Kidnapping insurance?"

"Correct, and he's running out."

"He's running out of a thirty million dollar policy? Explain." I glance at Knox, brows pinched with confusion.

"One week after Evelyn was kidnapped, her father received the first demand. That was April 1ˢᵗ and it was for one million dollars."

"I take it he paid it?"

"He did, but they didn't release his daughter. Two weeks later, he received the next demand. This time it was for five million."

"Is she alive?" I can't help it, but something doesn't add up.

"They sent proof of life."

"I take back what I said." I gnaw at my lower lip and mull over what I'm seeing. "So, he paid six million for his daughter?"

"Correct."

"But they didn't deliver her."

"Also correct."

"They're fleecing him." I give a shake of my head.

"That's our take on it. After he delivered the first five million…"

"First?" Knox's brows climb up his forehead.

"Yes. First. The next demand for ten million came the first week of May. Along with a picture of her holding a newspaper." Sam flashes another image on the screen.

It's Evelyn Deverough holding a newspaper with a fake smile on her lips. The girl looks terrified.

"A month ago, a fourth demand was made for another ten million."

"Don't tell me he paid that too?"

Sam shakes his head. "He did. Ransom paid on June fifteenth."

"Damn. That's impressive."

"He says they give him a week to collect and deliver the funds. He follows through. They fail to release his daughter and a week later increase the ransom."

"Fuckers." I can't help but glare at the screen.

"He expected to hear from them on the twenty-first. That would've been seven days after the last delivery."

"I take it he hasn't heard from them?"

"Nothing. No photo. No ransom demand."

"They fleeced him for twenty-six million. I bet they're done with him."

"And that's why he finally contacted us."

"Bastard should've called us after the first phone call."

"Not arguing that, and there's nothing we can do about it now. Our mission is to bring his daughter home."

Slaves are expensive, for many reasons. The operation we're tracking sells girls for anywhere from a few hundred grand to a million, maybe two million tops. I've never heard of them auctioning off a girl for more than that amount.

"So, they found a cash cow, and a man desperate enough to answer their ransom demands with money." Knox slams his fist into the top of the table.

"Correct."

"But still." I lean forward. "It's been months. Why didn't he go to the authorities? Or hire us back then?"

"Threats." The muscles of Sam's jaw bunch. "They told Mr. Deverough if he involved the police or any other law enforcement branch, they would start taking her fingers."

"Fucking pigs." Knox grinds his teeth beside me. An unsettling sound, it makes the hairs on the back of my neck stand up.

"Did they…?"

"No mutilation as far as we know. Our client states he met their demands, but they never released his daughter."

"And his policy is for thirty-million? I take it he realized what was happening?"

The kidnappers were taking more and more, until he was unable to pay.

"So, he's out twenty-six million. He's run out of cash." His policy only has four million left on it. "Why isn't the insurance company investigating?"

"They are, but this is beyond them."

No doubt about that. Something like this is way beyond what a pencil pusher can handle. "Why didn't his insurer contact us when this all started?"

"He told them not to because of the threats."

"I can't believe they listened." I pull at the roots of my hair. What a cluster fuck. "It's been three months."

"Yes."

"Anything could've happened to her."

"Which is why we need to get to her as soon as possible." CJ, who's been silent during the entire briefing, finally speaks up. "I want Alpha on this case. Bravo's not fully functional. Delta's on a domestic assignment. Charlie is working another case. I need your team."

"Okay, so the money is running out and he finally wised up that they're never going to release his daughter."

"Correct."

"And he hasn't approached the authorities?" I glance at Knox and read him. He's with me. We're taking this case. "And he told his insurer to stand down."

Knox leans back and crosses his arms. Like me, his attention hasn't shifted from Evelyn's terrified face.

"Yes, and yes. It's just us." CJ drums the table with his fingers. "When it became clear they were milking him for money, he realized they had no intention of letting her go."

"Any idea where they may be holding her?" I glance at CJ.

"The newspaper's in Spanish. Mitzy's looking." He gives a sharp shake of his head. "Our guess is Colombia."

"Well, shit." Now it's my turn to tap the table. "Someplace in Colombia is a lot of territory to cover." We've gone on missions with much less than this, but this one feels all kinds of complicated.

"Like I said, it's complicated." Sam picks the words right from out of my head.

"I'd say." I glance at Knox. "How are we expected to find her? She's a ghost."

"We're hoping the proof of life photos will help. Mitzy and her team are already working on it."

"How can that help?"

"Mitzy Magic?" Sam holds up his hands and shrugs.

It's a running joke. Mitzy accomplishes the impossible like it's nothing. It's magic.

"Let's hope she can work some of her famous magic." CJ shifts in his seat and crosses his arms.

"I want to meet Mr. Deverough in person. I have questions." From the look on Knox's face, he has questions as well.

"Already anticipated that. We're sending a helicopter to pick you up. You and Knox will meet with Carson Deverough. The rest of Alpha team will stay here and finish the interrogation." Sam lays out our next steps. "Once we have something actionable, I'll call them back."

At least Griff and the rest of the team can finish up with Julian Townsend. We're not abandoning that mission.

"You've got twenty minutes to pack your things before the helicopter gets here." CJ glances at his watch.

"Copy that."

With that, Knox and I go have a talk with the team. In less than twenty minutes, we board a helicopter and head back to land.

THREE

Eve

ONE MONTH AGO

~

"Evelyn." Tomas Benefield snaps his fingers, calling me to his side.

Despite the heat and humidity, he's decked out in black trousers and a crisp, white shirt with matching black jacket. The red satin of his tie matches the scarlet peeking out of his left breast pocket. Dark hair, slicked back, matches the onyx of his eyes. His oily gaze takes me in and sends another chill rushing down my spine.

I smile and give the slightest inclination of my head, as if it's my choice I join him here.

The stifling unease, which is my constant companion, intensifies. I brace for an uncomfortable evening and harden my emotions to withstand the torment that will come later tonight.

As for the guests, they are older men with too much wealth, too much power, and too much free time. The thought of any of them touching me makes me want to retch, but the only man in this room who will dare lay his hands on me is the man with the black hair and oily gaze.

Tomas Benefield, Satan in the flesh, Lucifer incarnate, with his infernal appetite for power and control, holds out a hand, beckoning me to his side.

He controls everybody and everything, then justifies what he does with ethics the devil would be proud to call his own.

I smile as I put on my game face for the evening. It's Auction Night. A banquet is being prepared. After all is said and done, six girls will take one further descent into a living hell as their new masters make them vanish from this world.

"I hope you had a good day with your guests?" Exchanging pleasantries with a monster is now a part of my new normal.

As for this day? Today is the day the guests get to sample the girls they will shortly bid upon.

"It has been a very good day." He draws me to him and insists on pulling me in to kiss my cheek. I hold perfectly still as he takes a deep breath, flooding his senses with the noxious perfume he forces me to wear. "How was your day? Did you enjoy the spa?"

The spa again.

He sends me to the spa on Auction Day, wanting me to look my best for the banquet and subsequent festivities.

I've been pampered from head to toe, and I do mean head to toe: hair, facial, manicure, pedicure, full body waxing, and a full body massage. I endured a luxurious day while the guests defiled the girls. Guilt weighs heavily on my shoulders.

"Yes, it was very relaxing." Eyes cast down, in deference to the power he wields, I wait to serve.

"Be a good girl and pour our drinks."

"Of course."

I glide around the room while powerful men debate the fate of the women kneeling at their feet. They masquerade as men of culture with their whiskies and Cuban cigars. Yet, they're obsessive in their quest to destroy innocent lives.

Prostrate and naked, the women are defenseless. Earlier today, they demonstrated new talents drilled into them through fear, coercion, and punishment.

I wish I could hold them and tell them things will be okay.

But they won't.

They never will be again.

We're all prisoners with one thing in common. Our fate is very grim.

The buttery smooth silk of my evening gown brushes across my skin. It's the exact same shade of scarlet as Benefield's tie, a subtle reminder to the guests that I belong to him.

I move around the room, serving the men their drinks.

"Come, Bethany." Mr. J barks at one of the girls, calling her to him. "I want to feel your hands on me again."

Bethany Weatherfield is all of eighteen. Younger than me, she's a pretty brunette with copper-colored eyes and a heart-shaped face. She's pretty—beyond pretty—and she's terrified. Mr. J shows far too much interest. At the banquet tonight, I bet he finalizes his purchase.

This is how time passes: week by miserable week, month by deplorable month.

How many girls have passed through The Retreat since I arrived? Thirty? Forty? It feels like hundreds.

If I'm ever released—and my hopes diminish with each passing day—I want a record of their stolen lives.

Poor Bethany crawls to Mr. J's feet.

"Touch me, girl." His command isn't one she can refuse.

I tense as her small hands reach for his ankles and travel up his shins. It's a delicate touch, a sensual touch, a touch drilled into her from the very first days she arrived. All the girls are trained to be visually, physically, and most importantly, sensually pleasing.

Tomas Benefield is selling more than a girl. He's selling an entire fantasy of devotion and abject adoration.

Mr. J slouches back and spreads his legs, preparing for what comes next. Bethany's hands travel up his legs and over his thighs, caressing and stimulating a monster.

Too disgusted to watch, I turn my back and fill the rest of the glasses with the finest whiskey money can buy.

The men sit in the Oasis. They gather here to finalize their selections before the banquet and subsequent auction that culminates their stay at The Retreat.

Conversation never falters as they speak of shooting clay pigeons, fishing in the sparkling waters, riding horses, or tearing up the trails on ATVs. But no matter how civil their words, none of these men are friends.

They're all adversaries, and the real power-struggle will occur later tonight when they battle against one another to secure the slave of their dreams. Money is power, and at The Retreat, that saying is never more true.

There are plenty of slaves-in-training to take care of their needs. As for the girls in this room, they will either leave with their new master or they'll be transferred to one of Benefield's many brothels scattered across the globe. Frankly, I don't know which fate is worse.

The idea of serving one man twists my stomach. To feed that vileness day after day surely is a living hell. But is a brothel any better? Instead of one man, there's a never-ending stream of monstrous men taking what's not freely offered.

There is another option, not one I would take.

In this place, the only freedom is through the sweet embrace of death. There have been three girls since I arrived who found their freedom through that route.

I no longer believe my father will come through and pay the ransom demands which hold me hostage. This is my fate.

It's a living nightmare, and I'm terrified I'll be next in line, auctioned off to the highest bidder.

"Come, Evelyn." Benefield pats the armrest of his plush leather chair.

No need to ask what he wants. Benefield isn't interested in me, not like that. He's far more interested in showing his guests that he gets to touch what they may not.

As for me, I waste no time responding to his call. With that same plastic smile fixed to my face, I gently lower myself down and sit on the armrest of his chair.

Benefield places a possessive arm around my waist while Bethany serves Mr. J's pleasure. I give in to the pressure of Benefield's embrace and lean against his hard, unforgiving, frame.

"Your father refused our demands again." Benefield's oily voice raises goosebumps on my arms.

I don't believe him. I can't. There's no scenario on earth that would make me believe Benefield. But my faith wavers. It weakens with the passing of every day.

I believe my father will do whatever it takes to bring me home. I just don't know if he can.

"Maybe he needs more time?" My voice shakes more than I like. There's no need to give Benefield more ammunition than he needs. As far as his patience, I only hope he has more than me.

"Your father has had plenty of time." Benefield snaps his fingers and points at Lisette, a pretty blonde with springy curls. "Attend to Mr. B, girl."

All the guests go by a single letter. Benefield calls the women, his prisoners, *girl*. Only the guests call them slaves. I don't know why, but for me, he uses my name.

No one uses my full name. My father calls me Evie. My friends call me Eve. Each time Benefield uses my full name, a little piece inside of me shrivels up and dies.

No man should have this much power over so many lives.

Wealth leads to power. Power wields control. I don't know who Benefield is except he must be an extraordinarily wealthy man.

As far as power and control go, Benefield's guests surrender all means of communication with the outside world while at The Retreat. The only thing they're allowed is the presence of a single bodyguard to protect their interests while they are guests beneath Benefield's roof.

"If your father does not come through by the end of this week..." He lets his words draw out, torturing me with what he might say next.

"My father will pay."

Benefield touches my thigh with the pad of his thumb and draws a lazy circle over the smooth silk of my gown. His vile touch makes me want to retch, but I control my emotions and hold onto the only power I wield in this despicable place. Benefield feeds off fear. I refuse to give him what he wants.

"If he does not, you will pay for him."

I shouldn't fall into his trap, but I can't help it. I give him exactly what he wants. I *feel* the blood drain from my face. I let my mouth gape and my eyes round in fear.

I can't stop my chin from trembling or the tears pricking at my eyes. I blink furiously, trying to regain my composure, but the damage is done. He got exactly what he wanted. My fear feeds his endless appetite to hurt others.

"Yes, my dear. One way, or another, you will earn your keep around here."

From the glimmer in his eyes, I don't want to know what that means. I duck my head and swallow against the bile rising in the back of my throat.

Death may not be such a bad option. I understand the decision those three girls made.

"My father will come through." Keeping my voice level comes with great difficulty. I have to believe my father will free me.

"If not..." He drags his hand down to my knee, then digs his fingers into my flesh until I hiss with pain. "Your lessons will begin."

I grasp his fingers as he digs in, hurting me. The first thing taken from the girls who pass through here is their resistance. I forgot that lesson amidst the pain.

Benefield tested me, and I failed. No doubt, I will pay for that later.

FOUR

Max

PRESENT DAY

~

As promised, a helicopter arrives in twenty minutes. I brief the rest of the team who will stay behind to extract the information we need from Julian Townsend.

Knox and I board the helicopter and rise above the trawler as we head back toward land. With exceptionally favorable weather, it's a pleasant flight; no chop and beautiful views of the ocean as we approach the California coastline. I'd call it idyllic if not for the reason behind our flight.

We land at Guardian HQ and take a moment for a meeting of the minds. That means bringing the incorrigible Mitzy into the mix. She is the brains behind our impeccable intelligence network and incredible technical team. We sit with her and Sam going over what we know about our new case and new client.

"Can you cut to the chase and tell us what's important?" I'm tired and strung out, which makes focusing difficult.

Mitzy's been talking nonstop for the past five minutes, inundating me and Knox with information overload, but I can't make head nor tails out of her techno-speak.

Sam and CJ mentioned she would be using the proof of life photos to narrow down where Eve's being held. Mitzy's giving a dissertation on the topic and the tech behind such a task.

"Actually, I need help from you." Mitzy pauses. Her gaze flicks upward as if she just had a new, and interesting, thought.

"Me?" I point to my chest. "How the hell am I going to help you? I've understood one word in twenty of whatever you said, and most of those words were when you were hemming and hawing."

Mitzy gives me a look, like I'm an idiot. "I do not hem and haw."

"Ummm… Okay… Ah…" I toss back her words and love the way her expression heats.

"Whatever." Dramatic eye roll engaged, Mitzy blows out a puff of air. "I need you to get them to take a picture outside."

"Outside?" My lips twist. "You want me to ask the kidnappers to take Eve outside for a photo op? I'm sure they'll be pleased as punch to do that." I inject as much sarcasm as I can, responding to such a ridiculous request.

"Yes, that's exactly what I want, a picture outside."

"And how does that help?"

There's absolutely no way that's happening, but I'm curious about Mitzy's thought process.

Mitzy blinks at me, like she's dealing with a child and must explain the most basic things. She's trying to maintain her cool, and I'm trying not to bust a smile.

Knox sits silently beside me, absorbing every detail. Sam sits across the table with a smirk plastered on his face. I don't know if that's for me getting Mitzy riled up or for her getting me all twisted. Honestly, it could go either way.

Annoying Mitzy is a fine art, one I excel at. Knox fights the grin tugging at the corner of his lips. He's stony-faced on the best days and is enjoying this far too much.

I try to reel it in, but I can't help it. Mitzy simply draws out the argumentative side of my character. It's probably because I hate it when people talk down to me, and Mitzy is exceptional at talking down to people.

It's something I should've gotten over years ago, but that kind of shit stays with a person for life. Growing up, I was never the smart guy. I was always the dumb jock busting my butt to barely pass my classes.

Physically, I excelled. Academically, I failed. I hated the smart kids back then, and I suppose I still hate them now. Only after high school, when I enlisted in the Navy, did I receive a diagnosis that explained my failures.

Dyslexia validated my academic difficulty, but the sting of all those comments about being a dumb jock sticks to this day.

I stay in my lane, and I expect Mitzy to stay in hers. Except it doesn't work. She doesn't understand why the rest of us can't keep up with her incredible brain.

"Asking kidnappers to parade their hostage outside for a photo op? You're crazy if you think something like that is going to happen."

"It helps," she says, "because we can confirm their location." Her lips press into a hard line. I'm not the only one holding back my frustration with this whole exchange. "That's what you want, right? Find the girl? Or did you forget what it is you do for a living?" Her growing frustration is fun to watch.

"We all want to bring Eve home." My tone takes on a sharp edge and a growl vibrates in the back of my throat. I will bring Eve home.

Want someone taken down? A facility breached? Need hostages rescued? I'm king of the hill in those scenarios.

Ask me about the intel and tech behind all of that, and I happily hand the reins over to her. She can be the queen all she wants when it comes to that. But when she openly questions my goals? All our goals? I won't let that slide.

We don't have time for this back and forth kind of crap. "Why would we consider something like that?" I inject enough impatience into my tone to get my point across without being rude about it.

Okay, I'm semi-rude bordering on rude-as-fuck, but what do I care?

"Evelyn is being held in Colombia," Mitzy states that as fact.

"Then why do you need me if you already know where she is?" I'm sure there's some kind of science behind it. Something to do with the position of the sun, or shadows, or some such shit like that. Or it could be as easy as reading the newspapers in the photographs. I don't understand Spanish, but someone here must.

While I'm happy we've narrowed down Evelyn's location, it's still not good enough. Colombia is known for its varied climate. Most of its population lives in the mountainous west or along the coastline to the north. Bogotá is their largest city, but Mitzy's given me no indication Eve is near the mountains or the coast.

"So, do you know anything? Just Columbia? Nothing more specific? Like a city?"

Without better intel, Eve's as good as lost.

"Of course, there's more to it." Mitzy props her hand on her hip and gives me one of her I-can't-believe-I-have-to-explain-this-kind-of-shit looks.

"Such as?"

"You're aware of geolocation?"

"Yes."

Geolocation is the nuts and bolts behind how my men get around. That, at least, is hard-wired into my brain. First in the military, where I trained to be a SEAL, and then with the Guardians as I learned how to use all their high-tech gear.

"Every picture taken from a cell phone is tagged with geolocation," she says.

"Right, and we all turn that shit off."

Everyone with an ounce of military training, or baseline paranoia about Big Brother, knows to turn off that particular feature on their cell phones.

Embedded in every picture is a set of GPS tags, which locate precisely where the photo was taken.

It's something the technical conglomerates imbed in their phones to assist in providing all manner of location services for their customers. Not only does it help influencers, friends, and families tag their locations on social media, but it also allows all the various apps to give directions to virtually any place in the world or to offer up any nearby restaurants, hotels, gas stations; pretty much anything a person might want. It does that because the phone always knows exactly where it is in the world.

Integrally connected to our digital footprint, nothing is ever truly private.

But geo-tagging can be turned off. It's relatively simple, although buried deep in the general settings of our phones.

"Exactly." Mitzy gives a nod like her dumbass student finally paid attention.

I love Mitzy to death. We all owe her our lives, in one fashion or another, but sometimes her superior attitude challenges my patience.

"Exactly, what?" I lean forward, waiting for her to spill. "I'd be pretty surprised if the men taking those photos failed to turn off that fancy little feature."

"They did, of course, but it's never really turned off." She cocks a hip forward, looking impressed with herself. "Or at least, the data is always there. It's a simple matter of turning it back on."

"Then why do you need me to get her kidnappers to take a picture outside? Just wave your magic wand and tell me where she is."

"That's what we want to do, but the geolocation is only so accurate. I want to match up what we have with Google Street View to get the most precise location possible."

"More precise than Columbia, I hope."

"Much more precise, asshole. Evelyn Deverough is being held in Colombia. We've stripped that much data from the metadata of the photos, but you want precise. Right?"

"Of course, I want precise." It amazes me how little privacy remains in the world. This is one bit of trivia I know. "But we're not making that request." I stand by my earlier decision.

"Why not?"

"It puts our target at risk."

Mitzy is wonderful, but she lives in a bubble. Intellectually, she understands we deal with some of the worst humanity has to offer, but that's where it stops. Her belief in human decency hasn't been shattered like the rest of us. It makes a difference in how we approach everything.

"I agree with Max." Knox shifts in his seat beside me, finally backing me up. "We're not going anywhere near that."

He's been quiet, listening, as Mitzy and I rile each other up. From the way Mitzy keeps yanking on her psychedelic hair, her frustration meter is pegging pretty damn high. That means, I'm in the lead.

"I agree with Knox." Sam leans back and taps the top of the table with his index finger. "If your intel is good enough, it makes more sense to get boots on the ground and eyes in the sky. We can do local recon."

"I need an outside view." Like a dog with a bone, Mitzy's not giving up.

"Why?" Sam asks.

Mitzy glances down. "There's this organization who can do exactly what we need."

"Do what?" I'm interested. Despite my difficult relationship with technology, I'm interested.

"They can pinpoint any location where a photograph was taken."

"That's a pretty bold claim and rather specific." I lean back and cross my arms. I'd like to see something like that in action. As if reading my mind, Mitzy pops up a picture on the screen.

"In this picture, they took the shape of the ridge in the background, coupled with the declination of the sun to locate this building in Madrid. That, along with the vegetation and that bird in the upper left of the photograph..."

"A bird?" Knox snorts beside me. "They used a bird to narrow it down?"

"You'd be surprised what you can do with the right equipment." Mitzy gives a little snort of indignation, not that Knox said anything that should twist her panties in a wad. "Anyway, the bird, along with that foliage, combined with street view cams and a bunch of fancy tech, which combines the date this was taken with the location of the sun, and..."

"Whatever." I'm tired of the tech talk. "You don't have that in any of the other photos? No outside views?"

"We don't."

"No declination of the sun?"

"No."

"Well, there's no way we're giving directives to these people without raising their suspicions." I look to Sam for support.

"You've got to work with what you have so far, Mitzy." Sam leans forward. The leather cushion of his chair creaks. "Put Max and the rest of the team as close as you can get. Send one of your dragons in the air, and we'll locate it the good old fashioned way."

"And what way is that?"

"Boots on the ground, babe." He gives her a wolfish grin, as if he maneuvered her into that answer.

"Don't call me babe." Her eyes pinch with irritation.

Mitzy's not happy, but she's not one to dismiss what we have to say. As tiresome as she can be, she listens to the input of the entire team. "I'll send what we have to my guys. See if there's anything more they can pin down."

"I know you'll be able to narrow it down further. In the meantime, I'd like to take a look at the photos."

"Okay." The way she elongates the word makes me bristle.

Not that I'm going to explain myself. In my experience, people often overlook the obvious when they're laser-focused on a particular goal.

"Tell me about Carson Deverough." Something isn't sitting right.

FIVE

Eve

2 WEEKS AGO

I AM NOT ENSLAVED—YET.

I am not chained in a cage—yet.

I have not been beaten into submission—yet.

These words are my mantra, reminding me how tenuous my existence is and how quickly it can change. My confident steps abandon me as that sinks in. Abject terror, my constant companion, whispers in my ear and erodes any hope that I'll be rescued.

My fate is here, which leaves me to make some difficult decisions. Survival is my goal. It's all that matters.

Summoned again to Benefield's side, I brace myself to face whatever he has planned. It'll be cruel, despicable, and inhuman. That is the holy triad upon which his existence rests.

Emotionally, and psychologically, I've experienced tragedy. I learned how to survive, how to endure, and to do it all with a gracious smile plastered on my face.

Etiquette training, in my family, was more important than regular education. I've been groomed to become one of society's powerful elite from when I was a little girl. I'm polished, sophisticated, and can carry on a conversation with a rock if I have to.

As for surviving, I'm not belittling the lives of others. I grew up with privilege and never wanted for physical things. My mother adored me, but there was no one there to comfort me after she took her life.

Many people would say I've lived an idyllic life, but to a child, the emotional vacuum I fell into after my mother's suicide crippled me.

Father never grieved mother's death, and I wasn't allowed to either. *Deveroughs,* he said, *are strong. They push through. They don't show weakness. Chin up, Evie, put a goddamn smile on your face, and face the world with strength.*

Weakness?

Grieving for my mother showed weakness?

From that day forward, I hated my father. He never held me in his arms—that showed weakness. He never told me things would get better—that fed weakness. Most importantly, he never told me he loved me.

Because love is weakness?

I never understood that.

I learned to bury my emotions and face the world with a gracious smile. Those are the lessons I lean on now. I become what's expected: pretty, delicate, and invisible.

When I peer into the faces of the other girls, they look back with emotion hemorrhaging out of their eyes. That's their first mistake. For some, it will prove fatal.

Either they plead with me, thinking I can somehow change their fate. As if that kind of power is at my disposal. It's not, and it kills me every time I see that hopelessness in their eyes. My gut churns with the injustice of it all. If they're not pleading, they rage at me with fury and outrage as they see me walking free.

As if I truly am an honored guest.

They see no shackles, no cuffs, no rope leads attached to my neck. My body is free from lash marks, cuts, or bruises. My face remains fair and unmarked. I'm allowed clothing where they are not, but most importantly, they see me walking free.

But I'm still a prisoner.

Those girls hate me, but they don't know the truth. I'm as much a victim as they are. The only difference between them and me is my torment is coming.

Until then, I wrap myself in my emotional armor where nothing can touch me. I hold my head high, dignified, but I'm really terrified and frightened for the day when I do become one of them. My emotions are on strict lockdown, buried so deep I appear as cold-hearted as the monster who holds me captive.

I glide through arched doorways with wrought iron gates designed to let breezes flow through. Hot and humid air rushes through the courtyards. Most of this place is open to the outdoors. High, arched ceilings allow heat to rise but do nothing to ease the oppressiveness of the tropical heat.

The open-air concept of the compound, affectionately called The Retreat by its master, lends a sense of serenity to the air, although I'm not fooled. This may look like a paradise, with wealth and opulence dripping down the walls, but it's a devil's oasis with Lucifer himself ruling from his gilded throne.

My unease intensifies as I approach one of the open-aired courtyards capped off with a ceiling to keep out the monsoon rains. The deep rumble of male voices is indistinct. I can't make out any of their words but come to a halt when I hear a softer, desperate cry layered on top.

I harden myself against whatever madness this might be and brace to endure the next few hours.

Last week's previous guests are gone. Mr. H with his hungry leers departed with his newest slave. Mr. J took two girls with him. I didn't keep track of the rest of the guests, but the girls they bid upon are all gone now. New ones will take their place. I may be one of them if what Benefield said is true.

I both like and hate the break when the guests aren't here. I hate the men who descend upon The Retreat with the sole intent of ruining a life to feed their carnal desires, but I love the emptiness when they leave.

For a moment, I breathe easier. Not that I lower my guard. The time between guests is a time of training, something I've been spared, but I have a feeling that will change.

Is this the day? Is that why I've been summoned?

My father still has time to respond to the latest ransom demand. Maybe this time, Benefield will let me go?

Can he afford to let me go?

I've seen too much. I know too much.

The voices of the men grow louder, more boisterous, as I step up the pace. No guard trails behind me. Not that there's a need. There's literally nowhere to run. The absence of a guard is more telling than anything else. Benefield no longer fears I'll try and escape.

Located inland from the coast, I haven't seen beyond the walls of this place, but we're surrounded by a lush tropical jungle. It feels as if we're at the end of the world, forgotten by the rest of humanity.

Although there's no guard, my progress is meticulously tracked and reported by the guards stationed at every door and every gate. Benefield does this on purpose, giving me the illusion of freedom within the walls of his estate, but always beneath the watchful eyes of his men who report everything directly to him.

My unsteady steps guide me under an arching hallway and down a long hall. As I draw near the courtyard, my painted lips curve into a soft, gentle smile. It's the only armor I'm allowed, and I need every bit of that added strength.

I turn the corner and my hand flies to cover my mouth as I swallow a strangled scream.

Benefield wants a reaction, and I deliver right on cue.

I plant my heels on the hard travertine stone and come to an abrupt stop. My mouth gapes and my smile falls away on a tattered scream.

The potent stench of male body odor floods my nostrils, but layered on top of that is the coppery tang of fresh blood.

Lots and lots of blood.

Guards line the walls, weapons held in steady hands. They cheer and shout as two men attack each other in the middle of the room.

More of a covered courtyard than a room, the floor slopes gently toward the center, where red rivulets of blood slowly make their way down a drain set in the lowest part of the floor.

Beside the drain, a sturdy iron pillar rises ten feet in the air. A rope loops through a ring at the top and ends on a pair of iron cuffs attached to a naked girl's wrists.

A gag covers her mouth, stifling her screams. Blood splatter coats most of her body, but it doesn't belong to her. It belongs to one, or both, of the men engaged in a deadly battle in front of her. They hold long, curved blades in their right hands and circle each other with menacing scowls.

Blood streams down their bodies. Deep cuts across their chest, arms, bellies, and thighs pour crimson down to the floor. It's more blood than I've ever seen. One of the men slips on the sticky substance, unsteady as he shakes sweat out of his eyes. His opponent takes the opportunity to lunge forward, knife arm raised to slash, maim, and kill.

"Ah, Evelyn…" Tomas Benefield calls out from the far side of the room. He sits on a dais—his throne in this miserable place. "Come here, girl." He cups his hand and raises his voice. "Step aside and let my dearest pass."

My shoulders lift to my ears with his use of *my dearest*, but I quickly school my features and reaffix the smile to my face.

The fighters break apart. They take two steps back and to the side. The guards lining the walls go silent as I gather the silken fabric of my gown and lift it above the blood soaking the floor.

Minding where I step, I try to navigate a safe path around the blood, but there's too much to avoid it all. In stoic silence, I stroll, with as much dignity as I can muster, all the way across the room where Benefield waits for me on his throne.

SIX

Max

PRESENT DAY

~

When I ask Mitzy to tell me about Eve's dad, she gets excited.

"Now there, I have plenty of intel." Mitzy's mood lifts.

"Lay it on us."

"Carson Deverough took over his father's import/export business after his father's death twenty years ago. Carson was thirty."

"Something tells me you think his father's death was *not* from natural causes?"

"Hard to say. The documentation is spotty. It just feels wrong."

"How's that?"

"His father was athletic, in perfect health. When I pulled his medical file, there was nothing that pointed to anything odd. Then he died from a massive heart attack. Sounds convenient."

"It happens." Knox glances up from walking a button across the back of his fingers.

"True, but I don't like things when they come tied up in a neat little bow. I'm not saying anything bad happened. It just feels off."

"Okay?" When Mitzy says something feels off, there's usually something going on. "How does that factor into our current case?"

"It doesn't, except to say Carson Deverough inherited a wildly successful import and export business and then went and turned it into a multi-national, multi-billion dollar enterprise."

"He's rich."

"Correct."

"How rich?" Knox gnaws at his cuticles. He's a quiet man. Seldom does he really participate in our briefings, but the man takes everything in. He's got perfect auditory recall and can recite conversations nearly verbatim from years ago. It's kind of spooky.

"Rich enough to take out a thirty-million-dollar kidnapping policy on his daughter when she decided to head to Cancun for spring break. The more interesting tidbit is the whole import/export business." Mitzy sits on the edge of the table and glances at the screen with the picture of the ridge in Madrid.

"His daughter had no protective detail?" I look at Knox. That's more suspicious than the death of her grandfather due to a heart attack. "That's almost asking for her to be kidnapped."

"Yes, and no," Mitzy says.

"What does that mean?"

"From what I can dig up, Evelyn and her father were not on speaking terms. Haven't been for years."

"Any reason why?"

"I presume it has something to do with her mother's suicide. That's when her social media basically goes silent on the dad front."

"How old is she?"

"Twenty."

Eight years younger than me. It wouldn't be a stretch to… Holy shit.

My mind went to the gutter fast. I remind myself to remain professional. Evelyn Deverough's rescue is an active case, not an emotional entanglement. Like I need something like that in my life right now.

Except, I'm full of shit. After one look at her photograph,

something shifted within me. She's a total stranger, yet something feels different. It makes no damn sense.

"When she announced she was going to Cancun with a bunch of college friends," Mitzy continues, oblivious to my sudden distraction, "her father said no. Outright refused. She, evidently, gave him the finger."

"Bad blood between father and daughter. Not the first time that's ever happened."

"Let's just say, there doesn't appear to be much good blood between them. According to Mr. Deverough, he took out the policy when she refused to allow him to assign a protective escort. He upped the standing five million policy to thirty million."

"Who underwrites that kind of thing?" Knox is interested now. "Can't imagine they would underwrite something like that and not place their own security detail on the client."

"Who takes out a thirty million dollar kidnapping policy?" That's what I want to know. It's an exorbitant sum.

"Good point." Mitzy lifts a finger and pauses. "I'll look into that."

"Especially if they've been paying out."

"Nearly all of it, evidently." Mitzy purses her lips. "One million, then five, then upped to ten million after that. The demands kept escalating. Another ten million followed, then silence."

"He's tapped out." Knox taps his finger on the table.

"A man like that is never really tapped out. Not with a net worth in the billions." Sam crosses his arms. The expression on his face is murderous, and I don't blame him. Deverough's stupidity placed his daughter in grave danger.

"His company is valued in the billions. He is only worth four-hundred million." Mitzy looks up from her computer screen.

"Still…" I give a shake of my head. Only four-hundred million? "What's his daughter's life worth? I'd think a father would bankrupt himself to get his daughter back."

"Maybe he finally realized what we've known all along." Knox's voice comes out like a low growl.

"And what's that?" Mitzy's eyes widen.

I answer for Knox. We're all thinking the same thing. "The kidnappers know about the ransom insurance. They've been systematically escalating, leaving enough room for hope. Now that they've taken it all, they'll kill Evelyn or make her disappear. She's a liability, especially after so much time, and bound to have seen something she shouldn't have or heard a conversation she shouldn't have heard."

My gut says Evelyn is more likely to disappear. She's a bewitching beauty. Men will pay millions to have a piece of that. There's no doubt in my mind she's headed into the slave trade. My gut churns with that knowledge and fire burns in my veins. My protective instincts rage.

Don't worry, Eve, I'll rescue you.

"Max is right," Knox says. "Evelyn's beautiful, which makes her a commodity. No doubt she'll be in high demand when it comes time to sell her to the highest bidder."

An idea forms in my head. "Mitzy, you said Evelyn had a security escort in Cancun?"

"Right. Her father sent three men down there to observe her, but she was unaware of their presence."

"Then how was she taken?"

"That's a little unclear."

"How can that be unclear?"

"Have you ever been to Cancun during spring break?"

"No."

"Well, it's not much different from spring break in Florida. There are massive parties, beach jams that bring in huge crowds. It's a mess."

"I get the picture."

"They lost her in the middle of a crowd." Mitzy goes on to explain what is known about the abduction. "According to the security detail, she was there one second and gone the next. Just —disappeared."

I don't doubt it. Something similar happened to Axel's girl. Kidnappers picked Zoe Lancaster off a busy street. It happens all too easily.

"I don't like that the people who took Evelyn Deverough are the same ones who took Zoe Lancaster." I curl my lower lip between my teeth, biting down. It's a thing I do that helps me think.

"Why's that?" Sam asks.

"The ones who plucked Zoe off the streets are human traffickers. They hunt for the prettiest girls. They're not even subtle about it. Zoe was snatched off a busy street filled with people. Evelyn was taken in the middle of a crowd. These men are bold. It doesn't make sense they knew about the kidnapping insurance on Evelyn. I have a feeling they found that out later, then leveraged the information."

"Makes sense." Knox agrees with me.

"Good or bad blood between father and daughter," Sam says, "Mr. Deverough certainly cared enough for his daughter to take out that policy."

"At least, he finally got his head out of his ass and came to us." Our services don't come cheap, but if the father has any hope of seeing his daughter alive again, he'll pay the price we command. "We need to piece together whether Evelyn's capture, like Zoe's, was one of opportunity or one of design. And we need to figure out how to either breach that facility and take her by force or infiltrate it and buy her out from under them."

The first option is riskier with greater opportunity to lose Evelyn in the chaos. The second option is no less risky and requires a bit of preparation. Fortunately, we're a step ahead as far as that goes.

"Right." Sam glances at Mitzy.

"On it." Her team will be hard at work putting together possible scenarios and connections. I don't think Mr. Deverough understands how thorough we dive into the personal affairs of our clients.

In my experience, our clients only ever tell us what they want us to know, rather than what we *need* to know. It's in the weeds of their personal lives where true motivations surface.

Those motivations always dictate our next steps.

"I'm taking point. Build me a different cover story." I lick the seam of my lips, not a big fan of that plan.

"What're you thinking?" Mitzy asks.

"We're not totally blind in this. Not after Townsend. You mentioned we now have access to their server, client lists, orders, deliveries, and upcoming auctions? You said you picked that off Townsend's phone."

"Yes, we do—kind of." Mitzy's brow arches with interest. "We stopped working on that when this case came in."

"It's all connected." I slap my palm down on the table. "Zoe and Eve were transported together. When Moira was taken, she was transported on the same ship. That's no coincidence. Figure out how it's connected." I look at her expectantly. "I have a feeling Eve is going to lead us to the heart of their operation. I need to be there, working on the inside. Is there any mention of an upcoming auction? Someway to put me in play?"

We talked about inserting men into their operation, either as a buyer, or hired muscle, or some combination of both.

"I'll get my team working on it," Mitzy scratches her head.

"Three girls. One ship. Find that connection." My gut says something's there.

Sam shakes his head. "We don't have time to discredit Max and turn him dirty like we planned. Make an alias. Send him in as a buyer. Townsend will crack. We'll use him to arrange an invite for Max. Anything you can piece together about buyers or auctions, do it."

The original plan was to turn me dirty, discredit my reputation as a Guardian, and wrack up a mountain of debt. We were going to use that to flush out Townsend, Moira's wannabe kidnapper. We went a different direction, putting Moira, herself, directly in the line of fire. Which worked brilliantly.

Townsend is ours and, hopefully, he's spilling all his secrets as we speak. I have no doubt in Griff's ability to crack Townsend's stoic exterior.

"I'm on it." Mitzy taps the screen of her phone. "Sorry I don't have it already. I got sidelined with Evelyn's case. But I'll get my team back on it."

"If we're scrapping the discredited Guardian scenario, we'll need to build up my alias. We can still use the gambling angle."

"Max," Knox cautions, "you sure you want to open yourself up to that?"

My aversion to gambling is well known in the teams, but not for the reasons I've let everyone believe.

A long time ago, during my team days with the SEALs, someone suggested I didn't gamble because I'd racked up significant debt. Which was true at the time. To shut everyone up, I let it slip it may have to do with an addiction to gambling.

Funny how people react. Suddenly, all the razing from my buddies stopped. They focused on helping me overcome my addiction. It's how the damn buttons came into being.

The thing is, addiction has nothing to do with why I no longer gamble. My ability to read people makes me an excellent poker player. I'm not so stupid as to say I never lose, but I rarely do.

Knox has his near-perfect auditory recollection. I read people. We all have special skills.

As for the rumors, I did rack up a huge debt, but that was only to bring down a total tool from high school. He was a smart, rich prick who berated me one too many times. Like I said, I was the dumb-as-shit jock, good for only one thing. He made my life a living hell.

So, I got even.

I baited him. Plain and simple, I set him up. I wanted him to think I sucked. I purposefully lost and racked up debt, then I roped him into a game where I took him to the cleaners.

What I did was malicious, cruel, and devastating in the end. Scott Connor took his life when he couldn't pay his gambling debt to me. That's a black mark on my soul, and I carry it for life. I swore never to gamble again.

For Evelyn Deverough, however, I'll break that vow if it helps to bring her home.

"I've got this." I give Knox a look which says we'll talk later. It's about time I came clean with the team.

"You sure?" he asks.

"Yes." I turn to Mitzy. "Do your Mitzy Magic and build me an alternate life."

"Any specifics?"

"Rich, arrogant asshole. Should be old money. Trust fund baby. Spoiled—shit like that. Never worked a day in my life. Love the ladies, but get bored with them too. Build in domestic abuse with past girlfriends. Something that says I'm a hothead, prone to losing my temper, and not afraid to take it out on a woman. Something that shows I have no issue with hitting women and have the kind of lawyers who can get me off abuse charges. Maybe throw in a dirty judge somewhere in the mix."

"Damn…" Knox gives me a look. "I don't know whether to be impressed or pissed off. I kind of want to punch you in the mouth for abusing those fictitious women."

"I feel ya. I kind of want to punch myself as well, but we need some pompous entitled prick to make this work."

"I'm with Knox. It's kind of scary how easily that rolled off your tongue." Mitzy gives me a long hard look.

"Curse of the job." The thing is, in this kind of work, we see the worst of the worst. "I know how men like that think."

"Speaking of douchebags…" Knox clears his throat. "Let's talk about Deverough for a second."

"What about him?" Mitzy shifts her troubled expression from me to Knox.

"I don't get why he didn't report his daughter missing all those months that he's been dolling out that insurance policy." Knox's not happy with that bit. "After they didn't return her following the initial ransom demand, he should've called in the authorities or come to us. I don't get why he waited."

"You're being a bit judgy." Mitzy gives Knox a look. "He said he was scared they would kill her if he involved anyone else."

"All I'm saying is something doesn't add up." Knox is not giving this up.

"I'll do a deeper dive, but nothing's popped on him yet." Mitzy gives a tug of her psychedelic hair. "I'll also work on the pictures. We should be able to extract a location soon enough, but that doesn't mean they haven't moved her around." Mitzy's fingers fly across her screen as she delegates tasks to her team.

"True." I hadn't thought of that. "Not to rush you, but I have a feeling our job is going to get complicated real soon." My mind is still at work, looking at all the angles.

"How's that?"

"Now that they have what they wanted out of our client, the next thing will be to put her up for auction. I need to be at that auction." And my team needs to be ready to make an extraction.

"Will do." Mitzy looks between Knox and me. "Anything else?"

"Knox and I will have a face-to-face with her father. I need my team." This isn't a two-man operation. "And, Mitzy?"

"Yes?"

"Build out that alias."

"On it already. We're going to make you one righteous bastard."

"Make it two." Knox leans forward and props his elbows on the table.

"Two?"

"Yeah, a shithead like that needs a bodyguard." He gives me a wink. "Not sending you in alone."

"Good thought." I turn my attention to Mitzy. "We good here?"

"I'm on it." Mitzy gives her version of an affirmative.

I hope Griff and the rest of the team are getting Julian Townsend to spill his secrets. We're going to need that intel to make this work.

With that, Knox and I hop on the company jet and head to our next destination.

The last time we were in New Orleans, we pulled Moira Stone off the deck of a cargo container ship. I'm beginning to think New Orleans is a bigger player in the slave trade than we ever imagined.

SEVEN

Eve

2 WEEKS AGO

~

Not a real throne, per se, Benefield reclines on a chair carved out of a single piece of wood. Intricate designs of naked women getting fucked by men twine up the legs. Erotic acts of every sort are carved into the wood and would be admirable if not for the subject matter.

He taps his leg, patting his lap, and spreads his arms wide. Benefield's touched me more in the past day than in all the weeks before, and that bothers me.

My smile stays in place as I arrange myself in his lap. He hooks his arm around my waist and pulls me tight against his chest.

"What do you think?" He gestures vaguely towards the fighters.

I take a moment, he'll allow me that much, and gather my thoughts. I could ask him to elaborate, but this is one of Benefield's tests.

"What does the victor get?"

"Why, the prize of course." He gestures to the girl tied to the pole. "She's a virgin. They're fighting for the right to break her in."

"What happens to the loser?" As the words fall out of my

mouth, I know it's a mistake to ask. There's nothing to do about it now. I give him the opening he baited me to take.

"Why, my dearest Evelyn, it's a fight to the death."

For the right to deflower a defenseless virgin? Nothing about this place makes sense. I've been kidnapped and placed in the middle of a horror show. Only, there's no way out of this hell.

"Oh." I glance toward the girl as my heart breaks for what she's about to endure.

Tears streak her cheeks. Her eyes are puffy, round, and wide with the terror flowing through her body. Her tiny feet teeter at the base of the pole, and I realize the horror forced upon her.

Benefield tied her so that only the tips of her toes touch the ground. She must balance on tiptoe or hang by her arms. Benefield's cruelty knows no bounds. I can only imagine the strain on her calves, her shoulders, her entire body. And when they do cut her down, her torment will only intensify.

Hot pricks of misery heat my eyes, but I can't let Benefield see me cry. In that, I can thank my father for teaching me how to bury my emotions. Who knew such a thing would ever come in handy?

"Engage!" Benefield claps his hands and the fighters launch at each other with snarls and murderous expressions filling their faces.

Since I'm trapped between his arm and chest, I get jostled in the mix and shoved hard up against him. I don't think it's a mistake. He's testing me.

I brace myself, placing my palm over the hard muscles of his chest while suppressing my revulsion and sudden need to throw up my lunch. When he places his hand over mine, I take a risk and give him a cautious smile.

"What do you think of my fighters?" He pulls my hand away from his chest, turns it to expose my inner wrist, which he then brings to his lips to place a kiss.

His cold, calculating eyes take me in: assessing, measuring, judging. The heat of his breath whispers over my skin: warm, foul, and disgusting.

So disgusting.

A shiver works its way down my spine, and I suppress it by

locking my jaw. He gives a chuckle like he's won some great bet. I don't think he realizes that's a shiver of disgust rather than desire.

But twisted men have twisted minds. He sees what he wants to see and I do my best to deliver.

"I don't understand why they would bother. It's not like bedding a virgin is some great prize. That's not worth risking their lives over."

"And yet they are…" He glances at me, menace, and all things dark, swirling in his eyes. "Do you know why?"

"No."

"It's because this is a gift bestowed upon them by me. It's a great honor."

"To deflower a virgin?"

"To deflower a virgin in front of all the men. That gives a man great power."

"If you say so."

"I do, my dearest. I do at that."

"I've never understood violence for entertainment."

"I doubt you would. You're a delicate flower who has been kept hidden from the real world. There is so much you've yet to see—to experience."

I won't see any of it locked in this hellhole.

Revulsion rips through me, but I swallow it all down, burying it deep within me. This is the game Benefield wishes to play. My fear is his drug. The more I feed it, the worse things will get.

He kisses the inside of my wrist again and places my hand back on his chest, patting it firmly. That's my cue not to move.

"Does violence disturb you?" He coos to me.

Those four words crystallize my future. I see it with perfect clarity, and I suddenly know how I'm going to survive this nightmare.

"You know it does." I turn my cheek when one of the men slices the other's chest. More blood pours over his skin.

Impossible to know who's winning, they circle each other like drunkards from the loss of blood. The slick floor makes their feet slip when they lunge, forcing them to grapple instead of slice and dice.

"You're a sensitive creature. A delicate flower. Utter perfection." He takes a strand of my hair and twirls it around his finger.

"I don't want to watch this."

"No, my darling, you need to stay. Watch the men. See how they fight, knowing only one of them will win. Only one will claim the right to have the girl."

If he's still standing after this. The brutality of the fight is beyond comprehension.

The girl sags in her bonds, her calves too fatigued to bear her weight. The pain etched on her forehead makes my heart bleed as her arms take the weight.

"Why does one of them have to die?" Not that I care about the men's lives, but I'm against senseless violence. Benefield, however, thrives on it.

"It increases the stakes. Makes them work for it. Failure is final. Don't you agree that proper motivation drives a person to perform at their best?"

His words never come without a test. Benefield is an intelligent man.

"Is that why you asked me here?"

He leans back, and I swear he's impressed.

And there it is.

The reality of my situation slams into me with all the subtlety of a freight train. He hasn't kept me here for the ransom money. Money means very little to a man like him; a man who has anything money can buy.

Benefield wants me.

But he doesn't want me as a slave.

Holy mother of… What a wake-up call. But I can use this. He wants my surrender.

As that knowledge surges through me, I make a vow to kill Tomas Benefield. Whatever it takes, I will watch him take his last breath.

I blow out a breath and put pressure on my palm. I use it to press myself away from his chest and wriggle to get out of the foulness that is his lap.

"Where do you think you're going?" He grabs my wrist, tightening his grip painfully. He yanks me against him then grabs my throat. His fingers dig into the soft tissues of my neck and close off my airway.

At this point, any sane person would struggle. I do not. I hold his gaze fearlessly and wait. My life is literally in his hands, and I'm telling him I don't fucking care.

When he doesn't get what he wants—my fear—he pushes me off his lap. I crumple to the floor, where I sit at his feet with the fabric of my dress in disarray.

With our gazes locked in a deadly battle of wills, I slowly, determinedly, gather my skirts and spread them around me as I methodically kneel at his feet.

"You think you want me kneeling at your feet. Calling you sir." I bend forward slowly, listening to the slow drag of his breath. "You want me afraid to take the next breath. Fearful of you, knowing my life is in your hands." I make a show of kissing the toes of his shoes, then lean back on my heels. "You want me to fear the power you wield and tremble beneath you."

He doesn't move a muscle. His entire body vibrates with rage, but he doesn't react. I doubt anybody has spoken to him with as much disrespect as I show him now.

Fury heats his blood as he watches me. But something's shifting in the air. His enraged demeanor shifts to that of a man captivated by lust. He wants me more than he wants to kill me.

"I offer an alternative."

"You have nothing to offer me." His low, warning growl turns my blood to ice, but I don't stop.

I rise gracefully, using everything I learned during my etiquette classes to make a statement.

In the back of my head, I scream as I lose my mind. A part of me says what I do is madness. It goes against every survival instinct I have. Yet, I silence those thoughts. They serve no purpose here. If I want any hope of surviving this madness, I must do the unthinkable. I'm not making a deal with the devil. I'm joining him.

Once I'm on my feet, I lean forward and grasp his hand. He doesn't resist. I'm stunned I still exist among the living, but he watches me. He watches me closer than any man ever has.

Slowly, I reposition myself in his lap. I take his hand and lift it over my head, placing his arm behind me with his hand on my shoulder. I kick off my bloody heels and draw my legs to my chest, placing my feet on his leg. My toes curl, digging into the muscles of his thigh. It's an intimate touch and he reacts.

I snuggle into the pocket formed between his arm and his chest and let my body relax. I wait for a count of ten, then I place my hand on his chest and allow my fingers to curl in the fabric of his shirt.

"What if this is what you had instead?"

"Do you desire death?" He grits his teeth and his words rumble with ominous intent.

"I desire life." I make a point of glancing out at the men fighting for their lives. "It's up to you to choose how that looks. Will you break me, like all the others? Or, will you allow me to come to you of my own free will?"

"You will never come to me willingly."

"What if I did? I have nothing to lose. If I don't please you, you'll sell me, or kill me." I shift subtly in his lap, but there's nothing subtle about what I'm doing. "If you can only have me after breaking me, nothing separates you from your guests. You're as brutal as they are and lack the power to truly make me yours."

"Is that what you think? That I lack power?" The agitation in his body accelerates.

I walk a very thin line, but I've already seen my future. I'd rather live in a hell I create than one created for me.

"You don't lack the power to make me do exactly as you please, just as you don't lack the power to make those men fight each other to the death for the fleeting act of deflowering that poor virgin. But that only serves to show your men, and your guests, that you control others through the threat of violence and death. What would happen if your guests see one of your captives willingly stand by your side? What does that message send?" I lean close and whisper in his ear. "You'll beat me because you want to. You'll hurt me because it's in your nature, but I'll stay because it's what I choose. How much power does that grant you?"

"You think to seduce me with your silver tongue? Many women have tried that before, thinking to control me from my bed. Do you know what I did to them?"

"I have no interest in being bedded by you. I'm not offering you sex. Sex means nothing to you. Sell me, kill me, control me as you will, but true power comes when I choose you."

To my utter horror, that's the one comment that makes his body react.

I'm going to endure hell before this is over, but one way or another, I will make Benefield pay.

That begins and ends with surrender.

I will most likely have to endure his sweaty body huffing and puffing over mine, but my father taught me how to bury my emotions.

No matter what, I will survive.

No matter what, I will kill this horrible man.

"Now, I don't care to watch this." I lift his hand, cupping my shoulder, and kiss his knuckles as I crawl out of his lap. I glance at my bloodied heels. "My shoes are ruined."

While he stares at me, I kick my bloodied heels to the side and stand with my back to the men locked in mortal combat. Their grunts sound behind me, laced with pain and fear.

"Yes or no? May I go?"

I don't mean for that to rhyme, but it does, and it sounds silly. The absurdness of this entire situation finally hits me, and I can't help but laugh. I cover my mouth as a nervous giggle escapes me.

Benefield gives me a once over, taking me in from head to toe. He claps his hands and I can't help but flinch. Wasn't expecting that.

The sounds of the men fighting behind me stops. Benefield bows at the waist and makes a sweeping gesture.

"As you wish, my love."

I smile and pray it comes off as genuine.

He raises his voice and addresses his men. "Let her pass."

I glance at the blood on the floor, truly afraid of slipping in it. No way do I want to walk through it. "Can you carry me?"

I lift my hand and wait for him to take it. If he does, I might survive the night. If he doesn't, I'm already dead.

To my horrified delight, Benefield takes my hand. I give the slightest slant of my head and look at him—directly at him.

"Thank you—Tomas." To my knowledge, I'm the only person on the planet to use his first name.

Tomas Benefield sweeps me into his arms and carries me across the room. He stops at the threshold and gently places me on the ground. He glances at his men gathered in the room behind us, then turns to me.

"You are playing a very dangerous game, Miss Deverough. I hope you don't think you can play me."

"Please, call me Evie."

I hate that name. I despise it greatly. The only person who calls me Evie is my father, and I hate him.

EIGHT

Max

PRESENT DAY

~

WHEN I THINK OF RICH MEN, I THINK OF THOSE I KNOW.

Forest: easy, approachable, a bit rough around the edges, fiercely intelligent, he and his sister command billions. It's a sum I can't imagine.

Griff has money too, nothing the scope of what Forest commands, and Griff hides it well under his gruff exterior. The thing is, for both Griff and Forest, you'd never know they were rich. They're just ordinary guys.

For me, when I think rich, I don't think of men in polished suits waging war from the comfort of their boardroom battlefields.

Money craves the unscrupulous. Sooner or later, it finds cracks in a person's moral code, tenacious and hungry to corrupt those with the noblest intentions.

That's how I think about money.

It's a vice for far too many.

It mirrors my experience; what it did to me, or rather what it made me do to poor Scott Connor, is reprehensible.

Money and power are indifferent of the virtues upon which they feed. They sink in their claws, weaken the strong, and allow sin to creep in. Impure thoughts take root until powerful men believe the lies they tell themselves. Vice and temptation, sins they once resisted, are openly embraced as mercy and compassion move aside.

But not all men.

Forest, the creator of the Guardians, is one example of how goodness can shine through. Griff, overly modest about his wealth, is tough as nails and not afraid of hard work. The man is a Navy SEAL, toughest of the tough, and I'm proud to call him brother.

I imagine Deverough is a pretentious, pin-headed, pen-wielding, boardroom warrior. He would like to think he's squeaky clean, but I bet my last dollar he's hiding some kind of filth. Perhaps Mitzy will uncover it. Perhaps she won't. Either way, I stand by my gut. It never steers me wrong.

What motivates a man like that to take risks with the lives of his family? I'm having a hard time rationalizing his actions.

I want to know more about his wife's suicide. Something in that man's past stinks, and I'll ferret it out eventually.

The company jet touches down and taxies to its gate on the private side of the airport in New Orleans. Knox and I spent most of the past few hours reading background information on our client. I've been staring at the photos sent by Eve's kidnappers.

"You okay?" Knox taps the heel of my boot.

"Yeah, why?"

"You look constipated." His flippant words get under my skin. I'm not that easy to upset, but my reaction betrays my mental state.

"What the fuck?" I lob his comment right back at him, like a child. "You look constipated."

What's bugging me?

What's bugging me is there's nothing in these photos that gives one bit of information about where Eve was when they were taken. One had a window, but the quality of the photo is grainy and poor, purposefully altered. Maybe Mitzy can strip whatever filter was used to do that?

"Bug crawl up your butt?" Knox is not letting this go.

The thing is, I'm thinking hard about Evelyn Deverough. I love the way her name rolls across my tongue, but I love it better when I breathe out a simple *Eve.*

It's like a whisper of desire flowing through me.

Not Evelyn Deverough, but rather my Eve.

This kind of possessiveness is new and sucks all the more because she's going to hate me on sight.

I'm going to be right smack in the middle of her worst nightmare, posing as one of the monsters determined to ruin her life. That's what my Eve is going to see the first time she sees me. It twists my gut, but there's nothing I can do about it.

Her safety is our priority. My priority. I'm a Guardian—part of a brotherhood of men dedicated to bringing those who've been taken home.

Her rescue is my mission. Doesn't matter what she thinks of me. As long as she's safe in the end, it's a job well done.

But damn if I don't want a different option.

Bug up my butt, or not, I bristle with the mission to come.

"Dude, whatever it is, you're thinking too hard. I can practically see the steam coming out of your ears." Knox gives me a hard look.

"Fuck you."

"Whatever." Knox unbuckles his seatbelt and grabs his things while I mull over his words.

He's right.

I'm thinking way too hard and judging myself even harder. Still, I want to figure Carson Deverough out. If I had a kid, nothing in the world could keep me from getting them back.

Nothing.

I'd move heaven and earth, bathe myself in the blood of my enemies, and I would bring my kid home. Just like I'll bring Eve home.

I join Knox in the aisle, grabbing my stuff, and file out of the jet behind him with my thoughts a muddled mess.

The moment we exit the plane, New Orleans' stifling heat and humidity slams into us. Sweat pops up on my brow as I tug in a thick breath of the sweltering air.

"Any word on the team?" Knox holds the door to the town car

while I slide inside the plush interior and welcome the bracing cold of the air conditioning. We didn't have this kind of comfort in the Navy, and we definitely didn't have this with the SEALs.

In many ways, I miss my Navy days. People think we fight for our country, defending life, liberty, and the pursuit of happiness. What they don't know is that when the bullets fly, we fight for our brothers; the man standing to the right, the one kneeling on our left, the one in front of us, and the one to the rear. In combat, you fight for your brothers.

There is nothing else.

I check my phone and arch a brow at the texts filling my screen. "Looks like they'll be joining us." I grin at Griff's short text. "Mission accomplished."

"Really?"

"Yup." I turn my screen so Knox can see the text Griff left on my phone. It says *Bingo*.

I don't need to know what information Griff obtained. My trust in him is solid. He got what we need.

Our mission is a go.

"Now, that's a bit of good news." Knox settles in the seat beside me and glances out the window as our driver takes us to our meeting with Carson Deverough.

No need to think too hard about what Griff may have found. He not only wrung information out of Townsend, but it's actionable data. Fingers crossed it helps with this case.

Julian Townsend is a man with a history with the Guardians. He's the cretin who paid to have Griff's girl, Moira, abducted. She was to become his slave.

The thing is, the men who took Moira also abducted Zoe, Axel's girl. Eve is one of the girls who was part of the shipment which carried Zoe to Colombia.

It doesn't take a rocket scientist, or any of Mitzy's brilliant technical crew, to put that together.

It's all connected. The traffickers who took Eve and Zoe work for the same people who Townsend used to put in the order for securing Moira.

But Townsend's past with us is far more complicated. Over a year ago, he was in Manila. Alpha and Bravo teams went in on a mission to take down Forest and Skye's nemesis, John Snowden. That mission became a colossal clusterfuck. Forest was taken, his nephew, and Sara, who became his wife afterward, were also taken.

Their kidnappings resulted in Forest trading his freedom to secure theirs. Snowden only released the boy, and we lost both Forest and Sara to a monster. But during that mission, we also rescued a score of women who were abducted and destined to be sold as slaves. Moira was one of them.

Townsend, as it turns out, was there. He was one of the guests at that despicable event, and his sights were set on Moira.

The Guardians rescued her, and she spent the next year at The Facility, a home for those we rescue and a place where they can rebuild their broken lives. Victims become survivors as a part of the comprehensive program offered by The Facility.

Moira spent a year there, never venturing off The Facility's grounds. The first time she did, the men Townsend hired lay in wait. They took her and Zoe Lancaster. Stole them out from under our noses, but we got them back.

And we got Townsend.

Bottom line, don't fuck with the Guardians. We save those who've been taken, and if you dare to steal one of those we've saved, we will hunt you to the ends of the earth.

Townsend learned this lesson at the end of Griff's fist, along with all the other implements he brings to his grisly task. The thing is, Griff is tenacious as fuck. If he wants a man to spill his secrets, nothing will keep Griff from achieving his goal.

I have no doubt Townsend sang like a goddamn canary, trading secrets to save his own pathetic life. I want those details, but that will wait for a face-to-face with Griff.

In the meantime, Knox and I have someone of our own to put to the question. Carson Deverough will spill his secrets. One way or another, the bastard will come clean.

Who leaves his daughter in the hands of a madman for months?

No one. That's who. No fucking man would do that to his kid.

Something shifts within me, a centering of sorts. It's the feeling I get before a particularly nasty mission. It tells me all the pieces are falling into place.

"We've got this." No need to say anything more. Knox understands what that means.

"Great news." Knox slides in beside me. "I kind of wish I'd been there to watch Townsend sing."

"Me too."

"It must be good if they're coming here."

"That's what I think." Like Knox, I look forward to that debrief.

"Good. I don't like wasting time like this. That girl's situation is only getting worse by the minute."

"I second that. We don't share this with Deverough."

"Gotcha."

Not one to trust easily, I like to keep my cards close to my chest, revealing only what I must. Knox understands this about me.

There's not much else to say on the matter as our driver maneuvers the SUV into the press of New Orleans traffic.

"It feels good, knowing the rest of the team will be here soon."

"Ditto." I unbutton my suit jacket and try to get comfortable. "What do you think about Deverough?"

We're dressed as executives. Our cover is that we're here to speak with Deverough concerning a new business venture.

"Seems legit. Inherited young. Took the reins of the company like he was born to lead. Turned a million-dollar company into a billion-dollar industry. He's a leader. Happy wife, untimely death, never remarried, and a daughter's affection he tries to buy instead of earn. Says they haven't been civil since the wife's death."

"That's what I read, but the wife's death was a suicide."

"True, I meant before that. Nothing to show issues with the marriage."

"Gotcha." Odd for Knox to ping on something like that.

We read the exact same dossier on Deverough, but I always like to hear what my team thinks. My dyslexia was a problem in school and remains a flaw I've grown to accept.

I've learned tricks to overcome it as best I can, but there are still things in written briefs that escape me. Or, rather, I should say, I don't always trust that I didn't miss something important or misread some pertinent fact. That's not the same with mission briefs. Those use a combination of visual aids, words, and written stuff. It's the written stuff that gets me twisted in a knot.

"Nothing to tie him in with organized crime." Knox leans his head back and pinches the bridge of his nose.

"Does that surprise you?"

"Only that the import/export business deals with docks, inspectors, trucking companies, and ships. Those industries are rife with graft and organized crime. I find it interesting he's kept himself as clean as he has."

"Maybe Mitzy missed something?"

"Or, he's really good at covering his shit."

I glance at Knox. "Good point. What do you suggest?"

"We always do a deep dive into our clients. This one needs to go deeper."

"Point taken." I whip out my phone and send a text to Mitzy.

I stare out the window, watching the city go by. It's a pretty city but shows signs of its age. New stands next to old. Poverty surrounds pockets of wealth. Then there are the mausoleums—cities of the dead coexisting with those of the living. New Orleans freaks me out with its cemeteries.

Dead people do not belong above ground. Total creep shows. Although, the alternative is worse.

I'm told the water table is too high, or the city's too low. Either way, that makes it impossible to keep the dead buried six feet deep. They tend to rise, floating to the surface, like something out of a horror show.

"If there's something dirty about Deverough, Mitzy will find it." Knox leans back and takes in a slow, deep breath.

"You feeling okay?" I glance over at Knox and catch him pinching the bridge of his nose.

"Just a bit of a headache. This heat doesn't help, and I always forget about the humidity. Feels like I can't breathe." He tugs at the front of his shirt.

I feel him. I hate the constriction of ties wrapped around my neck. One of the best things about the military uniform, at least for the enlisted in the Navy, is the absence of throat-throttling ties. Same goes for our Guardian gear. I don't know how businessmen handle this day after day, but I'm with Knox. These ties feel like nooses around our necks.

"I feel ya." I'm no fan of the humidity either, but I grew up in the South.

This is normal for me, nostalgic even, like the air has substance to it. It carries the weight of the centuries, grounding me in the present.

Sometimes, the dry California air feels insubstantial, leaving me grappling for purchase. I feel as if the slightest shifting of the winds will blow me away.

"So, we play this like any other job?" Knox stretches his neck and rolls his shoulders. Not like him to fidget like this.

"Yup, as far as we know, Deverough is clean, passed Mitzy's background checks. He's a grieving father who..."

"...left his only child in the hands of kidnappers for months." Knox shakes his head. "I'm telling you, that's wrong on so many levels."

I get the feeling Knox is far more invested in this than I am. His anger is palpable, a breathing, seething, living thing. Although, I'm right there with him.

"I thought we decided to give him the benefit of the doubt?" I glance at Knox, taking a read on him, weighing the state of his mind. Knox is not one to let his emotions guide him, but he's terribly conflicted. I'll need to watch that.

"You decided. I'm judging the bastard. He could've come to us at any time. We're discreet as fuck. We would've extracted her less than twenty-four hours after that very first call. Instead, he left her there for months." Knox pinches his eyes closed. "Fucking months."

"Let's not get into a blame game right off the bat. We're here to listen and figure out the next course of action."

"Next course of action is flying to wherever the hell in

Columbia we need to go and rescuing that girl. I hope Griff and the guys got something solid to work from."

"I feel ya', Knox. I feel you." The idea of Eve in the hands of kidnappers tears up my gut, but there's nothing I can do about the past. I can't go back in time and rescue her months ago. "All we can do is figure out where to go from here. You solid?"

I never ask Knox if his head's in the game. I've done that to others in Alpha team. I questioned Axel's fitness for duty when his best friend's little sister went missing. I questioned Griff when it became clear his relationship with Moira went beyond that of teacher and pupil, but I've never questioned my second.

The two of us are tight. We met in BUDs, found our way through that hell together. When I was weak, he carried me. When he wanted to quit, I shouldered his load and kept him from ringing that damn bell. We graduated together and operated on the same team for three grueling years. I know his every thought before he does. I've bled for him, and he's bled for me. He's more than my brother, he's my anchor.

And I don't get where this anger is coming from.

"I'm solid," he says.

"Good. Let's hope Mitzy's worked her magic and figured out where in Colombia this guy's daughter is. If Deverough doesn't know, maybe Townsend does."

"Fingers crossed." Knox lifts both hands and crosses his fingers.

While I don't understand all of Mitzy's tech, I believe in her capabilities. We'll know where Deverough's daughter is being held soon enough.

In the meantime, we need to prep the team and discuss how we're going to get her out. It's hard to do that when we don't even know where she is.

Hold on, Eve. I am coming. I will rescue you.

NINE

Eve

PRESENT DAY

~

It's been two long weeks since I became Benefield's girl. In front of all his men, I declared my willing union with the devil himself. *Make a deal with the devil and you will pay...*

Whoever said that is smarter than they look. I've paid a terrible price to secure my place. And for what?

I'm no more free today than when I spouted off that nonsense to Benefield about power and choice.

Not a slave, but not free.

Each day, I look in the mirror and hate myself a little bit more.

If I thought I was privileged before, it's nothing compared to this horrible self-loathing. I used my position to save myself, all the while others around me endure appalling torment.

I'm surviving and it's the hardest thing I've ever had to do in my life.

It's early and I dress for a run. Part of my new status is restricted access to parts of The Retreat previously denied to me.

I live in a fortress within a fortress. Three layers of walls separate this abhorrent place from the outside world.

An eight-foot wall surrounds the main buildings and courtyards. Two access points allow entry to the interior. Within that layer of security, girls are put through their paces, brutally trained by a staff of monsters.

Outside that wall, quarters for Benefield's men surround The Retreat. Those buildings form a square, performing the same functions as the inner wall. They're designed to keep slaves in and people out.

Decorative wrought iron bars cover every window and fortify every gate. Their artistry would be breathtaking, if not for their dreadful function.

"Good morning, Miss Deverough." One of the guards steps out from his post. He gives me a cursory once over. "Going out for a run?"

"Yes." I walk over to the door of his guard post and place my finger over our current position. Over the past two weeks, I've slowly memorized this map. "I haven't tried this path. What do you think? Easy? Hard?"

"That path heads through the jungle. Uneven ground, plenty of hills. It will challenge you." He speaks in broken English, since I don't understand Spanish.

"Sounds perfect."

"How long will you be out?" He hands me a tracker. I hold it on my wrist while he locks the device in place.

My status may have changed, but my every movement outside these walls is monitored and tracked.

"Five miles?" I drag my finger over the path I intend to take while he watches over my shoulder. "Does that sound right?"

"Yes, Miss Deverough. Would you prefer something shorter?"

"No. I feel a need to stretch my legs, and Tomas doesn't require me until after lunch."

I'm the only one who calls Benefield by his first name. Funny how much power lives in a name.

I put my earbuds in but stop at the sound of Satan himself calling out my name. Satan, Lucifer, these are the names by which I refer to the man loping into a slow jog toward me.

I force a practiced smile to my face and wait for Tomas to join me. "Tomas, this is a surprise. Are you joining me today?"

Dressed in shorts and a light t-shirt, he's ready for a run. My question is rhetorical and bile churns in my gut. I enjoy my time away from him. It's the only time I'm able to relax, so this is entirely unwelcome.

"I thought you might enjoy my company." His soulless eyes wait for my response.

Playing my role, I take half a step toward him and wrap my hand around his bicep. Lifting up on tiptoe, I kiss him on the cheek.

"I was just talking to Miguel here." With a light tug, I pull Tomas over to the map hanging on the back of the guard's door. "I was thinking about this route, but we can do something shorter. I thought you had an engagement for lunch?"

"I canceled it." He drapes his arm over my shoulder and peers at the map. "Why that run?" His eyes narrow with suspicion.

"I haven't been on that path yet, and it winds through the jungle. The shade helps with the heat."

"I see." He places his finger on the map, where we're standing. "Yesterday, you went this way? Did you not?" He drags his finger along the exact route I took yesterday.

"I did." I lean into him and point at one of the small lakes on the property. "I wanted to see the lakes." I place my finger beside his and tap the map. "I thought I could stop for a bit and bird watch, but all I saw were alligators, turtles, and snakes. Good thing I didn't stop for a swim."

"Yes." He tugs me tighter to his side. "And the day before that, you ran here." His finger shifts to a different quadrant of the map, and he traces out where I ran.

"I did. I wasn't up for a long run and it was a nice loop around the fields."

"The day before that..." He methodically presses his finger over a different part of the map.

"I wanted to see the stables." I turn into him and place my hand over his hard chest. "Have I done something wrong?"

"If I didn't know better, Evie dearest, I'd say you were checking out the property."

"I am." I've learned not to lie to Tomas. He can see right to the truth, but I've also learned how to shift the truth to my advantage. I inject enthusiasm into my voice as I twist the truth. "I hope to explore all of it, over time, but I'm not in a rush. This place is much larger than I ever imagined, and it's beautiful. If you don't want me to..." I let my words lift into a question.

He brushes a strand of hair off of my face and kisses my temple. Tomas Benefield is the only person on the planet with cold lips. I lean into the press of his mouth. If I don't, he'll sense the revulsion rippling through my body.

Afraid he's going to take this small freedom from me, I wait for what he says next. Whatever it is, I'll accept it with grace and a smile on my lips. I take his hand from my shoulder and twine my fingers with his. While I stare up at him, I place a kiss on the top of his knuckles.

"I'm thrilled you have the time to spend with me. If you don't want to go for a run, maybe we could go horseback riding and you can show me more of this place in person?" I'd certainly get a better feeling for the scope of his property.

"A run sounds perfect. I, too, like to stretch my legs. It does wonders to relieve my stress."

"Is there anything I can do to help?" I release his hand and stare at the map.

"Just run by my side, my Evie."

"Of course." I draw out a set of wireless earbuds. "I like to listen to music when I run. Do you want?" I offer him one of the earbuds, not sure if he'll take it.

The player is an older design, storing only music. Benefield doesn't allow me access to anything that can reach beyond the walls of my prison, but he does like to shower me with gifts. When I mentioned wanting to listen to music while I read in his office without bothering him, he presented me with this gift.

"Depends what we're listening to." He eyes my player, dubiously.

"Hard rock?"

He lifts a brow.

"Is that a surprise?"

"I didn't take you for a hard rock gal."

I glance at the player. "That's all I have." I didn't download the music. One of his men did it for me, part of the whole no access to internet thing going on.

"Hit me." He sticks the earbud in his ear and I make a note to disinfect it later.

I hit my favorite playlist and place the earbud in my ear. As soon as the music plays, I bounce my head and look up at him with a grin on my face.

The look he returns is cautious and wary, but there's something else there as well. I see loneliness.

I lope into a slow jog and Benefield joins me. I'd rather run alone, but it is what it is.

That seems to be my new motto.

It is what it is.

And there's nothing I can do to change my fate. If there is, I haven't found it yet.

We head out beyond the secondary fortifications. The estate stretches for over a thousand acres. That's a guess on my part. I bet it's more, but I haven't been able to explore all of it yet.

I'm slowly, methodically, finding where the property boundary is located. When I make my break, I'm going to need to know how far, and how fast, to run.

Within this space, Benefield built a nine-hole golf course he maintains for his guests. We jog around the first and second tee before veering off onto a dirt path. He keeps pace beside me, cutting his stride short to match mine. His easy breathing tells me much, not that it's any surprise. Benefield's in peak physical condition. I won't be escaping if he's the one chasing me.

I turn onto one of the many paths crisscrossing the estate with Benefield right beside me, watching me. His comment about checking out the property gets filed away.

Still a prisoner, my status is that of protected guest. Mornings are typically mine to do as I please, and I take every opportunity to head outside.

During my runs, I imagine I'm free, that this whole place isn't surrounded by a ten-foot wall hemming me in. Benefield's measured breaths beside me are a reminder never to lower my guard.

If I want, I'm allowed to take out one of the many horses reserved for the guests. I haven't yet taken advantage of that. I don't trust myself not to make my interest blatantly obvious.

While remaining in Benefield's good graces, I gather all the information I can about this hellhole during my runs, mapping out not only the property but the movements of his men.

How many guards man each of the gates? When do they switch? Where are they positioned? Where are the cameras that surveil Benefield's kingdom? Where are the blind spots?

I've found two, and I've also discovered plenty of cameras in the woods.

"Do you like my country?" Benefield surprises me. We're a mile into the run and have been silent so far.

"It's beautiful, although I admit I know little about it." We're in Colombia. That's as far as I've gotten to figuring out where I am. I glance toward the far hills, which are covered by the tropical jungle. "When I was little, I used to watch nature shows. My favorites were the ones in the rainforest. I always wanted to see one up close."

"It is awe-inspiring, but the jungle is thick with bugs that bite and suck your blood."

I laugh at that comment. Biting bloodsuckers are the least of my worries.

"What about snakes? The guards have warned me to watch the ground in front of me, lest I trip over a snake."

"It's not just the ground you must watch."

"It's not?" My breaths deepen.

Unlike Benefield, I'm not the kind of runner who can run and talk. I'm breathless with those few words and focus on my breathing.

He points to the trees crowding us in. Soon they will arch overhead, nearly blocking the sun. "The snakes can drop out of the trees." He grabs around my neck and I give a little screech. Real laughter spills from his lips.

I wipe where he touched and shiver, then pull to a stop to catch my breath. "That was mean!" Making a show of a very real whole-body shudder, I pretend that's because of his snake joke, but I hate when he places his hands on me.

It's all about twisting the truth, and he believes me by the grin on his face.

"You do not like snakes?"

"Nobody likes snakes."

"This is not true."

"Well, it's true for me." I'm sure those will be words I regret someday.

I should know better than to give him any ammunition to use against me. If I don't watch out, or he ever gets tired of me, I might just find myself chained inside a snake pit.

Benefield's presence increases my stress. I come out here, not because I enjoy running. I'm not a runner, or a jogger. I come out here to escape the oppressiveness of The Retreat. Instead of releasing stress, he builds upon it.

Since he appears to be able to run and talk at the same time, I use that to my advantage.

"Tell me about your country."

"What do you want to know?"

"Anything. I don't know anything about my new home." His stride falters, but he recovers quickly.

New home? The thought makes me want to gag.

"There's not much to know."

"Does it all look like this? Valleys and jungles?"

"Colombia is a mountainous country. You've heard of the Andes?"

"They're here?" I glance away from him.

Benefield goes on to describe his country in great detail while the miles pile behind us. I learn all about the Andes, the coastal lowlands and the central highlands.

We're in the central highlands, surrounded by lush rainforests, which sucks. If I ever escape, I'll have to find my way through dense jungle.

He says most of the people live in the mountainous west, which means there will be very few nearby who can help a runaway. No doubt, most of those people work for Benefield, and will be more likely to return me for a reward than help me escape.

As for my knowledge about Colombia, the geography lesson is good. All I know is what I see. The Retreat lies in a valley with steep hills all around. Impassable jungle sprawls over those hills. There's one main road in and one road out. I've yet to explore the entire perimeter, but I'm slowly changing out my runs to see as much as I can.

As for the ten-foot wall, it only covers the front of the estate. Massive, and intimidating, it comprises less than a fraction of the entire perimeter. Not that the boundary doesn't continue. Instead of a wall with guard towers at the top, ten-foot electrified fences with video surveillance take over the job of keeping unwelcome people out and the guests inside.

Sweat beads on my brow, and I blink away the salt as it drips into my eyes. Hot and sweltering, steam rises off the ground from the morning rains. I've grown used to the humidity and draw in the thick air, taking in the wonderful scents of the outdoors.

The running path I picked today is one of the ATV paths through the jungle. I keep my step light, my pace comfortable, and my eyes alert.

Although Tomas is with me today, I'm checking out a part of the grounds I haven't visited before. My shoes splash in puddles along the dirt path. Muddy water covers the backs of my legs as my arms pump and my chest expands with the illusion of freedom on every breath.

The jungle thickens around me, forming a canopy overhead, which blocks most of the light. Sunbeams shine through the thick foliage where tiny bugs flit and dance together. The squawk of a macaw sounds in the distance, answered by the hollering of monkeys in the hills. The chirping of birds and the happy croaking of frogs round out the symphony.

My attention fixes on the road ahead, eyes alert for any snakes which might cross the dirt trail ahead of me. Although, as the branches hang lower, they're more likely to be slithering through the trees.

Somedays, I feel invigorated, as if there's a chance of escape. Other days, like today, defeat surrounds me. There's no way I'm getting out of this hellhole. Not for the first time, I wish for a guardian angel—someone who will rescue me.

I thought to charm the guards, using my beauty to my advantage, but to the guards, Benefield is Boss. They speak his name with reverence, almost as if they worship his power and status. They're not going to help me.

When I use his more familiar, first name, the men look at me with confusion. They don't understand it, but they respect that my status is not the same as the other girls.

While it turns my stomach to speak his name, I use it to my advantage. Some way, somehow, there must be a way to escape. I devote every waking minute to discovering my way out of this hellhole.

Speaking of Hell, each day, I'm presented with a schedule. Mornings are mine to do as I please. I spend them scouting the grounds, going on runs beyond the second set of walls. When not running myself ragged, I retreat to the spa, or the palatial pool, where I show off my good behavior to the guards.

They ogle me, which is what Benefield wants. He loves parading me in front of his men, touching me as much as possible while they obsess over what they can't have. He likes it even more when I reach out to touch him. I find that vile and disgusting, but there's no way around it.

My wardrobe is nothing I would normally wear. While all the important bits are covered up, I've never worn such revealing clothing in my life.

And I'm no prude.

I have a nice body, blessed by my mother's genetics and my father's roguish good looks. In the past, I liked to show it off. Now that I'm forced to do so, I find myself in the odd position of feeling incredibly shy, almost demure.

The guards don't understand why Benefield allows such leniency with me, but they respect it. They admire me, but they're not dumb enough to trust me.

I will find no allies among them.

So, if not them, who else? The guests?

Doubtful. Those leeches are here for one thing, and one thing only. No way are they going to help free a slave. That's all they'll think when they see me.

Honestly, that's all I am. I'm a glorified slave to a monster.

This day can't get any worse.

"My dearest Evie, I have news." Tomas chugs along beside me as our run comes to an end.

"Yes?" Light and pleasant with my reply, I brace for whatever he wants to say.

"We're having a special auction this month. Our guests begin arriving in three days. I want you to help me greet them."

I practically trip over my own feet.

"Of course, it would be my pleasure."

My heart races as we stop at the guard shack. I hold out my hand as the guard removes the tracking device from my wrist. With a smile to Tomas, I take his arm and reenter the gates of hell.

"Whatever you need…" My smile lifts all the way to my eyes because I've learned how to lie. "I'll be right by your side."

"I'm counting on it." He leans over and kisses my cheek, then leads me back inside his hideous domain. "I have developed a great fondness for you over these past few weeks."

I lower my gaze as if overwhelmed, but I'm really fighting the urge to claw out his eyes. "As have I."

I can't stand the woman I've become, and I hate the man beside me. But this is my life—for now.

TEN

Max

THE SUV PULLS UP TO A STEEL AND GLASS MONSTROSITY. IT'S nothing like the quaint New Orleans architecture the city is famous for.

Part of the new, the skyscraper towers over the old, a grotesque testament to the ability of man to overcome and overshadow that which should be persevered and honored.

We exit the car and make our way inside. Knox and I check in at the massive reception desk on the first floor to announce our arrival.

I figure the receptionist will buzz some secretary upstairs who will approve us through. We'll meet Deverough somewhere upstairs, but I'm wrong.

Carson Deverough waits on us. The moment I say our names, a man in a suit, sitting on a couch by the wall, stands and adjusts his tie. He hurries over to us, looking nervous as he glances around the crowded lobby.

Not the best move. I doubt Deverough ever greets clients himself, let alone in the lobby of his building. If he's under surveillance, and I have no reason to believe he's not, it's a stupid move. It screams all kinds of not-my-usual-M.O.

"Mr. Sage? Mr. Alexander?" His hand shoots out for the obligatory meet and greet. "It's a pleasure to meet you." With a sweeping gesture, he guides us to a bank of elevators in silence. "Please, come with me."

Knox and I exchange a look after the awkward, formal but rushed greeting. We stand on either side of Carson Deverough, in complete silence, staring at the numbers counting down above the elevator cars.

I almost—almost—want to make a bet with Knox as to which of the twelve different elevator cars, six in front of us and the six behind, will win the race and open for us.

Mr. Sage and Mr. Alexander are our aliases. We aren't taking a chance of being associated with anyone in law enforcement.

Kidnapping cases are traditionally the realm of the FBI, which we kind of look like with our Men-in-Black getups, all the way down to our dark sunglasses, but we also look like businessmen from out of town.

Okay, neither Knox, nor I, look like businessmen. We're both well over six feet. We tower over those around us, and if not for our height, our brawn screams secret service or private security. Any way it's measured, we're formidable, and that attracts attention.

At Guardian HRS, our size, and bulk, means nothing. Every Guardian is built. Well, almost every Guardian. We do have two female Guardians. Members of Delta team, our unit that works with the FBI on domestic hostage rescue cases, Jenny, Delta-One, and Charlie, Delta-Six, are female. On first blush—not remarkable.

However, Jenny is tough as nails. She grew up in the slums of Brazil. Sam discovered her talents and recruited her to the Guardians. Charlie, aka Charlene, is a blonde-bombshell with perky double-Ds and a roundhouse kick that's landed me on my back more than once. Feisty and wickedly smart, she's a firecracker. Delta team is our only team with females, but that doesn't mean they aren't deadly. People underestimate them. It's their first, and last, mistake.

As for Knox and myself, not many people wear full suits in the heat and humidity of New Orleans. That makes us stand out as out-of-towners. Which is totally okay. If people look into our company, all they'll discover is a small start-up firm from New York interested in the import and export of Central American antiquities.

Following Deverough's lead, we say nothing during the ride up to the fifty-fourth floor and nothing as he escorts us to his corner office.

His secretary glances up from whatever she's doing and rises to greet us. "Gentlemen, welcome to Deverough Enterprises. Can I get you something to drink? Water? Tea? Whiskey?"

Whiskey?

I forget how southern businessmen conduct their affairs. It is after noon, but Knox and I are technically on duty. Not that it would stop us if we were undercover, which we are.

I smile at the woman. "Ice water would be great, and maybe a splash of that whiskey on top." I say it tongue in cheek as if we're getting away with something, but it's just par for the course around here.

"I'll have the same." Knox gives me a wolfish grin. He likes my style.

"This way, gentlemen." Mr. Deverough ushers us into his office, anxious to get us alone. Or maybe he doesn't trust his staff? "Jenny, please hold all my calls."

"Of course, Mr. Deverough." Jenny departs to get our drinks while Knox and I take in Deverough's spacious office.

Being a shipping mogul pays off: corner office, monstrous mahogany desk, leather of the finest grade in the couches and chairs, expensive art hanging on the walls, He knows how to make a statement.

"Thank you for coming all this way." He unbuttons his suit jacket and sits behind his massive mahogany desk. Knox and I settle into the overstuffed leather chairs facing him and make ourselves comfortable.

Knox pulls out his phone and turns it on. It looks like he's checking messages, but he's really completing a scan of the room for bugs and other listening devices.

"Our pleasure." I settle into the chair, kick a heel over my knee, and spread my arms out wide over the back of the chair. It's a power move, not that I need it to intimidate Deverough.

He may be a powerful mogul in his world, but Knox and I physically outmatch him. Our very presence is sufficient to establish the pecking order. We're trained killers, and we don't hold our punches. It's a powerful statement.

I'm actually enjoying the chill air piped through the air conditioning system. My balls are sweaty and my pits are damp from the sweltering summer heat outside. I'm just letting everything air out as I enjoy the cool office air.

"I don't really know where to begin." Deverough spreads his hands out wide over his desk.

Immediately, I read his body language. Dyslexia may have plagued me as a child, but I've always been able to read people. It's why I'm such a great poker player—or was. I no longer gamble.

Deverough is scared. He feels out of control, which is why he's grounding himself on the desk. That's the center of his power, and he's drawing what strength from it he can. He presses down on the wood, then pauses to look up at me. "How do we begin?"

My impression is he's never had to ask that question in his life and shows how desperate the man is to bring his daughter home. Maybe he isn't such a self-absorbed asshole after all?

I take a moment to read the rest of his body language, taking in every nuance. From the depths of his breaths to the pulse hammering in his neck, I read his facial expressions, the way he holds his body, and the subtle tells we all possess.

Still can't believe he waited as long as he did to call in Guardian HRS. No matter the concern he displays today, I don't trust the fucker.

"We have our tech team looking at the photos you sent earlier. Any other communication you have with the kidnappers we'll need to see." I broaden the spread of my knees, taking up more space, garnering more power. "Have you been contacted recently?"

Deverough may be our client, but he works for me now. Not the other way around.

"Just the last time. When they…" He swallows thickly. His

Adam's apple rises then lowers nice and slow, and his eyes close. They remain shut for a beat too long. Deverough clears his throat. "When they... when they asked for another ten million."

"I see." I need to ask intrusive questions, but we can dick around with the easy stuff first. "How long ago was that?"

"Less than twenty-four hours. That's when I called you."

It shouldn't surprise me, but I continue to be amazed by the speed with which Guardian HRS moves. Moments after Sam accepted the case, Knox and I were on the phone, yanked off that trawler, briefed at Guardian HQ, and put on a jet to speak with Deverough in person.

I bet it hasn't been but twelve hours. The military never moved with this kind of speed. Some days, I miss my time in the military, but those are few and far between.

"Okay. And did they send any proof of life photos with that request? Our team didn't receive anything."

"No. They just asked for the money."

"And how are you to contact them?"

"I have information for a money drop."

"Is there any reason to think they're aware of the kidnapping insurance you took out on your daughter?"

"No."

"Is she aware of the policy?"

"I'm sure Evie is peripherally aware, but I don't discuss those kinds of things with her."

"Would she have been aware of your baseline policy? The one for five million?"

"I don't know. Maybe? I mean, we've discussed it in the past, but that was a really long time ago. Evie and I... We're not as close as I would like." Truth rings out in those words, both the distance between father and daughter as well as his regret about the current state of their relationship. His concern over his daughter is real.

"We need more than maybe."

His expression darkens. "I'm sure she knew, but I honestly don't see how that matters." Frustration edges his tone and he almost loses his cool with me, but Deverough is a master of his emotions and tucks his shit up tight.

"It matters because we have to assume they've interrogated her." I hate using the word interrogate. It's a strong word, evoking powerful images, but Deverough is kind of a prick, and I don't have time to hold his hand.

"She's a smart girl. She probably did."

"You're sure about that?"

"Yes, but I don't..."

"Did she know about the thirty million?"

"Mr. Sage, I don't see why this matters?"

"Just answer the question."

"No. She didn't. I only did that because she..." Redness fills his face. He's a cultured man. Deverough once again puts a lid on his temper. "My daughter wouldn't know about that."

"Any reason to think she knew about the security detail you put on her?"

"Absolutely not."

"You're sure about that?"

"Yes."

"In my experience, children like her tend to be a bit more savvy about things like that."

"What does that mean? Children like her?"

"Only that children who grow up with the kind of wealth that demands personal protection details and kidnapping ransom insurance generally know when they're being protected. Would it be safe to assume she knew?"

"Yes, but I don't see how any of that matters."

"It matters because it determines the kind of information her kidnappers are able to extract from her. If they knew a five million dollar policy existed on her, it makes no sense why they initially asked for only one million." I wait to see if it sinks in.

Deverough returns a blank stare. He doesn't get it.

"Mr. Deverough, your daughter was targeted." And he was tested. I don't think he grasps what happened. It was a test he failed.

"Whoever kidnapped your daughter, more likely than not, knew about the secondary policy."

"How do you know that?"

"I don't know, but I'm very good at my job. A big part of that is reading people."

We fall silent as the door behind us opens. His secretary enters with our drinks. I'll need Mitzy to run a background check on Deverough's staff and find out which of them would've known about the additional policy.

One sniff of my water and I note the splash of whiskey on top is a generous pour, and very expensive. I'm surprised Deverough doesn't break out the Cuban cigars. A man like him, in the business he's in, probably has a few laying around. He's not totally squeaky clean.

Every man has secrets and I intend to discover his.

"Thank you." I put the drink to my lips and take a long slow sniff. "Damn good whiskey." I lift the glass. "To bringing your daughter home."

Deverough lifts his glass, as does Knox, but I don't take a sip. Knox does the same. We place our drinks on the table between our chairs, leaving them untouched. We wait for Deverough's secretary to leave before continuing our conversation.

"How could they know?" Deverough downs half his glass. Unlike our drinks, his is all whiskey with one large cube of ice inside.

"I'm guessing someone at the insurance company who underwrote the policy or someone within your company leaked that information."

"Why? Why would someone do something like this?"

"Two reasons come to mind."

He gives me another blank stare. For a shipping mogul, I'm not getting smart vibes from our client. I'd like to make allowances. The man's daughter has been missing for months, but it's difficult.

"First is the obvious. Money. Although, I'm surprised they didn't ask for the whole amount at once. Although, I have a theory."

"What's that?"

"It has to do with the second reason."

"Which is?"

"Your daughter is uncommonly attractive. Are you aware the men who took her are known human traffickers?" I wait a beat for that to sink in.

"As in sex trafficking?" His eyes grow wide, but they're a beat too late. I wouldn't have noticed if I hadn't been watching for something. He says it as if it comes as a shock, but I'd bet a million bucks he's known all along. He's a fucking idiot for sitting on his ass all these months.

All he accomplished was giving the kidnappers the time they needed to build up hype around Eve's future sale. The girl is a knockout, and with her family background, owning and breaking her are a perverted monster's wet dream.

"Yes, Mr. Deverough." I find it difficult to keep my voice level. "It's my belief they never had any intention of releasing your daughter. The escalating demands are merely a ploy to get their hands on as much of that money as possible. Once you stop paying, your daughter will serve her real purpose in their organization."

All the color in his face drains away. "My Evie…" So much pain in so few words. His fear guts me.

I understand it very well, but that's only because I've had up close and personal experience with the men who took Eve.

I don't tell him how lucky she is. Eve was put in the back of the right truck. With the exception of Axel's girl, none of the others in the second truck survived.

"What do I do?" His hand shakes as he reaches for his drink. The remainder of the whiskey disappears as he swallows it in one gulp.

"You said they didn't send a photograph with this last demand?"

"They didn't."

"Well, at a minimum, you need proof of life. This last request is for ten million."

"Yes."

"That demands some concessions." Maybe we can get that photo for Mitzy. If not outside, the geo-tagging will give us the most up-to-date information about her current location. It wouldn't be a stretch to imagine they've moved her around more than once.

Knox sits beside me and dips his finger in his drink. He slowly twirls the ice inside, making it clank against the glass. He's silent on purpose, putting that amazing auditory recall of his to work. We'll go over this conversation several times, pulling out all we can from it, before moving on.

"Do you have a way to contact the kidnappers?"

"No."

"They initiate?"

"Yes."

"Through what means?"

"My cellphone."

"Give it to me." I hold out my hand.

Deverough hesitates a second before handing it over. "What are you going to do to it?"

I turn the phone on, then hand it back to him. "Unlock it, please."

Deverough lifts the phone to his face and unlocks the phone. He hands it back to me and I pass it over to Knox.

Knox takes the phone and gets to work establishing access for Mitzy. She and her team will download whatever it is they do to mirror the phone and trace all incoming calls, texts, emails, and anything digital: past, present, and future.

"When's the drop?" I ask.

"I told them I needed time to get that much cash together. They gave me a week."

"They want cash?"

That's pretty old school and doesn't make sense. Extracting that much cash always sends out alerts to various governmental agencies. Not to mention logistics about cash drops, which exposes the person collecting it more than the one dropping it off. Honestly, if true, it makes our job a thousand times easier.

"That's what they said."

Maybe they want Deverough to alert the authorities? That's an interesting twist.

Knox hands back the phone. Deverough doesn't look at it before placing it back in the inside breast pocket of his suit. If someone handled my phone, I'd be checking out what they did.

I tap the arm of my chair and stand. Knox follows suit.

"Thank you for your time. We'll be in touch."

"Wait. That's it? What are you going to do? How are you..."

"Mr. Deverough, the less you know, the better." I point to his phone. "When they call, keep them on the line as long as possible. Demand a photo of your daughter. A video would be better. Tell them you want to speak to her. It's the only way to know you're not being fed an older photograph."

That's not true, but he doesn't need to know that. I thought all kinds of things like that until I met Mitzy and her crew. Fucking amazing what they can do.

"Like I said, we'll be in touch."

My phone alerts with an incoming text. Our team is inbound and will be here within the hour.

I can't wait to hear what Griff discovered after his conversation with Julian Townsend.

ELEVEN

Eve

_____

IT'S A FEW DAYS BEFORE OUR GUESTS DESCEND ON THE RETREAT. Tonight, Benefield will hold court with his men.

The girls are to be tested, and I get to sit front and center beside Benefield as he determines which will be offered to his guests and which will go to his brothels.

Benefield's depravity knows no bounds, and this is yet another test of my commitment to stand by his side.

I've doomed myself. In saving myself from being turned into a slave and auctioned off like a piece of meat, all I've done is traded one horror for another.

So damn stupid.

I thought I was buying time. I thought I was smart, gaining his trust while I worked out a way to escape.

Once free, I dream about returning to this horrible place with avenging angels by my side—righteous men hell-bent on destroying men like Benefield.

But really? It's a fantasy. I'm in the middle of Colombia. All the local police are in Benefield's pocket. How far does that corruption extend? How am I going to find anyone willing to go up against such men?

I don't even know if it's the FBI or the CIA that would care. Who would I even call? And if I can work my way through that bureaucratic red tape, how long is it going to take? How many more girls will be sold around the globe before I can get anyone to listen? To act?

My aspirations are unrealistic, hopeless, but they're all I have. I cling to those when my mind turns down darker paths.

Maybe I'm the one who's deeply flawed? Creating this fantasy in my head about, not just a rescue, but a complete dismantling of this whole wretched industry.

What terrifies me the most is that I created this fantasy to justify the actions I took, and continue to take each and every day.

Stand beside Benefield?

What the hell was I thinking?

The truth is I'm selfish, looking out only for myself. I'm no hero. I'm simply another monster. I'm willing to stand by his side while others suffer in front of me.

I hate myself.

I join Benefield for lunch and then spend the afternoon with him in his office reading a book and listening to music through my earbuds while he conducts last-minute business.

He sits with one of his captains, Lucian Torget, going over the guest list.

"An interesting repeat so soon." Benefield hands a dossier to Lucian. "Was Mr. B unhappy with his prior purchase?"

My ears prick up, absorbing everything the men say. If I get out of here alive, there's no telling what little bit of information will be the one that hammers home the last nail in Benefield's coffin.

No matter what, I will see this monster taken down.

"Exactly the opposite." Lucian clears his throat. "He's very pleased with Lisette, but interested in acquiring an additional slave."

I look up at the exact moment Lucian glances in my direction.

Benefield follows Lucian's gaze and the muscles of his jaw tick. I squirm in my seat, uneasy with the subtle non-verbals being exchanged. Mr. B is a wretched man, disgusting on so many levels, and showed too much interest in me when he last was here.

"Interesting," Benefield flicks his fingers, demanding the dossier back. He flips through the pages, looking through the list of financials and other things. "Repeat customers are good for business. I don't see where he's referred any clients."

"He has not." Lucian shifts on his feet.

"Finalize the invitation."

Referred clients? I suppose that makes sense. This kind of wretched business probably only works through word of mouth. It's not like they can advertise on the internet. Or can they?

I honestly don't know where Benefield finds his clients, although it appears referrals provide a base.

"Yes, sir." Lucian retrieves the dossier and places it on the smaller of two piles. He hands the next to Benefield. "Mr. S, a first-time client, referred by Mr. T."

"I see." Benefield flips through the short stack of papers. "An import/export company?"

"Dealing in antiquities."

"Legitimate? Or…"

"Legitimate and seem to be expanding operations. They've seen impressive growth in the past five years."

"I wonder what kind of antiquities they sell?"

Lucian grins. "Do you want to extend an invitation?"

"Dig a little deeper. See what you can find. I need leverage, and I don't see it here."

"Yes, sir."

"Is this his first purchase?"

"Yes, sir."

"Jumping into the deep end? Bold move. Suspicious."

"He does show a predilection."

"Predilection? How so?"

Lucian extends his hand, requesting the dossier back from Benefield. He quickly flips to someplace in the back half of the document and hands it back.

"He's been active on several online escort sites; specific requests were made. Two of those resulted in assault charges."

"A man with money and a record. I like that."

"No record, sir."

"Really?"

"All charges were dropped."

"Dropped? He paid the girls off?"

"It doesn't look like it. We checked their financials for any large deposits. None were made."

"How did he get the charges dropped?"

"I assume leverage and a savvy lawyer. His family retains legal services. There are also several ex-girlfriends with similar stories."

"I'm intrigued. Go on." Benefield flips through the dossier.

"Same thing, assault charges. All were dropped."

"Impulse control issues?"

"Aggressive sexual encounters, from the charges filed."

"I like that even better." Benefield's gaze flicks over to me.

My head stays buried in my book. My earbuds are in, but turned off. I bob my head to the beat of silence, leaving Benefield to think I'm engrossed in the book and oblivious to their conversation.

I hang on every word.

He's far too trusting, which terrifies me. The longer I'm around him, the more dangerous it becomes for me. My life expectancy decreases each and every day because Benefield doesn't keep liabilities lying around.

"His finances seem in order." Benefield steeples his fingers beneath his chin and gives me another hard look.

This one I see, as I'm staring at him. I beam a big smile back at him, displaying an affection I do not feel. I'm supposed to be here by choice. Standing by him, because it's what I choose. A woman who chooses him, rather than a slave forced to serve, gives him immeasurable power.

I'm going to make a mistake. Or, he's going to get tired of me. Or, he'll wake up one day and decide I know too much. He'll get rid of me, or kill me. Either way, he'll ensure there's nothing I can do to hurt him.

The afternoon wears on. The two of them discuss a dozen potential clients, selecting six in the end to join us for another round of destroying lives.

We join the men for a boisterous dinner, where the slaves-in-training are put through their paces. I sit through that horrible evening with my gut churning and my heart breaking for those girls. All the while, Benefield watches me.

He loves the idea of a woman who might truly sit by his side. Not an equal by any means, but someone worthy of that status. We are cautiously finding our way while I grow more nervous each and every day.

Benefield thrives on torture. Physical or psychological, it doesn't matter. He's toying with me, and my time is running out.

After dinner, he retreats to the Oasis with those slaves who've been chosen to be offered to the guests. Tonight, they'll demonstrate their new skills of seduction on him.

I'm dismissed for that, and his nightly exertions with his slaves continue to keep him out of my bed. I don't know how much longer that will last either.

Like I suspect, his desire isn't about sex. Benefield is more interested in parading me around his men, the prisoner who chooses him.

If I had access to a knife, I'd slit my wrists and free myself of this despicable existence.

But I don't.

As always, Benefield knows my mind better than I do.

TWELVE

Max

_____

"Mitzy with her Mitzy Magic comes through again." I sit with Alpha team going over our plans while ignoring the photo in front of me.

Knox sits next to me. Axel and Griff sit on the opposite side of the table. Liam is by the window, ear to his phone, getting last-minute updates. Wolfe is out fetching the pizza our late-night strategy session demands.

Sam, CJ, and Mitzy join us virtually through the screen. Mitzy's eyes move constantly, darting from here to there. No doubt, she's utilizing all four of her massive computer screens. Actually, I need to stop watching her eyes bounce around. It's making me nauseous.

"I'm sending final files to you now," she says. "Details on your business in case you get questioned."

That's my homework for the evening. I'll be memorizing five years of fictitious trades in the off chance someone shows too much interest in my business dealings. The likelihood is slim. I can't imagine that the kind of people at these events share too much about their personal lives, but being over-prepared is being just barely prepared.

I want my shit locked down tight. If there are hoops I have to jump through, I'm going to be laser targeted with perfect execution of my non-savory alias.

"Did you get what I sent about the girls?" Mitzy's gaze briefly flicks up to the camera, making it appear as if she's looking directly at me.

"Yes. I've already looked at it."

That was last night's assignment, learning all the details about the women I've abused. Knox helped me out, grilling me as we went over the disgusting information in detail.

I'm a Guardian. Saving others runs in my blood. This Maxwell Sage guy, he's horrific and makes me want to slug myself.

Acid burns in my throat knowing I'll have to step into those shoes for an agonizing week. What's worse is that I'll be exposed to women who've been taken with no way to save them. It goes against everything I believe, but in this, the argument for the greater good prevails.

I will keep that in mind. It's the only way I'll make it through.

"Knox, you need to know those too." Mitzy's gaze flicks to Knox.

"We went over it together."

"You don't need to know everything about the business, but Max's history with women…"

"I know. I'm the muscle that guards his ass. Don't worry. We're on it." Knox makes the emphasis for my benefit. He knows this doesn't sit well with me, and he reminds me I won't be alone. Knox will be by my side the entire time as my personal security detail.

The Retreat allows all guests one bodyguard. What they don't allow are cellphones, tablets, or computers with recording devices of any kind and access to the internet. That's okay; we won't be bringing any of that shit. At least, nothing more than a cellphone, and maybe a laptop, for them to confiscate.

A fourth face pops up on the screen, turning the three boxes into a square of four.

"Good morning, team." The icy blue eyes of our fearless leader stare out of the screen. Forest Summers, the visionary behind the Guardians, joins our pre-mission brief. "What have I missed?"

"We're going over their aliases." Mitzy takes over and gives a rundown on what we've covered so far.

We don't know how thorough the background check will be on Maxwell Sage, but even here, we go for overkill.

As for the women Maxwell Sage assaulted over the years, Mitzy's got that covered. We have people to help with this kind of thing, a network of previously rescued slaves more than willing to help the cause.

If contacted, each of them has information about me and the details surrounding our purported relationship. They also received detailed information about my tattoos and where they're located.

"Have we secured the invite?" Forest's deep voice rolls through the speakers and settles deep in my chest, where it resonates with restrained fury.

He's not happy about the connection between Julian Townsend and John Snowden, the man who terrorized him and his sister, Skye, when they were young.

Snowden's dead. But there's a new player in town. Not unexpected, but Forest's enraged.

The invitation is the last piece of the puzzle. Julian Townsend described, in exquisite detail, the steps required to secure an invitation to The Retreat. He gladly offered to make a referral after a little push from Griff.

In my honest opinion, he would've sold his soul if it meant Griff ceased the interrogation. Griff's like a dog with a bone, and nothing holds him back when he's got a prisoner with secrets to spill.

Until this mission is done, Townsend remains on an extended personal vacation, locked up in a cell where he will never be found.

Eventually, we'll release him.

Maybe.

Over the next four hours, we continue the strategy sessions, going over every scenario.

My eyes sting from lack of sleep, too much caffeine, and not enough pizza. I catch myself dozing off when Mitzy's voice jolts me to attention.

"Well, isn't this perfect timing."

"What is?" I stretch and yawn. Scrubbing at my eyes, I try to force myself to some state of awareness beyond sleep-deprived.

"We have a photo." Mitzy's screen blanks out for a second, then pops up with a picture of Evelyn Deverough sitting on a chestnut mare with a smile on her lips.

"What the fuck?"

"It's a photo, dumbass. And it's outside."

"I see that, but what the fuck is she doing on a horse?"

"Don't care about the damn horse. It's an outside shot, idiot. Outside. You know what this means."

It means Evelyn isn't locked in a dungeon with chains around her wrists and ankles.

I'm not sure what enrages me more. The thought of someone locking her in chains, or the proof that she's not.

Something funny is going on.

My phone chirps with an incoming email. With my mind spinning over that photo, I read the details and feel as if my heart has been ripped out of my chest.

∾

My Evie and I welcome you to a week of fun and recreation at The Retreat. Please refer to the body of this email for important instructions to secure your place at this week's exclusive event.

∾

I toss my phone on the table.

"Townsend came through. I got my fucking invitation."

THIRTEEN

Max

ON MY WAY TO A PLACE CALLED THE RETREAT, TENSION MOUNTS IN my shoulders and knots in my neck. Reality sets in as I accept the gritty truth. Masquerading as a wealthy businessman, I'm on my way to a secret compound where women are routinely sold to lecherous men.

I tense with revulsion; everything about this disgusts me, but what pisses me off most is how this whole despicable place is touted as a grand gentleman's retreat.

All manner of activities are provided for the guests' entertainment: ATVing, skeet shooting, fishing, horseback riding, and more. The Retreat is billed like a goddamn resort, with the ultimate pièce de résistance, an auction at the end with satisfaction guaranteed.

Makes me want to hurl.

But going undercover is my idea. I signed up for this knowing there will be things I must do that violate my moral principles. I'm a protector, a Guardian, yet for the next week, I'll do vile things under the pretense of doing good.

It's an odd mental space and I've got less time than I'd like to wrap my mind around it. Soon, I'll be at my destination.

I've been searched. No weapons of any kind are on my person. The bastards even took my three-inch pocketknife and my fingernail clippers. What kind of damage can I do with those?

The only thing I have on me is my phone, which I've been told will be confiscated upon my arrival. They cite security concerns, and I don't doubt it. No way do they want photos of what goes on in there getting out.

After trying to make light conversation with my driver, I give up after he responds in monosyllabic grunts. Every second of the drive is unbearable, but I don't show any unease. Instead, I lean back and pretend I'm enjoying the ride.

For now, I'm comfortable. The vehicle's air-conditioning blows cool air in my face. This is probably the best it's going to get from now until the end of the week.

My attention remains focused outside the SUV. I stare out the window, taking in the local terrain as I cement landmarks to memory. Being over-prepared is a requirement in this line of work.

We have plans, contingencies, and backups to those. Doesn't mean shit won't still hit the fan. When that happens, resilience and adaptability are my best friends.

We travel outside the city, heading inland toward what appears to be deep jungle. It's been well over an hour, with no signs we're close to approaching our destination.

Appearances, however, are deceiving. Despite the thick foliage, there are plenty of buildings alongside the rugged road. Ragtag structures that try to beat back the encroaching jungle—a battle they're destined to lose.

Columbia's a poor country. More people ride bikes than cars, although there are a fair number of motorbikes zinging along. The farther we get from the city, the more the bicycles and pedestrians predominate over cars and trucks.

Rusted hulks of cars line the road. Thick vines weave through open windows and up and through hoods and roofs.

Without my team, I feel unsupported, but this was the final decision. Not that I'm completely alone. Maxwell Sage does not travel without a bodyguard. I still have Knox.

Sage is not my real last name, but Maxwell is my real first name. A precocious name for a little boy and far too stuffy for a Navy shipman. It is, however, a name I'll answer to, especially under duress. Some of the best lies are those which incorporate the truth. So, I keep my name.

As for my bodyguard, Knox sits upfront with the driver, the proper place for the muscle that will keep me safe. Like me, he memorizes the route, marking important landmarks.

I don't like going in without the support of my team, but it's the best we could do on short notice. Not that they aren't spinning up. Once inside, Knox and I will complete our reconnaissance. That information will aid Alpha team in determining the best breach points for entry when the time comes.

What's strange is that my nerves are throwing a bit of a fit. I volunteered for this mission, and I'm highly skilled to operate independently. I should be chill as ice.

Only, I'm not.

My heart bangs around inside my ribcage like a kettle drum, hammering out a frantic beat. Highly unusual, I chalk it up to the fact that if I fail, or my true identity is revealed, Knox and I will be lucky if they shoot us. More likely, we'll be treated to torture with dismemberment and death to look forward to.

That's not the outcome I desire. Not to mention that would mean Eve will be lost. Maybe that explains my unease?

Whatever the reason, I need to get my shit together.

Half an hour later, we pull up outside a heavily fortified compound. Ten-foot walls surround a massive estate. Guard towers stand tall at the corners and rise above the land. I glance up at them as we pull to a stop.

My driver hands over a manila envelope to a waiting guard. Inside is my official invitation, along with dossiers on myself and my bodyguard.

The guard peers into the front of the car, taking a long hard look at Knox, then steps to the back window opposite me. The driver lowers the window and sweltering humidity rolls in. The guard peers at me, matching up the photo on the dossier with my bored expression and disdain.

He gives a grunt, hands the packet back to the driver, and we slowly roll through the checkpoint. The winding drive through a lush canopy suddenly opens up as we arrive at our destination. Extravagantly landscaped, the driver pulls around a sweeping drive. He parks at the base of a set of stairs leading up to a massive compound.

It's a goddamn fortress.

Mediterranean in theme, graceful archways stretch between thick stucco walls, and monolithic columns rise upward to support the tiled roofs. Wrought iron bars cover the windows. The same black iron sweeps intricately in curves to form gates that add an extra layer of security to the massive wooden doors. Those doors currently stand open to welcome guests.

I am not the only guest for this week-long retreat, and I have a feeling those gates are more often closed than left to stand open.

There's no shortage of guards. Either from turrets lining the walls to those patrolling outside, I note both their position and number.

Knox opens the door to the car and I step out. As soon as I stand, I button the jacket of my suit despite the stifling heat and humidity. The driver hands me back my documents and gestures for us to head inside.

With Knox beside me, we ascend the travertine steps and enter the first circle of hell. I'm certain there are far more inside.

We enter a massive courtyard. All around us, a perimeter of building forms an outer fortress guarding what looks to be a grouping of even more ostentatious and elegant buildings inside. Like a fortress within a fortress.

One glance clearly reveals the outer grouping of buildings house the guards who provide security for the inner compound.

A man waits for us.

"Mr. Sage, it's quite the pleasure to have you." An older man dressed in a light linen suit greets us, thrusting out his hand like we're long-lost friends. "We have your suite prepared. If you're in

need of anything, my name is James. Please don't hesitate to call."
He glances at Knox. "Your man will stay…"

"…with me." I cut James off before he can insist on separating
Knox from me.

"But we have separate accommodations for the…"

"My man stays with me. Will that be a problem?" With no idea
how they manage their guests' lodging, I might have just consigned
Knox and myself to share a bed. Although, from the looks of this
place, I don't think that will be an issue.

"Of course, Mr. Sage." He gives half a bow. "We will make the
necessary adjustments."

"Thank you." I make a show of looking around as if I approve
of the sprawling facility.

The outer buildings surrounding us leave little to the
imagination as to their purpose. It is a defensive fortification with
barracks sitting atop massive footings and walkways along the top of
the walls. Turrets crown the corners where men stand guard. They
glance down from their lofty perches, weapons at the ready as they
take in the newest visitors. Huddled in corners, groups of men bend
over what looks to be games of cards. I file that away for future
reference.

It's an impressive show of force, and without a doubt,
intentional.

Unlike the outer fortifications, the inner grouping of buildings
stretch out in an impressive display. Intentional here as well is the
display of hypercars parked out front. Ferraris, Porsches, and
Lamborghinis, they're a testament to wealth.

While scanning the perimeter, I don't forget my place and take
time to ogle the cars. They're there to impress me with the wealth of
my host. A car enthusiast, most of those cars sit in the high six-
figure range. One or two are valued much higher than that; millions
apiece.

My host struts his wealth like a goddamn peacock, measuring
the length of his dick by this outrageous display.

James walks us past the collection of cars, making a vague

gesture toward them. "For our guests' use while here. Maybe you'd like to take one out for a spin later on?"

"That would be fun." Although, I can't imagine they'd let me take one of their precious cars outside the walls. Too much liability comes with that.

James picks up with his spiel, welcoming us to The Retreat. "If you will follow me…"

Once inside the outer walls, a sprawling grouping of buildings meets my gaze. The place has the feel of a luxurious resort blended with the oppressiveness of an open-air fortress. It's, at best, disquieting.

Breezeways connect the various buildings. Guards look down from their perches overhead. At every intersection, and at every entrance, another pair of guards stand at the ready.

My shoes click against the travertine stone as Knox and I follow the direction indicated by the driver. We enter a portico with a wrought iron gate that, in addition to the six-inch thick wooden doors, give me pause. Once those close, nothing short of explosives will get them open.

This place is like a fortress within a fortress within a fortress. Alpha team will have to breach the outer perimeter, where we went through the checkpoint with its ten-foot walls. Then, they'll have to breach the first set of inner walls. After that, they will still face this inner realm. Our job is quickly becoming more and more complicated. Unless, I can get Eve out by other means.

We're prepared to breach the compound, but we're not prepared for an all-out war. This is vital information for our team. It's no longer a job solely for Alpha. We'll need our brothers in Bravo and Charlie.

Despite the tight security, I'm impressed by the artistry used to disguise the fortress. Lush gardens, cascading fountains, and smaller pools fill out the many courtyards we pass.

If not for the armed presence of the guards, the grounds are surprisingly soothing. Exactly what a wealthy businessman needs to relax and de-stress from the rigors of the corporate grind.

Some of that tension knotting in my shoulders eases, but then I remember why I'm here.

My guide takes me through an opulent estate. We pass beneath arched doorways and walk down halls with domed ceilings. The open design allows air to flow through, mitigating the sweltering heat and humidity of the tropical climate. My guide, in his light linen, isn't sweating bullets like me in my designer suit. Knox feels the heat too. Sweat trickles down his temple. It's hotter than hot.

Voices drift from unseen rooms as we continue through, headed to what I presume are my rooms. Deep rumbles of male desire anchor lighter, feminine sounds of sexual foreplay. It sounds innocuous and normal for a den of sin and desire, but I harden myself against all of it and brace myself for the battle to come.

We turn the corner and I feel as if I'm transported into a Sultan's palace. Women, many far too young to be legal, lounge in a rotten paradise. Flowers of every color and variety spill out of exquisite flower beds, and fountains spray water into the air. Surprisingly, the mist cools rather than adds to the humidity.

Silks of every color waft gently on the lightest breeze, flowing in mesmerizing waves as they drape down from overhead.

Adorned in gauzy scraps of fabric, which reveal more than they hide, girls of all shapes and sizes mill around the space. Some of them recline on chaise lounges. Others carry serving platters and meander around the room. A few dance to the sultry beat of music piped in through speakers hidden in the walls. A few men are present. Stripped out of confining suits, they lounge and admire the women, but they do not touch.

"Welcome to the Oasis, Mr. S. Once you have freshened up from your journey, feel free to retire here. Whatever you need will be provided; our host has only one rule."

"And what is that?"

"You may look, but you may not touch. The girls are here for your enjoyment, but any..." He clears his throat. "Carnal delights are reserved for later in the week. And, of course, there's the night of the banquet and the auction that follows."

Once again, this is a resort designed to entertain depravity, trading innocent lives for more money to fuel the disgusting indulgence of our host. Knox spins in a slow circle, taking everything in and capturing photographs of the room, and its occupants, for Mitzy's team.

We may have been stripped of our cellphones, laptops, and tablets, which are forbidden, but that doesn't mean we're not armed to the hilt with all manner of surveillance. Every step since we entered this place is recorded and transmitted to Mitzy's team. Over the first few days, Knox and I will map everything out to the best of our ability.

The women within these walls did not come here willingly. And while the men are not allowed to touch, the women are obviously encouraged to do so. Small hands travel over men's shoulders, rub up and down their arms. The girls lean in close. Their legs brush against the men's thighs, a constant susurration of sensual movement with the illusion of desire.

The girls look willing, but their eyes are vacant. A shiver rolls down my spine. The first girl blinks and all I see is despair and loss of hope. Another girl turns toward me, and gut-wrenching emptiness stares back despite the alluring smile on her lips.

These are the women broken beyond hope, tame and fitting to greet the guests.

An admirer of the fairer sex, I adore women in all their forms. Give me legs that go on for miles, voluptuous tits to lose myself in, small tits to worship and adore, hell, give me anything with tits, and I'm entranced.

Whether skinny, curvy, tall, or petite, the graceful lines of the female form intrigue me. No matter the shape, size, or ethnicity, put me in the arms of a willing woman, and I find heaven. I bow to the inner strength of women, and I've never found a woman lacking in mind, body, or spirit. I am simply in awe of them.

What I am not in awe of are the empty husks I see before me. Beaten into submission, these women are the docile ones. Any hope they had is dead.

Any will they had—extinguished.

Certainly, there are other captives hidden away somewhere on this estate, those who have yet to be broken, who await an unspeakable fate. I've never felt so sick in my life.

How much longer do I need to keep up this facade?

Which girls are the ones who are sold? The docile ones I see before me now? Or those who remain full of fight, waiting to be broken?

Despite my disgust, I make a show of taking in the sensual offering of unwilling female flesh. It turns my stomach to see these poor girls forced to serve rotten, old men, but they do it with grace and false smiles plastered on their faces.

Most of the girls bear evidence of fading whip marks and the marks from a cane, brutally trained to provide the illusion of consent over coercion.

"I look forward to spending time in the Oasis." I make sure to ogle the girls, leering like a horny bastard as if I'm eager to begin.

"It's our hope you enjoy your stay."

"I think I'll spend all my time in this enchanted place." I turn to him. "But no touching?"

"Most of our guests do enjoy their time in the Oasis, but we respectfully request no touching of the girls."

"Seems odd, considering…"

"You will have ample opportunity to meet the girls and select those you wish to spend more time with, but not here."

"Of course, I am your guest. I will adhere to your rules, just curious how I'm to choose a girl when I'm not able to sample her assets."

What a repugnant thought.

None of these women, these girls, are here of their own volition. While the girls in the Oasis sounded eager and flirtatious, I remind myself this is not by their choice. They'd rather die than endure the torments of the horny bastards touching them. But like everything else in their lives, that choice has been stripped from them.

"Completely understood. Do not worry, you'll have plenty opportunity to select the perfect girl for your tastes." He gives me a moment to get my fill of the girls. "The Oasis is not all we offer.

Later today, you may enjoy time on the green. We have a nine-hole golf course…"

"I abhor golf."

"No worries. There are several jogging trails and a group heading to the skeet range before dinner."

"That sounds more up my alley." A jog around the premises is exactly what we need. "My man will accompany me."

"Of course. There is a full list of amenities listed in your suite. This way…"

James continues his brief tour and reiterates the rules.

As a guest, the rules are quite clear. I am not to touch any of the girls. They may touch me, but I am to refrain from touching them. I'm curious as to how much the girls are forced to interact with the guests. Touching can mean any of a thousand things.

What am I going to do if one of them touches me? This is what I don't like about this whole plan. Going undercover means there will be things I must do that I abhor. When that time comes, I'll navigate those muddy waters with great care while reminding myself of the bigger picture.

At least one thing has been answered. I won't have to force myself on any of the girls. Fucking, at least, is off the table, and that comes as a great relief. Now, as far as touching with hands and mouths, I don't know what the hell I'm going to do about that. But I'll figure something out. Just because I must live in the company of monsters for the next week doesn't mean I need to act like one.

As for getting here, a little Mitzy Magic mixed with Julian Townsend cracked wide open like an egg—Thank you, Griff!—getting an invite was only monumentally difficult rather than impossible.

My invitation came after a thorough background check following Townsend's sincere recommendation.

Funds were placed in escrow to secure my seat at the auction. Those funds will be verified tonight and placed in accounts neither party may access until our business here is done.

I admire the thought behind the checks and balances. In exchange for surrendering my funds, my host has done the same.

Sitting in escrow is the tidy sum of five million dollars. If either of us double-crosses the other, those funds sit there forever. It's a lot to gamble, but Forest doesn't care about the money. Unfortunately, from the look of this place, my host probably doesn't either.

It's not ironclad, but it provides some protection for both parties.

At the end of the week, when I make my purchase, funds will shift. Until then, Knox and I are trapped within these walls.

No coming or going.

No cellphones.

No communication with the outside world.

We are ensconced in a paradise designed to cater to the depravity of men. For the next week, I will act the part of a monster.

It goes against my nature, but if I'm successful, we can bring down this operation and free countless women from a fate far worse than death.

The click of high heels turns my head. Long, shapely legs draw my gaze. Sun-kissed skin and legs that go on forever steal my breath.

My insides heat as I take in the sinuous curves of shapely hips, a narrow waist, and perfectly proportioned tits all draped in crimson silk. Long, loose curls spill over the woman's shoulders and cascade all the way down to her tiny waist, and those sea-green eyes take one look at me before moving on to our guide.

"Miss Deverough," James says, "a pleasure, although I'm surprised you're out and about."

Her ruby red lips curve into a gracious smile. "Tomas said our guests would be arriving today." She closes the distance between us.

My lips press hard together as my brain attempts to process whatever the fuck this is.

"Mr. S has just arrived. You may remember Mr. H and Mr. B? They are relaxing in the Oasis."

The smile on her face slips, but only for a moment. Eve lifts her delicate hand and drags crimson-coated fingernails along my jawline. An intimate, and forward gesture, it's all I can do to hold my breath.

Her attention shifts to Knox, but swings back to me when she identifies him as my personal protection detail.

"You're younger than our usual clientele. Definitely more handsome." Her sultry voice drips seduction.

I find difficulty focusing amidst her intoxicating perfume and the heady fog of arousal clogging my mind. More stunning in person, an ethereal glow lights her skin and her mesmerizing eyes, the most unusual shade of green, make me want to lose myself in their depths.

Our?

My mind pings on that word. What the fuck does she mean by *Our?*

"Welcome to The Retreat, Mr. S." Her fingertips lift off my jaw and fall to my chest. Delicately, she walks them down my chest. She drifts back a step, but not before I practically lose myself to the potent swirl of her perfume. "I am at your disposal."

"It's a pleasure to meet you."

"The pleasure is all mine. I assure you, Mr. S."

"Please call me Max." I grasp her wrist.

She instinctually pulls away, but then the resistance in her arm disappears. It's there and gone in a flash, making me think I imagined it.

Her smile broadens. "If you will excuse me, I must greet our other guests." She waits for me to release her, then departs with a smile. Confusion swirls in the depths of her eyes as she leaves us.

Eve isn't chained in a cage. She bears no marks of having been beaten into submission. Her confident steps take her toward the Oasis, and I can't erase the way her painted lips curved into a smile, but never made it to her eyes.

What the fuck just happened?

Why is Eve wandering around dressed to the nines? She's the only female fully clothed, and as far as I can tell, there's no guard following her around.

It's going to be a very long week, and my first task is going to be figuring out what the hell is going on.

FOURTEEN

Eve

HELL WEEK.

That's what I call the last week of every month. It's when the monsters descend.

Just met one of them outside the Oasis. Tall, dark, handsome, one look and he stole my breath. When I touched him, a surge of electricity shot through me, lifting the fine hairs of my arm, and jumpstarting my heart.

I've never reacted to a man like that. For a split second, an overwhelming sense of calm washed through me, as if he could save me from this living hell.

That only goes to show how much I struggle. Seeing a savior when Mr. S is really a devil on the inside. My mind is playing tricks on me.

They're all devils, which doesn't explain my reaction.

It's official.

I'm crazy.

As I make my way to greet our new guests, my attention wanders to the cameras embedded in the ceilings, the walls, at every crossing hall and down each long corridor.

How did I ever think I'd escape this place? Because I'm crazy, that's why.

Max? Why did he have to tell me his name? I met his gaze with a smile fixed to my face, wholly unprepared for the warmth in his eyes and the gentleness of his smile.

But when I looked deeper, losing myself to the crazy fantasy he might save me, danger swirled in his eyes; a lethality which took my breath and made my belly flutter. I barely escaped before a flush rose on my neck.

A flush?

An entirely odd reaction for an entirely unexpected man. He held my gaze for a beat too long, almost as if he recognized me and hated what he saw. Or maybe that was confusion scrawled across his face?

Either way, it doesn't matter. I know his type all too well. He's the kind of man infused with insidious dominance. On the surface are smiles, go a layer deeper to uncover the lies. Bored, with far too much money, he's the kind of man who can have whatever he wants and still isn't satisfied.

He's here for the thrill. His desire to obtain the unobtainable drives men like him to this god-forsaken place.

Needles stab at the back of my eyes as I prepare to enter a den of sin. In the Oasis, girls in training, not the ones to be sold, practice their newfound skills. My chest squeezes for them, for the pain they endure, and hot fire sears my throat because I'm not one of them.

This feeling isn't new. It's my constant companion. Revulsion mixed with relief. Revulsion that I saved myself from that fate, and relief not to share it with these girls. I mourn those girls. I grieve the lives stolen from them. I weep for the pain they endure. But I don't let my crippling sorrow break my spirit. That kind of lapse isn't one I'll come back from.

With a deep, shaky breath, I twist around, looking back the way I came.

Why?

Because I can't get Max out of my head.

Benefield doesn't share the particulars with me concerning his guests. They come from all over the world, eager to take and claim. Max is an American. We don't get many of those. His accent, friendly and sounding of home, penetrated my senses and awakened a searing ache.

I wish for nothing more than to go home.

A big man, he took up not only the space his body occupied but a good portion of the air around him with a menacing threat he could do serious bodily harm if he so chose. But my first sense of him is that he's not here to harm. A gentleness resides within him.

Goodness.

But that can't be. Not if he's here. Not if he's one of the guests that make my stomach turn.

I sensed him in a way I can't describe. Like he was all around me, heat swirling off his body to lick against my skin. I felt the intensity of his stare like a physical blow, and I didn't like the judgment in his turbulent gaze.

His bodyguard, no less lethal, no less potent, made me pause. Max doesn't need a man like that to keep him safe. He's capable of doing that all by himself.

So why bring a bodyguard at all?

Max?

None of the others ever offer their first name to me. I'm female, and therefore have no status in their world.

But Max saw me.

He saw me, and I felt the walls pressing in, restricting my breathing, and making my pulse race. It won't be possible to avoid him, but I make a vow to limit any interactions with that man as much as possible.

There's something about him that screams, *Stay the hell away*!

Why then do I yearn to get closer?

I make my way into the Oasis and brace myself to deal with the lecherous stares of the men.

Mr. B and Mr. H lounge in the Oasis surrounded by a bevy of girls in training. I wonder what happened to the girls they bought the last time they were here. Are those girls still enslaved? Or did something worse happen to them?

I give a little shake of my head and approach the men. "Mr. B, Mr. H, are you being treated well?"

Mr. H assesses me head to toe, lips twisting into a grimace. "I heard the rumors, but didn't believe. You are with our host then?"

"Tomas sent me to see how you were being treated. Is there anything I can do for you?" I pointedly turn my attention to Mr. B, the less repulsive of the two.

Mr. B leans his head back and opens his mouth as one of the girls feeds him a ripe grape. He arrived earlier today and already dressed down in shorts and a thin cotton shirt. Feet propped on one of the many cushions, he moans contentedly as two girls rub each of his feet.

The rules are clear. The men cannot touch the girls, but they can suggest. Good marks from the guests give the girls points back in the pens where they're held and trained.

Which only means the girls are eager to please.

Suggestions become insidious coercion and the perfect motivation to break any resistance a girl might have left. But that's not the worst offense.

These girls have been abducted, tortured, abused, and sexually trained. Misery unites them, but a fierce competition separates them. How much misery they experience ties directly to their performance with the guests. High marks are rewards, while low marks get punished.

I've seen them demonstrate their burgeoning skills on Tomas and his trainers. All I can say is competition is fierce. It never ceases to surprise me how low people can go to save themselves from misery.

I should know. I'm the worst of the lot.

When I look at them, chunks of my soul splinter away and shatter at my feet. There will come a day when all that remains of me is an empty husk. When that happens, there will be nothing separating me from the broken girls inside this room.

Before the evening bell is rung, there's no doubt in my mind what will happen. The scum-sucking rapists will gorge themselves on hedonistic pleasure, without regard for the cost in lives lost.

I chat briefly with Mr. B and Mr. H, as briefly as I can make it, then I take my leave.

My instructions are to greet the men and ensure their needs are met. Three more men will descend on The Retreat before the day is done.

What Benefield really desires is to parade me in front of his guests as the woman who chooses to stand by his side in this vile place.

When I return to Benefield's study, I slam to a stop. Max is there, as is his bodyguard. Their lethal presence vibrates in the air and sends a shudder ricocheting down my spine.

"Ah, Evie, have you met our newest guest?" Tomas makes a sweeping gesture toward Max.

"We met in the hall, when I was on my way to the Oasis. Mr. B and Mr. H are settling in well. The girls are seeing to their needs."

"Wonderful." He gives a flick of his fingers, ordering me to his side.

I glide across the room, aware all eyes are on me, and wrap my hand around Benefield's arm. His bicep flexes beneath my fingers, a display of strength he can't help but make.

I give a squeeze and brace for the inevitable. I refuse to openly embrace him, resorting to intimate touches such as this to demonstrate my loyalty, but he loves showing others my compliance.

His large hand reaches for mine. He lifts it, kisses the back of my hand, and wraps his arm around my shoulder, folding me against his hard frame. If I had a knife, I'd stab him. The only man in this room I want touching me is the one staring at me with thunderous anger. Max's hard gaze takes me in.

"Your woman, I presume?" His deep baritone rumbles in the air. It slams into my chest and presses on my heart. In any other place on the planet, I'd die to have his attention turned on me. Now, I simply want to crawl under a rock and hide from shame. Breathing out, I overcome my instinct to run.

"She is."

"You are a lucky man." Max's eyes pinch with simmering anger.

His bodyguard stands at the back of the room, his face as expressionless as the rest of his body.

"I was explaining the week's events to Mr. S." Benefield gives my hand another squeeze. Keeping my knuckles pressed lightly to his lips, he focuses his attention on Max as he feathers light kisses over the back of my hand. "He's a first-time visitor."

"Tomas runs an excellent establishment. Whatever your desire, we will meet it." I lean into Tomas, sealing my fate while battling the disgust and revulsion flooding my veins.

My words consign a poor innocent to her fate while doing what exactly? Saving my skin from a similar fate? I need a knife so that I can stab Tomas, then end my misery with a slash to my wrists.

"My tastes are—eclectic, but I have no doubt I'll find exactly what I seek." Max's hard gaze turns on me, eyes storming with malevolence and savagery. "For a price, I'm sure anything is possible." His attention shifts to Tomas, where the two men wage a staring contest for a beat too long.

Tomas' body stiffens, then suddenly relaxes. "Of course, everything has a price."

My muscles contract, a fear response, and I fall back against Tomas with a gasp, unprepared for the fury raging in Max's gaze.

"We can discuss—possibilities later, but pleasure before business." Tomas' grip on my hand tightens. He looks between me and Max as tense silence writhes in the air.

I return Max's glare with determination and conviction to survive this nightmare.

As one of the monsters, his need to destroy and inflict pain vibrates in the air around him, building up a dangerous charge in the air.

I feel it on my skin. I feel it in my bones. But most importantly, I feel it in my soul. This is a man who will destroy me.

I need a hero, someone to help me escape this hell, yet the universe keeps delivering monsters to my doorstep.

Max makes no secret of his interest in me. There is no hidden subtext in his exchange. His hungry gaze slides from my face all the way down to my toes, taking time to linger where he wills.

My body responds, bracing for war, and preparing for the battle to come. But Tomas is not a man who likes to share. That gives me some sense of relief.

"How interesting…" Tomas slowly lowers my hand. "I think I have exactly what you seek." Tomas releases me from his side. "Luv, why don't you finish greeting the guests." His attention swivels back to Mr. S. "Now, to facilitate your stay, let's speak specifics. The more I know about your tastes, the better offerings I can provide."

"Of course…" Max holds my gaze as I make my exit.

After the door closes behind me, I lean against the wall, breathing hard, and covered in nervous sweat. Nothing but words were exchanged, yet I feel as if I've fought a battle and lost.

I stumble back to my rooms, numb and shaking. There are a total of six guests this weekend. Three are here. Three are yet to arrive.

There's a change in the air. I feel it, and I fear it.

FIFTEEN

Max

I SPEW A LITANY OF FILTHY AND VILE THINGS, CEMENTING MY ALIAS as the words spilling out of me violate every moral principle upon which I stand. I tell Tomas about dark desires, forcing myself on girls who aren't in a position to consent. How I can't wait to find the perfect girl to dominate, and how I need to exert control.

I speak of being frustrated I can't touch who I want, when I want. We speak of dungeons and cages as my insides twist. But this is the job, and I'll wear this filth until this mission concludes.

One way or another.

As for Eve? Seeing her in person knocks me back a step. Her sea-green eyes and the way those long, thick lashes sweep over her cheeks unnerves me. The haunting arch of her brows which elegantly frame her face? She makes my skin heat, my blood boil, and my dick stir.

It's an instinctual response. I don't understand where this deep-seated need to protect and shelter her comes from. This isn't the same as any of my other rescues. I never felt *this* for any of those women. Not to mention, this is the kind of shit I definitely don't need complicating a mission. It's distracting, and I can't afford to be distracted.

I could fight it, but I'm realistic. I give up the pretense of emotional detachment, and I'll figure out a way to keep my head in the game.

Something primal draws me to Eve. It's animalistic and raw. Not a sense of her being mine, but rather this gut-wrenching need to protect, shelter, and save her from this hell.

Whether it's her enchanting eyes or her long flowing curls, I itch to reveal her secrets. And I'll be damned if I don't want to tan her hide for standing beside Tomas Benefield.

What the hell are you thinking, Eve?

It would be great to say he forces her to stand with him, but there aren't any signs of coercion. No marks on her flesh. No bruises. No cuts. Nothing to say she isn't here of her own free will.

The moment the door to my suite shuts, I let loose. "What the ever-loving fuck?"

"Eyes." Knox's short, clipped, reply reminds me of the ever-present cameras monitoring our every move. No doubt they're listening in on us as well.

We haven't had time to scan the suite they gave me for cameras and bugs, but no doubt they are listening and watching.

"Five." I lift my hand and spread my fingers wide, making a bet on how many devices we'll find strewn throughout the room.

"Eight." Knox holds three fingers, tilted to the side. It's how we count to ten on one hand. The first five, fingers go up; six through nine, fingers go sideways.

I rein in my temper, and disbelief, surrounding Eve.

As opulent as the rest of the place, our quarters for the next week consist of a master's suite, a smaller adjoining room for Knox, and a large sitting area. The master's suite comes with its own bathroom. Knox gets to suffer with a coffin-sized shower next to his coffin-shaped room, while I get to luxuriate in a shower built for ten and a jetted tub the size of a spa.

Our bags arrived in our absence, searched as expected. The backup cellphone and laptop are confiscated, along with a polite note they will be returned once our time here is done.

Knox, acting as manservant and bodyguard, unpacks my things

while I pace the room. After acquainting myself with the bar, I pour two fingers of whiskey and relax on the couch.

"Sir…" Knox hands me the note about the laptop and cellphone while I drag a hand down the back of my neck.

"Yeah, I forgot about that." I toss the note on the bureau, acting like I couldn't care less. "Who needs that kind of crap with what they have here."

"Did you see something which interested you?"

"I did."

"One of the girls in the Oasis, perhaps?"

Our conversation is for the benefit of those listening in.

"Those are too docile." I take a sip and brace against the alcoholic burn. "Don't you think?"

"They appeared well-trained."

"Too well-trained. There's no life in their eyes. No fight. All their resistance has been beaten out of them."

"I agree. The joy is in breaking them. Another then?" He pauses in his unpacking to leer at me. Something a close servant might do. "Someone less tame?"

"You would like that."

Benefield is no idiot, and after our conversation, he knows I reward Knox, sharing my women as I please.

"I would."

"As would I."

"The forbidden might be unobtainable, however. Perhaps take another look at what's offered."

"Everything has its price." If that doesn't cement my interest in Eve, very little will. "I had high hopes this trip would net something worthwhile."

I glance at one of the cameras mounted in the corner of the room and cock my head as if I only just realized what it is. My eyes pinch together and my lips twist. It's all an act, but the outcome is the same. Knox and I can't have eyes and ears listening in on our private conversations.

"Take care of that and any others you may find." I give instructions to Knox, then turn my attention to our listeners. "I don't mind being watched in the common areas, but I won't tolerate intrusions on my privacy in my quarters."

Knox makes quick work of the cameras in my bedroom, the sitting room, and the master bath. We find nothing obvious in his little room. Not much larger than a closet, it holds a twin bed, small bureau, and the micro bathroom.

This sweep is for show. No doubt there are other listening devices we haven't found, but Knox will go through the motions of a manual sweep while I use some Mitzy Magic to find all the bugs.

To my surprise, nobody comes to check on us. I would've thought security would be pounding on our door, but we're left to ourselves.

After unpacking, I take a deep breath and glance at the door.

"You ready, sir?" Knox comes to stand beside me.

He knows what's going through my mind and shares my sentiments. I take a deep breath and put on my game face.

"I am." I focus on the mission. Our first step is to map out as much of the estate as possible. I step out of the suite and turn left.

"Sir, the Oasis is this way." Knox gestures to the right.

Forced air blows cooled air through most of the building, but it does little to abate the heat, turning sweltering to merely warm and muggy.

We each wear a pair of specially designed contacts with Mitzy Magic embedded in them. They record everything we see, transmitting it back to base. All Knox and I need to do is walk as much of the grounds as possible.

"I want to stretch my legs."

"Of course." Knox steps to my side as I take off.

We wander for the better half of an hour, nodding to the many guards we pass along the way. Moving through one magnificent room to the next, we methodically map out what we can of The Retreat. In addition, facial recognition software tags each of the guards for future use. Mitzy says she never knows what information will wind up being useful.

I blink a couple of times, surprised the unique contacts are as comfortable as they are.

"Let's take a look outside." The sun dips toward the horizon, making the oppressiveness of outside bearable.

We wander into one of the many courtyards and glance up at the open sky. The contacts transmit to our watches. Those link up with Forest's impressive satellite network. We have ten minutes to kill while all of that happens.

Once outside, I wander around the fountains and gardens, pretending I'm admiring the intricate designs while Knox uses his watch to communicate with our team. Cellphones and laptops are not the only things that can record and communicate with the outside world.

Benefield's guards left our watches alone. Mine is a Rolex, flashy and expected, while Knox's is military grade. It's bulky, ugly, and fitted with the best spyware on the planet.

I move past the center of the courtyard to a row of cages holding colorful birds. The parrots and macaws give me the eye, ruffle their feathers, and squawk with excitement.

But I have nothing to offer them.

The click of approaching heels stiffens my spine and draws my gaze over my left shoulder.

Eve approaches, wearing a scarlet dress which molds to all her feminine curves. It's both modest and completely indecent at the same time.

Each time she steps with her left foot, the nearly thigh-high slit of the dress parts to reveal creamy skin and well-toned legs. It also draws my eye, hopeful for a glimpse of what she may, or may not be, wearing under that dress.

"Mr. S." She inclines her head in greeting. "Why are you not in the Oasis relaxing with the others?"

"It's nice to see you, Miss Deverough." I let her name spill off my lips, thick with lust and desire.

Until we're Mission Go, she can't know who we really are. It would jeopardize our cover. And I hate that. I hate that her first impression of me will be as a slave buyer.

I hold her gaze and lean close. "Please, call me Max."

Her eyebrow arches. "Tomas prefers I address our guests by last name."

"Mr. S is not my last name."

Eve clears her throat. "We don't use first names here."

I accomplish exactly what I set out to do, which is to make her uncomfortable around me. But there's something else there as well, deeply buried, it wakes and takes notice.

An electric charge fills the air, sizzling and crackling between us. It's nothing I've ever felt before. It's powerful, undeniable, and growing stronger with each breath we take. The urge to reach out and touch her overpowers me.

"Yet you use his, and he uses yours." I brush the back of my knuckles against the underside of her chin. "I want you to use mine."

I want a lot more than that. The moment I touch her, it's like getting hit by lightning. I feel her everywhere and my body responds.

"I can't."

"But I insist."

"Tomas won't allow it."

"Do you always do what Tomas says?"

"Yes." The shakiness in her breath is something I feel as well. A shifting beneath my feet. A pull on my heart. A desire stirring deep within me and heating my blood.

"Then we must keep it a secret between the two of us."

Something shifts inside me. The desire to shoulder her burdens, if only to take away her pain, consumes me. And I can feel her agony. It bleeds into the space between us.

"That won't be possible." She takes her time answering, carefully choosing her words and enunciating them clearly. Eve clears her throat. "Dinner will be served soon. We should make our way to the dining room." She glances at the birds in the cage. "You don't want to miss dinner. It's one of the highlights of your first day with us at The Retreat."

"And why would that be?"

"Because you'll meet those upon whom you will bid."

"And what if I have no interest in what I see?"

"Tomas will find you a suitable slave."

"Perhaps, although as far as tonight goes…" I make a show of checking her out like the lecherous man I'm supposed to be. "I'm quite delighted right now."

I again make a sweep of her body, but this time I stop at her tits, making it clear the value I place upon her is in her unique assets. To my surprise, Eve holds still beneath my stare.

She waits patiently, allowing the moment to stretch, and letting me know she tolerates such looks all the time.

I suddenly pull back, reminding myself that everything I do is being recorded and transmitted later to the team. I may need to rethink these contact lenses.

"If you will follow me, please." A hint of unease clutters her delicate voice—urgency laced with fear.

What happens if she fails to deliver me as ordered? I'm curious, but not enough to jeopardize her safety. Although, this damn role dictates my actions and the responses I give.

"I'm not here to socialize with the other guests. I prefer to stretch my legs and acquaint myself with my surroundings, unless that's not allowed? This is an impressive place, a true retreat from the outside world, but if your boss doesn't allow his guests to roam freely, that should've been explained. I didn't realize we were prisoners…"

"You're not prisoners. I was sent only to make sure you were aware dinner would be served soon."

I glance over at Knox. "Do you have my schedule?"

"Yes, sir."

"See, I'm perfectly capable of taking care of myself." I flash her a magnanimous smile.

"I didn't mean to imply…"

"You're merely doing as your boss desires, checking up on his guests."

"He's not my boss." Her expression darkens and she shifts a step away.

Something flashes in her eyes. It's there and gone before I can catch it, except I sense deep pain, longing, and despair.

"I'm surprised he lets his slave wander around unsupervised."

Her status in this place is of the utmost importance. We came here to rescue a kidnap victim, but if Eve intends to remain of her own free will, that makes things very complicated.

"I'm not his slave." Her emotions get the better of her as she snaps at me. That gives me pause, but I don't dig deeper. Not a slave then. Good to know.

What are you doing standing by his side, my dear Eve? What the hell is going on?

She turns toward the cage with the parrots. "Do you like the birds?"

"I do." They continue to squawk and beat their wings, rattling the cage. "They're beautiful. It's a shame to keep them in cages."

My comment gives her pause. "And yet isn't that what men do?"

"What's that?"

"Put beautiful things in cages?" She grabs one of the metal bars and turns to face the cage.

"Beautiful things are meant to be treasured, protected, cared for, and admired."

"I don't think the birds agree. They're trapped, unable to spread their wings. Caging them destroys their spirit."

"That's the price they pay."

"For what?"

"For being desirable."

"It's getting late. Dinner will be served soon." She takes in a deep breath. "Tomas does like to start on time."

"I'm flattered he sent you to fetch me instead of one of his guards."

"Like you said earlier, Mr. S, you are a guest, not a prisoner. We do not need to send guards to escort you to dinner."

"And which are you?"

"What do you mean?"

"You say you're not a slave. Are you a guest or a prisoner?"

"Neither." Her shoulders roll back and her chin lifts. "I'm here by choice."

"Choice?"

A loud gong sounds in the distance.

"That's the bell for dinner. Shall I tell Tomas you will not be joining us?"

"I wouldn't want to insult my host, now would I?" I clasp my hands behind my back and rock back on my heels. "I suppose I've done enough exploring for now. Maybe later, you can show me around?"

"If that's what Tomas wants."

She sounds as if she'd rather eat rocks than spend time with me, but damn if she doesn't tie up her words in a pretty, little bow. I've never seen a more brilliant smile.

Not a prisoner and not a guest, she's here by choice? That doesn't make sense. Getting to the root of this mystery will be interesting.

"Please, lead on." I gesture for her to proceed ahead of us and settle in a few steps behind her.

I admit, part of that is to enjoy the view. The way her tight ass sashays beneath that dress draws my eye, but Knox and I walk behind her to confer, using an altered form of code to discuss what comes next.

He also tells me I owe him a goddamn button. There were eight cameras in the suite.

As we walk back through the estate, following Eve, she keeps up a litany describing all the rare pieces of art, providing small bits of knowledge before we move on to the next shiny thing. I focus on what she doesn't address, like the hundreds of cameras tucked into every corner.

Eve takes us a different way from how we arrived at my suite of room, crossing several courtyards during the long trek. Not sure if it's my imagination, but I swear her steps slow as we exit the building and enter the protected courtyards.

"The Oasis is that way. You may wish to retire there with the others after dinner."

"What if I desire something else?"

"Such as?"

"A midnight stroll with a beautiful woman?"

"None of the slaves are allowed outside."

"I wasn't speaking of them."

Eve's steps falter. "I belong to Tomas."

"I thought you said you weren't his slave?"

"I'm not."

"Then you don't belong to him."

"There are many ways a person can belong to another. Tomas has my loyalty."

"Loyalty?"

"Yes."

Those words make me want to wring her neck. *Loyal? To a fucking monster?*

Knox clears his throat beside me, reminding me not to step too far out of line. I'm a buyer. It's a role I detest, but I know exactly how to twist that to my advantage. Maxwell Sage is a man with a dark and twisted past.

"In my experience," I say to her, "loyalty has a way of shifting."

"Not for me."

"Everything has a price, my dear Eve. Everything and everyone."

Her shoulders draw back and her chin lifts. Eve spears me with a malevolent glare that would sunder any other man. Fortunately, I'm not easily intimidated, but damn if that look doesn't stab deep into my heart.

Taking her is a card I need to play. If she's not a slave, not an employee, and is loyal to Benefield, that means she's untouchable. I need to break whatever hold he has over my Eve.

Good thing I'm used to accomplishing the impossible.

SIXTEEN

Eve

DINNER WITH MONSTERS IS QUICKLY BECOMING MY NEW NORMAL. Usually, dinner is spent with Benefield and his trainers. There are always opportunities to train the girls.

Opportunity to strip away more of their humanity, demeaning them at every turn.

In addition to their sexual education, they're trained to serve with grace. It sickens my stomach to see the girls gliding around the room, dressed in diaphanous silks that flow and lift as they flit around the tables filling glasses with water, wine, and misery.

Light, classical music carries in the air from a string quartet placed out of sight in an alcove at the far end of the room.

This week, Tomas entertains six guests. Some months there are only four. Other times there are upwards of twelve, or more. This is a smaller gathering, a more exclusive offering.

"What do you think of the girls?" Benefield lifts his glass, his words spoken to the table, but meant for his newest, first-time guest.

Max raises his glass. "They are truly exquisite."

"Let me know if there is one that draws your eye. We can ask her to serve you later in the Oasis."

Max's attention shifts to me. "There is one."

Benefield isn't an idiot and catches the direction of Max's gaze. He places his free hand over mine and gives a squeeze. "That is always good to hear. Not all the girls you see are available, however."

"That's a shame."

"Some are still in training. I wouldn't want to send you home with an unfinished slave."

"Your training is admirable. Although, there is joy in the breaking."

"This is true."

They continue a discourse about training slaves, breaking their spirit, and conditioning them to endure unspeakable things.

I sit through it all with the slightest of smiles on my face. It's the smile I learned to wear to the boring social functions my father forced me to attend.

I take a sip of water and choke as it goes down wrong.

"Darling Evie, are you okay?" Tomas looks at me with concern.

I cough a little, but I need to get up before I make a scene. I need to get away from this vile place.

An aching loneliness fills me and it pulses with unrelenting pain. Despite my issues with my father, I miss him. I miss his smiles. I even miss his frown when I try to get out of one of his boring social functions. What does he think happened to me?

"I'm sorry. I swallowed my drink wrong." I cough into my napkin, playing up that I aspirated my water. "May I be excused?" I touch my throat and cough.

"We haven't started the main course."

"Just for a moment." I grab my throat again and lean in close to Tomas. All eyes are on me. I feel each and every one of them. Making sure all those eager eyes get an eyeful, I place my hand on Benefield's shoulder. "I'll be back."

Tomas gives a nod. He scoots his chair back and stands. I wait for him to move behind me to help me with mine. With all the grace instilled within me through a lifetime of etiquette classes, I rise and make my excuses. Max is the only other man at the table who takes to his feet. He gives a half bow as I turn to leave.

Once again, I touch Benefield, placing my hand on his arm. This time, however, I lift on tiptoe and lightly brush my lips against his cheek.

"I won't be long."

My heart breaks for my father. For the pain he endures.

Instead of joining me on one of my runs, Benefield took me out horseback riding. I didn't know it at the time. My brain focused only on surviving the next moment. I pretended I was having the best time of my life, smiling for the picture Benefield took of us.

I assume he sent that to my father.

What did he think when he saw that? It had to have broken his heart to see me smiling and laughing with the man who took me.

With a momentary reprieve from the oppressiveness of dinner, I hurry out of the room and head for the restroom. There are no locks on the doors, something which still bothers me, but in this place women have no right to privacy. They have no right to anything, except that they will be used.

I lean against the vanity and my knuckles turn white as my grip tightens. This is how I cry now. It's my way to grieve. Instead of tears, I grip whatever I can. Harder. Harder. Hard enough to feel pain, my eyes remain dry as my tears feed the pain.

I gasp for breath and gulp the air as my head spins and my insides twist. I can't keep this up for much longer. There is no escape. I've run the grounds, as well as the entire perimeter with Benefield by my side. He's so confident I can't escape, or won't escape, that he no longer watches me like a hawk.

Doesn't matter if he does, or doesn't. There's nowhere for me to go. No holes in his security. No way out.

I look up, staring hard into the mirror and check my makeup. Not a single tear spilled, but I feel like I've sobbed for hours. I wash my hands and fix my hair, smoothing the strands and centering the diamonds Benefield forces me to wear around my neck.

A single chain of one carat diamonds, the necklace is symbolic. I belong to him, for now and for always, or until I'm dead. There's one thing I know with absolute certainty. Benefield is never letting me go.

As I stare at my reflection, I begin putting the shields back in place that allow me to continue living this horrible life. With a final breath, I fortify myself against the demons outside.

I grasp the door handle and yank it open. When I walk into the hallway, I pull to a stop.

"Mr. S, what are you doing out here?"

"Waiting to see if you were all right."

"I'm fine, thank you." I smooth the fabric of my dress.

"Fine?" He arches his brow, amused.

"Yes. I'm fine."

"Luv, in my experience, when a woman says she's fine, she's either testing me, is tired, doesn't want to talk, is stressed, is on her period, or wants a hug. Which one is it for you?"

"I meant what I said. I'm fine." I can't help but roll my eyes. He's really full of himself.

"You don't look like you're fine."

"Trust me, I am."

"You look stressed, like you're pushed past your breaking point, but have too much inner strength to be beaten down. I think you want a hug."

I put up my hand, palm out. "The one thing I will say, with absolute assurance, is that I do not want a hug from you."

"You sure about that?"

"Definitely."

"Hmm..." His attention shifts down. "I give the best hugs."

"I don't..." I nearly stamp my foot but catch myself. "Mr. S, thank you for your concern, but I'm okay. My water just went down the wrong hole."

"Call me Max, and I might believe you, except..." His eyes narrow, like he's caught me in a lie.

"Except, what?"

"Luv, you weren't drinking water. In fact, you barely touched anything on your plate. If you're going to lie, you need more practice."

"I'm not..."

He holds up a finger, silencing me. "Don't worry, your secret is safe with me. I'm good at keeping secrets." He glances down the hall, toward one of the courtyards. "I was going to head outside and check out the garden. Would you like to accompany me?"

"Mr. S…"

"Max." He rocks back on his heels and gives a shake of his head.

My attention shifts back toward the dining room. The hallway is empty.

"Max…" I give in and relent. Why I do this is beyond me, but there's something about Max that tells me I can trust him. I know it makes no sense. He's the worst of the worst. Perhaps not as malignant as Benefield, but Max is here to purchase a slave.

A slave.

He's not a confidant. He's not here to rescue me. He's a man who sees something he can't have, and he's doing everything he can to undermine Benefield's authority over me.

I grew up around powerful men. This is the same game I've seen played out a hundred times. Only, instead of a wife, or a mistress, I'm the woman he can't have. To a man like Max, that's intolerable.

"Will you join me?" He gestures down the hall.

"I'm sorry, but I need to get back. Tomas doesn't like it when I…"

"I see." He snaps his heels together, coming to attention. An odd move; it gives me pause. "Perhaps another time."

"Perhaps." With that, I excuse myself and make my way back to the dining room on shaky legs.

Max is quickly getting under my skin and I don't like it. I don't like it at all.

Benefield stands the moment I reenter the room. He pulls back my chair and offers his hand as I settle in place. I scoot in with his help then wait for him to sit back down beside me.

For a man who trains slaves, he's going overboard in treating me like—like what? Not a girlfriend. Not a mistress. Not a wife. So, what is it? Why does he extend all the social courtesies to me, but to no other woman in his life? I don't get it.

"How are you feeling, my Evie?"

Each time he calls me Evie, I cringe. With a false smile on my face, I give him my full attention.

"I'm sorry I had to leave." I lean close and whisper in his ear. "I didn't want to go into a coughing fit in front of your guests." I tap my throat again. "Still a bit of a tickle, but much better now."

"Good." He takes my hand in his and gives it a light pat. "Dinner will be served shortly. Did you see Mr. S in the hall?"

There's absolutely nothing to be gained by lying to Benefield. He knows everything, or will once he reviews the tapes recording the whole thing.

"I did. He wanted to take a stroll in the gardens. I think your birds fascinate him."

"Is that so?"

"I suppose so."

"Why didn't you join him?" The tone in his voice changes. I've learned his moods. Hell, I survive only because I can read him so well.

"I wanted to get back to you. The first night is the most important and my place is by your side."

"That it is, my dearest Evie. That it is." He keeps his voice low and his head tipped over, close to mine. "And what are your thoughts about our guests?"

I don't answer right away. Benefield expects me to give him my honest thoughts.

"Mr. B remains eager to grow his stable of girls. More equates to power with him, but he's rough on the girls. He will go through his slaves quickly and be a frequent customer."

"I agree. What about Mr. H?"

"He wants me." I could hedge and beat around the bush, but that goes nowhere.

"And how do you feel about that?"

"I'm happy here."

"Are you? Happy that is?"

"You've been kind to me when you didn't need to be. Happiness comes in many forms. I'm content and grateful."

"You never lie to me, do you?"

"I try my best to be honest with you. I told you I would stand by your side, and that is what I'm doing. Those men see it. They want it. Mr. H wants what you have. It's why he wants me. He doesn't understand the difference between forcing a woman to serve him and having one do so of her own free will. It confuses him and he covets what he doesn't understand."

"And what about Mr. S? He shows interest in you."

"Mr. S is testing boundaries. He's not interested in me."

"You don't think so? The way he looks at you…"

I place my hand over his. "He only looks at me that way to see how you react. He's testing you. I'm of no consequence, and for that matter, he won't be interested in your current selection."

"Why is that?"

"He wants his slave unbroken."

"That bothers you."

"What I think is of no consequence. I said I would stand by your side. I never said I was comfortable with any of this."

Our conversation is cut off with the arrival of the main course. Served by girls in training, they do their best to be graceful, but I sense stiffness, as does Tomas.

They're all beautiful, plucked from their lives because of their grace and beauty. These girls are just a tease of what's to come. They're docile, any rebellion in them is long gone, beaten out of them through weeks of intensive training. But they're still not ready to be sold. That doesn't mean they won't be used.

"Gentlemen." Tomas grabs the attention of the table. Once all eyes are on him, he continues. "I have a treat for you tonight." He gestures toward the girls. "After dinner, you will have an opportunity to choose who you want to spend the night with. Our selection is exquisite and the girls are willing."

"And the price for this treat?" Mr. B asks. He's a fat man, with greasy hair pulled over the bald spot on the top of his head.

"Complimentary." Tomas settles back in his chair while I draw my shoulders back.

Tomas never gives anything away for free. Some of the girls gasp, realizing their fate. The reality of their situation is only just settling in. Whatever glimmers of hope and remnants of free will linger, they'll be stripped of those foolish emotions after tonight.

"Now this is a treat. Does this mean we can touch?" Mr. B leers at the closest serving girl.

"No. And to make things interesting we will draw lots on who gets to choose first. The next man may choose a new girl, or steal from anyone who came before him. Each girl may be stolen twice, so plan accordingly."

"And if our girl is stolen?" Mr. H joins in the conversation.

"Then you get to pick a new girl, or steal another, but not the one which was taken from you."

"This sounds interesting." Mr. H rubs his hands together while I fight the urge to rush out of the room and empty the contents of my stomach.

They act like this is a game, which it is. Tomas makes it one, but it's no game to the poor girls who will be taken tonight.

Once again, that could be my fate. It can still be my fate. My exalted position is tenuous at best.

I spend the rest of dinner in relative silence, making small talk with Tomas and his guests.

The moment Max returns, the air shifts. I feel him when he enters. An electrical charge fills the air, crackling between us as he takes his seat. I should hate him, he's one of the monsters, but my body doesn't seem to know that.

That would be a lethal mistake.

Tomas repeats the rules of his sadistic game. In response, Max lifts a single brow and shifts his attention to the girls. Unlike Mr. B and Mr. H, his gaze doesn't linger. Instead, it's as if he dismisses them completely. Is he not interested in a night of pleasure?

Why the hell do I care?

Because he's ruggedly handsome. There's a brutal beauty about him.

In the months of my captivity, I've seen a lot of guests. Most are hideous, inside and out. None have been remotely attractive. Max with all his hard angles, muscled frame, and mesmerizing eyes, fascinates me. He doesn't fit the standard mold. Something is different with him.

Max catches me staring and wings up an eyebrow. The expression softens the hard lines of his face, revealing tenderness, concern, and undeniable interest.

Again, I come around to why he's here. Women must flock to him. In addition to his powerfully honed muscles and the way he carries himself with absolute confidence, he brings undeniable charisma into the mix. Handsome, intelligent, massively built, he's the epitome of potent, powerful male. It's an intoxicating combination.

He's every woman's fantasy.

So why does he have to pay for sex?

I leave off the other things, like his clean, woodsy scent, and the way his voice rumbles, getting under my skin. How my gaze naturally gravitates to his, lingering longer than it should. Or the way his lips curve up, not quite into a smile, but rather a cocky smirk.

His dark hair curls at the ends, giving a tousled look, like he just got out of bed and only had time to run his fingers through his hair.

But then I remind myself he's a predator. A man in a suit, he's nothing more than a wolf in disguise. While I admire the beauty of his face and his muscular prowess, it doesn't change what he is. Before the night is done, he will choose a girl, take her back to his rooms, and rape her. It doesn't matter which unfortunate girl he chooses, he's still a monster.

A prickling down my back makes me shudder and I lean back in my chair, folding my napkin over my lap. I pointedly make an effort not to look at him, and I don't like the thoughts swirling in my head, the jealousy and anger I feel because it won't be me.

Jealousy?

Anger?

This place is getting to me, making me think unthinkable things and desire the unspeakable. I'm slowly becoming a monster myself.

"Are you cold?" Tomas runs the back of his knuckles over my

arm. His fingers feather over the goosebumps lifting on my skin, making them worse. Turning them vile with revulsion.

I hate his hands on me.

The air is comfortable, but far from cold. The air conditioners chug along, but they can only do so much to beat back the press of heat and humidity from outside.

"Just a chill." I smile at him and wonder about my sanity. How can I be attracted to a man like Max? If that's even what this is.

Speaking of Max, he watches me, like a predator fixed on his prey.

He wants me only because I belong to Tomas. I'm unobtainable, and therefore, the subject of his lust. His eyes blaze, hooded by desire. His thick lashes lower with a slow blink as the corners of his lips curl into a smug grin.

Dinner winds down as the men discuss their plans for the morning. A hunt is scheduled, pheasant or quail, or whatever kind of bird is hunted down here. Men with guns are not my thing and I pray Tomas allows me to excuse myself from that activity.

Before long, the slaves clear the table.

"Come, let's retire to the Oasis for drinks, then we'll play our game."

The men push back from the table. I wait for Tomas to help me with my chair.

"You look pale, my dearest Evie. Are you well?"

I place my hand on his arm, knowing my every move is tracked by his guests. "A pinch of a headache. I'm sure it will pass."

"Do you wish to be excused?" His tone sounds sincere, but I know not to trust him.

"It's a minor inconvenience. I should stay by your side. Especially this first night?"

His cold hand pats mine. "Come, let us retire to the Oasis."

I hate everything about the Oasis. Built to resemble a Sultan's harem, its opulence is over the top. Silks drape down from the ceiling and undulate in the light breeze flowing through the room.

It's fake. Everything in this room is fake. From the breeze to the smiles on the slaves' faces, it all fake.

And Cruel.

And disgusting.

Mr. H and Mr. B make beelines for seats separated from the rest. Mr. J and Mr. Q, who arrived late, stand looking like they don't know what to do. It lasts but a moment, before they claim their own spots. They lounge back on the pillows and gesture to the girls.

No touching means they can't grope the girls, but the girls are encouraged to tease, tempt, and stimulate the men.

I settle in behind the plush couch Tomas chooses as his for the night. He sits in the middle and spreads his legs. With a flick of his finger he calls over the girls. Then he leans back and waits for me to give him a shoulder massage.

A girl comes over, goes to her knees in front of him. She unzips his trousers and proceeds to demonstrate how her oral skills have improved.

I tune it all out. Eventually, Tomas will dismiss me. Until then, I escape inside my head, and block out all the sounds.

As the evening wears on, I lean down to whisper in Tomas' ear. "Forgive me, but it's turning to a migraine. Will you be upset with me if I leave?"

"We haven't started our game for the evening."

I take in a deep breath and brace myself to endure more, but he surprises me by tapping my hand. A different girl bobs over his lap. Disgusting. However, one thing I've learned is sex makes him more agreeable.

"I will stay, if that's what you want."

"No, my darling Evie. You may retire for the night. I don't need you."

"Thank you." I lean down and brush my lips against his cheek using as little pressure as possible.

The room is full of hedonistic desire, men getting off on the suffering of others. When I stand, one chair is vacant. There's no sign of Max and his silent bodyguard.

Where the hell did he go?

SEVENTEEN

Eve

I TAKE MY TIME LEAVING THE OASIS, GLIDING ACROSS THE FLOOR AS if I have all the time in the world to make my exit. I project grace and elegance, with a serene smile plastered on my face as if the sounds of non-penetrative sex don't bother me and I'm pleased the men are enjoying themselves.

I detest what they're doing.

I hate them all.

Inside my head, the scene is much different. I flee toward the exit, racing toward freedom as swiftly as my legs can carry me. My chest constricts. Panic rises. Breathing becomes difficult.

Will Tomas change his mind and call me back to his side before I can make my break for freedom?

That shifting in the air is real. I felt it at dinner and again in the Oasis. I fear what it means.

I manage to make it to the doorway and glide into the hall with that damn smile fixed to my face. Then I navigate through the labyrinth of hallways, unwilling to spend the rest of the night in my room. It's suffocating in there, with the walls slowly closing in, encasing me within a tomb.

I need fresh air. I need the illusion of freedom. I simply need a break.

My steps take me through The Retreat to one of my favorite courtyards. It's the largest, which is probably why it's my favorite. Tall trees block out the oppressiveness of my prison, and I can pretend I'm on a stroll outside as if none of this exists.

In the center of the courtyard, a fountain sprays water into the air. The light sound of it falling back into the rippling pool at its base never fails to soothe me.

I wander the paths between the flower beds, where bushes rise above my head, again giving the illusion I'm not trapped in this feral place.

It's a warm night, as always, but the overwhelming humidity is gone, swept away by the coming of night. A light breeze flutters leaves all around me, and brings the aromatic fragrance of tropical flowers floating in the air. Torchlight flickers, lighting the paths. It's dark enough to escape, but light enough not to trip and fall.

I take it in and let the constriction in my chest ease. Three deep breaths push the headache away. I didn't lie about that. The low sound of male voices carries on the wind, and I come to an abrupt stop.

Suddenly alert, tension builds between my shoulders as I debate my next move. Can I tiptoe back the way I came? In heels? Did the men hear my approach? I wasn't trying to be quiet.

I listen, but no longer hear them. Adrenaline spikes in my blood as I debate whether to flee or stay put, hoping they move on.

The footsteps head toward me. Whoever it is, they're coming for me. Max and his bodyguard come into view.

"What an unexpected pleasure." A genuine smile brightens his face.

"Good evening, Mr. S."

"Please, call me Max."

"Good evening, Max."

"You look lovely." His gaze sweeps over me. Not predatory. Not revolting. He looks at me with genuine interest.

What is it about this man? When he's near, I find it impossible to look away, like there's some otherworldly pull that draws my eye.

Dressed in an immaculate suit, tailored to his massive frame, he moves with lethal grace, but there's more.

So much more.

Max is acutely aware of his surroundings. I've never noticed that in a person before, but he scans and takes note of everything around him.

How does he do that?

My head tips as I try to figure out this mystery, only to realize I'm doing it again.

I'm staring at him.

"Shouldn't you be in the Oasis?"

"Shouldn't you?" Immediately, I regret the harshness of my tone.

Dark hair, dark eyes, broad shoulders, thick arms, and muscled thighs, he's dangerous. It's riveting and intoxicating. Mesmerizing and terrifying. There's a solidness to him, a sense he can provide comfort, protection, and shelter to those around him. It grounds him, and unsettles me. If I didn't know why he was here, he's a man I could easily fall for.

Hell, I'm already falling for this monstrous man. And why? Because he's tall, dark, and handsome? Because I like the way his eyes burn when he looks at me? Because the corner of his lips tilts into a smirk?

I know why.

My world officially makes no sense.

He's a predator. My inner voice tells me to be wary, but I can't help but gravitate toward him. He feels like a savior, even though I know he's a devil. I can't stop my heart from wanting to believe a lie.

I don't know what it is, but I feel like I can trust him. It's almost as if he's strong enough to carry my burdens and lighten my load—if only I can trust him to do so.

This is the kind of thing I can't risk. Looks are deceiving. Don't fall for one of the guests.

"I preferred a walk outside." The way he looks at me makes my skin burn. I should find him as revolting as Tomas, but I don't.

"I only mean," I clear my throat, "it's your first night and you should enjoy yourself."

"Who's to say I'm not enjoying myself right now?"

I look beyond him, to his bodyguard, and wonder what the two of them are doing out here. We're nowhere near their rooms.

"Are you lost? Your suite is…"

"I know where my suite is." He takes a step toward me and it takes every ounce of willpower not to shift back. "This place is incredible and I thought to take a moment to explore my surroundings. Are your rooms around here?" His brow arches in question.

"They are not." My back stiffens at the intrusiveness of the question.

"Maybe we can take that walk together? I'm dying to get to know you."

"I don't think…"

"Relax, Eve, I don't bite."

I bite my lower lip debating my sanity. The thing is, I want to take a walk with him. There's something about him that tells me I can trust him, that he won't hurt me. I don't know why that is, considering he's all but announced his interest in purchasing me out from under Benefield's thumb.

I can't help but feel safe with him. It's easy to breathe when Max is near. The constriction in my chest eases. My breaths come more freely around him. The constant tension in my shoulders loosens its tight grip.

I dream.

I hope.

He's so different from the other guests who make my insides churn with disgust. His demeanor doesn't suggest he means me harm. I sense no cruelty in him. But I know better than to trust my senses. He's here for one, and only one, purpose.

"I belong to Tomas."

"What hold does he have over you?"

"He protects me."

"Is that what you think this is?" He gestures around us.

"It is."

"No." Max closes the distance between us. "You're one of those pretty little birds, trapped in a gilded cage, too frightened to venture out into the world."

"I'm not scared."

While I consider my options, he stares at me, drinking in my features. His gaze makes an unhurried exploration of my face while his brows knit together as if he's trying to unravel some great mystery.

"You're frightened out of your mind, Eve." The way he says my name is like a whisper, uttered with reverence and affection.

"I am not." My snappish reply is something I'll pay for later if Max reports it back to Benefield.

"I feel the terror flowing in your veins. Being held against your will, in a place like this, must be frightening."

"I'm not here against my will."

"Are you telling me you could walk out of here anytime you like?" His eyes spark, and his uniquely masculine scent floods my senses.

"There's no reason for me to leave. I'm content, here."

"Is that so?"

I can't help it, but the things he says make me feel weak, and after all this time, what I really need is someone who isn't out to hurt me. It's stupid, and crazy, and incredibly unwise, but I ache for the simple comfort of a hug. It's a desperate ache, which only grows larger when he's around.

He's a devil!

My inner voice is at it again, warning me off. The thing is—I'm tired.

I'm tired of pretending to be strong. I exist at the whim of a madman, and there will come a time when I am no longer of use to Benefield.

I'm terrified of that day. Is it wrong of me to lean upon a

stranger for help? Even if he's one of the monsters infesting this world?

Is Max standing closer than a moment before? Or am I the one who moved? This man has an odd effect on me.

People speak about chemistry. I've never felt it before. I don't know what it is, but something swirls in the air between us.

It's potent. Undeniable. And terrifying.

I open my mouth to tell him how loyal I am to Benefield, but Max lifts his index finger and gives a shake of his head.

"I'm going to save you the embarrassment of lying to me."

"I'm not..."

"When you lie, your eyelids flutter and you fiddle with the fabric of your dress." He points to my hand where my fingers are indeed playing with the buttery-smooth silk of my gown.

"How do you..."

"I'm an excellent read of people."

He slides a thumb along my jawline, and I realize I don't know when he closed the distance between us. I find myself leaning into his touch as he slides his thumb along my jaw. My breath falters.

"It's how I know you're not here willingly." His smug tone wakes me up from this weird trance I'm in. "You're just as much a prisoner as any of the other girls."

"You're wrong." My safety relies upon the illusion I stand by Benefield's side.

"Am I?" He presses closer, breathing in my strangled gasp. He stares into my eyes with concern instead of lust. "Whatever you're doing with Benefield, that man will hurt you."

"And you won't?"

The muscles of his jaw tick. "Have I given you reason to think I will?"

"You're here to purchase a slave."

"What if I was here for another reason?" His words give me pause. "Would that make a difference?"

"A difference as far as what?"

"In how you feel about me."

"I belong to Tomas."

"Beware the trust you place in others, especially men like him. Benefield doesn't have your best interests in mind. He cares only for himself."

"He cares for me."

"Is that so?"

"It is."

"I find myself drawn to you. If I placed a bid on you, what would he do? If the price is right, he'll give you to me."

"No." I gulp and put on my bravest face. "He wouldn't do that. I'm not for sale, Mr. S."

It's a lie, and he told me he can tell when I lie. I can't hide my true feelings, although I try. I need to tread lightly here, considering the interest Max displays in me and the unpredictability Benefield presents. Honestly, despite the depravity such a thing means, I'd jump at it. From the frying pan into the fire, who's to say Max is any worse than Benefield? But that's not something I can risk my life on.

"He most definitely would."

"Benefield will never let me go." That's the absolute truth. I'm never leaving this place alive.

"Benefield?"

"Tomas. I mean Tomas."

"I see. At last, I understand."

"You understand, what?"

"I don't know what deal you struck with Benefield, but you don't belong here. Good thing I'm here."

"And why is that?"

"Because, I'm going to get you out of this place." His eyes narrow and blaze with fire.

It's a punch in the gut and a reminder. The men here, all of them, only ever look at me as a thing to have. To take and claim. Hurt and destroy. Max is no different. He just laid it on the line. He wants me. He desires me. And he'll do whatever it takes to have me.

Unwittingly, Max signs my death warrant. He doesn't understand that Benefield never relinquishes his toys.

Never.

I'm a dead woman walking.

Although, Max makes me believe there's life beyond these walls, his interest consigns me to death.

I pull back from his touch and drop my gaze. "I'm sorry if I've given you any reason to think otherwise, but I truly am here by my choice. My place is by Tomas' side."

"You're very convincing, but I don't believe you. Given the chance to be free of this place, would you take it?"

That path leads to death.

I'd rather stay with the monster I know than leave with the one I don't.

"That is not for me to say." A tear makes its way past my defenses. It pools in my eye and trickles down my cheek. "My place is here."

Max brushes the pad of his thumb over my cheek, catching my tear. He puts his thumb to his lips and sucks away the salty essence. I want to grab his hand and demand he return my tear. He has no right to it.

"You don't belong here," he says.

"And yet, here I am. Didn't we have this talk already?"

"What do you mean?" His brows pinch with confusion.

"Men crave beautiful things. They put them in cages to keep them safe from the world, without realizing they destroy what they aim to protect."

I firm my chin and wrap my protective inner armor back around myself. Max gets under my skin. I lower my barriers when I'm with him, letting him see the weakness within me. Pain hitches in my chest as I turn away.

Max's arm shoots out. He grabs me and spins me around until I face him.

He's tall, massive, undeniably male, and I react to the potent swirl of masculinity engulfing me. His intoxicating scent hits my sensory receptors. Male. Virile masculinity. Power. Control. It's an aphrodisiac I can't escape.

"Some men set those they love free," he says, "hoping they will one day return. Not all men are monsters."

"The men who come here are." There, I said it. I called him a monster.

"I would never put you in a gilded cage."

No, but you would buy me and take my freedom. "I'm not for sale, Mr. S, but there are plenty of girls here who are."

Max makes me believe he can protect me. He makes me believe I'll find shelter in his arms. God forbid, he makes me believe he will rescue me.

I can't help but dream.

His masculine aroma slams into me. I try to turn away. I try to fight biology on its most primal level, but Max holds me tight in his grip.

I should shout, or scream. Only nobody will come to my aid. Not in this place. Not where such sounds are a part of business as usual. Only, I don't shout. I don't scream.

I need to believe, if only for a moment, that this man might care for me, even if it's not true. I need it because I'm weak and incredibly lonely. If these past few weeks taught me anything, it's that there is no hope.

I place my hand between us, meaning to push him away, but the moment my palm connects to the warmth of his chest, I breathe out all the torment and misery within me. I need a protector more than I need to breathe.

My head tilts forward, and before I know it, my forehead presses against the hard planes of his chest. My fingers curl in the fabric of his shirt as my shoulders shake with the sobs I refuse to let loose.

He grips my other arm. Instead of tightening—instead of hurting me—his bold hands glide over my shoulders, pulling me to him. In complete silence, he does nothing other than hold me while I silently fall apart in his arms.

Outwardly, all I do is stand still. Inside, I weep and sob and cry as I pour out months of terror and fear into his embrace.

I need this. I need a protector.

A savior.

I need to know I'm not alone in this desolate hell.

Why does he hold me? Why am I leaning into him? Why does it feel like that perfectly tailored suit is nothing but a shell? Like if I were to strip it away, I'd see the real him?

Is it too much to hope for compassion from a monstrous man? The solid beat of his heart steadies me. The slow draw of his breath centers me. I feel him all over, touching me and protecting me. I feel him humming in my blood, delving deep into all the hidden places inside of me.

The canopy rustles overhead as a songbird shifts in its roost for the night. The noise breaks this odd spell, clearing my muddled thoughts. I push away, but he growls deep in the back of his throat. His arms tighten.

"You're safe, Eve. You'll always be safe with me."

The funny thing is, I believe him.

An insect buzzes off to my left and a tree frog answers with a chirp. A light breeze tickles my cheek as his fingers float through my hair. His tenderness will destroy me.

When the backs of his knuckles graze my face, I hold my breath and tense. Reality comes crashing around me. This is a mistake.

It's a terrible mistake.

He cups my jaw, such a gentle touch for a massive man. It feels nice, but he's not safe. He's a man bent on bending a woman to his will. Maybe this is how it starts? Give a little tenderness to draw me in, then crush me beneath his strength.

My chin tips into his palm, unwilling to be rid of his touch so soon. There's something about him that draws me and compels me to believe his lies.

I look up at him, and tumble into his compassionate gaze. Mesmerizing and dark, his eyes shine vividly, promising protection and salvation. His mouth parts, and for a minute, I think he's going to kiss me, but he only presses his warm, pillowy lips to the top of my head.

This feels too heavy.

Too real.

Something shifts within me, a loosening of the iron-tight hold I keep on my emotions. There's a gravity to this moment, as if everything is going to change.

And that is dangerous.

I should fight this strange chemistry, but all I do is lean further into his embrace. I'm so tired of fighting, of pretending, of hating what I've become. I'm tired of everything.

All I want is for all of this to end.

If I'm to become a slave, is this man any worse than the others?

Then it hits.

His tenderness will be the thing that breaks me.

In the fight for freedom, I've already lost.

EIGHTEEN

Max

IT TAKES FOUR DAYS TO CLEAR MY SUITE OF ALL THE BUGS. WHILE we identified all of them that first day, removing them in one sweep would've raised red flags. As a result, we moderate our conversations.

Knox gets up from his knees with the last of the listening devices pinched between his thumb and forefinger. He walks into the bathroom and crushes it beneath his shoe and the hard tile.

I breathe out a sigh of relief.

"Finally." Not that we're going to suddenly reveal our true identities, but it's one less thing to worry about. I don't have to spew filth to Knox about the girls I'm considering.

So far, I've let Benefield know none of them will do. Too tame. Too broken. Too eager to please. I tell Knox about wanting to break in my own girl.

Benefield is yet to respond by offering different girls for me to sample. He still brings out those who've been meticulously trained with defeated eyes. He's holding back, playing a dangerous game. But then, so am I.

"You going to sit around all morning, or are you going to get your ass off the couch and join me for a run?" Knox snips at me.

Dutifully playing the part of bodyguard and manservant, he grows more and more restless with each and every day.

I get it. I feel it too. We're in a pressure cooker and Benefield is slowly turning up the heat. He notices my reticence to avail myself of the pleasures to be found in the Oasis, leading to questions about my authenticity.

As much as it twists my insides, it's time to step things up a notch. I know what needs to be done. The only problem is I can't stomach what I must do.

There must be a way to navigate this situation and keep my morality intact at the end. To do that, a leap of faith will need to be made, and it won't be me making that leap.

"Hang on, I gotta get these out." I blink against the irritation in my eyes. Mitzy's contact lenses are giving me a fit in this humidity.

"Still bugging you?"

"Just scratchy and itchy." I head to the bathroom and carefully remove Mitzy's incredible spy tech. We're not finished mapping everything out, but Knox is always with me. We can do with one pair of Mitzy's *eyes*.

After four days, Knox and I settle into a routine. We get up, head out for a run, lift weights in the gym, then join Benefield and the other guests for whatever activity is planned for the afternoon. After dinner, I head to the Oasis with the rest of the men, drink a whiskey, then excuse myself once the depravity begins. I tell Benefield I'm not interested in the docile slaves he offers and that my cravings turn toward darker things. If he is listening in on my private conversations with Knox, there should be no reason to question me.

"I'm putting my shoes on." I glance around the suite, trying to remember where I left my shoes.

"Looks like you're thinking about your woman again."

"She's not my woman."

"You sure about that? Because it definitely looked like something was going on the other night."

"That was three days ago and she hasn't spoken to me since."

Either Eve actively avoids me, or Benefield keeps her away. I've made no secret of my interest, but it may be too big of an ask for Benefield to hand over his woman to a guest. I've been working on that problem for the past few days, watching my host for anything I can use to my advantage. He's a prideful bastard, and that may be my lead-in.

"The way the two of you trade stares says something else."

"Whatever." I rise from the couch to grab my shoes. "This should be the last pass."

"Yup."

Our systematic mapping of The Retreat and its grounds is nearly complete. Mitzy and the rest of Alpha team pour over the data looking for a way in. The heavy fortifications make this particular job more challenging, but it won't be the first time we've accomplished the impossible.

Our goal is a coordinated breach on the last night when the auction occurs. Most of the girls will be in one place. Those in training will be in lockdown in the slave quarters.

While our mission is to rescue Eve, we'll do our best to save as many of the girls as possible. It's going to be tricky.

Knox and I head outside, waving to the guards as we go. One of the benefits of working out in the gym each day is Knox and I are getting familiar with the guards. We also make a point to sneak out and play cards with them at night.

The time I don't spend in the Oasis is time spent collecting valuable intelligence. No doubt the guards report back to him, bragging about how much money they win off my mediocre poker game. I win just enough to establish I'm credible while losing what I need to create the perfect setup.

Knox and I lope into a slow jog, warming up for a faster pace where we'll make a lap of the one section of the property we've yet to explore. I put in my earbuds. Knox does the same. Instead of music, our team comes online. The signal from Knox's watch gets a boost from the highflying drone overhead and patches us in.

"Status," CJ's clipped voice gets right to the point.

"Heading out now." Our daily runs are the one time we're absolutely certain no one listens in.

"How's the planning going?" I settle into an easy pace. My body's eager to work out the added stress this mission brings. Knox's words circle back around in my head.

My woman.

Eve is not mine, although I'm definitely interested. When I close my eyes at the end of the day, her face is what I see. Her delicate scent is what I smell. The way her small frame fits against mine is what I feel.

But she's kept her distance these past few days. Not sure if that's Benefield's doing or hers, it drives me crazy.

I settled one thing that night in the courtyard. Eve is definitely being held against her will. Whatever charade she has going on with Benefield is just that. It's an act that somehow saves her from the degradation the other girls suffer daily.

No surprise there. I'm not the only guest ogling the woman who stands by Benefield's side. Although, if any of those men dare touch my Eve, I will take their arm off. But how to get Eve away from Benefield?

"Infil is going to be difficult." CJ briefs the team on infiltration possibilities. "We've looked at several scenarios."

"Tell me." I turn my thoughts from Eve and refocus on the job.

Infiltrating this fortress is no small feat. Knox and I are well-positioned. We've memorized every room and hallway in both the inner buildings and the outer buildings that house the guards.

The mapping we've done allows Mitzy and Forest to create a virtual reality model for the team to practice on. They've spent a good part of the past few days doing exactly that. They'll be just as familiar with the layout of this place as Knox and I are.

Getting our team into the compound won't be difficult. Benefield doesn't watch for threats coming from inside. All of his forces look outward, beyond the gate. We're Guardians, which means we're all ex-special ops with extensive jump training.

Our team will parachute inside the outer boundary fence and work in from there. They need to make it from there to inside, where the auction is being held. That's where Knox and I will be.

"I don't see any scenario where we breach the walls without triggering an alarm. Knox and I won't have any weapons."

"I'm working on that." Mitzy chimes in. "I'm reconfiguring a drone to deliver you a package."

"Really?"

"We'll drop weapons to you. Sidearms only. You'll have to make do with those."

"It's not like I can hide a semi-automatic under my suit." Knox snickers.

"You sure about that?" I grin because Knox is more than well endowed. I've seen the man naked, and even I'm impressed.

I have to say I feel exposed behind enemy lines without a weapon on hand.

"Once we breach the outer wall, it's going to be chaos in there." Axel, Alpha-three is acting commander of Alpha team in my and Knox's absence. He'll lead Alpha into the fortress. "Do you know where the auction is held?"

"No, but we'll find out. Most likely, the banquet hall," I say.

"I need that info."

"Copy that."

"Max, I'm going to drop your weapons into one of the courtyards." Mitzy's back online. "Do you have a preference?"

"You don't think they'll notice a drone coming in for a landing?"

"It's not going to land. From what you've told us about their cameras, they're only looking at the people inside. Nothing is pointed up into the sky. The drone will fly in and lower your gear on a cable. I've done extensive work on the motors; it's virtually silent now, and black on black. Unless they know where to look, they won't see it coming, and I don't see any evidence of monitoring for aircraft overhead."

"Are we going to have to be out there to greet it because that's going to raise suspicions." Knox glances at me and rolls his eyes. Stealth drones delivering guns definitely has Mitzy's crazy signature all over it.

"Once you tell me which courtyard is the closest, I'll figure out the delivery. My plan is to hide the package in the canopy of one of the trees or in one of the fountains."

"Got it."

We talk for the next two miles of our run with the team, ironing out the details of where, when, and how.

"Heads up." Knox taps my arm.

Jogging toward us is a vision of loveliness. Eve's long hair is pulled back high on her head. With each step, it swishes back and forth. That tiny flick of movement mesmerizes me, but my focus doesn't stay there.

How can it when her tight body is on display? Perfect breasts lift and lower with each step. Her expression is one of intense focus. Looking down at the ground in front of her, she doesn't see us until we're almost in front of her.

I should move on, but I can't help but stop. How many opportunities have we had to get her alone? And away from the prying eyes of The Retreat.

None.

That's how many.

"Good morning, Eve." I stop right in front of her, forcing her to either swerve around me or stop for a polite conversation.

"Good morning." She gives us a curt nod as she jogs in place. It's a subtle statement that she's not interested in talking.

"I'm surprised to see you out."

"Why is that?"

"I wouldn't think it's allowed."

"I'm free to wander the grounds as I choose."

"What about outside the walls?"

Her gaze flicks to the left where a twenty-foot wire fence bounds the property. An electric fence Knox and I have extensively mapped. Today is the last bit of our reconnaissance.

Knox moves off a bit, giving his "Boss" a modicum of privacy. He continues speaking to the team. Or rather, listening. He won't blow our cover by talking to himself. I pull the earbud out of my ear so as not to be distracted by their conversation. They're talking about exfil, which is how we're going to get our asses, and the girls, away from this hellhole.

"I'm safer in here." Eve stops jogging in place, perhaps settling herself for a conversation with me, but she turns wistful eyes toward that fence. I bet she runs along the fence doing exactly what Knox and I are doing now. She's looking for weakness and opportunity.

That knowledge might come in useful. I file that fact away.

"Are you?"

"As safe as I can be."

"Is this where you wish to stay?"

"That is a complicated question."

"It's a binary question with only two answers. Either you want to stay or you don't."

"This is better than the alternative."

"What if the alternative is me?"

Something about Eve makes me restless and possessive. I probably shouldn't blurt something like that out, but I am here to buy a slave. Mr. S would definitely be interested in taking Benefield's woman. It's a power play between two powerful men.

Eve's gaze clashes with mine, flashing with anger, indignation, fear, and a glimmer of something else. I capture her gaze in mine, letting the moment stretch. Disgust curls her lip.

"I belong to Tomas."

"Is that what you think?"

"Step aside, please." She takes a step to the left.

Anticipating her move, I step with her, barring her passage. Eve huffs with irritation and steps back to the right. Again, I move with her, watching her irritation grow.

"I'm not done speaking with you."

"I have nothing further to say to you, Mr. S."

"Call me Max."

She gives an indignant snort and props her fists on her hips.

Knox's already stated she's my woman. I'm beginning to understand what that means. As for how to secure her freedom, I'm still working that angle.

We all are.

The difficulty of this mission lies in the other girls. Forest, Sam, and CJ need to make a decision if we extend our extraction to the girls or limit it to only Eve. Knowing Forest, he won't be happy leaving any woman in captivity. But there are limits to what even the Guardians can accomplish.

For now, I focus on Eve.

NINETEEN

Max

EVE IS ALWAYS WITH BENEFIELD, AND OTHER THAN THAT NIGHT IN the courtyard, I haven't been able to get her alone. Seeing her outside for a run, without guards, confuses me until I spot the device on her wrist.

Not any watch a woman would willingly wear, it's obviously a tracker. She's free to run outside the walls, but only at the end of an electronic leash.

More than ever, I'm convinced Eve's status in this place is unsettled. Somehow, she convinced herself standing with Benefield would protect her from his depravity, but Eve doesn't understand how psychopaths operate.

He's the cat. She's the mouse. And he's playing with his shiny new toy.

He dangles her freedom in front of her, waiting for the right moment to pounce. That's when he'll rip away her safety blanket because it amuses him. I intend to take advantage of that very thing.

Over the past few days, Knox and I debated how to proceed, arguing whether to let her know who we are or keep her in the dark.

At first, I made the case for telling her about our mission. Knox vehemently opposed, saying we couldn't trust her, that her allegiance to Benefield left too many unknowns up in the air. I relented after a day, deciding Knox raised valid concerns. We left it there, deciding to keep our secret and keep her in the dark.

Every day since, I try to get her alone, but Benefield tightens her leash.

With regret, Knox and I leave Eve to her jog and finish ours, heading in opposite directions. Then Knox surprises me.

"We need to tell her."

"Why? I thought you didn't agree."

"I've thought about it."

"And?"

"You need her willing."

"Willing? There are many ways to define that. If anything, it'll raise suspicions."

"You don't think she can pull it off?"

The willing part, in all honesty, is a foregone conclusion. Some wicked chemistry exists between us. I felt it just now, a crackling in the air, a heating under my skin, and desire blooming into undeniable need. From the way her breathing picked up, I'm not alone. She feels it too.

"Benefield will know something's up. If she comes to my bed willingly, he's going to want to know why."

"You still think he's not sleeping with her?"

"Without coming right out and asking, I don't believe so."

"She never leaves his side, and he's pretty free with touching her."

"There's a difference between letting him touch her and having no choice in the matter. If he's raping her, she wouldn't tolerate his touch like she does. And as for his touching her, it's platonic as fuck. He's possessive of her, but he doesn't touch her like a lover would."

It's true. He never lets his fingers graze her breast. His hand never slips down to her ass. He holds her like a brother would hold a sister. They're not having sex. I'd bet my life on it.

"You think a man like him is capable of love?" Knox glances at me as if I would know the answer to a question like that. The thing is, I do. The read I have on Benefield solidifies with each passing day.

"No, but he knows lust."

"I don't see it. We don't know he's not fucking her."

"Watch him."

"I watch all the time. All I do is stand around watching stuff."

"I mean watch how he touches the girls and how it's different from the way he touches Eve. With Eve, it's possessive. He reaches out, reassuring himself she's still there. With the girls, he grabs what he wants and pushes them away when he's done. There's a difference."

"You sure about that?"

"Definitely."

"To me, it looks like she's his lover."

"Benefield wants us to think that."

"Why?"

"It's a game."

"How's that?"

"She's the woman he can have whenever he wants. By not taking her, he shows restraint."

"That's fucked."

"Not really. His men sense it. They see a great man, with great power, showing restraint with his greatest asset. Eve gives him power."

"Like I said, that's fucked."

"Not arguing the point, but you can't deny it's effective. He's had every woman here. You see him in the Oasis. You've watched how he treats those girls."

"I do." Which is why Knox and I stay only as long as necessary in the Oasis, excusing ourselves for the night.

"He can have those girls whenever he wants. He directs their training, but his guests, and his trainers have those girls as well."

"That's because he's a psychopath," Knox says. "Those girls aren't human in his eyes. They're baubles and things. He uses them to scratch an itch."

"Exactly, but Eve is something else."

"How so?"

"You know how some kids keep their favorite action figures wrapped in their original packaging? Never opening them? Never playing with them?" I may have done something like that back when I was a kid. It was stupid. I threw out my action figures once my voice deepened and my balls grew hair. Never once did I play with the toy. Waste of time and money.

"Yeah?"

"Eve is that to Benefield."

"A toy?"

"A toy more valuable because he doesn't touch her."

"If you say so." Knox doesn't look convinced.

"There will come a time when he opens the package. And when he does, Eve will suffer the same fate as all the other girls in this place."

"Well fuck. We definitely need to tell her." Knox scratches his head.

"I thought you vetoed that?"

"I did."

"You told me not to open that door."

"Yeah, but if you're right, it's a ticking time bomb." Knox paces in a circle, staring at the dirt as he thinks about all the possibilities that might happen if we tell Eve.

"Precisely."

"That's why we need to let Eve know what's going on. She can help us." He sounds sure of himself.

I disagree. "She needs to stay in the dark."

"Come again?" He stops and looks me square in the eye. "This is what you wanted."

"I need to get him to give her to me, but it needs to be worth it. Or…" I take a breath, trying to puzzle it out. "Or, I need to force his hand."

"How will you do that?"

"What is it that Benefield craves more than anything?"

"A stable of women to sell to the highest bidder?" Knox shakes his head. "I don't know. Power, money, and religion are the big three motivators. It's nothing to do with religion. So, power or money."

"He's got more money than he can spend in a hundred lifetimes. Benefield craves power, and he'll do whatever he can to hold onto it. Which includes getting rid of things that no longer matter."

"How is that going to help?"

"Because he can't tolerate anyone who threatens him. He can't afford to lose."

"And that's your grand plan? Get him to lose?"

"Why do you think we've been playing poker with the guards?"

"We've been pumping them for information." Knox glances up like I've grown two heads.

"True, but I've been laying the groundwork."

"How does losing our asses in poker help?" Knox scratches his head.

"We haven't lost our asses. You've won a fair share. I have too."

"You've lost more than you've won. And I'm not happy about you gambling again. Not with your history."

"I'm not addicted to gambling." It's time to finally come clean.

"That's what an addict would say."

I take in a deep breath. "It's time I told you about Scott Connor."

"Who the hell is that?"

"He's the reason I stopped gambling." Blowing out my breath, I unpack the memories of how my arrogance and need for revenge ended the life of a bully.

Knox listens through the whole thing. At first, he doesn't believe me, but then I explain why we've been playing poker with the guards every night.

"Benefield keeps tabs on all his guests. Researches the hell out of them before granting them access."

"How thoroughly does he research. Our cover..." I get Knox's concern. Our cover is only as strong as the weakest link.

"Is tight. Mitzy and her team know what they're doing. I asked her to build in a history of gambling debts, large loses, moderate wins, but overall loss. Just enough to keep me at it."

"So, we weren't just pumping the guards for information?"

"Right, we're laying credible, first-hand accounts of my skill."

"Fine. So, poker? What's the play?"

"Get him to bet something he no longer values."

"And that's Eve? According to you, he places great value in her."

"For now. Once he loses to me, her shiny package status is gone. It puts her at even more risk. He'll part with her because she no longer has value to him. I'll think I'm getting his little trinket, and I'll lord that over him. He'll say he's tired of her, or something along those lines. That she's useless, or something. Whatever it takes to maintain his status with his men. We can't afford to let her know who we are. When he loses her to me, her reaction needs to be real."

"*If* he loses her to you." Knox is still not on board.

"Dude, no one can beat me in a game of poker."

"You ever play poker with a psychopath before?"

"No," I say with a shrug.

"Then don't get cocky. I've got your back, but I see a hundred ways this can go wrong."

"It won't."

"Whatever. So, we don't tell Eve?"

"Right. Her reactions need to be authentic."

"You do know what that means?"

"I do."

"She's going to hate you."

"It's all I've been thinking about. But I can make it work."

"You can't play with your new toy, and Benefield is going to be watching. For every bug I remove, they replace it with two more. There will be eyes and ears."

"I'm aware of that."

"You're not crossing that line."

"I'll do whatever I need to be convincing. We need to make it to auction night intact."

"What you're talking about can leave scars."

"I'm prepared to accept that."

"She's going to hate you."

"She already does."

"Bullshit. I don't know what the hell is going on between the two of you, but it's palpable."

I don't disagree. Electricity charges the air when Eve is near.

"If you noticed, odds are Benefield has as well. The girls he offers are too docile. That's not an accident. I've made my desires clear. Eve isn't docile. She's not trained. He can't afford for me to leave unsatisfied."

"What happens if it doesn't work out?"

"It will."

"And if not?" Knox isn't arguing with me. He's doing what a good teammate does. He's poking holes in my plan.

I get he doesn't think this makes sense, but I've been watching Benefield. He's getting tired of his little pet. He's getting aggressive.

It's day six of our weeklong stint at The Retreat. The auction occurs tomorrow night. I've got a little over twenty-four hours to figure something out. In my head, it's easy. Rope Benefield into a game, take him to the cleaners, then go all in. Make a bet he can't refuse.

"You really think you're good enough?" Knox gives me the side-eyes. "I get why you stopped gambling. Makes more sense. You've always struck me as a man who has his shit locked down tight. I figured it was your one flaw."

"One?"

"Everyone has a flaw."

"I'm sure I have more than one."

"I'm concerned."

"Why?"

"It's been years since you've played. Your skills may not be what they once were."

"What do you think I've been doing these past few days? Besides, the game is like riding a bike."

"Is that so?"

"Yeah, the rhythm settles back in. The cards never lie. And people are people."

"What does that mean?"

"It means, players lie all the damn time. Know how to read them and the game's a breeze."

"You can still lose."

"There's always that risk."

"Is it worth Eve's life?"

"When all hell cuts loose tomorrow night, I want her by my side. I'm counting on you to help me get her out of this place."

"I'll be right there, brother." He claps me on the arm and gives a firm squeeze. "When Alpha comes knocking on the door, it's going to be chaos around here."

"Organized chaos."

Sam decided to activate all our teams. Well, all except Delta. That team handles domestic kidnapping cases in tandem with the FBI. Not that Jenny and her team can't kick serious ass, but we can't afford to have all our teams on one mission.

Charlie, and the four operational men in Bravo team, will coordinate attacks on the slave pens, where they keep the girls. Alpha is taking on the main house during the auction.

Benefield will protect his assets. The Guardians will interrupt his plans. This is what we live for.

TWENTY

Max

ANOTHER NIGHT IN THE OASIS.

"You don't seem interested in my girls." Benefield reclines on his sultan's couch. Numerous cushions surround him, as do half a dozen girls.

They massage his arms, his hands, his legs, and his feet. A girl straddles him, facing away, and rubs her ass shamelessly against his crotch in what's supposed to be a sensual grind.

Benefield looks bored.

Bile rises in the back of my throat.

The no-touching rule appears to be one Benefield holds himself to as well as his guests. I've yet to see him fuck any of the girls in the Oasis. Not that there aren't plenty of hand jobs, blow jobs, and lap dances going on.

"These are too tame for my tastes." I pointedly glance over his shoulder, making my interest in Eve obvious. "Although, one of your girls has caught my eye."

Benefield reaches over his shoulder and wraps his fingers around Eve's delicate wrist. "Are you interested in a virgin?" He deliberately deflects. "I have several."

"Virgins are delicate treats, but short-lived fantasies. The moment you deflower one, she's no longer special. Then you're left with just another whore. I prefer mine to have more—experience." Again, my gaze cuts to Eve.

Her stormy sea-green eyes rage with fury. I don't blame her. I'm talking about rape. Not that I ever would, but she doesn't know that.

Eve presses her delicate lips together, forming a hard line. Guys talk about getting stuck in the friend zone, but I bet no one has ever found themselves where I am right now. There's no recovery from this. Which I'm okay with. My mission is to rescue Eve, not to make her mine.

My desire comes secondary to securing her freedom.

There's fear in her expression. I read each of her emotions, but it's not necessary to be an expert to decipher her body language. Her lower lip trembles and her entire body tenses.

From the look in Benefield's eye, her exalted status is on a precipice. I have no doubt he'll toss her over the edge just because he can. It's what a monster would do, and Benefield is a monstrous man.

I rise from my seat and press out the wrinkles of my pants. Knox kicks off from the wall he's been holding up, getting ready to follow me out.

"Heading out?" Benefield's tone takes a dangerous turn.

"Need some fresh air."

"Fresh air? Or are you looking to lighten your wallet with my men again?" He cackles, thinking it's a funny joke.

"The thrill of a good game is hard to pass up."

"And here I thought you came all this way to purchase a slave."

"You've yet to provide one who suits my interests." I make a sweep of the room. "Docile. Trained. Accommodating. You create the perfectly trained pet." I want to add for weak-willed men, but hold my tongue. No reason to start an argument. "I crave resistance, fight, and a bit of spitfire. A woman who kicks and screams is far more fun, and worth her price."

"You crave power over the one you own."

"I crave dominance."

He absently rubs at Eve's wrist. "Power comes in many forms."

He twists his neck and pulls on Eve's hand. While staring at me, he kisses the inside of her wrist. "You can force a woman to serve, or she can come to you willingly. Which one gives you more power?"

"Both."

"How so?"

"One you take because you're more powerful. The other is earned because you have power."

"My slaves are trained to be submissive." He glances at Eve and releases her wrist.

Eve places her hand on the back of Benefield's neck, continuing her massage.

"Your slaves are vacant inside. Good enough for an effortless fuck. I can lie on my back and any one of them will crawl on top of me and serve my needs. Where's the fun in that? There's no fight, no victory when you pin her down and take what you want. My slave will respect me. She'll fear the consequences of not pleasing me. I'm not looking for a woman whose will is broken and mind is shattered."

"You like your slaves to resist?"

"I like them to fight back." Again, my gaze cuts to Eve. "The moment they realize they can't win, that's when I truly own them. That moment is better than any sex in the world. Not to mention it keeps things interesting."

Benefield needs to understand who I crave, in addition to what and why.

I'm sorry, Eve. One day, you'll forgive me.

As for Eve, the tension in her body builds, magnifying by the second as I describe in excruciating detail how I like to discipline my slaves. After this is done, I'll need a shower to wash away this goddamn filth.

"Perhaps we've wasted each other's time. I was under the impression you could deliver whatever your client needs."

"I've never had a client complain about the goods I have for sale."

"Perhaps you've never met a man like me."

Benefield is a cocky prick, claiming no man leaves The Retreat unsatisfied. Well, I'm not like any of the men here. I have morals.

Benefield is a psychopath with a god complex. Power is the currency he wields. Money means little to him.

In a business where word of mouth is king, he can't afford an unhappy customer. My bet is he'll do everything in his power to meet my demands, but—and here's the kicker—he's going to make me pay for it. How he intends to do that remains to be seen, but it's coming. He'll force an unsavory choice on me if I fail to play his game.

"Don't be so hasty. I'm certain I have something that will meet with your approval. My ability to provide my guests the perfect gentleman's companion is unrivaled. None have left unsatisfied."

Gentleman's companion?

It's a grotesque euphemism for a broken woman. Men like him belong six feet underground. His dark, soulless eyes glimmer with anticipation.

My gaze cuts back to Eve. "You have my attention."

Benefield crooks a finger and gestures to one of his men. It's James, the man who greeted us on our first day. James leans down while Benefield whispers something in his ear. With a nod, James departs.

I follow it all with interest. This part of the plan is a long shot.

He taps Eve's hand. "My darling Evie, will you please go with James?"

"Of course." Tiny lines furrow her brow as her troubled gaze cuts to mine. While I stare greedily at her, she takes a step back and gracefully departs with James.

Mr. H takes an interest in our conversation. He separates himself from his bevy of women and wanders over. "What's going on?"

"Mr. S and I are going to make a wager."

"What is the bet?" Mr. H looks eagerly between us.

A smug smile slides across Benefield's face. "Something of great worth."

"Such as?" Mr. H rubs his fat hands together. "Anything I might be interested in? Or is this a private offering?" His beady eyes shift between me and Tomas.

Mr. H is a tool. Oil rich, he's a pompous, self-inflated prick who shows no interest in a girl until one of the other guests does. He's the kind of man who gets off on depriving others of what they want. Men like him piss me off.

Honestly, all these men irritate me.

Benefield takes a moment to consider his next move. He claps his hands. "Usually, for our last night, I let you pick one girl to spend the night with. Sample the merchandise before the auction tomorrow. Let's shake things up. I have something different in mind for this evening's entertainment."

I don't like the sudden change in the air. Involving the other guests is not a part of my plan.

Mr. B notices us gathered in front of Tomas. He ambles over, moving his enormous bulk to stand beside Mr. H. "What is this?"

"Tonight, I'm putting up something valuable for your pleasure." Benefield looks at each of his guests in turn.

"Really?" Mr. H rocks back on his heels. "And what might this be?"

"Something special." He takes his time, drawing out the anticipation. "Mr. S wants a challenge."

"A challenge?" Mr. B wipes the spittle from his chin. "As in, what?"

"A woman who fights."

Mr. B's face screws up with distaste. "Fuck that. I get enough of that from my wife. That's why I'm here. I want a woman who doesn't fight me. One who does what I say, when I say it, keeps her trap shut, and her legs spread. Not interested."

"You don't have to participate. It may be more fun to watch."

I have to give it to the man, he takes perversion and depravity to a new level. As for the girls, they wisely move to the edges of the room, huddling against the walls until called upon again.

Men enter the room. Two of them carry in a card table. Four others carry two chairs apiece.

"We're playing cards?" Mr. H rubs his hands together again. "I fancy a good game of Texas Hold'em."

No doubt he does. Mr. H is a Texan, and he fits all the stereotypes: thick lazy drawl, bit of a swagger, a belt buckle two sizes too large—although he's not wearing a belt now. One of the girls removed it during an earlier lap dance and subsequent demonstration of her oral skills.

A repeat customer, I'm curious as to how many slaves he's purchased. Those questions will not be answered by me, but rather by Mitzy and her team of tech whiz kids.

"Poker?" Mr. B gives a nod. "It's been a bit since I've played, but I'm interested."

"I thought you said you weren't."

"I like the game." Mr. B shrugs. "What's the buy-in?"

Benefield looks at me. With a grotesque grin, he answers, "Five million."

"Five? Five million?" Mr. B takes a step back. "That's awfully steep."

"We're playing for money?" Mr. H doesn't sound as interested as he did a moment ago. "I thought we were playing for a slave."

"In a way."

"What way?" Mr. B pulls at his chin. "Five is a bit steep, don't you think? I want enough for the auction tomorrow." He turns and waves to one of the girls trying to remain invisible.

She catches him waving at her and returns the slightest flick of her fingers. She's smart enough to know how to survive. I feel sorry for the girl, but hopefully, there will be a real smile on her face in twenty-four hours instead of the illusion of one.

"And what are you offering as the prize?" Mr. B may think the buy-in steep, but he's definitely interested.

"Now, this is the interesting part." I don't like the way his tone turned. Benefield is letting his crazy show.

"How's that?"

"The winner of our little game will get a chance to fight for the right to have my Evie for one night."

"One night?" My voice deepens. "For five million, I expect more than one night."

"She belongs to me, Mr. S. Surely, you didn't think I'd give her to you."

"I think the word you're looking for is lose her to me."

"But you misunderstand." He gives a slow shake of his head and clucks his tongue. "Winning our little game only gives you the opportunity to fight for her."

"And what does that mean?" This is the payment piece. I brace for whatever madness he's planning.

"Are you interested in playing, or not?"

Fucking bastard. I'm interested in ripping his head off. Scratch that. I want to rip his balls off, feed them to him, then finish it off by shoving his dick down his throat.

My game face is on. I've played enough poker to know the real strategy begins long before the first card is on the table.

"Your Evie? No strings? I can do whatever I want to her?"

"That is what you wanted, is it not? A woman with fight in her. If I win, you walk out of here empty-handed and forfeit your deposit. I like games where the stakes are high. Makes it more interesting."

"I came to purchase a slave. Not to walk away empty-handed. If I win your woman, she's mine, not just for one night. I leave with her."

"Then let's hope the cards are kind to you. Of course, you can always decline. I'll have James take you to the stables and you can pick two slaves for the price of one."

"What about me?" Mr. H whines like a child. "Why does he get to pick two?"

"Mr. H, if you win, you may do the same." Benefield's head tilts back as he laughs.

I glance at the others in the room, gauging their reactions. Something's up. I don't know what, but I'll figure it out.

Mr. H and Mr. B trade nervous glances, but then they cautiously join in with Benefield's laugh.

I don't.

There's nothing funny about any of this and I refuse to be manipulated. With my feet planted shoulder-width apart, I stand my ground. Knox's a little behind me and to the left. I see him in my peripheral vision. He rocks forward, putting his weight on the balls of his feet.

As guests, we're unarmed. Our contact with the outside world severed. That doesn't mean Knox and I are defenseless. The guests pose no threat. They're eager to get in and get out of this place with their identities protected and a girl sold into slavery.

Benefield poses a mild threat. He's rich, arrogant, keeps himself physically fit, but knows nothing about fighting.

I worry about the guards. There are scores of them in the compound. Half a dozen stand duty in the Oasis. The same number are within shouting distance. Each one of them is armed.

Knox shifts position, placing him close to one of the guards with a Russian AK-47. At my signal, he'll secure that weapon for himself and toss me the 9mm attached to the guard's belt.

I'm not worried about taking out the guards. My concern is what happened to Eve. Where did Benefield send her?

"Let's play."

TWENTY-ONE

Max

_____

THE NIGHT TAKES A TURN, GOING FROM SOMEWHAT RELAXED TO downright dangerous.

Benefield's men set up a card table. One of them flicks a white linen tablecloth into the air. A man standing on the opposite side catches the other end and they lower it in place.

Seven wooden racks of chips are placed in front of each seat. Crystal water glasses go down next, then ashtrays beside each player. A humidor is brought out and we make our selections. I set my cigar down beside the ashtray, leaving it unlit for now.

I don't trust Benefield. Who's to say the tip isn't laced with some drug that will muddle my senses. Mr. H doesn't share my concerns; he lights his cigar and puffs on it until bluish-gray smoke coils toward the ceiling.

Mr. H, a total tool, keeps rubbing his hands together like a greedy little fuck. No way am I losing to him. Mr. B joins us; he looks at the deck of cards like they're going to bite him. The other guests, who generally keep to themselves, gather around with interest.

Mr. J is a banker. More than a banker, he owns a financial powerhouse. Mr. Q, a little man with beady rat eyes, licks his lips while the table is set. The last of the guests, Mr. Y, watches from a distance, but that's only because one of the girls is on her knees in front of him.

Yeah, no touching, but the girls are free to do as they please. There's no doubt in my mind that girl is not willing. Coercion comes in many forms, and no doubt Mr. Y strongly suggested she perform fellatio on his miserable cock.

Me and the alphabet soup of secret identities gather around to play cards. I'm not supposed to know what the other guests do for a living. Our anonymity is one of the things Benefield protects. Not that we can't share those bits and pieces of ourselves with one another if we so choose.

Only an idiot would. Wait, Mr. H tells us all how oil rich he is. Such a fucking tool.

What I know about these men comes from Mitzy and her marvelous tech team. Using facial recognition, she identified all the players. I have no doubt these men will be visited by someone from Guardian HRS in the near future.

"Mr. H, you mentioned Texas Hold'em?" Benefield sits at the table while the rest of us follow suit.

"Sure did." Mr. H scoots in his chair. He rubs his hands together as his gaze darts around the table.

I'm a bit more reticent, although this is exactly what I need. Benefield's words keep sounding in my head. Winning here only gives me the right to fight for Eve.

Fight?

How?

I take my seat and push my concerns to the back of my mind. It's time to get serious and that means all my attention needs to be focused on the game.

Knox comes to stand at my six, making sure none of the girls or guards tries sneaking behind me where they can see my cards. Then I remember the cameras.

Would Benefield sneak that low? He might, but that's okay. I know how to keep my cards covered.

"Mr. Y, will you be joining us?" Benefield calls out, not bothering to look at Mr. Y.

Finished with the girl, Mr. Y tucks himself inside his pants and zips the fly. "I heard poker?"

"Texas Hold'em," Mr. H announces. "Best game on the planet."

"Sure thing, deal me in." Mr. Y strolls over to the table and takes a seat to my right.

"What are we playing for?" Mr. Y asks. "I assume this isn't just for fun?"

Benefield points to me. "Mr. S is interested in my Evie. If he wins, she's his."

I note how he leaves off the part about me needing to fight for her and take a breath. Good to know that's off the table. Whatever it was.

"Interesting wager. Are we all playing for the same thing? Because —and I mean no offense—but I'm not interested in your woman." Mr. Y glances around the room. "How about first choice at the auction?"

"First choice?" Mr. B perks up. "How would that work? It's an auction."

Mr. Y and Mr. B have been eyeing the same two girls the entire week. No doubt there will be fierce bidding between them tomorrow.

"Hm, now that is interesting." Benefield leans back and pulls at his chin. "How about this, whoever wins gets to choose whatever girl he wants." His sharp gaze makes a sweep of the table. "No bidding. No auction."

"At what price?" Mr. B glances around the room. His attention focuses on the girl Mr. Y had bobbing between his legs.

"No price. The winner wins the girl of his choosing."

"Now, I like that." Mr. H cracks his knuckles and shifts in his seat. "Let's play."

With us all around the table, and the stakes clearly stated, Benefield gives a snap of his fingers. The girls detach themselves from the wall. They bring drinks and stand at attention for any demand placed upon them. The speed with which they respond to commands sours my stomach. No woman should ever be trained to perform like an animal.

I push away the girl who tries to give me a neck massage. That's a distraction I don't need.

"High card takes the deal." Benefield taps the deck in front of him. With everyone seated, Benefield tosses out seven cards face up.

I get the two of clubs, while Mr. H draws an ace. Benefield hands over the pack of cards to Mr. H while we all toss our single cards toward him.

"Let's do this." Mr. H looks to Mr. J, who sits immediately clockwise to him. "Ante up."

Mr. J places the small blind, the first forced bet of the game. Sitting next to him, Mr. B tosses in his chips. We all add our ante to the pot and Mr. H deals two cards, face down. Betting begins.

We all check, declining to bet. Keeping our cards, we wait for the flop, the first three cards dealt face-up. These are community cards we all get to draw from in making our best five-card hand.

Betting begins on the flop with Mr. J, who sits to Mr. H's left. Mr. J checks. Mr. B places his bet. Mr. Q meets the bet, declining to raise. Benefield tosses in his chips, staying in the game. Mr. Y does the same, as do I.

With betting completed for the flop, the fourth card is dealt face up. We go around again, checking, betting, raising until that round concludes. I hold a shit hand, two minor cards that don't match anything on the table, but I'm good with losing for now.

We continue to play, nothing serious, as each of us settle into our game. Texas Hold'em is not a game of chance, nor is it a game of skill. It's a game of incomplete information. In this, it's not much different from everyday life.

At the start, I know very little. Nothing about the cards the other players hold, and very little about them. I draw on the past week, knowing the general personalities of the men around me to base decisions upon, but that's not good enough. I need to learn how each of them plays at the table.

With each hand, I accumulate more knowledge. I learn enough to guess at the cards they hold and how aggressively they play.

It's Benefield's turn as the dealer. He shuffles the deck while we ante up. He deals us each two cards, ending with his cards, then he places the deck on the table. We bet pre-flop before the dealer turns up the first three cards.

Mr. Y, who's first to bet this round, drags his cards to the edge of the table and peeks at what he holds. The girl in his lap shifts, tightening her grip on his shirt. He places his bet.

I'm next. I look at my cards, queen of spades and a five of hearts. Not even the same suit, but I might be able to do something with it depending on what's on the table. I check, staying in the game, and betting continues around the table.

Mr. H, sitting next to me, checks as well. No surprise there. He's cocky and arrogant, but I respect his game. I nail his tells, those that are real and those that are pretend, like the way he gnaws at the end of that cigar. An aggressive player, he calls no matter what. He's got experience, but I'm far better than him.

Mr. J, our banker friend, is as miserly with his chips as he probably is with the rest of his money. He's got skill. A player to watch, but ultimately, he'll bow out when the pressure rises. For now, he makes the first bet of this round.

Mr. B looks at his cards as if they'll bite him and he handles his chips like they're precious. He folds. Either the man doesn't know how to play, or he's stringing us along. One thing I notice is bigger bets make his play more chaotic.

Mr. Q, our beady little rat man, continues to lick his lips with anticipation. A nervous individual, he constantly wipes his hands on his pants. He does it with a good hand as well as a bad hand, which tells me it's an ingrained habit and not a tell. What is his tell is the way he twists his wedding band, the one missing a stone. He hasn't replaced it for a reason, not that I care.

One of the things which made me an excellent operator in the military, and now as a Guardian, is my ability to get a read on people with very limited information.

Give me a minute with a person, and I can tell you how they're going to react. Poker is no different. I lose several hands, on purpose, to learn about the players. Sometimes it's worth losing to extract information that will be extremely valuable later on.

The one person I can't read at all is the psychopath sitting nearly opposite me. The man is stone cold. Benefield, unpredictable and chaotic, doubles the bet.

Mr. Y plays with a girl propped in his lap. The very same girl Mr. B wants to add to his stable of slaves. Y's head isn't in the game. He's more interested in the girl on his lap than playing cards.

He's the first to fold and excuses himself back to the couches. It's no surprise when he takes the girl with him and sets up for round two of fellatio. Fucking putz. I want to beat him to a pulp for what he's doing.

Mr. B's poker game improves as the night wears on. Either he's learning as he goes or threw those first few games on purpose.

Mr. H holds his own, losing as much as he wins. On the balance, it's enough to keep him in the game.

Mr. Q drops out a few hands later when he loses a particularly large pot. Mr. B sits taller as he rakes in more and more chips. Time to pay a little more attention to him rather than Benefield. I can't ignore a legitimate risk, but B falls flat on his face two rounds later. He's out of the game.

A new round is dealt, and I settle in to win. This may not be a battle fought with knives and bullets, but it's a battle just the same. Eve's future is at risk. I've got a ten and an eight, both hearts. It's not much.

Benefield continues with his unreadable poker face and I swear he's hiding a smirk. He's smug about his game, but that's okay.

Mr. B, although out of the game, remains at the table. He glances over at Mr. Y and the girl they both want. He turns his attention to Benefield. "Where do you get your girls?"

"Why?" Benefield caresses his chips. He has something.

"I was curious if you took orders." Mr. B leans back slightly.

"Orders?" Benefield scans his cards and tosses a chip onto the pile.

I add a chip to the pile, staying in this round.

H glances at his cards. He tries to look cool, but from the way he puffs on that cigar, he's got nothing.

"Yeah, like if I have a specific request." Mr. B continues his line of questioning while we play this round.

"I aim to please. If you have specifications, we can get you a girl who matches them."

Mr. J glances at me, checking for my tells. I return his flat stare with an expressionless face. As the dealer this round, he holds the pack of cards. Mr. J deals out the flop, placing an ace of diamonds, a jack of clubs, and nine of hearts face up on the table.

Benefield looks at his cards. Does he have the king? King and queen? There are still two remaining cards to be dealt. He places a bet.

With my ten and eight, I don't have a hand. Not yet, though there's a chance for a straight if a queen or seven is dealt in the remaining two cards. I do some quick math and don't like the results.

"Check." I'm not raising the bet with that smug expression on his face. I could win this round, but my chip pile is embarrassingly small compared to Benefield's.

With nothing in his hand, H must fold or risk losing the rest of his chips. Despite his poker game, Benefield's the real threat here.

"Fold." H tosses his cards down. Smart play. The odds are against him.

Mr. B's question raises an alarm. Julian Townsend put in a specific order. More than specific, he requested Moira by name.

"How specific of a request can you fulfill?" I lean back and wait for Mr. J to check, raise, or fold.

"As specific as you need, for the right price of course." Benefield's gaze sweeps around the table. What does he see when he looks at his guests?

None of us are friends. None are business partners. He probably only cares about the dollars in our pockets and very deep bank accounts.

"If there is a particular woman I'm interested in, could you fulfill that request?" Mr. B isn't letting his question go.

"I can. It costs more and takes longer."

"Good to know." Mr. B looks over at Mr. Y and the slave in his lap.

Mr. J lays down the fourth card and we go around the table again. Benefield's smile alarms me, as does the size of his bet. He puts two million into the pot. That's all I have left. I can fold, or I can check. What I can't do is raise the bid.

"Fold." With the odds against me, I place my cards on the table.

Mr. H is out of this game. Surprisingly, Mr. J goes all in, raising the bid to two and a half million. Benefield calls. Mr. J deals out the last card.

It's a seven. I could've had a straight.

"Shit." Mr. J tosses his cards on the table, revealing nothing. He'd been bluffing.

Benefield lays down his hand. Two jacks.

I don't react. A straight beats three of a kind, but I'm already out of the game. Benefield rakes in the chips, not bothering to count them. He takes the deck from Mr. J and shuffles for the next round.

With less than two million left, I need to step things up, or I'll be out.

There are only three of us left in this game: myself, Mr. H, and Benefield.

I make up my losses over the next several rounds. The three of us are nearly equal as far as our chip count goes with Mr. H having the least, a few million shy of the astounding sum I sit on now. In my lifetime, I've played a lot of poker, but nothing like this.

It's my deal. Two cards down, we begin the bidding. Mr. H looks at his cards. He'll bid first. He puffs hard on that cigar. I haven't looked at my cards and won't until it's my turn to bid.

Mr. H checks. Across the table, Benefield's face is glacial cold. The stakes are high. I have a feeling everything will come down to this one hand. He, too, checks. With no reason to place a bet, I follow suit and check as well.

I deal out the flop; the first three cards face up. Mr. H stares at the pair of twos and eight of hearts. It's a strong hand, a pair out of the gate, but we all get to use that pair to our advantage.

Mr. H checks. He's not confident in his hand. Benefield pushes in a large stack. A quick glance reveals five million in play. I need to play my hand cautiously, or I'll run out of chips before it's over. Good thing I'm the dealer this hand. It puts me at the end of the betting.

"Check." I check Benefield and must meet his bid or fall out of the game. Five million go into the pot.

I deal the fourth card. Another eight.

We all stare at the cards. Two pair, another impressive combination. With two pair on the table, the only way for any of us to win is to beat that with three of a kind, a full house, or four of a kind. A straight and flush are out, both ranked higher than two pairs, but those combinations aren't possible with what's on the table.

Mr. H looks at his chip stack. There's no way he can stay in the game. Benefield and I have far more at hand. He'll have to fold.

"I'm out." Mr. H tosses in his cards; a king and four. Smart move. He had nothing.

The stakes couldn't be higher. I either win this hand now, or I'm out. Benefield is more than capable of making me sweat.

He leaves his cards face down on the table. I'm not sure, but his breathing is a little bit deeper than usual. Does he have a good hand? Better than mine? There's no way to know, considering I've yet to look at my cards.

Or, is he simply feeling close to victory. If he has a two or an eight, that gives him a full house. Very hard to beat that. I itch to look at my cards, but if he's figured out any of my tells, that'll ruin me. I keep my wrists balanced on the edge of the table and stare him down.

To my left, Mr. H's gaze darts left to right, as if unsure about everything. He's anxious to know how this plays out.

Benefield taps the top of the table, looking relaxed as hell. Not an ounce of tension fills him. He ogles the girls, taking his time, then turns back to me, inquisitively raising an eyebrow.

Damn straight I'm watching you.

He appears as if he doesn't care about the outcome of this

game, but if I win, Eve is mine. I don't think Benefield thought he could lose to a man like me.

He lifts a finger and calls over one of his men. The man rushes to Benefield's side and leans down. Benefield whispers something into the man's ear. The man gives a sharp shake of his head and rushes out of the room.

"I wonder what you'll do to my Evie?"

"Isn't it obvious?"

"What's not as obvious is what you'll do when you leave here with nothing." He points to my cards. "You haven't looked at your hand." When I don't answer, his brow furrows with confusion. "I see…" He drums his fingers on the table, tapping as if he's got all the time in the world. "Winning this game doesn't give you my Evie."

"That is not what we agreed."

"Yes, it is. If you win, you have the option to fight for her." He tilts his head to the side. "How badly do you want my girl?"

"Enough to beat you at a game of poker. Are you going to place a bet or keep talking all night long?"

We've been at the game for hours.

"I say we play the last card, and see who wins." He pushes in all of his chips, and I about feel my heart drop to my stomach.

The odds say I'm sitting on a crap hand. If I don't win Evie, I might lose our chance to rescue her. Knox shifts behind me, and I feel his unease.

But there is no going back.

"Check." I push in my chip stack and stare at nearly thirty-five million dollars. I've still yet to look at my cards.

"Let's see what the last card is, shall we?" Benefield leans back.

I draw the top card from the deck and flick it on the table. It's the king of diamonds.

Benefield crosses his arms over his chest and the corner of his lip ticks up. We're both out of chips. There's no bet to be placed. All we can do is reveal our cards.

Benefield turns over his hand, revealing a four and an eight. "Full house."

There's no way for me to win, unless I'm holding a pair of twos. Three eights and a pair of twos beats three twos and a pair of eights.

I tap my top card and close my eyes. But there's no reason to delay. I flip over a two of clubs and cringe. I've got a full house as well, but it's lower in rank compared to his.

He leans forward, and stretches out his hands to collect the chips. I turn over the last card and feel the earth stop.

It's another two.

Benefield's eyes widen as he takes it in. Mr. H covers his mouth.

"Four of a kind."

It's the lowest ranking of four of a kind, but it's a heart, diamond, club, and a spade—four twos staring up at me. My heart beats inside my chest as a surge of adrenaline runs through me.

I won.

I fucking won.

Benefield stares at the cards and shakes his head. "Well played, Mr. S. Very well played."

"Where's Eve?"

"Evie is waiting for you."

"Where?"

"She's in the arena."

I don't know what that means, except I don't like it one bit.

Benefield claps his hands. "Come along, we don't want to keep Mr. S's girl waiting." Without another word, Benefield turns on his heel and strides out of the room.

I glance at Knox and rush out, following a madman.

TWENTY-TWO

Eve

ONE BREATH.

That's all it took for my world to fall apart. Not like I was standing on solid ground, but still.

This day, it's been coming for a long time, but I foolishly held onto the belief I would be rescued. That this hell would end.

I made the mistake of thinking I controlled my fate, all the while knowing it rests in the hands of a madman.

I've been here before, weeks ago. This is the courtyard where I told Benefield I would stand by him. It's here where men bled and that poor girl cried.

I remember thinking she must be in great agony. Arms stretched overhead. Made to balance on her toes.

I didn't know the half of it.

James said nothing as he wrapped my wrists in iron. There was no humanity in his eyes when he strung me up, tying me to the pole. The steel is cold against my skin, rusty and abrasive.

I cried. I begged. I sobbed and howled.

All he did was lift me higher until I, too, balanced on my toes.

It's been hours, grueling hours of torture as I alternately hang by my arms and balance on my toes. My calves cramp again as I cry out. I can't bear it anymore. My shoulders burn and my sockets protest the weight I place on them as I hang to relieve the stress on my toes, my calves, and my legs.

I blink and my eyebrows pull in as misery sweeps through me. What's going on? Why now? What nefarious plan does Benefield have for me?

Strings of hair hang in my face. They get in my mouth, and twist around my shoulders. I spit out the hair that finds its way into my mouth and ignore the rest.

My bare breasts glisten with perspiration. My sweat attracts bugs that bite and sting. Hot, itchy, and naked, I've been stripped of dignity and forced to stand naked in a courtyard where men fought for the privilege to deflower a virgin.

I'm no virgin, but there's no doubt something similar will happen tonight. This isn't random. Benefield has something horrendous planned.

The sound of booted feet coming my way grabs my attention.

"Gentlemen…" Benefield's voice rings out loud and clear. I cringe as he stops at the entrance to this hell. "We've arrived at the part of the evening where Mr. S may choose to fight for the right to have this girl or leave empty-handed."

"You said she would be mine." The menacing growl coming from Max sends shivers down my spine. The tiny hairs on my arms lift and my nipples pebble despite the evening heat.

Girl.

It's the first time Benefield uses that derogatory name on me, and it means everything.

I'm no longer his. No longer protected.

The chains clank as I squirm against the cold metal at my back. Max is going to fight for me.

Mine.

I don't react to Max claiming me as his with the same revulsion I did when Benefield said it. When I look in Max's eyes, I don't see the soulless dispassion that steals my hope like I do with Benefield.

But who? Who will he make Max fight?

"Now where is the fun in letting you have the girl?" Benefield's sugary sweet voice grates on my nerves.

I glare at Benefield, focusing all my hatred into that stare. I'm not one of his timid girls, broken and subdued, their minds splintered and cracked from the suffering they endured. He rebuffs me with a flick of his lids, as if I don't exist.

Too easy to fall.

Rage rips through me.

"You bastard! I hope you rot in hell." My fiercest weapons are my words. It's all I have left, and I'm not sure if those words are meant for Benefield, or the man who gapes as he takes me in.

And Max's jaw is open and gaping. His eyes pinch and his fists curl. Fury bunches in his shoulders as rage fills his face.

Evidently, he's pissed at Benefield. From their conversation, I take it Benefield promised me to Max, conditionally, and only just now is Max realizing what that condition will be.

I suppose I'd be upset too, except I'm the one whose life they're ruining.

Men are such dicks.

Naked and chained to a post, I'm not feeling very confident about the outcome of this night. I don't know much about Max, except for the perversions Benefield told me about.

Max wants a challenge, a woman who will fight him. He wants a girl who will claw at him and bite, screaming vile obscenities as he forces himself on her, raping her over and over and over again.

I pinch my eyes shut and struggle in the chains, knowing it's futile. If this truly is my fate, I will fight and I'll take him down with murderous passion. It's either me, or him, and I won't let Max break me.

I'd rather die.

"Explain what this is…" Max's tone is sharp, deadly. He's not happy. "I won the rights to her fair and square. And why is she naked?" His tone is oddly protective.

Why does he care that I've been stripped and tied up like any other slave? This is what he likes, isn't it?

Benefield told me all about the darkness swirling in this man's mind. It's repulsive, but the way Max stares at me says something else. Murder swims in his gaze. Anger bunches in his muscles. He's about to explode with all the fury building inside of him.

"Ah, but this is the way it must be." Benefield coos, enjoying Max's reaction. He's a manipulative sadistic twat. "You won the right to fight for her. You've yet to win the right to have her."

"I don't know what game you're playing, but…"

A tall man emerges from the opposite side of the courtyard. He steps out from the shadows. Splatters of blood stain his shirt. Everything about him radiates violence. From his malevolent stare to his hard-set shoulders, the man's a professional killer. Lucian is Benefield's right-hand man. If he's here… I suppress a shudder of revulsion.

I don't want Lucian to win whatever fight this is.

I know little about Benefield's business, except trafficking slaves is but one small part of it. He's involved in drugs, growing and transporting, as well as the movement of guns, ammunition, and weapons. Lucian runs all of that, and he's known for making people disappear.

"The rules are simple," Benefield says.

"Is that so? And what are the rules?"

"To the victor go the spoils." Benefield gestures toward Lucian. "You are not the only one with eyes on my woman. Lucian desires her too, and just like you, he enjoys a woman with a bit of fight in her."

"This is not what we agreed to." Max's eyes storm with fury.

"Oh, I remember exactly what we agreed on. Win the game and I give you the chance to fight for her."

Max glances at Lucian. His eyes pinch and I wonder what he's thinking. No doubt he's debating whether he can win.

They appear evenly matched. Lucian radiates violence, but Max isn't backing down. From the way he holds himself, he's not afraid of Lucian.

I'd tell him to be careful, except rooting for one monster over another isn't a mental space I can handle.

"Fight?" Max glances at me, then his attention shifts to Lucian.

"That's what I said."

"And when I win? She is mine, not for a moment, not for a night, but mine to take home?"

"If you win. More likely, Lucian will crack your skull."

"Sir," Max's bodyguard speaks up. "You can't do this."

"I was wondering how long that would take." Benefield's face spreads into a wide grin. He snaps his fingers and two men come running. They carry something bulky.

My arms can no longer take the strain of my weight. I press my toes against the concrete beneath my bare feet and grimace as I slowly transfer my weight from my sockets to my toes. My calves protest immediately, threatening to go into another agonizing cramp.

It's a balancing act I won't be able to maintain for much longer. A sob escapes me as my weight shifts, but at least the pressure on my arms eases for a bit.

"What is this?" Max takes a step forward while Benefield unfolds what one of the men carries.

"Your weapons, of course. Choose whatever you like." Benefield lifts a knife and moves it slowly through the air. Lamplight flashes on the steel as he makes a slashing cut through the air.

"Knives?" Max's displeasure grows by the second.

"To win a great prize, you must be willing to sacrifice something equally precious."

Benefield's gaze cuts to me. He takes one last look at me, and I feel the moment he lets me go. No longer of use to him, he has no further use of me. I am now simply one of the girls who passes through this hellacious place.

"Sacrifice what?" Max adds.

"Your life of course."

"Sir..." Max's bodyguard's tone turns menacing.

Max takes a look at the knives. His sharp gaze cuts to me, then back to Lucian. His lips press into a hard line and he takes a breath.

"If I kill him, she's mine?" He glares at Benefield. "Not mine for the moment, or the day. She leaves with me?"

"Sir..." His bodyguard isn't happy about this.

Honestly, I'm not either. I don't care one bit about Lucian. It would be wonderful to watch Max carve him into tiny pieces. But Max? Somehow, I don't want anything bad to happen to him.

I squeeze my lids together and don't mind the tears. Benefield had men fighting to the death over a virgin. This shouldn't come as any big surprise.

Benefield truly is mad.

As for Max, he wears his anger in the harsh lines carved deep into his face. I feel mine burning from the inside out. My anger is a hot ember. It burns through my emotions, turning everything to ash inside of me.

Fake torchlight, spaced too far apart, provides little light. Shadows dance with darkness in this hellish place. They flicker erratically, turning this whole place into the seventh pit of hell.

Why seven? Hell if I know. I just picked a random number out of the air on a whim.

As soon as Max selects his weapon, the man holding the bundle crosses in front of me and stands in front of Lucian. Lucian doesn't take long. His hand darts out and he lifts a wicked curved blade straight out in front of him.

"You want to spend the rest of the night chatting? Or you ready to fight?"

Max shrugs out of his dinner jacket and gives it to his bodyguard. There's a brief exchange. I can't hear what they say but read enough of their body language to figure out the gist of it. The bodyguard isn't happy.

Max is putting his life on the line for me.

My left calf cramps, pulling tight with searing pain. I cry out, drawing the attention of both men.

They glance at me. One with rabid hunger, reminding me of my naked state. The other with a promise to take me from this place forever.

I sag and hold in another shout as all my weight transfers back to my shoulders. They need to hurry and get started because I can't handle much more of this torture.

Men file into the courtyard, lining up against the walls. The fake torchlight flickers, turning brighter as someone turns up the juice.

The lights illuminate the perimeter while casting the center, where I'm tied, in shadows.

The murmurs of the guests and guards rise in pitch. At first, it's indistinct, but then I hear bets being placed. Their voices rise as Max moves into the courtyard. His gaze cuts to me, to my wrists which bleed, to my muscles which shake from exhaustion, and finally to my eyes which fill with tears. There's compassion in that gaze.

He doesn't look at my breasts and he skips over my private parts.

Lucian drinks in my nakedness, making me want to crawl into a dark hole and die. Beneath his terrifying gaze, I feel violated in the worst possible way.

Max lowers his weapon. His right hand fists the handle of the blade. My nerves are wrung tight, but what is he feeling as he faces what is most surely his death?

Why? Why are you doing this Max? I'm not worth your life.

But then I look at him again, seeing not a deplorable businessman, but a man with virtually no body fat. Broad shoulders cap a hard, honed physique that I doubt was refined inside a gym.

There's a lethality to Max's gaze, which tells me he's fought before. He's killed before. His eyes practically glow as he takes in his opponent. I can't imagine what's going through his mind.

Suddenly, Max seems far more dangerous in his dress shirt and trousers than Lucian does in the blood-soaked shirt he wears.

Max directs his fiery gaze one last time to me. He holds me there with a promise. Max intends to win.

He then turns his focus on the man standing a few steps from him. Lucian bobs back and forth, placing most of his weight back on his heels. Max carries himself differently. Shifting forward. Readying himself for battle.

"Fight to the death!" The cry comes out from the crowd.

To the death.

My breaths accelerate as panic sets in. I don't want to be here. I don't want to watch this. One of these men is going to die, and I pray to God it's not Max.

But there's not a damn thing I can do about anything.

TWENTY-THREE

Max

ALL IT TAKES IS A SHOUT TO SEND BENEFIELD'S MAN CRASHING toward me. He slashes with his knife, a burst of energy that will wear him out. Unless he gets me with that blade of his first.

Not that I'm worried. We trained for this as operators during my team days and again as a Guardian.

Lucian's technique is sloppy.

Mine's spot on.

While he slashes wildly with his knife hand, I grapple with his arm, twisting and putting pressure on the nerves until his grip fails and the knife drops. I should cut him right there, but he slips out of my grasp.

With a kick, I send his blade skittering off to the side before he can grab it again. Pissed I disarmed him so quickly, Lucian launches a burst of punches.

He's fast, but he's not fast enough. I counter his punches with hits of my own, moving at a blinding speed. I slice across his bicep, but it does nothing to slow him down.

My hope is to knock him out in the first minute. Claim my victory. And get the hell out of Dodge.

Knox is already in communication with our team, moving up

our rescue by a day. With luck, we'll be out of this place before dawn.

I miss a block, opening myself to an attack. Lucian gets his hands on me, lifts me off my feet, then slams me back-first down to the ground.

The only reason he doesn't knock me out is because I tense my abs on the way down, keeping my head from smacking the hard stone, but I lose my blade in the process.

Lucian wastes time looking for his knife. In that half second, I draw in my knees then kick out, launching myself up to land on my feet. A quick spin puts me behind Lucian, where I wrap an arm around his throat in a chokehold.

Lucian rears back with his elbows, trying to hit me in the solar plexus. I brace for the impact and absorb the pain. It feeds my fury.

My opponent's arms turn sluggish as I deprive his brain of oxygen. The sound of metal scraping on stone grabs my attention. Lucian wraps his hand around the hilt of his knife. He jabs back, slicing across my thigh.

Ignoring the sting, I don't let the injury slow me down.

Lucian staggers. He gains his feet. Death fills his face, but I don't care. We're matched in strength, but my skill surpasses his. He's going to figure that out pretty damn soon.

We crash together. I disarm him for the second time as we trade a burst of punches, but not before he slices across my chest. More pain that I ignore.

Hit. Smash. Crunch.

I shove the palm of my hand against his nose. Cartilage and bone give way.

Lucian howls. He drops his blade and holds his bloody nose. It's the perfect opportunity to get in a few more hits. I dodge his next blow. Deflect a kick. I jab upward and connect with his chin.

He screams in pain and spits out a wad of blood. He staggers as he comes at me, sneering as he attacks again.

The force of our blows intensifies. The brutality of the fight turns deadly. Initially, I thought to spare his life. Now, I just want this to end.

Hit. Crunch. Smash.

I get in another punch to his jaw. As his head whips back, I grab his shoulders, steadying him for a knee jab to his solar plexus. Once. Twice. He staggers back, but the bastard doesn't go down.

He shows no sign of giving up. Not that I blame him. Victory or death are the only two paths out of this.

He comes at me, swinging. I block out the pain from the few hits he manages to land. Someone kicks the knife back into play, but I kick it back. I don't need a weapon to kill this man.

A snarl fills Lucian's face. It's lopsided and comical, considering all the bruising and swelling on his face. Not to mention the weird angle of his nose.

He and Benefield are pure scum. Neither deserves to breathe, but I only get to end one life tonight.

Lucian's technique isn't disciplined. From the way he moves, he learned everything on the streets. In those fights, raw strength prevails. I don't fight like that. I fight with my heart and the knowledge I'm on the side of greater good.

But the thing that will win this fight is my instinct to protect and defend. Eve is all that matters. Getting her out of this hellhole drives every kick, powers every jab, and lands each and every punch.

Pressure builds in my muscles as I tense to deliver a killing blow. Lucian stumbles toward me.

I grab him and lift, twisting him around. Back to the ground, I power bomb him, dropping him over my thigh. His spine snaps and his body goes limp. The bastard still breathes, but he's paralyzed from the waist down. Maybe higher. There's no movement in his arms.

I stand and take two steps back as the courtyard falls silent.

Lucian stares at me, surprise etched in his face. His labored breathing is not quite right. More than likely, he won't survive the night.

"You have to kill him." Benefield walks into the center of the courtyard. He stares down at his man then hands me a knife. "Those are the rules."

I take the knife from Benefield and spit on the ground. "Not my fucking rules. I'm taking my woman."

Benefield's eyes narrow. A moment passes between us. Rage fills his expression, then bleeds away as if it was never there in the first place. Benefield's dispassion is scarier than his anger.

Who flips a switch on their emotions like that?

A madman, that's who.

Benefield calls out. "The bitch belongs to him."

I head to the pole where Eve's strung up. Her eyelids flutter and she slowly focuses on me. I take the knife and cut her down.

I barely wrap my arms around her before she collapses, falling over my shoulder. Knowing all eyes are on me, I can't do the one thing I crave above all else.

I can't be gentle.

I glare at Benefield. "Give me the key to her shackles."

Benefield looks to one of his men and gives a nod. That man fishes out a key and hands it to me. I shove it deep in my pocket, making sure everyone sees. Then I march out of that damn courtyard with Knox falling in step by my side.

Behind me, Lucian takes his last breath.

I wish it had been Benefield. I've killed men before. Vile, despicable men who deserved death. I've killed with bullets, knives, and my bare hands. But I've never killed to save the life of a woman I cared about.

No escaping the emotions raging within me. I'll do anything to keep Eve safe. My chest squeezes with that realization.

While I don't have a claim on Eve, she is mine. I'll always think of her that way. As for what she thinks of me, I can only imagine the hatred flowing in her veins.

"Do you want me to carry her?" Knox steps alongside me as we retreat to the suite.

"No. I've got this." My heart beats, pulsing with the need to explain to Eve that she's safe. But I can't do that. Not yet. I hand Knox the knife, afraid of accidentally slicing her delicate skin.

Knox wipes the blood away on the cuff of his pants and grips the knife as his head swivels, looking for threats.

There are eyes in every corner and ears hidden in the walls. There's not one bit of privacy in this godforsaken place, and for every bug we remove in the suite, we return to two, or three, more. No doubt there will be more in the suite when we arrive.

For the duration of the night, until our team gets here, I must continue to be Eve's tormentor.

Eve stiffens as she comes back around. She goes from limp to squirming in less than a second.

"Put me down, you scum-sucking perv."

A smile tugs at the corner of my lips. Damn if I don't like the way she fights.

It has nothing to do with the vile things I told Benefield. I'm not into that kind of shit, but give me a woman with spunk, who's not afraid to face her challenges head on, and I'm smitten.

Smitten is a funny word, but it fits.

She squirms again, kicks her feet and tries to punch my back.

Aware of all the eyes watching our progress, I smack her hard on the ass.

"Stop squirming."

"You vile pig. You despicable worthless excuse of a man…"

"Is that really the way you want to start? By calling me names? Sorry, Eve, but sticks and stones may break my bones, but words will never harm me."

"Seriously?" She squirms again. This time, she plants her bound hands on the small of my back and tries to buck off my shoulder.

That's not happening.

Knox chuckles beside me. The shithead is having fun with this. He knows how I feel about Eve and the uncanny attraction which pulls me to her.

"Laugh it up, fuzzball." I give him a look.

"You have to admit—it's funny."

"Not funny at all."

Knox shrugs as Eve's seething anger keeps her tiny fists pummeling the small of my back.

"Keep doing that, Eve. I like a good massage."

She continues to kick and buck in her shackles as I carry her over my shoulder to the suite. Anger spews from her mouth, vile obscenities directed at me.

I lied.

Her words hurt. They dig deep and wrap around my heart, squeezing it with regret and shame. This woman hates me.

Probably time to nip this in the bud.

Coming to an abrupt stop, I lift her off my shoulder and place her against the wall. Knowing cameras watch every move, I lean in close, crowding her in.

"Fight me, if you want, but I like it." I cup her chin and force her to look at me. Her eyes burn hot with rage. "Kick and scream. Hit me if you like. All you'll do is wear yourself out and turn me on. If you want to make it through this, stay by my side." She won't understand why, but some part of me hopes she can see through this disgusting ruse.

Eve's shoulders twitch. Dried tears streak down her face. I continue, putting on a show for Benefield.

"If you harm me, or my bodyguard, I will make you pay. If you run and force me to chase you, I will hunt you down and hurt you."

Those words twist my insides. It's not fair that she doesn't know, but Knox is right. Eve's safety depends on her belief that I'm a monster.

I tilt my head. "Any questions?"

"I hate you."

The point of this display in the halls is to scare her with threats of what I could do, rather than resorting to hitting her outright. Benefield expects physical violence, but he appreciates the subtlety of instilling fear.

Only, I know I'll never hit Eve. She believes the lies I've told, and Eve reacts to the truth in her head. She flinches when I move in, terrified of what I will do to her.

"I expect nothing less, but there will come a time when that's no longer the case." At least that's what I hope.

"You're wrong. There's nothing you can do that will make me change my mind."

"We'll see about that. Now, do you want to walk to my suite, or shall I carry you?" I keep my gaze fixed to her face, avoiding looking at her nakedness. I don't think she notices, but that's not the point. I don't do it to impress her. I do it because it's the right thing to do.

Her eyes flash as she stares me down.

This line I walk is precarious at best. I must scare and subdue her with verbal threats instead of using my fists. I don't want to hit her, but if I must, there will be no hesitation on my part. There's an audience expecting just that.

The next few hours are critical. Benefield will have certain expectations. I need to deliver on those without crossing a line with Eve that I can never recover from.

"Walk or carry. Your choice."

Her strength and resilience make my heart swell. The stubbornness in her expression makes me want to cheer.

So much strength.

I'm proud of Eve, and I know she'll survive this tragedy.

"I'll walk." Her teeth grind together as her attention shifts between me and Knox.

"Fine." I gesture down the hall. "To my suite then."

Eve takes one step. Her leg gives way and I catch her before she falls. Her hands go to her calf and my eyes follow.

Hard, contracted; the muscle of her calf cramps. Gently, I lower her to the floor and place my fingers on the back of her calf.

Eve jerks out of my grip, but I simply grab her leg and drag her in front of me.

"You've got a charley horse. Let me…"

"Don't touch me." Eve yanks her leg, but I'm much stronger.

"Let me help you." I grip her foot and gently flex it up.

Eve screams in pain, but I don't let up.

"You've got to stretch it, keep pressure on the muscle until it fatigues and relaxes."

"It hurts. It hurts so much." She wraps her hands around mine and huffs against the pain. Rock hard, the cramp is a bad one.

Knox stands guard over us. To this point, we've been left alone. My guess is Benefield is not done with Eve. He will try to take her back.

I kneel beside her, putting pressure on her calf muscle while simultaneously flexing her foot. Slowly, the muscle gives up. It relaxes and her pain fades.

Eve looks up at me, relief and gratitude fill her face, but they're wiped away with blinding fear.

I'm sorry, Eve, but you don't need to fear me.

I wish I could tell her, explain who I am, but I can't. All I can do is offer her a hand up.

Eve looks at my hand like it's a poisonous snake that will bite her. I give a shake of my head.

"Sometimes, an offered hand is simply that. Someone reaching out to help you stand on your own." She won't understand the subtext behind my words, but it doesn't matter.

I do.

Eve takes my hand reluctantly and I pull her to her feet. She takes one shaky step before I shake my head.

"You're in no condition to stand, let alone walk." I glance at the manacles shackling her wrists. "Give me your hands."

Eve wobbles on her feet, looking like she's going to tip over any second while I pull out the key from my pocket.

She doesn't lift her wrists for me. I move to stand in front of her and take her left hand in mine. While she watches closely, I unlock the manacles by touch alone, keeping my gaze locked to hers.

Maybe she'll understand what I'm doing? How I'm not looking at her nakedness? Honestly, it's torture not to take in all her amazing curves, but I'll respect her boundaries. I'm pretty sure she's not a fan of strange men ogling her naked body.

It takes a second. I fumble a bit with the key and the lock, but I get the restraints to unlock. I turn my attention to her wrists as I remove the shackles. Red, raw, and bleeding, there are deep cuts and areas of denuded skin.

"How long?" The damage to her wrists is impressive.

"Excuse me?"

"How long did he keep you chained to that pole?"

"Why do you care?"

"Because I do. How long?"

"I don't know. Hours?" She reaches up to rub her shoulders.

"Where else are you hurt?" I take a step back, realizing how intimidating it must be with me towering over her.

"My shoulders hurt. My arms." She glances at the wounds on her wrists. "My wrists. My calves."

I give a shake of my head. "Put your arm around my neck."

"Why?"

"Because I'm going to carry you, and I don't want you draped over my shoulder."

"Why not? Isn't that exactly what men like you want?"

"You have no idea what I want." How can she not know how I feel?

It's a rhetorical question. It's not like the past six days are magically erased because I don't want to carry her to my suite caveman style.

"Put your arm over my shoulder, or don't. I'm still going to carry you." Without waiting for her to decide, I scoop her into my arms. Well aware she's naked, I take several deep breaths to center myself.

Actually, there's nothing sexy about any of this. My feelings aside, Eve's pain doesn't arouse me.

Not one damn bit.

Carrying Eve in my arms, however, almost puts me over the edge. This feels right.

I cradle her, and to my surprise, she doesn't resist as we continue the long trek back to the suite.

Once we draw near the suite, Knox moves ahead of us. He opens the door and steps inside. I carry Eve over the threshold and take her straight back to the master bedroom.

Her entire body tenses when she realizes where I'm headed.

"Relax." I lean down and whisper in her ear. "I'm not going to hurt you."

Eve jerks away. Her rosebud lips press into a hard line and her eyes narrow with suspicion. I completely understand. If I were her, I'd be thinking the same thing too.

I gently lower her on the mattress and release her. Eve scoots back, placing distance between us. Her attention shifts to the door.

"You can try and run, but you're not getting past Knox."

Her eyes cut back to me, fury and spite flaring in the turbulence of her gaze. She holds her arms over her bare chest and folds her legs to hide as much as she can from my view.

I leave her and head into the bathroom. There, I start filling the massive bathtub with warm water. It would be better if she took a shower, but I don't think she's steady enough to stand on her own. I could help her, and I still may need to, but putting me naked in a shower with Eve sounds like far too much temptation.

I'm not a teenaged boy anymore. I can control my body's reactions, but I can only resist so much.

I grab one of my shirts and bring it to her. Eve's eyes flash, but she doesn't say a word when I toss it to her.

"You can put that on while the tub fills." I give her my back, letting her cover herself.

At first, I hear nothing, but then she scrambles to put on the shirt. Her whimper of distress, however, spins me around. Her head is half in, half out of the hole. One arm is bound up inside the shirt. She struggles, and obviously can't see me.

"Here, let me help."

Eve flinches when I draw near. Huddled in the middle of the king-sized bed, I have to place a knee on the mattress to reach her. She doesn't draw back, however, as I gently guide her arm through the armhole and get the shirt to pull over her head. With her eyeing me the entire time, I help her place her other arm through the sleeve.

"Why?" she asks.

"Why, what?" I move away and off the bed.

"Why are you being nice to me?"

"What did you expect?"

Her lips press together and her brows tug tight.

"You need a bath and I need a shower. How's that for an answer?"

"I just thought…" Her voice trails off, and I'm reminded to

watch what I say. Knox is sweeping the suite for new bugs, but he hasn't made his way in here. He's giving Eve space, and me as well.

"You're going to have to rethink a lot of what you think you know about me." I glance toward the door. "It's a big tub. Takes long to fill. Stay on the bed. Don't try to walk around on your own. I don't want you to break a leg."

"Whatever." She draws her knees to her chest and pulls my shirt over her legs. My shirt swallows her much smaller frame and I can't help but take a moment. I love seeing her wearing something of mine.

I'm a protector and a Guardian, but I'm still one hundred percent male. I'm not completely immune to her charms.

My gaze slides back to her face. That energy is there again, crackling in the air. If only I could take her in my arms, comfort her like I want, and promise her that everything will be okay.

Instead, I turn on my heel and walk out of that room before I do something I can't take back.

TWENTY-FOUR

Eve

MAX LEAVES ME ON HIS BED. MY ONLY WEAPONS ARE THE DAGGERS I shoot from my eyes, and they're as effective as they sound. He dismisses my unblinking glare and leaves me.

Okay, now what?

My fingers stretch out, feeling the softness of the sheets.

He slept here last night.

And tonight?

Tonight, I will too.

Not sure how much sleeping there will be, but… It smells good in here. He smells good. I lean down and sniff the sheets, flooding my senses with his uniquely warm, masculine scent.

My eyes drift closed and I do nothing but breathe.

One breath. Two breaths. Three breaths. One more.

Why does he have to be one of them?

Another place. Another time. Things may have been different. I can't help this feeling. My gut says he's not one of the bad ones, but wishing and hoping do nothing to change hard, cold facts.

Max is a monster, and sometime later tonight, sooner rather than later, he will rape me. It's what men like him do. If I believe what Benefield told me, Max's bodyguard will too.

My fingers curl in the sheets as I fight back tears. There's no place for them. Not in a place such as this.

Max leaves me in the middle of his bed. He leaves me alone. He and Knox speak in subdued voices from the other room while I curl into the fetal position, hugging my knees to my chest.

The only escape is my mind. It's time to build the shields I pray will keep my sanity intact.

Max.

I bury my nose in the sheets, taking in his scent. *Why can't you be one of the good guys?*

When he looks at me, all I see is compassion, concern, and a need to protect. And I definitely notice how he doesn't stare at me like any of the other men. I didn't feel naked when he carried me. Even his bodyguard keeps his gaze to himself.

I'm naked, stripped of all dignity, but the two of them don't make me feel that way. The deference they show, just in how they avert their gazes, confuses me and muddles my mind. It makes me believe in the impossible.

I rub at my legs, lightly soothing the itching from countless bug bites. A heaviness weighs me down, extreme fatigue from my ordeal. Sleep calls to me, but I need to remain alert and ready for the fight to come.

Mosquito bites cover my legs, my arms, my belly, and my ass. I itch everywhere.

The rumble of their voices grows louder. A door slams, and then there's silence. Well, as much silence as there can be over the sound of water filling the tub and my frantic breathing.

I'm not sure, but I think I'm alone now.

With him.

With Max.

His large frame darkens the doorway. "I sent Knox to get a medical kit and to fetch your clothes."

"Because you want to be alone when you rape me?" I cock my head, knowing I shouldn't push, but if I'm going to be defiled, I will go down fighting.

"I have no intention of raping you."

"Really? You fought for the right to take me and you're going to do what? Give me a bath?"

"For now, that's about right." His low chuckle shouldn't sound that sinful, but it does. It makes me want things I can't have. Max cocks his head and gives me a long hard look. "How bad off are you?"

"What do you mean?" I cringe when he steps into the room.

"Come here." He moves to the foot of the bed.

"No." My refusal is funny as shit because he can make me do whatever the hell he wants. He's huge, like massively built huge. I bet he could press me over his head with one arm.

"Don't make this difficult."

"I should just let you rape me?" I glance behind me. "Like lean back, spread my legs, and let your tiny dick poke at me."

Max's entire body stills.

It's frightening how quiet he becomes. Terrifying. I don't know if I pushed too hard. Although, let's be honest, he's going to do it eventually.

Mirth crinkles in his eyes. It's the weirdest thing to watch his stony face turn into a beautiful smile. The only thing better than that is the low resonating laughter that follows. He shakes his head and laughs at me.

"You're not going to push my buttons, sweetie. I'm not going to rape you, and I promise, tiny has never been a word used to describe me. As for lying on your back, I want you in the tub, soaking, relaxing, and letting your muscles loosen up after being tied to that pole for hours."

"You want me to soak? In the tub?"

"Pretty sure I didn't stutter. That's what I said." His stony stare brooks no argument, but I can't help but poke and provoke a reaction.

"Just soak?"

"You have a problem with that?"

"You're not going to…" I make a vague gesture pointing to the bed.

"It's late, and I'll admit I'm insanely attracted to you, but I'm tired, you stink, and I'm not so fresh either. You need a bath. I need a shower. We'll have a nice long talk once Knox returns."

We.

That's what Benefield said. He said Max likes to share his women with his bodyguard. I don't understand something like that. It's weird as shit. I guess people would say it's kinky.

I'm as far from kinky as kinky can get. Although, I guess I no longer have a say in that.

Given the chance to choose between two evils, Max is certainly the man I'd rather be in this situation with. My mind goes dark when I think about how this would play out with Benefield. Not that I'm all Stockholm syndrome when it comes to Max.

I'm leery of him, and honestly? This kindness is the cruelest form of torture. I don't want to like my captor.

I like Max. I feel like I can trust him. He's one of them. Yeah, I know. I know he is, and that part hurts the most.

Max is a monstrous man. I'll never forgive him for being the kind of man who buys women for fun. But when he smiles, and that smile lights up his eyes, it's almost possible to imagine him as a different kind of man. A man bursting with warmth, compassion, and perhaps even love.

He checks out the progress of the tub. I peeked inside the bathroom, as much as I could see from the bed, and it's plenty large enough for the three of us.

Eww.

A shiver worms its way down my spine. I don't get the sharing thing at all.

Max returns. "Can you walk? Or do I need to carry you to the tub?"

I bite my lower lip and debate a thousand ways I can answer that question. I come up with something lame.

"I think I can." No hostility. No fight. Nothing which shows my anger. I should fight him on everything. Show a little spunk? Something?

Honestly, I'm drained. Physically exhausted, my arms hang like dead weight and my legs aren't making me feel good about staying upright when I stand. I don't have it in me to put up much of a fight.

I clamp my lips together and wriggle my way off the bed. Keeping his shirt pulled low to cover all my private bits, I place my feet on the floor and slowly transfer my weight to my legs.

I wobble and debate the wisdom of crossing the impossible distance between here and the bathroom on my own.

"Damn, they really did a number on you, didn't they?" Before I know what's happening, I find myself once again in Max's arms.

My arm naturally drapes around the back of his neck, resting on his shoulder, as he effortlessly lifts me and carries me to the tub. His skin is warm. His muscles hard. My hand presses against his chest as I close my eyes and sniff him like a crazy woman.

Steam rises off the water pouring into the tub, looking exactly like what I need right now. I'd love to sit in a tub and do nothing other than relax.

"It's a shame," I mumble.

"What?"

"No bubbles."

"You want bubbles?"

I'm too tired to respond. As the adrenaline surging through my body burns itself out, I'm left with profound fatigue and a listlessness I simply can't fight. My body drapes in Max's arms as he slowly lowers me into the steaming tub.

It's only a third filled, but I don't care.

Then I realize he left me in his shirt. Why didn't he strip me down?

"Easy there. Settle yourself in. It's a big tub and I don't want you to slip."

Max digs through the cupboards. He comes back with a smile on his face.

"Bubbles it is."

"I like bubbles." My voice sounds far away to my ears. My eyes drift closed as the water splashes into the tub.

The scent of strawberries fills the air and I take a peek. Max stands near the faucet, squeezing what looks like half a bottle of bubble bath under the running water. I can't help but giggle.

"Silly, you put too much in. I'm going to disappear under all these bubbles."

Indeed, bubbles begin to cover my feet and legs, and they're growing. A thick head of foaming bubbles rapidly fills the tub.

"You're pretty when you smile." Soft, gentle, melodious, his tone takes me by surprise. Then I remember where I am and what my fate will be later tonight.

I slip beneath the water and let the bubbles cover me up. Only my head is exposed as I stare up at him and wish again that he was a different kind of man. I clamp my lips tight and pray for the impossible.

Please, someone rescue me. Take me from this living hell.

"Tell me how you got here." Max sits on the side of the tub. His broad shoulders draw my eye, as does the swath of red on his arm.

"You're bleeding."

He glances at his arm and shrugs. "A flesh wound."

I can't help but giggle thinking of the Monty Python skit about *Just a flesh wound*.

Max looks down at me as if I've lost my ever-loving mind, and he may not be wrong. I shouldn't feel as comfortable as I do, laying in a tub, half-naked, with a man who killed another man for the privilege of making me his.

"Sorry." I peek up at him and notice the bubbles are growing fast. My entire body is covered.

He glances at his arm and pokes his fingers through the cut in his shirt. "I've had worse."

"How?"

"What do you mean, how?"

"I thought you were a businessman dealing in Central American antiquities."

"So?"

"It doesn't seem to be the kind of job where the owner is exposed to flesh wounds."

"You'd be surprised." The corners of his eyes crinkle as he

smiles, turning his rough and rugged face into a thing of beauty. "Now, how about you remove my shirt?"

Here it comes. The violation. My body tenses.

It's too easy to let down my guard around this man. It's the easiness of his smiles, something Benefield never showed.

Max stretches out his hand and gives a little flick of his fingers. "I'm not going to bite."

I don't know whether to trust him, or myself. There's a small part of me, a part which is growing rapidly, that wants something close to that. Not a real bite, but a little nibble?

Damn, I've officially gone insane.

"Come on, Eve, don't make me come in there and get it." His words are teasing, but I can't separate the truth from the rest of it.

I slowly work his shirt up and over my head, handing him the dripping, wet fabric coated in sudsy bubbles.

Max puts the shirt in the sink. I watch as he yanks his shirt open and peels it off his muscular frame. Dear lord, the man is built. Every muscle's defined. Every ridge, cut from granite, is hard and pronounced. His back flexes as he rolls his shoulders back, then he pulls his arm forward to get a look at that cut.

My eyes are glued to the tapestry of his back, and the tattoos printed into his flesh. It's a 3D rendering of an avenging angel fighting the demons of hell.

"Wow." I clamp my hand over my mouth as Max spins around.

"Yes, bubbles?" Mischief twinkles in his eyes as he smiles at me.

"Bubbles?"

"Yes." He points at the tub. "You look like you're floating in a cloud of bubbles. You may want to turn the water off before the bubbles overflow."

I feel around and realize the water doesn't fill half the tub. All the rest is a thick layer of bubbles. I can't help but smile. Talk about a bubble bath. I scoot to the end of the tub and turn off the water. Then I turn around and sit sideways, my legs tucked up under me, crisscross applesauce, as I scoop up a massive handful of bubbles. I blow on the bubbles sending a cloud lifting into the air.

Max stares down at me with that gentle smile on his face. That's when I see the dark stain over his left thigh.

"Max, your leg."

He glances down. Looks at it. Shrugs. "Forgot about that."

"You need to clean that out. The wound on your arm as well."

"I'd much rather watch my *bubbles* blow bubbles." He crosses his arms and a light-hearted smirk trades places with that smile.

Bubbles? Did he just call me bubbles?

"Can I trust you to stay in the tub while I shower? Or do I need to wait for Knox to return with your things?"

I glance toward the door, but the idea of streaking through The Retreat covered in nothing other than bubbles doesn't sound like a good plan.

"I'll stay."

"Promise?"

"Yes. I promise."

"Good." He reaches for his belt and I can't help but tense. "Relax. I'm just going to take a shower. Consider this fair play."

"How's that?"

"I've seen you naked. Now you get to see me naked."

Nope. Not going to happen. If I see the rest of him without clothes, any restraint will fall away. No matter how good-looking, no matter how lickable his eight-pack looks, I am not going down that road.

I spin around in the tub, placing my back to him. Not that it helps. There are mirrors everywhere, and he's not shy about stripping out of his pants. First, he shucks his shoes, then he unzips his pants. In one fluid movement, he's naked as a jaybird, reminding me I, too, am wearing my birthday suit.

Max says nothing as he strides over to the shower built for a committee. He turns on the faucet, then winks when he catches me peeking.

I'm not peeking. I'm staring.

My jaw hit the floor when I saw the size of him. Not a tiny, limp dick. Oh no, Max's package is built in proportion to the rest of him.

He faces the stream of water, steps under the spray, and grabs a bar of soap.

Holy mother of... I can't take it and slip beneath the bubbles before I see more, or say something I shouldn't.

Why does my tormentor need to look like a Grecian god out of the history books, and that tattoo? I need another look at that tattoo.

I stay buried beneath a foot and a half of bubbles for as long as I can. When I surface, Max stands with his injured leg propped up on the bench seat in the shower.

I see everything, only this time, instead of soft and flaccid, his member is semi-hard and rising.

He cocks his head, catches me staring again, then casually goes back to examining the stab wound on his leg.

As for me, I don't know what to do. I feel marginally better. My arm sockets ache, but that deep, pulsating agony is gone. My calves feel—relaxed. Maybe this bubble bath is doing what it's supposed to do?

A shadow darkens the doorway and I tense. Knox saunters into the bathroom, like it's nothing for him to walk in on his boss in the shower and a chick in a tub full of bubbles.

"Got a medical kit and gear for..." His attention swivels over to me. He gives a slow shake of his head. "Maybe I should've knocked?"

"Nah." Max turns off the water and steps out of the shower. He makes no effort to hide his nakedness from me. Knox hands him a towel and Max rubs at his head. "Any word on the dragons?"

Dragons?

"On time. On target." Knox pats his chest. "You gonna get dressed or are you planning on doing this naked?"

"Ha ha." Max gestures for the medical kit. "Just need to wrap my leg and slap something on my arm."

"Gotcha." Knox looks at me with compassion. "Don't worry, kid. Everything is going to be all right."

All right?

I don't think anything will ever be all right.

Max and Knox leave me to my bath overflowing with bubbles.

Their low voices drone on at the threshold of my hearing. I decide to take advantage of the moment and enjoy the warm water and the bubbles as they pop and fizz all around me. At some point, I even take a moment to rub them through my hair.

Many minutes later, Max raps on the frame of the doorway. "Time to get out, bubbles."

"Bubbles?" Knox laughs his ass off.

"Shut up, fuzzball."

I love their easy banter. I like the way they include me. I hate that I'm nothing more than a slave to Max. I wish I was more.

But I follow Max's command. I get up and stand in front of him as bubbles stream down my body.

Knox sees me and immediately turns around, giving me his back. Max rushes into the bathroom, snagging a large, fluffy towel. He wraps it around me, then helps me step out of the tub.

Knox twists around. He averts his gaze and hands Max a pile of clothes. My clothes.

Max takes them and puts them on the counter.

"Dry yourself, then get dressed." He retreats to the bedroom. "ETA?"

My brows scrunch together, but that last bit wasn't for me.

"Thirty minutes," Knox responds.

"What's happening in thirty minutes?" I dry myself quickly and wait for an answer. Neither of them responds to my question, leaving me to wonder. What the hell happens in thirty minutes?

TWENTY-FIVE

Max

IT WON'T BE LONG NOW. KNOX CALLED THE TEAM, GIVING A STATUS update on the past few hours. Eve is in my possession, but I'm not such a fool to believe Benefield isn't, right this second, thinking of a way to take her back.

He made a show of throwing her away, of downgrading her to a worthless whore, but it doesn't change the fact I took something precious.

To him, Eve isn't a person, but rather an object, a shiny toy that's all his. Nobody got to touch her, except now she belongs to me.

We've swept the suite for cameras, more times than I can count, and still find new bugs to destroy.

"Eyes." Knox points to his temple, reminding me to put Mitzy's magical contact lenses back in.

"No go." I keep my reply short and to the point while pulling my pants back on.

Instead of a suit, I dress in black tactical pants, a black long-sleeved t-shirt, and black boots. Not the attire of a businessman on vacation.

Knox doesn't like my answer, but I refuse to be held back by anything that might degrade my performance. Itchy, dry eyes that blur my vision are non-starters. Not all of Mitzy's tech works perfectly.

As I dress, my body's acutely aware of Eve in the bathroom. She's putting on clothes I desperately wish I could keep her out of, but that is not my place. I'm not here to start anything with her, as much as I'd like otherwise.

Focus on the mission, Max!

I berate my distraction. Distracted minds are dangerous. My team deserves one hundred percent of my focus. Until this op is done, Eve is nothing more than a package which needs to be moved from point A to point B.

Except she's a whole lot more than that. I've never mixed personal with business in my life. Laser-focused, I concentrate all my energy on completing the mission objective. I shouldn't be thinking about Eve, at least not in that way.

But I can't help myself. I can't help but feel something for her. And that totally sucks.

"You dressed in there?" I call out to the bathroom rather than take a look myself. If I walk in on Eve half-dressed, I'm afraid I won't be able to control my reactions.

"Almost." Her light, lilting voice is like a warm blanket settling over me.

I lean down and lace my boots, tugging tight on the strings as I lock them in. I hear her approach and brace for impact.

That's how it is with Eve. Every time I look at her, it's like getting hit with a ton of bricks. The woman doesn't just steal my breath, she makes the very foundation of my world shake.

"Can I ask a question?" She pads over to me in her bare feet.

I inch up my gaze, hoping the rest of her is clothed. Sure enough, denim clads her legs and a dark t-shirt covers those tits I can't stop thinking about now that I've seen them.

"Shoot."

"Um..."

"Um—what?" I love the way her brows push together when she's not sure of herself.

"Why am I wearing this?" She makes a vague gesture with her hand, moving it up and down her body.

My gaze follows the sweep of her arm. I catch and trip on her tits that I can no longer see. I fall down her narrow waist and slide across the flare of her hips. Hips which a man could definitely grab a hold of during sex. I fall past her legs, especially where they come together. I ache to explore more of what she has between her legs, but that is not something I will ever get to do.

I'm Eve's rescuer. Not her lover. I'm not her boyfriend. I'm nothing to her. My gaze continues its journey down her body and then back up. I lick my lips.

"What's wrong with what you're wearing?"

"It's just…" She shifts her weight off her heels. Her bare toes curl into the carpet. "I thought…"

"You thought, what?" I finish tying the laces of my boots and sit up straight.

"I suppose… I just figured…" She twists at the waist, looking back toward the tub. "I guess I thought you'd want to…"

I put a finger to my lips, a gesture for silence. Knox cleared out the cameras, but I can't be sure there aren't any bugs that can still hear.

"Your job isn't to think, now is it?"

She takes a step back, eyes widening. The tone of my voice scared her. Which sucks. It's not meant for her but rather anyone listening in.

Knox pokes his head into the bedroom. "You gonna stay in there all night, or bring the party in here?" Again, Knox speaks for an audience, which may, or may not, be listening in.

Eve's entire body tenses. Her fear slams into me, hard. But then I put two and two together. My girl isn't that hard to read.

"It's not what you think." I move toward the door.

Her wide eyes track me all the way out of the room. Knox gives me a look. He taps out in our special code.

Knox: What's up?

Me: She thinks I'm going to share her with you.

Knox shakes his head and slaps his knee. "Come on, boss, hurry up, bring her in here. I wanna taste of that fine ass."

"No. No. No!" Eve takes a step back.

I lift my finger to my lip, commanding her to be silent. With a flick of my fingers, I point to a pad of paper and pencil near Knox. He scribbles something on the paper and takes it to Eve.

She takes her time reading it, then her eyes round with surprise. She glances at Knox, then turns to me. I have no idea what he wrote, but it's clear Eve's now in the know about our plan.

Tears leak out of her eyes. It starts slow, then, as if turning on the faucet, she sobs. Her hands lift. She covers her face. Then Eve falls to the ground.

I rush to her, intending to catch her before she falls, but she comes to her knees and just kind of stalls there. Deep, soul-gutting sobs escape her.

I look to Knox, not knowing what to do.

He gestures back toward Eve, telling me *Go to your woman, dickwad.*

I rush to Eve, crouch down beside her, and wrap her in my arms. Her deep sobs intensify, but then they're suddenly cut off.

Eve twists toward me and loops her arms around my neck. She buries her head against my shoulder and whispers so softly, I'm not sure I hear.

"I knew a man couldn't smell that good if he wasn't..." The rest of what she says is cut off by another round of sobs. Only this time, they're joyous and filled with relief.

All I know is I've found heaven. My arms wrap around my woman. Her arms wrap around me. I never want this moment to end.

Knox clears his throat, interrupting us. A growl escapes me, but Knox is insistent.

"Max..."

"A moment..."

"Boss..." The switch to Boss grabs my attention.

I release Eve, thrilled to see happiness in her eyes. She beams with joy and I can say I've never seen anything more beautiful in my life.

"What's up?"

He leans close and speaks for my ears only. "Team's on the way. We need to be in place."

In place.

This is the tricky part. How to get the three of us out of the suite to the rendezvous spot.

I don't see a path forward. In our suite, we're safe. Expectations are that I'm sampling Eve's assets as we speak. There's zero reason for us to head outside.

Unless.

"I have an idea." I turn to Eve and debate my sanity. I crook my finger, calling her over. When she's near, I lean down and whisper in her ear. "Do you trust me?"

An odd question, considering everything she knows about me. Knox told her who we are, but she's still processing. I'm not sure the amount of trust I need is something she'll give me.

Eve nods. In that moment, my heart just about breaks.

"Knox, get me the shackles."

Knox gives me the eye, but he doesn't hesitate. Eve, however, tenses.

"What are you going to do with those?"

"Silence." The sharpness in my voice isn't for her. I mouth a soundless *I'm sorry* and *Trust me.*

Knox returns with the metal cuffs and I cringe at the drying blood on them. Eve's blood. No way in hell am I putting those back on her, at least not like that.

I stomp into my room and yank a shirt out of one of the drawers. I tear strips out of the soft cotton and I take these back to Eve and wrap them around her wrists.

"There. How's that?"

"You're a monster." Eve joins in, playing to our silent crowd.

"You have no idea." I wrap the manacles over the soft cotton, making sure her skin's as protected as it can be. Knox arches a brow, wondering at my plan. "Grab a belt. A thick one."

"On it, boss." Knox smirks, he knows exactly what I plan.

We gather at the door for one last check. I cup Eve's cheeks and press my forehead against hers. "You okay?"

"Yes."

"Things might get intense out there."

"I'm good." Her soft whisper sends chills down my spine.

She doesn't understand what I'm about to do. I glance at Knox and give him the okay.

Knox grabs Eve's manacles and jerks her out of the suite. He waits for me in the hall while I take the broad leather belt and loop it around her neck.

She wobbles as I cinch it down, tightening it against her throat. Out here, cameras are everywhere. I give a yank and head down the hall with my slave in tow.

Knox follows beside Eve, keeping her shuffling behind me.

TWENTY-SIX

Eve

YOUR FATHER SENT US.

Four little words change everything. Suddenly, the constriction around my chest, my constant companion for the past few months, eases.

My father sent Max and Knox.

Giddy with joy, I almost forget where we are. I'm just relieved it's over. But then, the care with which they handle their words reminds me this isn't over. They still need to get me out of The Retreat.

How?

The obvious answer is I'll leave as Max's slave the morning after the Auction. As great as that sounds, the idea of spending another minute in this hellhole concerns me. Benefield is known for changing the game midway through. I don't want to give him a minute to turn all of this around.

Not now.

Not that...

"Tone it down." Knox's low voice cuts through my joy and kills the spring in my step.

Giddy. I'm giddy with relief.

Max marches in front of me. The end of the belt wraps around his wrist as he keeps tension on the leather.

Knox's warning reminds me to stay in character.

In character.

Right. Max is scum of the earth. He won me in a poker game and fought to keep me.

Nope. It's not working. A grin keeps tipping up the corners of my lips. I need something to bring my spirits down.

But I can't help it. Knowing Max isn't one of the bad guys changes everything. I can't keep that kind of joy inside. It's bursting within me, eager to find a way out. I want to skip and leap for joy.

I'm free. Free from this hellacious place where girls are—wait a second.

I stumble over my feet. The belt pulls tight around my throat. Max takes a step, yanking me forward, as I choke and sputter.

"Keep up, slave." Max turns to berate me, but all I see is concern in his eyes.

Knox grabs my arm to steady me as I pull at the belt around my throat.

What about all the other girls? I can't leave them.

But what can you do about it?

Nothing. I can do nothing, but surely Max and Knox wouldn't leave those girls here to suffer.

Would they?

My father only paid them to get me out of here. He doesn't care about the other girls. I know all their names. Those no longer here, having been sold off to monsters, as well as the girls currently undergoing training. It's the list I've kept in my head since the day I arrived and realized what was going on.

The men I know only by a single letter, but there must be a way to track down the men who bought them. There has to be a way to save them all.

I need to tell Max. I don't know the names of those men, but I know how to find out. Old school, Benefield keeps tabs on his guests. It's all meticulously recorded in a ledger he keeps in his office.

Max sets off again and I stumble after him. How do I tell him? Once we're out of this place, there will be no way to get that information. It'll be gone, as will all trace of those girls.

I'd like to think some of the privilege I enjoyed here was worth it. As hard as I try, however, I don't see what I can do that won't jeopardize everything.

Max marches us down covered walkways. He takes shortcuts through the extravagant courtyards. Beauty surrounds me, lush vegetation, beautiful blooms, and a heady fragrance from the flowers flood my senses. I've been kept prisoner in a grotesque paradise.

We head toward the front gate and I'm horribly confused.

During our long walk, Max and Knox remain stoically silent. What are they thinking? Max can't walk me out the front gate.

"Four," Knox calls out beside me.

I glance at him, and pinch my eyes in confusion.

"Copy that." Max steps up his pace.

We wind through the massive estate, passing guards at their posts. So far, Max remains unchallenged. But how long will that last? Our progress is, without question, being relayed to Benefield.

We arrive at another one of the courtyards, the largest one at The Retreat. Four guards round the corner. When they see us, their hands go to their weapons. They come right toward us.

The leather around my neck draws tight as Max yanks me into the courtyard. Knox follows half a step behind me.

The change in the two men is palpable. No longer do I see Max and his bodyguard. I see two men, highly skilled, working as a team.

Max draws me along a narrow path lined with chest-high bushes. He comes to a gap in the hedge, where a perpetually flowering tree drapes pink flowers over the walkway. The light floral fragrance, normally soothing, feels thick and cloying as Max ducks under the limbs and heads deeper into the vegetation.

Max pulls me after him. Knox walks behind me. His hand moves inside his suit jacket as he faces toward the rear. Max gathers in the slack on the leather belt until I practically step on his heels.

"What's…" Max silences me with a finger to his lips and a stern shake of his head.

I want to put a hand on his shoulder. Something to steady me as I navigate over the raised roots of the tree, but I'm supposed to be an unwilling slave. That means no seeking comfort from Max.

My attention swivels to the opposite side of the courtyard. Benefield's office isn't that far, but we're walking in the opposite direction.

"We've got company," Knox calls out.

"Copy that. How many?"

"Four."

"Damn," Max curses. "Alpha?"

"Two minutes out."

They speak in short, clipped phrases. It sounds like code. Most of it I follow. There were four armed guards who rounded the bend when Max yanked us into the courtyard, but what does Alpha mean?

He cuts through the meticulously manicured foliage, ducking under trees, stepping over small streams, and squeezing through gaps in the bushes.

Max makes a beeline for the opposite corner of the courtyard, still headed toward the main gates.

I high step it behind him, keeping my feet from tangling in the roots, which suddenly seem to be everywhere underfoot. I'm also loud, like an elephant stomping through the underbrush kind of loud. Max and Knox move silently, stealthily.

How? How the hell do they do that when they're wearing combat boots and I'm in sneakers?

But we're not silent enough.

Several sets of footsteps approach directly in front of us. The men call out to one another in Spanish. I've learned enough to know they're looking for us. Not that it's hard to miss the urgency in their voices.

"Shit." Max stops between two bushes and drops to a crouch. I follow suit. First, because I'm copying everything he does. Secondly, because he yanks me down with a harsh tug on the damn leash.

"Plan B?" Max directs his attention to Knox.

Just then, a massive explosion sounds someplace in front of us. The ground rocks beneath my feet, and a concussive blast rustles the leaves all around us. My ears pop.

"Plan B." Knox's expression turns grim. "They're early."

"No shit." Max draws out a gun from under his jacket. Knox follows suit.

How the hell did they get firearms? Benefield is ruthless in ensuring none of his guests carry weapons of any kind. I suspect there were problems in the past.

Max releases the end of the belt and frees the loop from around my neck. I guess we're beyond pretending I'm his slave.

Early?

Who's early?

Another concussive blast rips through the courtyard. It's closer than the first one. I feel it in my lungs and in my throat. My ears ring from the shockwave.

Max wraps an arm around me, covering me with his body as limbs and leaves fall all around us.

Adrenaline spikes through my body, racing around as it preps me for fight or flight.

I glance up at Max, terrified, but also reassured. I trust him. I trust him with my life.

He presses close to whisper in my ear. "I've got you. Stay by my side and I promise I'll get you out of here."

I lay my hand on his forearm and give a little squeeze. I'm too terrified to speak, and with all the ringing in my ears, I don't trust myself not to shout.

That odd dichotomy back in his suite disappears. No longer do I see a vile man interested in purchasing a slave. I see the man he's always been. He's a protector. A savior. And Max is going to rescue me.

Shouts sound out not ten feet away from where we're hiding. Those must be the men from the hallway.

Benefield wants me back.

A whole-body shudder overtakes me. I can't go back. There's no more pretending.

Another concussive wave slams into us as a third explosion tears through the air. Max places his hand over mine and gives a reassuring squeeze.

"Don't worry, I've got you."

I want to believe him. I really do, but it feels as if the world's gone crazy. We're in the middle of a war zone. As if to punctuate that thought, another explosion, closer yet again, rattles the air.

"Max." I look up at him. "I'm scared."

"Don't be. That's our team softening things up."

I don't know about softening things up, and I'm not sure why we're still hiding in the bushes. Shouldn't we be running? Either away from, or toward, those explosions?

I'm no expert in this kind of thing, but I kind of feel like staying in one place makes us a sitting duck.

"His men are moving off." Knox pivots in his half-crouch.

"Copy that." Max taps his ear, pushing inward. "Gate's a no-go. Heavy resistance."

"It's still closer…" Knox tilts his head, as if listening to something in his ear.

Then I get it. They've got some kind of communication gear on.

"Deliver packet to rear wall." Max's lips firm into a hard line. "Exit the breach?"

"Sounds like a plan." Knox shifts again, this time looking around the bushes. "On me?"

Max holds up a finger, telling Knox to wait. He leans toward me and cocks my head to speak directly into my ear.

"Put your hand in the back of Knox's trousers. Grab his waistband. Stay close. Head down. I'll have my hand at your back." He reaches to my back and slips his fingers beneath the waistband of my pants. His fingers curl, gripping the fabric tight, demonstrating what he wants me to do with Knox. "Our team is going to breach the rear wall. On the count of three." Max stares at me until I nod, telling him I'm ready.

Honestly, I have no idea what I'm supposed to be ready for. They don't teach this kind of stuff in etiquette class.

"One. Two." Max keeps his eyes on me and flicks his gaze toward Knox's back.

Oh right. I'm supposed to... I slide my fingers down the small of Knox's back and grip the back of his trousers.

"Three." Max completes the countdown.

I lift a little, getting ready to run, sprint, walk, or stroll, but nothing happens. Instead of moving, Knox lifts his hand next to his head and forms a fist.

Max's grip on my jeans tightens as Knox sweeps his weapon toward the sound of footsteps. His entire body tenses.

Lights swing back and forth, looking for us. The courtyard is huge, but it doesn't have any lighting inside of it, except for the fake torchlights along the paths. The bushes we crouch behind should keep us hidden.

Knox creeps forward. I shuffle behind him. Max is right with me. The warmth of his hand calms me. It's the only thing keeping me from crawling out of my skin.

The men stop. Knox's arm lifts. Two shots ring out. Knox surges forward and I lose my grip on the back of his pants. Not that I need it. Max propels me forward. Just before I clear the bushes, he bodily picks me up and places me to his side.

Knox takes a knee at the bodies of two of Benefield's guards. He bends over one, shoves something metal and black into his pocket. Then he shifts to the other body. Again, he leans forward. This time, instead of putting whatever it is in his pocket, he tosses the metal clip to Max, who catches it. He tucks it inside his back pocket.

"You ever use a pistol before?" Max arches a brow.

"I have." Meaning, I've watched a lot of television and handled a real gun once in my life.

"Hand here." He puts the grip in my palm. "Safety." He shows me how to flick the safety. "Aim where you look. Don't think too hard about it. You good?"

Hell no. I'm not good at all.

My heart's banging away a mile a minute. The air suddenly feels thicker. Harder to breathe.

Knox tosses a bigger gun to Max. It's one of those automatic rifles the guards always carry. Knox passes back another pistol to Max.

He takes it, and just like with the rifle, he checks the chamber. I didn't check the chamber of the tiny gun I carry. Not that I'd know how, but I trust Max knew what he was doing when he put it in my hand. I don't even know how many bullets are in my gun.

"Time to beat it." Max glances over his shoulder. He takes my free hand and shoves it at the small of his back.

Now, I get to grip his pants. I hold the gun he gave me out to the side, making damn sure my finger's nowhere near the trigger thingy. Just as Max stands, Knox's hand is on my back. He doesn't hang on to me the way Max did a second ago.

Max moves out. I follow because I'm holding onto him. Knox takes the rear, running backward and sideways at the same time.

This is definitely not their first rodeo show. Another explosion rocks the ground. This one's farther away, but those gunshots are pretty damn close.

Gunshots?

Yeah, that *pop, pop, pop* is definitely the sound of gunfire.

We move in silence, which means I can't hear Max or Knox. For the life of me, I can't keep silent. When I try tiptoeing, my calves nearly cramp up. They're still not fully recovered from the whole being tied-to-the-pole thing.

More gunshots ring out. These are a bit farther away. Max continues to move. We travel quickly down hallways, pausing at intersections while he checks to make sure it's clear.

We're not too far from Benefield's office. I tap Max on the shoulder to get his attention. When he doesn't answer, I call out to him.

"Max…"

He turns around, face calm and devoid of any emotion. It's scary as shit; it's a whole other side of him I never want to see again. Cold, calculating, he's a killer.

I bite my tongue and glance right as we head left.

TWENTY-SEVEN

Eve

I SHOULD BE ONE HUNDRED PERCENT LASER-FOCUSED, ON GETTING out of here alive. It's the smart thing to do, but that doesn't mean it's the right thing.

If Max and Knox really can get me out of here, then I need to make my time here worthwhile. There are other women to save. Other lives to recover. We meander down the hallways of The Retreat, backtracking as much as we move forward. If Max senses people in front of us, we duck down a connecting hall, then renegotiate our way toward the back of The Retreat.

Max's knowledge of the layout of this place astounds me. We're in areas few of the guests ever go. Not that they aren't allowed. It's simply the men who come here tend to spend their days in the Oasis as much as they can.

Our haphazard progress brings us closer to Benefield's office, then frustratingly farther away.

Max leads us down another long hall. The shouts of men sound out in front of us. He yanks me back to an alcove, plastering our backs to the wall as five men run past us carrying guns. Too focused on where they're going, they fail to see us as they rush past.

Max waits for several long seconds, listening for the sound of more men. When I can't hold it in any longer, I tug on his sleeve to get his attention.

"Max…"

He turns to me, expression hard as granite, eyes dark and focused. I should remain silent. Let him lead. But I can't.

"We need to go back." I point down the hallway those men just went down.

"No. I'm getting you out of here."

"Benefield's office is that way."

He gives a sharp shake of his head, dismissing me. I tug on his arm again.

"We have to go back."

"Why?" He gives a slow blink and his expression completely changes. No longer the fierce warrior, he looks like the nicer version of Max I prefer.

"The ledgers."

"Come again?" His brows pinch together.

"Benefield's ledgers." I realize he doesn't understand. "He keeps written records of every transaction. Every girl who's ever come through here. Every client who's ever purchased a slave. We have to get it."

Max glances back the way we came. For a moment, he looks like he's considering it, but then he gives a sharp shake of his head.

"Can't risk it."

"We have to."

"You're our objective. Your safety is my priority."

"I won't be able to live with myself if I don't at least try." I try to convince him.

"Max, we need to move." Knox, who's been listening to the entire exchange, is watching down the hallway.

Max grabs my arm, but I shake out of his grip. "I'm not leaving here without those ledgers."

"I'm not leaving here without you." Max gives Knox a look.

The two men stare at each other for a long moment. I swear they communicate telepathically. A whole host of facial expressions parades across their faces. I look back and forth between them, wondering what the hell they're saying. Finally, Knox speaks.

"If it's what she says it is…"

"I know." Max turns to me. "Are you sure, absolutely certain, that's what's in those ledgers?"

"I've spent months in that office. I've seen him write everything down. Every name, the price paid, and girl sold."

"This could be invaluable," Knox says.

"I know." Max taps the device in his ear. He gives a quick rundown of what I told him to whomever is on the other end of that device. Once he's done, he cocks his head, listening to whatever is said back. At least, that's what I assume he does.

The two men nod at the same time, leaving me guessing as to what's been decided. I don't like not being involved in whatever is being said about me, but I don't have much of a choice. Honestly, I want to get out of here as fast as possible.

Who knew this much adrenaline could spike in a person's body. My heart's racing. My pulse slams in my throat and roars past my ears. I hear myself breathing, rapid and shallow. It feels as if I'm running a race, but I'm not.

We're not moving.

But then Max puts his hand on my arm. "Eve, it's your call. If we go now, you'll be free of this place. If we go back…"

"I have to go back." I point in the direction of Benefield's office. "It's not that far." Max glances where I point. "If we cut through there…" A shiver ripples down my spine as I point in the direction of the courtyard with the steel pole driven into the ground. PTSD much?

But I don't care. If that ledger helps Max and his team recover just one of the girls who passed through this place, it's worth the risk.

"You're sure about this?" Max glances out into the hall. It's been strangely quiet these past few minutes, but that can change any second.

"I am."

Max and Knox do that thing again, their weird telepathic communication, then Max kicks off from the wall.

"You stick to me." He grabs my wrist and places it at the small of his back. I grip the waistband of his pants and nod.

"I stick with you."

"Let's move out." That comment isn't for me, but rather Knox.

The two of them move as one, with me trailing behind Max. I tighten my grip on his waistband. No way am I getting separated from him.

We make our way to the end of the hall. Max glances right and pivots in that direction. I yank on his pants.

"It's quicker through here."

In front of us lies one of Benefield's many trophy rooms. Long and narrow, the room cuts right through the center of The Retreat. From there, Benefield's office is a quick walk through that horrific courtyard with the pole.

I have questions. Questions I can't ask. Questions like, what are all the explosions? The gunfire? Who are Benefield's men shooting at? It feels like an all-out war is in progress, yet again, there's an eerie sense of dead calm.

It's been minutes since we've seen any of Benefield's men, heard any gunfire, or felt another explosion.

What's going on?

The not knowing makes my anxiety spike. As if it's not already spiking.

I point to the door to the trophy room. Max moves up to it. He halts right outside. Slowly, he grips the door handle. A glance to Knox. A nod exchanged.

Max opens the door, kicking it with his foot, as Knox charges in. Knox sweeps his weapon left then right, then aims it straight ahead.

"Clear."

The moment Knox calls out, Max draws me into the room. He closes the door behind us. He and Knox move stealthily toward the opposite door while I bumble along behind them.

Seriously, how do they do that?

It's a long, narrow room filled with precious art, stuffed trophy animals—mostly endangered species. A black panther stares down at me. His glassy green gaze judging. We move past a Bengal tiger, rearing up with paws raised, mouth wide, canines ready to rip and rend. There are beautiful birds, with incredible plumage in all colors of the rainbow, mounted on the walls, dangling from the ceiling, and posed on the floor.

This room always fascinated me with its macabre beauty. With no regard for life of any kind, Benefield snuffed out the lives of these animals solely for the purpose of putting them on display here. I hate how the lives of these magnificent creatures were brutally taken, but there's beauty here as well. A weird dissonance consumes me as I admire and hate everything in this room.

Max continues forward. The slow chugging of his breath the only sound I hear. Knox finally comes to the far end of the room. He places his hand on the door and closes his eyes. Next, he leans close and puts his ear to the wood.

Long seconds pass.

With a look to Max, he gives the signal.

Again, Max is the one to open the door. Knox is the first one through. Max follows, and I trail behind them both. Once in the hall, I point to the left. We head that way until we come to the entrance of that courtyard I hate so much.

It stands empty, except for that pole. Last time I was here, I thought Max was a monster fighting for the right to have me. Little did I know the truth. It's sobering, really, knowing he willingly put his life on the line to save mine. I don't think I would be that brave.

I could never be that selfless.

Max and Knox pause yet again. It's incredible watching them work together. We move at what seems to be a snail's pace yet continue to cover a great deal of ground.

As we work our way to Benefield's office, I'm well aware how far it takes us from getting out of here.

Knox mentioned something about a breach. I can only assume those explosions created holes in the defensive walls which surround this place. Those holes are, more than likely, heavily defended by Benefield's men by now.

I don't see how we're getting out that way, but Max doesn't seem concerned. If he's not worried, I won't be either. He asked if I trusted him.

I trust him with my life.

We cross the courtyard without incident. I give that pole a heated glare as we pass, but that's it. There's no time to think about the agony I endured tied there for hours or the fight between Max and the other man.

Once we pass through the courtyard, we turn left at the next intersection.

Distant gunshots sound off to the right. I want to ask Max about that. Who are Benefield's guards shooting at?

"Second door on the right," I whisper to Max, although there's no reason to tell him where to go. He and Knox seem to know this place nearly as well as I do.

Knox pauses at the door. He listens again. Another nod. Max reaches for the doorknob. He twists. It doesn't budge.

Locked.

I didn't think about that.

Not that it stops Max. He takes the butt end of his weapon and slams it down hard on the handle. The doorknob falls to the floor, and just like that, we're in.

Max moves us inside, then shuts the door behind us.

"Where?" He glances around the room, but he's not going to find the ledger.

Benefield keeps it hidden.

I release the death grip I have on Max's waistband and head directly to the small secretary desk pushed into an unobtrusive corner. Benefield's massive mahogany desk dominates the room, but he doesn't keep anything important there.

I also know where he keeps the key to the secretary's desk. I fish around in a nearby fern until I find the long metal key. Moving quickly, I unlock the desk, roll back the top, and locate the secret compartment where the ledger is kept.

I pull it out and hold it tight to my chest.

I have it. I have all the names. All the lives. And if I don't know what to do with it, Max and whoever he works with certainly must. A stack of papers on the desk catches my eye. I lean forward.

"Eve, we need to leave." Max joins me at the desk while Knox guards the door.

My hand moves on its own to the stack of papers. Not papers really. They're bills of lading. I flip through them, not believing what I'm seeing.

"Eve?"

Bills of lading. Documents of title. Receipts for shipped goods. Contracts between a carrier and shipper. Documents that accompany shipped goods, signed by authorized representatives of the carrier, the shipper, and the receiver.

Benefield's name flows across the paper. Then there's another name, one I don't know. Finally, there's a third name. A name I know all too well; Carson Deverough.

My father.

The bottom drops out of my world. My father. His name is on every document. I flip through the sheaf of papers as everything I thought I knew turns into one big lie.

The dates.

They go back years.

"What's wrong?" Max places a hand on my shoulder.

I show him the documents as tears pool in my eyes. "My father." I point to the damning evidence. "He's in league with Benefield."

"What?" Max takes the papers and flips through them. His eyes round as I grab at my stomach and sway on my feet.

"He's in business with Benefield. They're partners."

Partners.

Suddenly, my kidnapping takes on a whole other meaning. Was the ransom just a lie? Did my father intend for me to become just one of the hundreds of Benefield's victims? Is everything I thought I knew about my father a lie?

"Max…" The floor tips beneath me. The only reason I don't fall is that Max wraps an arm around my waist. He holds me up. He grounds me. Max provides the only truth I know right now.

He's here to rescue me. As for my father? Benefield? I take a shaky step back.

"I'll figure all of this out." Max turns me to face him. He grabs both my arms and gives the tiniest of shakes to get my attention. My tear-filled eyes greet his grim expression. "I've got you." He stares deeply into my eyes. "Eve…I've got you."

His words shake the foundation of my world. I believe him. This man who came into my life as the most monstrous of men is now the one who will save me. I trust Max. I believe him.

I've got you.

I cling to those words. They're the only thing that makes sense right now.

He tucks the papers and the ledger inside his shirt, securing them in place. All expression is gone. Max, the cold, calculating warrior is once again in place.

I thought to take evidence of all the girls whose lives had been stolen in the hopes they could be found. Instead, I found evidence of my father's betrayal.

I also found hope.

TWENTY-EIGHT

Max

TIME'S RUNNING OUT AND THIS DETOUR IS MESSING WITH OUR extraction plans. Knox and I are supposed to be at the south wall. Instead, we're rummaging around Benefield's office finding the unspeakable.

Eve discovered an unsavory truth. Those papers, more so than this ledger she's adamant we find, reveal a connection between her father and Benefield.

Carson Deverough's in business with Benefield.

Even I, who've seen all manner of vile and disgusting things, struggle to frame what we found into something which makes sense.

The bills of lading span a five-year timeframe. Meticulous shipping records not of cargo, but human lives.

Her father.

Benefield.

Their signatures side by side.

It's damning evidence.

But I have questions.

Her kidnapping? How does that work into this?

The ransom demands? Those make no sense.

Why would Benefield extort millions from Deverough if they're in business together?

Money laundering? It's the first thing that comes to mind.

Blackmail? That comes in as a close second.

It's the most obvious answer, although the man Knox and I met in New Orleans certainly played the role of desperate father perfectly.

He was worried.

Scared.

He feared for his daughter's safety.

It's the kind of desperation that can't be faked.

What's the angle being played here?

Nothing we're going to solve in the next few minutes. This is the kind of stuff we give to Mitzy to chew on until it makes sense. My job is to get Eve out alive, and I'm one hundred percent dedicated to that task.

A task I'm currently failing at achieving.

"Max," Knox calls out, telling me we're running out of time. "We'll miss exfil if we don't step up the pace."

Our operation is planned down to the minute. If we don't make our window, we'll be left here without support.

I turn to Eve. "You with me?"

She returns a shaky nod, telling me she totally doesn't have her head in the game. I need to get her attention and shake her out of this trance.

I grip her arms and force her to look me in the eye. "All of this…" I tap my shirt, where I stuffed the damning evidence. "We'll deal with it later. Right now, I need to get you out of here. I need you focused."

The stare she returns is one of turmoil. Eve isn't on board; she's barely hanging on.

That's okay with me. I'm trained in dealing with unwilling hostages. If I have to sling her over my shoulders and carry her out, I'll do it.

I snap my fingers in front of her face. Eve blinks. It's the slowest, most ponderous movement I've ever seen, but it works. A veil lifts between us. Her vision clears. Her eyes focus. Eve sees me. She trusts me. Talk about a sledgehammer hitting my heart. Her trust hits me where it counts.

If only she could look at me that way with something more than desperation. I'd give everything to have her look at me with affection instead. Desire for her rushes through my body. It's carnal, needy, and undeniable.

And there goes the kind of stray thought which is dangerous.

Thinking about a relationship right now is not where I need to focus. Not that she'd ever want me. Time to bite the bullet and accept the hand I've been dealt. Mission first.

Get her out alive.

I focus on that.

"Eve..." I grab her arms and shake her, "you with me?"

Another slow blink, but her vision clears. Her lips press together. Eve looks at me with the grit and determination I've learned to expect from the strength of her character. This girl is a survivor.

"I'm getting you out of here."

"Okay." She moves toward the door. The door Knox guards. "We need to head to the west wall."

"Exfil is to the South." Knox gives a shake of his head, dismissing Eve's instructions.

She looks at him. "I don't know what 'exfil' means, but we're closest to the western fence. There's a gap where an animal tried to break through the fence. Benefield's men haven't mended it yet. I don't think they know it's there, and the cameras don't look that way."

"Are you sure about this?" I grip her arms, tight, still kind of giving her a hard shake. If her mind's not in the game, it could mean certain death for us.

"Sure as I can be. A pig, or a tarpon, doesn't matter. It dug a trench through the stream, pushed up the bottom edge. It's covered by a bush growing over the stream. It's been there for weeks. Either he doesn't know about it, or he doesn't care. Either way, we're closer to the western fence than the southern wall. What does exfil mean?"

"It means that's where our team expects us to meet them." Knox looks to me like I'm crazy to contemplate Eve's suggestion.

I turn to Eve. "What's between us and the southern wall?"

"His whole army, I suppose. Honestly, I don't know, except he doesn't guard the western approach like he does the southern exposure. It's all heavy jungle that way. Nobody moves through the jungle. It's impassable."

"All the more reason for us to stick to the plan." The muscles of Knox's jaw bunch.

"What do you know about Benefield's men?" I ask.

"Only what I've learned over time. The majority of his forces guard the southern exposure. It's where the roads come in. Like I said, the jungle to the west is impassable. I've seen gaping holes in the fences that took weeks to repair. He's not worried about an attack from that direction."

I glance at Knox. This goes against our teams' plans. Unlike me, Knox still wears the contacts that report our every action back to base. CJ, Mitzy, and Sam will know everything, at least as soon as Knox is able to upload the data to the satellites. That requires a clear view of the sky and communication with the satellites our organization commands overhead.

"Knox? Your call."

"Mine?" He points to his chest. "What does your gut say?"

"It says there's only three of us and scores of Benefield's men between us and the exfil site."

"Then we head west." Knox grudgingly agrees with Eve's suggestion.

The ground trembles beneath our feet as another explosion rips through the building. I tap at my earbud as it squeals in my ear. Plaster and dust rain down from the ceiling.

"That was…"

"…too close." Knox finishes my sentence.

"How's your comm? Mine's fried from those first explosions."

"Same here." He taps the side of his head, trying to get his comm to quiet down as well.

What's with all the explosions? This wasn't a part of our plan.

"Whatever we do," Knox says, "we need to do it now."

I glance at Eve and make a decision. She's not equipped to make her way through the dense vegetation of the jungle. Not in those shoes.

"We keep to the plan. Head to the southern wall. Meet up with the team there."

TWENTY-NINE

Max
———

KNOX TAKES A STEP AWAY FROM THE DOOR. THE KNOB'S BUSTED from when we came through. He places his hand on the wood, feeling for any vibrations that might indicate movement on the other side.

I move up beside him. Eve's my responsibility; therefore, I give him the lead. Doing this as a two-man team brings several disadvantages. There's no good place to put Eve. In a full contingent of six operatives, she'd be placed in the middle of the group. Two operatives to take the lead and sweep for threats. Two more would provide coverage to the rear. The middle two would keep tabs on the package, moving her through danger until we made it to the extraction point.

Knox and I must take all those roles upon ourselves. This leaves him in the lead, unsupported, and me bogged down with Eve and a thinly supported rear position.

I glance at the weapon Eve carries with a mind to tell her to be careful of the trigger, but there's no need. Her trigger finger lies along the barrel rather than sitting on the trigger itself.

She's one smart cookie.

I nod to Knox, who now presses his ear to the door. We go on his signal. Eve gives a start when I wrap my fingers in the waistband of her jeans, but then she settles down. It's not the best solution, but I can push her forward, or pull her back, as needed; better this way. It also keeps my right hand free to handle my weapon. The rifle Knox appropriated from Benefield's men rides over my back. Eve carries my sidearm, and I have the 9mm kindly supplied by Benefield's man.

Knox moves us out into the corridor and down to the first intersection. Head cocked, he listens for any sign of movement. I would too, but my attention is split by watching Eve and guarding our back.

We cut across a courtyard, moving silently, when all of a sudden Eve pulls out of the grip I have on her.

"Eve..." I growl out her name, ready to chastise her for breaking the line, but she stands in front of one of the many cages.

"I have to let them go." Eve works the clasp on a cage holding half a dozen tropical birds. The metal squeals as she opens the door.

The birds inside give her the eye and hop to the back of the cage, keeping their distance.

"We have to go," I call out to her, but she looks back, determined to free the birds.

"They're scared of you. Leave the door open. They'll figure it out."

Knox crouches not too far from us as I get Eve to leave the cage with the birds. I think we're ready to move out when she heads to another enclosure. It's the one with the butterflies. She opens this door too and props it open with a rock. Three butterflies escape, flitting over her head as she kicks the rock in place.

"One more." She heads over to the last enclosure in the courtyard. It's the one with the spider monkeys in it, and it's on the opposite side of the courtyard from where we are.

"Eve, no!" I shout as movement on the rooftop catches my eye.

Eve freezes mid-step as a burst of gunfire lights up the courtyard. Knox returns fire as I launch myself at Eve, sweeping her to the side and behind the cover of a neighboring tree.

Her wide, frightened eyes nearly pop out of her head as I force her to scramble deeper under the canopy of the tree. We've got marginal cover, but it's not bulletproof.

Knox shoots off a volley toward the rooftop, then overwhelming silence fills the air.

"We go, now." I grab Eve, hauling her to her feet, and head back toward Knox.

"I'm not leaving them caged." Eve pulls away from me, batting at my hand to force me to let her go.

I do, but only because another shooter appears on the roofline. One shot and he's dead. The body falls into the courtyard and lands with a thud. Knox rushes over to the body, not because he gives a damn, but to salvage the man's weapon and unspent ammo. He tucks a couple of magazines into his pants and gives me a *What the fuck* look. I return a shrug.

Eve's already up and on her feet, sprinting to the far side of the massive courtyard. A quick scan reveals no more movement on the roof, but that won't last long. The gunfire will attract unwanted attention.

I make it to Eve as she opens the door to the spider monkey enclosure. While she looks around for a rock to hold open that door, two monkeys move to the opening, chittering loudly as they realize freedom is just a step away. Neither of them takes that final step, however. A third hangs back, cowering in fear with tiny hands clasped tight to its chest.

"Eve, we *have* to go." I'm not happy about the delay.

"Why aren't they leaving the cage?" Eve turns soulful eyes to me. She squats down and holds out a hand.

One of the monkeys gives her a dubious look, but then it jumps in her hand and scampers up her arm where it clings to her shoulder. It grips her hair as its tiny feet dig in for purchase. The second monkey follows its friend, chattering as it climb up to perch on her shoulder.

Eve leans into the cage, hand outstretched, trying to get the last monkey to come out.

If we weren't in the middle of an escape, I'd laugh at the sight of Eve, two monkeys on her back, trying to cajole the third monkey out of the cage. The two on her shoulders chitters, talking to each other, or maybe they're coaxing their fellow to take a leap of faith.

Either way, the last monkey finally gets brave enough to sit in Eve's palm. Its tiny hands grasp her thumb, and that's all I need.

With my hand in the back of her pants, I yank Eve to her feet and spin her around. The monkeys scream at me, but I couldn't care less what they have to say. I push Eve back into the courtyard. My head's on a swivel as we rejoin Knox, who's guarding our backs. He gives me another *What the fuck?* look when he sees the screeching monkeys clinging to Eve. All I can do is roll my eyes.

No way is she leaving those monkeys behind. Which sucks major monkey balls, pun intended. I don't need this added stress.

Although—totally being honest here—I love this about her.

Insisting we circle back around to Benefield's office to get the names of the girls who've moved through this despicable place, shows a depth of character too few people have these days.

She's a protector, a rescuer, willing to put her life on the line to save others. How can I not respect that? She's phenomenal.

"Keep them quiet, Eve, or ditch them."

I growl out the command, knowing she won't let them go, *and* I'd never force her to leave those damn monkeys behind.

Knox takes off again, heading south, toward exfil. We're already late. The delay may prove costly. CJ marshaled the combined forces of Alpha, Bravo, and Charlie on this mission. Once Forest received confirmation of the stable of girls, there was no way he'd leave them. Which means they won't delay extraction of the abducted girls. If we don't make it on time, Knox and I will be on our own until we can reconnect with our team.

Knox and I have one mission objective.

Extract Eve.

We have her. Now, to get her out of this despicable place. If we don't make exfil, it's not the end of the world. It's just not the best option as it keeps us here until we can figure out an alternate extraction plan.

Another explosion rocks our world. This one's closer; felt in the chest, and rings in the ears. It sets off the birds in the first enclosure.

Their screeches and squawks escalate and change in timbre as they finally find their way to freedom.

Eve pauses to watch the multi-colored birds fly off into the night. The butterflies are on their own; no doubt they'll find their way free as well. The spider monkeys cling to Eve's shoulders; their long limbs and prehensile tails wrap up her arms and around her neck. In addition to their loud, prolonged screams, I swear I hear something like the yipping of a dog or the whinny of a horse.

There is *no* way we're making it out of here with any kind of stealth.

"We gonna move or stand around here all day?" Knox isn't pleased with the delay.

I'm right there with him.

"Shortest route?" I look to Knox, hoping he's more mentally engaged than I am. As leader of Alpha team, I find myself at a great disadvantage. Eve commands all my mental faculties and I am, without a doubt, the weakest link in this chain.

Eve corrals her troop of monkeys. Eye's wide, she's as fierce as fierce can be.

"Max," she tugs on my sleeve, "there's a servant's corridor just this way. It goes directly to the kitchens. We can get out that way." Eve's instructions are coherent, to the point, and devoid of emotion. She's thought this through, more than once.

I love her to death, but do I trust her to lead our way? One of the monkeys grabs a strand of her hair. It meticulously grooms it, looking for nonexistent lice, or whatever it is monkeys look for in the grooming of their troop.

"Show us. We can hook up with the rest of the team once we're out of here."

Knox gives a sharp shake of his head, agreeing to the plan. The three of us take off. Knox is in the lead. Eve points the way, coming to a stop at the end of a long hallway. I cover our rear but keep one hand on Eve. I'm not going to lose her.

Distant explosions and gunfire rumble down the halls. We head away from those.

"There." Eve stops at another crossing corridor and points to a small, nondescript alcove. "Tucked in right there."

"Let's do this." I release the grip I have on Eve; she's shown me her head is in the game. I'm not worried about her getting separated.

Knox holds up a fist, telling me he hears something. I place a finger over my lips, telling Eve to be silent. The monkeys glance nervously down the long hall, chirping nervously, but thankfully none of that hooting and hollering from before. They seem to understand the need for quiet.

I tilt my head and listen with Knox. Booted footsteps approach our position, but they suddenly stop and turn away. We stand there, more exposed than I like, until all sounds fade away.

Tapping Knox on the shoulder, I indicate readiness to proceed. His body tenses, getting ready. This time, I take point, crossing the hall in front of Knox, with Eve on my heels. Knox remains where he is until Eve and I navigate our way to the alcove. There's barely room for the two of us, let alone Knox.

"You sure about this?"

The alcove looks normal. No sign of a door.

"Yes." Eve slides around me, brushing against me as she reaches out to a panel on the wall. She presses against the tile. A soft click sounds. Her eyes light up as she glances back toward me and slides a portion of the wall to the side.

I'm impressed and waste no time in getting Knox to join us. Eve makes to head inside the darkened hallway, but I pull her back. Doing things by the books is a habit deeply ingrained in everything we do. I enter first, peering into the darkness, looking for threats.

A light flickers some distance down the hall. I enter the hall as Knox joins Eve in the alcove. He'll watch our back. The lightness of Eve's steps follows me into the narrow corridor.

I wish I'd known about these. It might have helped our team. I tap my ear, trying to get my earpiece to stop ringing. It's the only link I have to the Guardians, but it's been ringing since that first concussive blast. The light pouring into the hallway dims as Knox joins us.

"How do I close this?" His words pull us to a stop.

I keep my attention focused down the dimly lit hallway.

"There should be a plate set into the side of the wall." Eve twists away from me. Their movement sounds behind me as I remain laser-focused on the path ahead.

"Eve, are we missing a light switch?" Not happy about leading us down a dark passage, I'm thinking this is a poor design.

"Yes, it's around here somewhere…" Eve runs her hands along the wall as the door we came through slides closed, plunging us into near darkness. "Ah, yes—here." Another switch engages and a string of flickering lights disappears into the distance.

"How do you know about this?" I take a step forward, eyes alert for any threats. I doubt Eve's freedom extended to these small passages, and I wonder how she knows it connects to the kitchen. We can't afford for her to lead us the wrong way.

"The dining hall is just down the way. I watched the servants coming out of here with platters of food, but the kitchen is some distance away. Benefield didn't like the servants out where his guests could see them. The whole place is littered with these hidden passageways."

"And you're sure this goes to the kitchen?"

"Absolutely. I memorized everything."

I tug at my ear. "Knox, my comm is acting up. All I'm getting is static. Are you receiving?"

"No. Lost mine back in the courtyard."

"Copy that."

We're out of communication with our team. Not the best scenario, but we plan for this. With my radio non-functioning, I rip it out of my ear and shove it in the front pocket of my pants. The feedback interferes too much with my hearing.

The servant's hall is long. The flickering lights of the bulbs give enough illumination to guide our way. We come across only one crossing hallway and I pause.

"Where does that lead?"

"The Oasis." Eve's lips press in a thin line. "At least it's in that direction. Along with the servants, Benefield moved the girls along these halls."

Another shudder rocks the building. Eve's troop of monkeys complain, screeching and reaching out to each other for comfort. Eve takes their tails, unwraps them from around her throat, and gives me an apologetic smile. Silence is our greatest ally right now, and that's difficult with screeching monkeys. At least, they're on her back, not mine.

My team is out there, fighting to free dozens of abducted women. Not happy about being separated from them, I hurry us along until we come to the end of the hall. There, I pull to a stop to check for potential threats on the other side. Eve's monkeys settle back down.

She checks the wall to my left, looking for the switch that will open the door. Her contingent of spider monkeys look at me with wide eyes, but otherwise, keep their chattering conversation to a minimum. Knox points his weapon back the way we came, ever alert for threats.

Palms pressed to the door, I lean into it, listening for anything, or anyone, who might be on the other side.

"I found it." Eve's excited voice takes me by surprise.

"Hold up." I reach out to stop her, but I'm too late. The door begins a slow slide.

Four men turn at the noise, staring down the barrel of my weapon; three guards and one man I know all too well.

Weapons lift. Gun barrels swing.

They aim at Eve.

THIRTY

Eve

THERE ARE FOUR MEN STANDING ON THE OTHER SIDE OF THE DOOR. All of whom aim their weapons at me. One of whom is my nemesis, Tomas Benefield.

Max shoots.

The harsh bang makes my eardrums pop. The monkeys on my shoulder screech and holler, terrified of the loud noise. They cling to me, ducking behind my hair, as they try to find someplace safe to hide.

Max's aim is spot on. He shoots one of the men in the center of his chest. Knox takes out another man with his gun. Both men crumple at Benefield's feet, dead before they hit the ground.

The third man is quicker with his weapon. It swings up.

Points at me.

Before I know what's happening, Max jumps in front of me. He pushes me behind him and shields me with his body. The monkeys continue screeching.

The gun fires, and Max's body shakes. A grunt escapes him; he stumbles back. My heart leaps into my throat as he sags against me. I loop my hands under his arms, supporting him, until he roars back on his feet, enraged.

His body shudders, then braces. *Please be okay.* If anything happens to him...

I don't want to think about anything bad happening to Max and stop that train of thought.

The monkeys go ballistic, barking and howling. Two of them scamper down, using their long limbs and prehensile tails to swing down to the floor. They continue with their loud, prolonged screams.

Benefield bends down. He grabs a gun. With a malevolent glare, he aims it right at me.

Knox takes out the third guard. The loud retort rings in my ears. More screams from the monkeys. His next shot misfires. He racks the slide and pulls on the trigger, but nothing happens.

"Shit." Him cursing is not what I need to hear.

Benefield closes the distance. The barrel of his gun points directly at me. I slam my hand against the door release on the wall. The door slides closed but not fast enough. Benefield gets off a shot. Once again, Max grunts in pain.

It's dark again in the hallway. The flickering lights seem to have given up for the most part. But every now and then, we get a flash. It's barely enough to see. I look at Knox as Max bends a knee.

"I don't know how long it will hold." Actually, I don't think there's any way to lock that door. "We have to go back."

"Max?" Knox moves to the side and gestures for me to get behind him. No doubt, he's thinking the same thing as me. That door is going to open soon.

"I'm good." Max responds, pain threads through his voice, sharp and wavering. "Got my arm and leg, but I'm good."

He doesn't sound good.

Max took two bullets for me. I want to hug him, kiss him, but now isn't the time.

Will there ever be a time when I can show him what he means to me? We may have started out on the wrong side of things—at least that's what I thought—but he's always been there for me. Even when I thought the worst of him, he was literally there to rescue me.

I hoped to be wrong. I hated the weirdly insane attraction I felt for him, back when I thought he was nothing more than a despicable slave buyer, but now…

Now?

Now, I just want to make it out of this hellhole alive. I want to see if whatever this thing is between us is real. First chance I get, I'm going to find out. Before that…

"Can you walk?" Knox helps Max to his feet.

"I'm good." Max breathes through his pain. "Back the way we came?"

"Either that or reopen that door?" The two men confer while I soothe the screeching monkeys. They're back on my shoulders. I guess I'm their safe place.

Max does something to his gun. All I hear is the sound of metal scraping against metal.

"There are probably more of his men out there," Max says. "We go back."

I don't like the way Max braces against the pain. The urge to go to him, help him, overwhelms me, but he looks up at me with a fixed stare. I read his message. Now is not the time.

"Eve, lead us out of here." Max issues a command. That tone, it's sexy as fuck, but I need to focus on getting out of here. Not on naked fantasies with Max.

Naked fantasies?

Yeah, that's totally what's going through my mind right now. Me and Max, together, skin touching skin, hands seeking hands, mouths colliding as desire consumes us.

I give a shake of my head. Definitely not what I need to be thinking about right now.

Turning on my heels, I take us back down the long passageway. We reach the section leading off toward the Oasis. For a split second, I almost take it.

Max wants to meet up with his team on the south side of the compound, but if we go back to where we started, I can take us to the western side of the estate. We can escape into the jungle and find his team later.

Whatever timetable his team is on, we've already blown through it. Or, so I assume. Also, there's a second reason I head back. Benefield may not know where the access panel is to the door from the kitchen side, but one of his men will know. We've got seconds to get out of here before we become sitting ducks. I don't know how to lock the door, but that alcove had a bookshelf in it.

We should be able to push it in place and block his men from following us.

I take Max and Knox back down the hall. Max loops an arm around Knox's shoulder. Knox helps him walk. We make it to the original door we came in when I hear the sound of a door scraping against the floor in the darkness behind us.

We exit into the alcove. Max looks like shit. There's something shiny on his sleeve and on his pants leg over his thigh.

Blood.

Two bullets meant for me.

"Knox, they're coming," I warn Knox.

He grabs Max and gets ready to move.

"The bookcase." I point to the massive bookcase. Just as I speak, shots ring out. No need to explain what I'm thinking to Max or Knox.

They get it.

Knox glances at the large bookcase and exchanges a look with Max. Max gives a nod. He steadies himself on his good leg and leans into the bookcase. The floor-to-ceiling bookcase scrapes over the floor.

I wouldn't be able to make it budge, but the two of them get it shifted in place. While they do that, I do my part for our team.

Max is losing too much blood.

Working with a troop of monkeys on my back is challenging, but I use my teeth and rip off a strip of fabric from the hem of my shirt. Turning to Max, I tie it tight over his arm.

His smile is something else; talk about swoon worthy. Every girl should have a protector like Max, but not Max. He's all mine. Or will be if we ever get out of here. I rip another section off the bottom of my shirt and tie it around the wetness covering his thigh.

Knox gives an approving nod as Max shifts his weight to the bad leg. A grimace fills his face, but he soldiers on. The three of us take off at a slow jog with me leading. I head to the western side of the building.

It's not too far, and there's no sound of pursuit behind us. At the very least, I hope half of Benefield's men headed to the Oasis. We could use a break like that.

Knox isn't happy with the direction I take or that I don't stop to check before turning a corner. But we don't have time to stop at every corridor or at every door. I barrel forward, more concerned with reaching the jungle than what I might run into ahead of us.

But I know Benefield. He'll concentrate his men at the roads leading out. The jungle's thick. Many say impassable, but I don't believe them. If a group of pigs can make their way through, we can too.

Max and Knox jog behind me. Knox supports Max, whose breaths grow more labored as we turn into a back hall.

"Almost there." I try to provide what encouragement I can.

"Hold up at the door, Eve. We're not walking out into another mess." Max speaks, issuing orders.

I hold up at the door. While Knox pushes it open, I turn my attention to Max.

"You're bleeding."

"Just a flesh wound." He returns a cheeky grin. It's meant to disarm me. To keep me from worrying, but I saw how hard it was for him to keep up.

I tighten the temporary bandage I put on his arm, then do something crazy. Lifting on tiptoe, I lean in and gently brush my lips against his. I know, it's crazy, but I can't help it. I want to feel far more than his lips on me. Then I wonder what the hell I'm doing.

I don't know Max. He could be married with four kids, or dating some gorgeous woman. A man that looks like him can have any woman he wants.

Right when I pull away, feeling awkward for kissing my rescuer, his uninjured arm wraps around my waist and pulls me tight against his body. A low grown escapes him as his lips crash down on mine. Every nerve in my body takes notice as he bends down, strong and powerful despite his injuries, to kiss me back. My body thrums as he sucks on my lower lip.

I burn beneath the rush of his exhales, breaths turn ragged, not from pain, but from desire. His hot mouth comes with an expert tongue. He licks and nips, kisses and consumes.

My senses swim, taken over by his hunger, unprepared, but deliriously happy to know he wants me as much as I want him. The kiss deepens.

He deals relentless strokes of his tongue, demanding entrance to my mouth, until I give in and let him sweep me away. He's not gentle or slow. Max takes, ravenously, and mercilessly, groaning with each breath.

Hungry and relentless, he takes my hesitant kiss and turns it into something else. My hands reach up to catch in his hair as my entire body trembles beneath the ferocity of a single kiss.

Each thrust of his tongue inside my mouth comes with a promise of something more. Heat simmers in my blood, burning my insides, and shaking the foundations of my world. I want what he promises in the thrusting of his tongue. I desire it like a madwoman driven drunk on lust.

My nerves sizzle as he shows me exactly what he wants. Holy hellfire. If this is what kisses feel like, what will the rest be like? A low moan escapes me as Knox interrupts the most perfect kiss in the world.

I swoon in Max's arms as Knox clears his throat.

"If you don't mind taking a moment from that lip lock, I'd like to get out of here."

Max's laugh is a low rumble. I think he'll pull away, but I'm wrong. He tugs me even tighter against his body. My chest rises and falls with a shuddering breath. In his embrace, I feel fragile yet protected, grounded yet sublimely free.

Max ends the kiss. He cups the side of my face, sweeping his thumb along my jawline. "You have no idea how long I've wanted to do that." He looks down at me like he wants to hold me forever.

I'm cool with that. Then what he says makes it through the fog of my mind.

"You have?"

He leans down as I offer my mouth, pleading for him to kiss me again. Our current predicament aside, I never want this moment to end.

"From the very first time I saw you." He shifts, testing his injured leg. "How far?"

That question isn't for me. His attention swivels to Knox. This is when I think Max will release me, but he clings to me as if holding me in his arms is the most natural thing in the world for him to do.

Like this is where I belong.

That kiss, and the way Max holds me now, doesn't faze Knox. He glances down at Max's leg.

"Twenty yards to the vegetation. About the same until we're covered. It's either this or make our way back to the south side of the building and try to connect with the team."

Whatever they decide, it needs to be quick. No doubt Benefield and his men are hot on our tail.

"We go for the jungle. Contact the team later. How are your eyes?"

His eyes?

That's the weirdest question ever. "Functional, but it'll take time to connect and upload." Knox looks back outside. "Don't know how that canopy out there will affect that."

"We go and figure it out later."

"Agreed." Knox gives a little flick of his fingers, telling me to move away from Max's side.

I don't want to move. I like where I am. The heat of Max's body sinks into me, and I have no intention of removing myself. Except, Max gives me a little push.

I wobble on my feet as Max shifts his weight. He lifts his arm. Not for me, but to drape it around Knox's shoulder. I wish I was strong enough, big enough, to help, but there's no way I can support Max.

Max gives me a long hard look. "You ready?"

"I am."

"Once we're out that door, you run."

I nod, vigorously.

"You don't stop. You don't slow down, not for me. Not for Knox. You get to the trees. Head into the jungle. Run until you can't run anymore."

"I'm not leaving you."

"You'll do exactly as I say." Max gives me a look that brooks no argument. "Follow the water. It will lead you to a trickle, then a stream. The stream will turn to a river. Follow the water and my team will find you."

"What about you? I'm not leaving you behind."

"I have no intention of being left behind, but if something should happen…"

"Nothing. Nothing will happen."

"Knox can't carry me and guard our escape. If they get here before you're safe, I'm sending him with you, while I…"

"No. Don't say it. Don't think it." I lift my pistol. "I'll never leave you. We'll fight…"

"Don't argue. We haven't come this far only to fail now. You will not fall back into Benefield's hands. Do you understand?"

I do, and I hate every word of what he's saying. My attention shifts to Knox, looking for support from him, but the expression on Knox's face mirrors Max's.

"Give me that." I point to the rifle on Max's back. "Let me help."

"Not giving you a weapon you don't know how to use. Not to mention it's heavy and will only slow you down."

"Don't leave me, Max. Don't make me go out there alone."

"I have no intention of leaving you, but if things go south…"

"They won't." And there's no way in hell I'm leaving him behind. Max may have come here to rescue me, but I'll do whatever it takes to make sure he gets out of here with me.

Whatever it takes.

"We ready?" Knox bends his knees, grabs Max's arm, and wedges into the fold of Max's arm to support him.

"Ready." Max's lips firm into a hard line. He looks at me, demanding I agree to his silly demands.

It's quiet. Too quiet.

Benefield's men are looking for us, and it will only be a matter of time before they discover where we are. I glance at Max's pant leg. The bleeding has stopped and a quick look behind him doesn't show any blood on the floor.

At least we're not leaving a trail of blood for Benefield's men to follow.

I push the door open and hold it while Knox and Max navigate their way outside.

"Run, Eve. Run as fast as you can, and don't look back."

I bite my lower lip and run.

THIRTY-ONE

Max

HOT KISS.

Hotter body.

Wickedly intelligent woman.

Brave. Keeps her shit together in a crisis.

Eve is definitely my perfect mate.

I finally have *my* girl in *my* hands, and damn if it doesn't feel like heaven.

Why the fuck did it take so long?

I know *why*.

This entire undercover crap is for the birds. I'll never volunteer for this shit again. My poor cock is ravenous and aching for a taste of Eve, and for the first time since I came to this wretched place, it feels like there may be a chance for us.

A chance.

Hell, I want forever, but I'll start with a chance.

Strawberries covered in sugar with cinnamon spice. That's what she tastes like. I can still taste her on my tongue. Knox and his whole *we need to get out of here* thing put a total damper on what is surely the best kiss of my life.

Knox slings my arm over his shoulder. There may, or may not, be men on the rooftops. Not that we can do a damn thing about it. We have to sprint for cover, then lose Benefield's men after a little evasive action in the jungle.

Both of our earpieces are defunct, but Knox's contact lenses still function. All we need is to get to a place with clear reception to link back up with our team.

Exfil, for us, is blown.

The team won't stay behind for us. They'll come back, but they won't stick around. The whole *Never leave a man behind* thing is just as pertinent now as ever, only Forest adds in the *Good of many outweighs the needs of a few.* This means our team will rescue all the abducted women and free them from a life of slavery. After their safety is ensured, our team will circle back to save our asses.

Until then, Knox and I fall back on the training we received in the Navy: survive, evade, resist, escape. S.E.R.E. is a brutal course meant to break the strongest man down into his most basic parts. That's where strength is found, and we lean on that now.

It's also learning how to trust your partner and let them carry the load when you can't. I do this with Knox. We perform the best three-legged race in the history of man. Which simply means we put my bum leg between us. Knox will shoulder as much of my weight as I need while we run for cover.

My leg hurts like a motherfucker. I can walk on it. I'm just not fast. I take a step on my good leg. Knox uses his leg opposite me, then when I put weight down on my injured leg, Knox bears the burden on his. We work together, a tightly run machine, and manage to make it to the edge of the jungle only a little behind Eve. My girl's got some legs on her, and despite what I said, she doesn't leave us behind. Eve runs a stride or two ahead, constantly looking over her shoulder to make sure we're keeping up.

Not that I thought she'd ever leave me behind. My girl, she's a Guardian in the making. Just look at the way she runs with those monkeys riding her shoulders.

Monkeys? I'd laugh, except I'm in a good deal of pain. I thought bubbles was a great nickname. Little did I know... I may have to change that to monkey.

We cross the open space between the buildings and make it to the edge of the trees without incident. There's no sign of pursuit. No gunfire shot from the tops of the buildings.

We see smoke. Tons and tons of acrid smoke fills the air. Our team planned on breaching the walls, a strategic strike meticulously planned to minimize loss of life, but they didn't bring that much firepower.

My assumption is Benefield's men fought back with more firepower than anticipated.

Left wondering about the degree of devastation, my thoughts turn toward my team, hoping none of them were caught in that.

"How're you doing?" Knox helps me through the underbrush. He's breathing hard, but so am I.

Eve stops. Glancing left and right, she looks like she's searching for something. Once in the trees, the monkeys screech and holler as they grab limbs and climb into the vegetation. Eve watches them scamper away, and I can't help but smile at their excitement to be reunited with the jungle they call home.

"Where to, Eve?" I bend down to look at the damage to my leg. There's blood, but not as much as I would've expected. I'll take a closer look later.

She peers into the forest, biting her lower lip in a way that makes me want to kiss her again. Holy hellfire, but that kiss rocked my world.

"This way." She glances at my leg. "How bad is it?"

"Bad enough to slow me down, not so bad that I can't move. We'll stop once we're in a safer place." I don't like being this close to Benefield and his men. It won't take much for them to track us down.

We follow Eve deeper into the vegetation until we come to a stream. She guides us along the water's edge until we reach the ten-foot perimeter fence. I sit on a rock, tending my injury, while she and Knox move fallen limbs out of the way.

Not happy about this either, we're practically telling any pursuit exactly where we're headed, but I don't see a way around it. We'll lose them as we head deeper into the jungle.

As for my leg, the bleeding's nearly stopped. The bullet didn't go all the way through, which is good and bad. Bad in that I'll need to get it out. Good in that the injury could be far worse. No major blood vessels were nicked. As long as I can keep it as clean as possible, I should be good.

Clean as possible? That's a laugh. I have to wade through water, and jungles aren't exactly the cleanest place on earth. Doc Summers better have some super potent antibiotics ready to inject into my ass. How long does it take for infection to set in? It's a serious question because it limits my operability.

Already, I'm thinking of several options to get out of this mess.

Once Eve and Knox have the way clear, I gingerly wade into the stream and duck under the wire fence. It's electrified, but none of the fence touches the water. I hold a hand out for Eve, loving the way her hand fits in mine, but what I enjoy most is how she doesn't let go once she's with me on the other side.

Knox does what he can to replace the fallen limbs on the other side of the fence, then he, too, ducks under the small gap and joins us. Maybe that'll buy us some time. Maybe not.

"How's your signal?" I turn to Knox, giving him a hand up the slippery bank, which is more mud than anything else.

We're all soaked from our knees down, which includes our feet. Obviously, it includes our feet. I only think about that because in the heat and humidity of the jungle, trench foot will become a serious consideration if we're here for much more than a day or two.

We've been outside for a good five minutes. Not long enough for the data to upload from his watch to the team. He glances at his watch and gives a shake of his head.

"No signal."

"We need to put distance between us and this mess. Find higher ground and an extraction point." I glance at Eve and look at her shoes. The uneven jungle ground with its raised roots loves to twist ankles. In her running shoes, she has no ankle support. I'll need to keep a close eye on her.

"Your leg?" Knox asks about how incapacitated I am.

"No exit wound. Bleeding's stopped. Hurts like a mother, but I can manage."

It's the truth. Not a comfortable truth, but one nonetheless. I will slow us down. All that means is we need to keep moving.

"Let's move out." My goal is to put as much distance between us and any pursuit. Then, I plan on finding a place where I can watch for Benefield's men while sending Knox and Eve on without me. This seems the wisest plan. Eve's safety is paramount.

He can get her out. I'm better suited to stay behind with my bum leg. My arm throbs, but the bullet only grazed the skin. It's a deeper wound than I'd like, down to muscle, but nothing like my leg.

We trudge through the dense underbrush for an hour. Eve keeps up without much difficulty. As suspected, the roots trip her, but she's a fast learner. Eve looks where she steps and lifts her feet high.

That's a challenge for me. Although after stopping to patch together a makeshift crutch, I gimp along fairly well.

The constant throbbing in my leg is tolerable. I check every fifteen minutes when I force us to take a break. The bleeding is manageable. I'm more worried about infection setting in; not that it matters now. In a day, or two, that might be an issue. Right now, I monitor blood loss. I'm not going to think about what was in the water at the fence line.

During our rest breaks, Knox tries to get a signal. The dense vegetation, along with the deep valley we travel through, make that complicated.

"You need to go ahead." I give Knox one of my looks. He reads me like an open book and his lips press hard together.

"Bad idea."

"You get that signal through and we get out of here."

"I leave you, and…" No need to finish that thought.

Knox and I are tight. Tighter than tight. We've been through the worst of times. More than either of us wants to admit. It started in BUDS and continued from there.

He and I served together overseas. A shit assignment in a poor country overrun by militant men eager to die in their fight against the enemies of Islam. We've been to hell and back again.

Knox was with me when we pulled what remained of our squad out of a burning vehicle. Together, we dragged our men to safety under active gunfire to a berm where we then did the unthinkable; the unconscionable.

Knox and I took stock of our meager supplies. We looked at our teammates—men we trained with, friends we knew for years. Together, we decided who would live and who would die.

That kind of thing leaves a mark on your soul. Knox and I shoulder that burden as one. Our meager supplies stretched only so far. We couldn't save them all.

Those are the tough decisions that come with the job, and we faced them together.

We did our best. We saved who we could. We prayed for the rest. Knox and I looked at one another, and between us, we made that choice.

He looks at me now, and I can read every thought in his head. He's thinking the same thing as me. I reach out to reassure him.

"You're not leaving me behind."

"Then why does this feel like all kinds of a bad idea?" Pain rolls across his features. Determination and grit collide with the inevitable. There is only one decision to be made. Knox knows it.

As do I.

"If you don't get that signal through, we're all dead." I glance at Eve as she leans against a tree gasping for breath. "Take her."

We've been moving hard. Hard for her, hell for me, but this is what I've trained for my entire life. I'm a warrior. A Guardian. I train to endure. To survive. To complete the mission no matter the cost.

Eve isn't trained for this kind of shit. She's at the end of her rope, barely holding on, and I've yet to push her through the pain.

"She'll only slow me down." And there is the Knox I know. The stoic warrior who does what needs to be done.

"This isn't a good place." I glance around the thick canopy. It's dark and we don't have anything to light our way. Not that we would if we did. Light would only draw the enemy toward us.

"Then we find a better place." His gaze cuts to my leg. "You've got twenty-four hours before infection sets in." Yeah, he's been thinking the same thing as me.

"Then we find a place I can defend. Send you on. Eve and I wait."

We'll wait for rescue, or the unthinkable. Knox won't say it, but I read it in his expression. I feel the truth of it. He's faster on his own.

I'm a liability, but then Eve is as well.

"We find a place." I give a sharp shake of my head. "You head up. Find a ridge…"

Knox clasps my arm. "It's a shit plan."

"I know."

We look at each other, communicating a lifetime of words in a single breath, but Knox knows this is the only way. He glances over at Eve.

"I can take her, but…"

I know. Eve will only slow him down.

"She stays with me." It's the best plan.

We need him to get clear, contact the team, and bring reinforcements to get us out of this place.

"I've been watching the trees. I have an idea."

Knox looks up. "It boxes you in."

"I know." He and I noticed the same thing.

In the jungle, the most dangerous place to sit still is on the ground. Once night falls, the creepy crawlies make the ground the worst place to be. I'm glad we don't have light. Eve would freak out if she knew what crawled on this ground.

We will move to the trees. Lose ourselves in the canopy overhead. Difficult with my bum leg, but not impossible. And it offers a certain advantage. Any pursuit will be by ground. No one will be looking overhead.

But going up provides challenges. We can't leave any evidence behind that we've moved overhead.

"Eve…" I hobble over to her. She looks at me with the

smoldering remnants of our kiss in her eyes. It's enough to make my heart skip a beat.

"Yes?"

"We need to talk."

The three of us gather around as I explain the conversation Knox and I shared. I'm not surprised when Eve agrees. Something tells me she would put up a fight if I tried to separate her from me. I both love, and hate, that about her.

We've been through hell to free her, but I need to go with my operational experience. I know what Knox is capable of on his own.

As for Eve, I don't know her limits.

With all of us in agreement, it's only a matter of placing Eve and myself in the best defensible position possible. The delay is one I'm not fond of, but it's unavoidable.

We backtrack to a tree both Knox and I independently identified. Broad of base, torturous trunk with plenty of handholds, it's the perfect place to hide. It's also one hell of a climb up, especially since we can't climb the tree itself. That would leave a sign for anyone following us.

Working out the best way to do this takes a moment, but we stagger our approach, climbing a smaller tree a few yards away, and by *smaller,* this one is merely ten feet in diameter. This jungle is home to some monstrous trees. Their limbs are broad enough to walk on. It's why panthers love the canopy. It's easy for a big animal to get around.

Right now, that means it's easy for the three of us to navigate our way through what's essentially a veritable highway of intersecting limbs.

Once the three of us scale the first tree, Knox leads the way across a bridge made of limbs. He helps me across, then assists Eve. From there, we climb another twenty feet into the air. The trees tower over our heads. The limbs, broad and sturdy, are large enough to sleep on, but we don't stop there.

Knox and I push up and onward. Eve and I need to be high enough in the canopy to evade pursuit from below. We need to become invisible. We also need to be safe enough, which means no falling off when we sleep. I've already accepted we'll be in the jungle through the night. Depending on how it goes with Knox, and then the response of our team, I'm looking at two to three days in a tree.

Days without water and without food. Doesn't matter. I've survived worse before.

Onward and upward.

Fifty feet into the canopy, we can barely see the jungle floor. We also can't see the sky. It's pitch black overhead, a ceiling made of broad leaves which blocks out most light. Or will, once the sun rises.

I find a hollow within the trunk of a tree. It's a crevice Eve and I can hide inside. Better yet, Knox can work his way back down to the jungle floor in a direction opposite the way we came.

The spot we find is small, cramped, but sufficient for our needs. Food and water will be problematic, but I place my trust in Knox.

Once we're situated, Knox and I clasp hands.

"Godspeed." I pray it's not the last time I see my friend.

"And you." Knox turns to Eve. "Take care of my friend. Don't let him play hero." He gathers her in a hug that's far too close for my tastes.

She throws her arms around his neck. I've never wanted to shove a knife in my friend more than now, but it's over and done before I can process the jealous rage.

"Here." I pull out the ledger and the bills of lading. "Make sure Mitzy gets these."

Knox gives me a look, but he takes the papers, tucking them securely inside his shirt.

There's a lot unsaid in handing those over to him. If anything happens to me, at least Guardian HRS will have what it needs to bring down this organization. Knox knows why I'm handing them over, and from the look on his face, he doesn't like it.

"Until you get back." I try to reassure him, but his scowl is fixed and not going anywhere until he returns with the rest of the team.

"Until I see you again, my friend." Knox grabs me and pulls me in for a hug. He thumps my back as I do the same.

We're Guardians, and we don't believe in goodbyes, but it never hurts to embrace one last time.

Knox gives me a corny salute, then scampers along a broad limb. He'll work his way to the ground, gradually, staying far away from the tree Eve and I hold up in. We follow his progress until we lose him to the vegetation.

Then we settle back as I take stock of our ammunition, acutely aware we're alone, together, for the very first time.

THIRTY-TWO

Max

"So, we wait here?" Eve peers out into the night. Her voice shakes.

The jungle can be scary at night. It's dark, noisy, and terrifying for those not attuned to the rhythms of the jungle. Eve jumps at every rustling leaf, every chirp of the tree frogs, and the buzzing of a multitude of insects.

Not that I'm particularly attuned to jungle noises, but I know what to listen for, what to worry about, and for me, the noise is a comfort. Only when things go quiet will I become concerned.

Eve doesn't realize it, but when we were walking, the jungle grew silent as we passed through. When we climbed high into the canopy, the same thing happened. Only now that we're relatively still have the denizens of the jungle returned to their nightly rituals. If quiet suddenly falls, that will tell me either Benefield has found us or my team is ready to extract us.

"We wait." I prop my weapon against the trunk of the tree. "You should try to get some sleep. We're going to be here a while."

"Do you think Benefield will come after us?"

"Not think." I give her a hard look. "I know."

Eve runs her hands up and down her arms, giving herself a little hug. I want to provide her that comfort and hate the awkwardness I feel now that we're alone. She belongs in my arms. I should be giving her the comfort she needs.

The hollow we sit in is the result of the parent tree losing its top some years ago. Smaller branches rose from the outer circumference of the remaining trunk, growing upward until they joined together overhead. We're in a natural teepee, with a floor that's relatively even. Most importantly, it's dry.

It's not such a bad place.

The sweltering humidity clings in the air despite it being nighttime. In fact, it feels thicker up here than on the jungle floor. The powerful scent of the forest surrounds us. The pungent aroma of rotting vegetation mixes with the loamy soil far below. That essence blends with the woodsy scent of our tree, home for the night, into a complex mixture of life, death, and decay.

It all combines into a musty aroma that invades every breath. Fortunately, light floral accents float on the wind, just enough to make it tolerable.

I don't say anything to Eve, but there are plenty of threats in the canopy we need to watch out for. My hope is this tree isn't a part of a major ant highway. The idea of them swarming over us as the night progresses is unsettling. I don't mention how perfect this spot is for a large animal to make its own den. Although, there's no scent of cat urine, which would indicate a panther lived here. As for monkeys, they live in the canopy and can be a nuisance.

"How are you holding up?" I shift my injured leg, picking it up gingerly, using both hands to straighten it out. The pain, no longer sharp and acute, is more an annoyance than a constant irritation.

Eve fits herself into the spot next to me, half leaning against me, but obviously keeping herself apart. Our shoulders brush and the heat of her body radiates outward. I feel every inch of her and tamp down the base desires rising within me.

I crave Eve.

It's a carnal, primitive need rising within me: to protect, to shelter, to claim, and to take. My desire to make her mine increases despite my attempts to tone it down. The last thing Eve needs right now is a rutting maniac, and that's exactly what I fear I'll become.

This feeling is new to me. I've had plenty of women in my life, couplings which eased my ache, but nothing about those compares to what I experience now. It's potent, overwhelming, and ultimately dangerous.

Dangerous for Eve.

The howl of a jaguar sounds in the night.

"I'm scared." She draws her arms inward, withdrawing from me. Only the vaguest outline of her face is visible.

"Don't be scared. I'm here."

"I know." She blows out a deep breath. "This feels like a dream."

"A dream?"

"Yes. All of this is—it's hard to believe it's happening. I thought I'd never get out of that place." She looks down and pauses for a moment. "Do you think any of the other girls got out?"

"I'm positive they did. The man I work for will make sure of it."

"You sure?"

"I am."

"How can you be certain?"

There's no easy way to describe Forest Summers. I admire what he's done with his life, especially considering the hell he endured as a child. He could've remained a victim, but Forest doesn't believe in handing that power over to his tormentors.

Everything he's built, along with his sister, Skye, is aimed at liberating those who've been taken and showing them how to take back the power they lost. Victims turn into survivors, and he does everything to make sure the life of his rescues is brighter than the darkness of their past.

"I feel like none of this is real." She turns toward me, and I love how the close quarters we're in forces our bodies to touch. Eve places a hand on my good arm.

"Someday, this will be a distant memory." I do my best to

reassure her. I imagine all of this is terrifying to someone without the training I've experienced.

The unknown doesn't frighten me. I focus on what's important and ignore the rest.

"Do you really think so?"

"I know so."

"I don't want to forget *this*." I don't know if it's me, or not, but the slight emphasis she places on that word gives me hope.

"What happened at The Retreat will always be a part of you, but it won't rule you. You're free of all of it."

"I meant us." Her hand tightens on my arm. "I don't want *this* to be a distant memory." She blows out a sigh. "Please tell me you're not married."

"I'm not married." A grin pulls at the corners of my lips.

"Tell me you don't have four kids waiting for you at home."

"I don't have any kids waiting on me, but I'd like to have some down the line." A low chuckle escapes me.

"No gorgeous girlfriends?"

"None." I lay my hand over hers. "I wouldn't have kissed you the way I did if I had any of those."

"Good." She blows out a breath. "It's not hero worship."

"Excuse me?"

"When I kissed you. It wasn't because I was emotional and kissed you just because you were sent to rescue me. It wasn't a mistake." Her fingers curl against my skin. "I've been attracted to you since the first time I saw you. Which was really unsettling, to be honest, but…"

"Eve?"

"Yes?"

"You don't have to explain yourself." I grab her wrist and lift it to my lips for a kiss. Gingerly, I press my lips against her skin. "You have no idea how difficult this week has been for me, or what kind of thoughts have been going on inside my head."

Eve lays an arm over my midsection and snuggles against me. She takes in a deep breath and blows it out. Her fingers draw little circles over my shirt, and I barely move, too afraid she'll stop.

"I'm really glad you're not one of the bad guys." She glances up at me. "I hated that I was attracted to you. It made me feel *squiggy.*"

"Squiggy?" I chuckle. "I made you feel squiggy?"

"Don't say it like that. It's only..." Those maddening circles her fingers make are slowly driving me insane.

"Only, what?"

"I desperately wanted you to not be one of Benefield's guests, but you were, and I hated you for that. I hated how much I wanted to be with you."

"I distinctly remember you avoiding me."

I grab her hand, unable to fully control my body's reactions to her touch. This is most certainly not the time, or the place, for what's going through my head.

"I couldn't stand to be in the same room with you, not with what was going on in my head. I've never..." Her voice hitches and lowers to a whisper.

"You never, what?"

"I never *fantasized* about a man the way I did with you."

"Oh really." I tug her close and kiss the top of her head. I have to keep things chaste for now, even if all I can think about is stripping her out of her clothes and showing her exactly what kind of fantasies I've been having about her. "Tell me."

"No." She gives a cute, little squeal and affectionately pats my chest.

"Why not? We've got all night, and I love a good bedtime story. Especially if it involves you and me in the same bed."

"You're incorrigible. You know that?"

"Definitely."

"I'm sorry if I was mean to you." She presses on my chest and lifts up to place a kiss on my cheek. It's chaste and utterly perfect.

"Mean?"

"Yeah."

"I should be the one apologizing to you."

"You were only doing your job, the one my father hired you to do."

"It may have started out that way, but it quickly became more."

She burrows more deeply against me. "I know that now." Eve peeks up at me. Her features are nearly impossible to see in the darkness, but I see a flash of her spirit flickering in her eyes. "I've never been kissed like that before."

"What do you mean *like that?*"

"With your whole soul." A breathy sigh escapes her. "It was phenomenal, swoon worthy, made my head spin. I'm still kind of floating from it."

"Floating?" What a way to stroke a guy's ego? "I'll take that kind of praise any day. Tell me more."

"It was awesome."

"I'll take awesome." I give another low, throaty chuckle. "If you only knew what I really wanted to do."

"Tell me."

"Oh no. I asked about your filthy fantasies first. You tell me yours, then I'll tell you mine."

It's too dark to see, but I swear her cheeks just turned the deepest shade of crimson. I feel her blush in her words, and that's sexy as fuck.

"I can't do that." There goes that tiny squeak in her voice. I can't wait to watch Eve blush where I can see all of her.

With that thought, I make a slight adjustment in how I'm sitting. My pants are getting uncomfortably tight in the groin.

Unfortunately, my attempt to find a more comfortable position results in a sharp pain shooting down my leg. I grunt and grasp my injured leg. That's one way to get my dick to calm down.

"I really should look at that." Eve leans forward, and as she does, the swell of her breast brushes against my arm.

I bite my lower lip and hold back a groan. My dick, the eager fuck, takes notice, growing harder, longer, and more demanding. The conversation needs to get off the topic of sex or it's going to be a very long and uncomfortable night.

"It's too dark. I don't think you can see anything."

"It must hurt so bad."

It hurts like a motherfucker, but I'm too distracted by her being so near to concentrate on the pain.

"Only if I move." I pull her back until we're sitting side by side. "It's getting late. You should get some sleep."

"What about you?"

"I'll keep watch."

"You've got to be exhausted. We should both sleep."

"Not gonna happen." I make a vague gesture toward the jungle floor. "I need to keep watch."

"How about me? I can keep watch and you can sleep. You're going to need all the rest you can with your leg." She shifts beside me. "And how's your arm doing?"

"My arm is the least of my worries. That, at least, is a flesh wound."

It's deeper than a flesh wound. The bullet ripped through skin and muscle. Unlike the bullet in my leg, however, that bullet continued on through. The one in my leg is most likely lodged against the bone.

"Well, you need to sleep. I'll take first watch." She's cute when she tries to be bossy.

"Luv, there's no way I'm getting any sleep tonight." And, it's not just because I need to watch over our position. I can't afford to fall asleep with Eve in my arms.

Eve draws her knees to her chest and peers out into the inky black of the canopy. Her attention shifts to my rifle.

"And you really think Benefield will come after me?"

"I do."

"Wow, no hesitation there."

"Sorry."

"Will we be able to hear them?"

"Not how you think."

"Huh?"

I explain to her about the rhythms of the night and how by listening to the jungle, we'll be alerted to any human approaching.

We continue talking, which means I explain what I'm listening for, and why, as well as where Knox went and what we expect from that.

"So, all we need to do is stay put?"

"Pretty much."

"I'm glad I'm here with you."

I lift my arm and drape it over her shoulder, not even thinking about the intimacy of such an embrace. To be honest, it feels natural.

It feels right.

It feels even better when Eve turns toward me, curling against my side. The thing about jungles is they're never silent, especially at night. That noise means we're safe.

"I wish we could stay here forever, just you and me, that the outside world didn't exist." She lays her arm across my midsection, getting closer.

"I wish for that, too." This moment is one I'll never forget. I've found heaven, and she's sitting right beside me, lowering her walls, and baring her soul. Nothing else in the world could be this perfect.

The wind rustles the leaves. Tree frogs and cicadas chirp and buzz at near deafening levels. Off in the distance, monkeys howl as they call out to their troop to settle in for the night. Most birds have found their roosts, but their evening song fills the air. Chirping and buzzing insects round out the noise, along with a slow drip.

Drip?

I take note of that sound in particular. Depending on how long we find ourselves here, that could be a viable source of water. I send a silent prayer to Knox. He won't let me down, and until he can return with the rest of our team, I will keep Eve safe.

But I pray they don't come too quickly. Like Eve, I never want this moment to end.

The pain in my leg keeps me awake most of the night, and despite the harsh discord of noise all around us, I'm acutely aware of the moment Eve drifts off to sleep while I hold her in my arms.

Trapped in a jungle somewhere in Colombia, hiding fifty feet in the air, I realize something profound.

I've fallen in love.

Eve is no longer a package to secure, a hostage to rescue; she's my everything.

And I'll do anything to keep her safe.

Anything.

My thoughts turn toward Benefield and our client. Carson Deverough.

What the hell are you two playing at?

THIRTY-THREE

Eve

THIS DOES FEEL LIKE A DREAM; ONE I NEVER WANT TO END.

Perhaps, I shouldn't cling to Max the way I am, but he's not pushing me away. As long as he lets me touch him, I'm going to get my fill. My greedy fingers eagerly explore the expanse of his chest. They dip down to rock-hard abs and linger there for a bit, enjoying the ridges and valleys of a body cut from stone.

I've heard of such things, but I've never really felt them on a man before; the six pack, or rather an eight pack. The amount of physical training it must take to maintain this level of fitness astounds me. And I'll admit to staring at Max's ass during the climb up the tree.

I struggled.

Not because there weren't plenty of hand and footholds, but because of how high we climbed. After the first ten feet, I was exhausted. Not Max. Even with a bum leg and injured arm, he climbed upward like it was nothing.

His leg worries me. I want to take a look at it, but in the darkness, what would I see? Nothing. And I don't need to be putting my dirty fingers anywhere near the injury.

I curl up against Max and listen to the sounds of the forest. All the noises only amplify my fear, at least until he explains everything to me.

And let's face it, curling up against a Guardian feels like the safest place on Earth. I know now what he is: a Guardian. He's a protector and a rescuer, devoting his life to saving people like me.

Not sure when I fell asleep, I remember the precise moment when I wake in his arms. It's to the soothing rhythm of his fingers combing through my hair. The gentle tugging on my roots relaxes me.

So perfect.

"Good morning, sleepyhead." The low rumble of Max's voice welcomes me to a new day.

I run my fingers over the expanse of his chest and breathe out a contented sigh.

"Is it morning?"

"Open your eyes, bubbles." His soft laughter makes my pulse race. Either that, or it's the ridiculousness of the nickname.

"Bubbles, huh?"

"Yeah, I'm never getting that visual out of my head."

My cheeks heat thinking about that, especially since I was completely naked in that tub. And he—he had no issue stripping buck naked in front of me and taking that shower. Which reminds me...

"Your tattoo?"

"What about it?"

"It's incredible."

"Thanks?"

"No, I really mean it. I've never seen anything like it."

"I'm glad you like it. Is that all you liked?"

"What do you mean?"

"That's not all your eager little eyes latched onto if I remember things right."

"I did not..."

"Luv, no shame in staring. I certainly got my eyeful of you. It's only fair that you got a look at me."

I swallow thickly, a little uncomfortable talking about seeing each other naked.

"Um..."

Another low chuckle rumbles out from him. "Just teasing." He pulls me close and kisses the top of my head. "Sleep well?"

I wipe the sleep from my eyes and peer out onto what I can only describe as the most magical place on earth.

Our lofty perch is nowhere near the top of the canopy. Still, sunlight filters down through the dense vegetation in hundreds of sunbeams. That light dapples the leaves as they gently flutter in the light breeze. Insects flit around in the columns of light, looking like tiny fairies dancing with joy.

As always, it's hot, humid, and sweltering. A light sheen of perspiration covers every inch of my body. I don't even want to think about what kind of funk I smell like. As for Max, his scent is heavenly.

How is that possible? I take in a long, slow inhale, trying not to look like I'm smelling him, but seriously, there's something deeply arousing about his rugged scent. I turn my attention to the jungle and away from the aching between my legs. I've got a major lady boner for Max.

Like M-A-J-O-R.

"Wow, it's really pretty here." Maybe he won't notice the way I curl against him? Maybe he won't notice the way I obliterate any open space between us?

"The most gorgeous sight on earth." Only Max isn't looking at the jungle. His eyes are just for me. "You make me ache in the best possible way."

If he only knew I feel the same, not that I'm going to tell him. I'm not that bold.

"That really is a corny nickname."

"So?" He leans his head back and his eyes drift closed.

"It's weird."

"It's perfect." A smile tugs at the corners of his lips.

"Perfectly weird." I shake my head and move away from thoughts of climbing into Max's lap, where I want to do very unladylike things to my stalwart rescuer. "Do you think Knox got a hold of your team?"

"There's really no way to know, but Knox is unstoppable."

"Unstoppable?"

"Yeah, he's got the stamina of a horse, the agility of a gazelle, and the stubbornness of an ox."

"That's funny."

"Yeah, we tease him about it, but it's the truth. Knox doesn't know how to quit. He can run any man down, and if he's being chased, he'll outrun whoever dares to pursue him."

"The two of you seem close."

"We're teammates, so yeah, close."

"Teammates?"

"We were in the Navy together."

"Tell me about that." I place my hand over Max's chest. To my delight, he places his hand over mine. He absently runs his thumb up and down my fingers and across my wrist.

"We enlisted at the same time. Were in the same class at BUDS."

"Oh, I've heard about that. Is it really the way they show it on TV and in the movies?"

"That and more."

Max takes a moment before continuing. It feels as if he's judging me, determining if I can be brought into the fold. I'm not sure what test I pass, but I make it through those defensive walls.

"It's brutal. It takes a stubborn man to make it through. People always think it's about physical strength, but that's not it at all. They break you down in BUDS, mentally as well as physically. Those who can't handle the stress ring out. Knox was there when I was at my weakest. He helped me, and I helped him."

"Sounds intense."

"We then went on to serve the next few years on the same team. Did some stuff. Saw some stuff. Our re-enlistment contracts came up the same year, and CJ reached out to us."

"CJ?"

"He's the lead for the Guardians. At least, for the pointy tip of the spear."

"Huh?"

Max laughs. "That's what we call the actual Guardians. We're the muscle that gets shit done. We have an awesome tech crew and intelligence group who back us up."

"The pointy tip?" I can't help but giggle. "A little phallic symbolism there?"

"You have no idea." His grin stretches across his entire face. Max is beautiful when he smiles. Fearsome when he doesn't. I love seeing both parts of him.

"I'd like to know more about the Guardians." I want to know everything about Max, and I'm thrilled he's talking. If I can just keep him talking, then I don't have to address what's going on inside of me.

I want Max.

Like I want-want him in the most depraved, carnal way a woman can want a man. I want him over me, demanding my surrender, taking what he wants, giving that to him. Yeah, that's what I want.

Instead, I'm here. Sitting beside my rescuer. Biting my tongue. Swallowing my desire. Wishing the impossible was true.

Hoping we share some connection.

Once his mission is over, I fear it'll be the last I see of him. So, I'm hoarding memories. I want to look back on all of this; me and Max, sitting in a tree…

K-I-S-S-I-N-G.

Oh wow, where did that come from?

Eve and Max, sitting in a tree, K-I-S-S-I-N-G.

"What just went through your head, bubbles?"

"That really is a weird nickname."

"It fits." He's not giving up on it, so I let him have his fun. "Answer my question."

"Bossy much?"

"Depends on what you like…" He tugs me tight and brushes his lips over my forehead. I still in his hold. "Eve?"

"Sorry." That sudden flash of heat is unexpected. Not heat. That was pure, unadulterated lust. Holy hotness. "What did you say?"

"I asked you what went through your mind just now, and you…" He shifts in his seat and coughs. Max clears his throat. "Anyway, tell me what you were thinking."

"I can't."

"Why not?"

"It's embarrassing."

"There's nothing you need to be embarrassed about with me."

"Easy for you to say."

"Doesn't mean it's not the truth." He gives me the eye. "Now, spill."

"Fine." I sniff and press my lips together, mortified that I'm really going to tell him, but he says not to worry. "I was just singing a little thing in my head."

"What kind of thing?"

"Just a stupid kids' song."

"And…"

"You're really not going to give this up, are you?"

"Not in a million years." He gives me a cheeky grin. "Spill it."

I sit up a little straighter, which means I pull out of his grip. His hand moves from my shoulder to my leg—my thigh more specifically—and that searing heat returns.

It licks between my legs and travels all the way through my body to heat my face. From there, it tunnels down, traveling deep to my core, reverberating and building, warming my blood, until it makes my heart race.

These sensations are new for me. Not that I've never had sex before. I'm no virgin. I've had my share of heated encounters and the sexcapades that followed, but I've never felt anything like this; a burning urgency building within me.

"You need to stop squirming like that," he says.

"I'm not squirming."

"Luv, you most definitely are, and it's a bit distracting." He shifts again, wincing with the movement of his leg.

That's when I notice a prominent bulge in his pants that wasn't there a moment ago.

Evidently, I'm not the only one affected, which makes this burning need within me a thousand times worse. I feel like a cat in heat, eager to rub myself all over Max and claim him as mine, but he's injured. We can't—I can't do what I want. Not to mention the whole hiding out in a tree thing we have going on.

I rub at my cheeks as our gazes clash together and tangle in a frisson of need. The moment stretches until the corners of his lips twist up into the most cocky, arrogant, and perfectly beautiful smirk I've ever encountered.

"Damn, Eve, the expression on your face, the way your face flushes, it's so fucking hot. If we were anywhere else…" He trails off, not needing to finish what he wants to say. Not that he needs to. Evidently, we're both thinking the exact same thing.

"Yeah…" A smile curves my lips. "Same page?"

"Fucking same page." He glances down at his lap and gives a shake of his head. "I ache for you in the best possible way."

"Is this weird?"

"Weird?"

"The way we feel?"

"There's nothing weird about what's going on." He wraps an arm around me, lifts me into the air like I weigh nothing, and spins me around until I face him. Gingerly, Max guides my knees to either side of his thighs as he positions me the way he wants. "Nothing weird at all about this."

Conscious of his injured leg, I turn my attention to his bicep and the long gash in his shirt. Matted with blood, dirt, and grime, I pull apart the fabric to take a look at the injury below.

"How does that not hurt?"

"Pain is but a state of being."

I look down at his leg, very aware that I'm straddling his injury. Shifting to keep my weight off the bullet wound, I explore the cut on his arm.

"I wish there was a way to clean this up. Do you have any idea how long we're going to be holed up here?"

"A day or two at most. Once the Guardians secure the other girls, they'll come for us."

"Let's hope it's sooner, rather than later."

"Why sooner?"

"I just figured you were ready to finish this mission."

"The mission, yes, but…" He gives me a long, hard look. "This thing between us is happening. We're only just starting. I think we can safely say we've gone beyond the point of no return."

"We've barely kissed."

"Doesn't matter." He thumps his chest. "I already feel you in here."

I bite my lower lip, trying to process what he says.

"The gears in that head of yours are working pretty damn hard. Do yourself a favor, and kiss me already." Max looks at me with mirth in his eyes, arousal flooding his words, and a promise on his breath for a future I can barely hope for.

I can't help but grin. "That's kind of what I was thinking about."

"What's that?"

I sing for him. *"Eve and Max, sitting in a tree, K-I-S-S-I-N-G."*

"Now that's something I can definitely get on board with. Kiss me. Stop tormenting me and put me out of my misery."

I lean forward and kiss him. He grips my hips, steadying me, as my lips brush against his.

Max takes over from there, applying the perfect mix of pressure and friction with his lips on mine. His hands move, traveling up my back, tangling in the hair at my nape. He tugs, forcing my head back as the kiss moves from my lips to the angle of my jaw, then to my earlobe.

A sigh escapes me as he sucks gently, then follows up with his tongue. He combines light licks, moderate suction, and dizzying friction to drive me insane. Combine that with the low vibrations of his moan and I about come right there.

The man is most definitely skilled. If he can turn me into a puddle of need with a kiss on my earlobe, what can he do in other places?

Sadly, I won't find out. Our current predicament doesn't lend itself to hot and sweaty sex. Not to mention, stripping down will expose my skin to a multitude of stinging, biting insects.

Max surrenders my earlobe and returns to my lips.

"You taste like sin." He pulls back to look at me. His gaze travels across my face, taking in my lips, my nose, my eyes, my hair. "So fucking beautiful."

"You're not so bad yourself."

Max reaches between us and makes a crude adjustment. The backs of his knuckles sweep against my inner thigh, and I'm acutely aware of how close his hand is to my core.

His attention shifts back to my mouth, gaze darkening with desire, hungry for more as well.

"We can't really..." I bite my lower lip, feeling a little shy. Talking about having sex with the hottest man I've ever met is difficult. Hard. Nearly impossible, but the kindness in his eyes helps.

Such dichotomy in one man is unusual. I've seen him laser-focused, a warrior intent on killing another man, and I've seen this. This beautiful man filled with tenderness and affection.

For me.

"I feel like I need to pinch myself."

"Why?"

"Like I said, this feels like a dream."

"You feel good in my arms." His hands drift down along my spine. He gently grasps my waist. His hands are so big, they nearly encircle my waist. "You belong here."

"Here?"

"In my arms. In my life." His hands slide down to my hips, then lower still until he cups my ass. "Anywhere else on the planet, I'd already be inside of you, sliding home. I ache to have you."

"We could..."

"Too distracting." He gives a sharp shake of his head and glances over my shoulder. "Not to mention, getting caught out here with our pants down is a bad idea." That cheeky grin of his returns and he lowers his voice to a whisper. "I'm also not packing."

"Packing?"

"Protection." He winks at me, and I about die right there. I might be a little shy talking about sex, but he hits it straight on.

I settle back on his legs, making sure to put my weight on his good leg and avoid the injury to his other leg. That gives me time to recover from the whole condom comment. Unfortunately, he has a point. Naked is a bad idea out here, and I'm not interested in getting pregnant any time soon.

"It is beautiful." I twist around to take in the beauty of the jungle and inadvertently place too much weight on Max's injury. Not wanting to hurt him, I reluctantly crawl off his lap and turn around until I'm once again sitting beside him. "So, tranquil."

Indeed, it seems as if the jungle holds its breath. An eerie calm fills the air. Beside me, Max's entire body tenses. He puts a finger to his lips, telling me to be quiet, and grabs his rifle.

We hold our breaths. Too terrified to move and make an inadvertent noise; my entire body stills. Far below, the sound of something large crashing through the jungle reaches our ears. Max taps his ear, cocking it forward while I press my back against our little hollowed-out tree.

That's when I hear the indistinct voices of several men. They push through the vegetation without a care for stealth. I still remember how silently Max and Knox navigated the dense foliage with barely a sound while I lumbered through it like an ox, tripping nearly every other step.

On full alert, Max's weapon is at the ready. We should be safe. That was the whole reason for the complex climb up to our perch.

Up one tree, cross the canopy to the next tree, using a bridge of limbs. Up again, only to cross over one last time. I thought I was going to die.

Knox moved like a leopard with lethal grace. Even Max moved easily, quietly, and he has a leg with a bullet still in it and an injury to his arm.

We wait for several long minutes, long after the last crash and crunch, before Max finally settles back beside me. He's warm, with sweat beading his brow, and looks exhausted.

Warm?

Sweat?

I'm warm, but the air's not that hot. The humidity of the day is still locked in the trees and leaves. I place my hand on his forehead and wince.

"You have a fever."

"Was afraid of that." He winces and casts his gaze out at the jungle.

I wait for what seems like forever, thinking he's got more to say, but when he keeps staring out at the leaves, I tug on his sleeve.

"We can't stay here. There has to be a village nearby. A pharmacy? Someplace to get medicine?"

Infection's setting in.

I can see Max try to deny it, holding his own council. The play of expressions across his face is comical, as if he's arguing with himself and losing. Just when I think I need to step in and demand we leave, he gives a sharp nod.

"We go." His bloodshot eyes give a slow blink.

Not sure if that's from lack of sleep or the infection. I wonder if we shouldn't stay here and wait for Knox to return with his team.

He stares back at the jungle, casting about for what? I lean next to him and stare with him, trying to figure out what he sees. Then I realize he's tracing out a path, following limbs to other trees and trying to find another way down.

"Max, if those men passed us, they probably aren't going to come back this way. Why don't we just climb down this tree?" I bite my lower lip. "Although, I don't know where to go from there."

"We head West. There's a rural village two clicks away. From there, we'll wait for a chicken bus to come along. Take that to…"

"A what?"

He turns to me, mirth filling his eyes. Okay, maybe he's not as tired as I thought. I don't know how that can be, considering he kept watch all night while I slept like a baby beside him.

"Have you never ridden on a chicken bus?"

"I don't know what that is, so I'm guessing no?"

"Ah, the magical chicken buses of Central America…" He gives me a playful shove. "They are a bucket list experience."

"Never heard of it."

"You've probably seen one in a movie, just didn't know the name."

"I take it there's something involving chickens."

"Not as much these days, but that is how they got their name." He lumbers to his feet, favoring his good leg. "I'll tell you about it on the way down."

I gulp as I lean out of our tree and stare down the dizzying height. A chicken bus is the least of my worries. I'm more worried about breaking my neck.

THIRTY-FOUR

Eve

SURPRISINGLY, GETTING OUT OF THE TREE IS WAY EASIER THAN THE climb up. There are so many roots and vines winding around the trunk that I have no problem finding hand and footholds. Climbing down a ladder is probably harder than getting out of this tree.

We stop twice on the way down, standing on broad limbs, while Max listens for the men. But he doesn't hear them, and neither does the jungle.

All the birds, bugs, frogs, monkeys, and all manner of beasts wake up and greet the day with a cacophony of hoots, hollers, chirps, tweets, and birdsong.

Once we get to the ground, I brush the dirt and grime from my hands on my pants and look expectantly at Max.

"Where do we go now?" I've never been this lost in my life. Max, however, shows no hesitation.

"West." He executes a precise pivot and points.

"How do you know that's west?"

He points overhead at the sun. "Rises in the east. Everyone knows that."

Max flashes one of his magnetic grins, teasing me. Then he pulls me to him, wrapping his arm around my waist as he leans down and kisses me senseless.

My blood goes from simmering to nuclear hot in a nanosecond as the firm pressure of his mouth devours mine. I turn into a puddle of sensation as his greedy mouth takes and claims, overloading me with sensation and burning desire. My body responds to the heat of his kiss with a gasp of wanting much, much more.

When I look up, the arresting features of his face make me tremble. Every nerve in my body is on notice, acutely aware of the promise behind his kiss. His thumbs rub tiny circles along my spine, which make me shudder and sigh in contented bliss.

The tenderness of his kiss is enough to make me swoon. The promise for more makes me burn beneath the rush of his exhales and the tiny whimpers coming from my mouth.

Kisses laced with promise. The man is an expert with his tongue. He kisses me in a way I've never been kissed before, engaging his entire body. From chest to hips we're bound together with the need rushing through our bodies.

Max isn't ashamed to let me feel every hard inch of his molten desire either, shamelessly grinding against me. But then, I'm pretty shameless myself, practically humping his leg.

Give me a roof over our heads, a warm bed, and the safety to strip bare and I'm there. I can't wait to discover what else he can do with that wicked tongue. Not to mention, I'm eager to wrap my hands around what he's packing in those pants.

He pulls back, winks, then executes a sharp about-face with a smug expression plastered on his face. Yeah, he knows exactly what he did to me, leaving me wet and wanting—for him.

As we march through the jungle, I pay close attention to Max. He walks in front of me, clearing a path, but I worry about his leg and the infection setting in.

The man is a total machine. The injury to his leg barely slows him down, but I sense he is moving slower than he'd like.

Like the night before, he moves stealthily through the underbrush while I sound like an elephant crashing through without any regard for silence. I swear I'm trying not to make this much noise. Those men are somewhere in this jungle too, and the last thing I need is to let them know exactly where we are.

But it's hard to be quiet when every twig cracks beneath my feet.

"How do you know there's a village this way?"

"I paid attention during the drive in. There's just the one road for miles, but plenty of small villages. Not to mention, there were bus tracks in the dirt. There's no way to know how often the chicken buses come around. Could be once a day, or once a week."

"Once a week?" There's no way he's making it a week without some kind of medical attention.

Through some miracle, Max manages to guide us out of the jungle. If I'd been left to myself, I'd probably be walking in circles, too confused to know that I did. Everything looks like everything else around us. Sure, there are small differences here and there, but the jungle, as varied as it is, looks like one solid patch of green and brown.

When we come to the road, Max holds up a hand, telling me to stay back. I crouch at the edge of the thick vegetation while he moves stealthily to the narrow, deeply rutted, dirt road. He glances up and down, then waves me forward to join him.

"We take the road. The jungle's slowing us down. It means we're exposed, so we need to be careful and keep an eye out."

"Okay." Suddenly, the jungle sounds like the better plan.

"They're looking for you, but Knox left a path headed away from here. Hopefully, that buys us time."

Personally, the idea of Benefield getting his hands on me turns my stomach. I'd rather put a bullet in my head than suffer under that madman's rule.

"Isn't Knox supposed to be on his way back to us?"

"Don't worry about Knox. He'll find us."

"How?"

Max reaches out and breaks the stem of a small woody plant. "I've been leaving signs."

Of course. Now why didn't I think of that?

Because, you're not a Guardian. You're not trained for this.

But I kind of wish I was.

I'd love to know everything Max knows. To move the way he moves. I wish I was strong and confident like him, and not terrified and weak and scared all the time.

"These tracks are old. No new vehicles have come this way in some time. Which is good." He crouches down, fingers brushing the dirt. "From the looks of it, a chicken bus comes once a day."

"How do you know that?"

He shows me tracks in the ground and explains about the depth of the grooves and the way the soil's eroded.

None of it makes sense to me, but that's okay. Max has one hundred percent of my trust. If he told me pigs could fly, there wouldn't be a doubt in my mind they were flying directly overhead.

Sweaty, exhausted, sleep-deprived, I'm glad we're going to use the road. Walking through the jungle requires far more effort than I ever imagined. I'm the one slowing Max down, yet he's the one with the bullet wounds.

This man is made from steel, and to be honest, he reminds me of the Energizer Bunny. When I want to stop, he patiently waits for me to catch my breath, but I see his agitation building.

We're exposed and vulnerable. One of us is definitely the weaker link, and it's not my Energizer Guardian Bunny.

Max holds out a hand. Together we head west and pray for a miracle. Meanwhile, Max tells me all about the brightly colored, retired American school buses, pimped out in garish colors and repurposed for cheap public transportation.

"There's no hill a chicken bus can't climb. No vehicle it can't overtake. And when you ride in one, you'll discover fat you didn't know you had jiggle and wiggle."

"Jiggle and wiggle." I don't believe him.

"Yeah, they're cheap, but far from comfortable."

"So, we just go to this village you remember and hop on board?"

"Hopefully, it'll stop for us." Max is flushed; the pink an unusual color on his olive skin.

"What does that mean?"

"The buses don't always stop to take on passengers. You've got to run and jump to get on and jump to get off."

"Sounds terrifying."

"Best not to think too hard about it."

We spend the next hour trudging along the dirt road while I envision what a pimped-out school bus must look like.

I never rode in a bus as a kid. I was Eve Deverough. My chauffeur drove me to school and picked me up at the end of the day. All I know is what I've seen on TV.

The ruts in the road get a little deeper, a little wider, more used. At one point, an older man heads towards us, weaving unsteadily back and forth on his bicycle. He gives us the eye but says nothing as he cycles past.

Over the next hour, we see no one. My legs ache. My feet throb. My running shoes are about done in. If I have to walk much farther, I'll be doing it minus a sole.

But signs of civilization begin to pop up. An abandoned hut on the left. The carcass of a car pitted with rust on the right. A tree grows out of the middle of its trunk. Creeping vines overtake an abandoned motorcycle with the rubber stripped from its rims.

The heat builds. The musty smell of the jungle infuses the air. Sweat beads my brow and drips down between my breasts.

We start to see chickens. One at first. A few more. Then we're surrounded by half a dozen as they peck at the dirt.

Max spies a ramshackle shack just off the side of the road. I would've missed it completely. He angles over to speak to an old woman with a huge gaping smile and only one tooth. He speaks in broken Spanish, gesticulating wildly. After a bit, he appears satisfied and pulls something out of his pocket. He gives her something shiny then returns to me.

"What was all that?"

"Just asking about our ride."

"And?"

"We're in luck." He points down the road. "It stops up the road sometime in the afternoon."

"How far?"

"A few kilometers at least."

I turn and look down the dirt road with a groan. "What did you give her?"

"A button."

"A what?"

"A button."

"Why would you do that?"

"Because it's all I have." When he takes off, his limp is worse than I remember.

"How's your leg holding up?"

"Best to keep moving." His tight-lipped expression tells me he's anything but good, and there's more color in his cheeks than there was a couple of hours ago.

I'm growing more and more concerned.

By the time we wander into a small, run-down village, sweat beads on Max's brow. The limp is worse. My concern skyrockets.

The village is nothing more than a collection of shacks and lean-tos strung out along the road. There is maybe a score, or more, on either side and more people than I expect.

Despite the drabness of the structures, the people are dressed in vibrant colors. Huge smiles fill their faces, and like the woman down the road, they have gap-toothed smiles.

I glance at the stands filled with fruits and vegetables I don't recognize and push my fist into my belly. Hunger is something new for me. I doubt I've gone a day in my life ever experiencing this gnawing pain. But we don't have anything to barter.

That's when I see a stall with what looks like pills in tiny bottles. I tug on Max's sleeve.

"What kind of medicine do you think that is?"

He peers at the shack, then moves toward it with interest. "Let's find out."

The rifle slung over his back draws every eye, but they don't seem nervous about a man walking armed into their town. It makes me think they're used to it. Max also has a pistol shoved in the back of his pants. I do too.

"Do you even know what to ask for?"

"We'll figure it out."

Which is exactly what Max does for the next ten minutes. In broken Spanish, with lots of wild gesticulation, Max draws a crowd. Seems to me that's not such a good idea, but infection is setting in. If we don't get some kind of antibiotics on board, we're going to have a big problem.

Then I wonder how Knox and the other men on Max's team are going to find us. He showed me how he'd been leaving a trail, bending back sticks that pointed in the direction we came from, rather than where we were heading, but once we reached the road, he's left no sign that I can see.

And I don't like the attention he generates with his questions, or the looks I'm getting. I stick out like a sore thumb, which makes me wish I had one of those colorful scarves to wrap around my head. I'm a brunette, not a blonde. Regardless, my hair is noticeable, memorable, compared to the deep black of the women's hair all around me. They keep looking at me, grinning, as they reach out to touch my hair.

When one of the women sees me eyeing her stall filled with the bright scarves, she waves me over. I hold out a hand, waving her off, but she's persistent. Not wanting to make a scene, I wander over. She immediately begins showing me brightly colored fabric, holding it up to her face, then points at my head.

It takes a minute, but I finally figure out what she wants. I pull out one of the pins in my hair and hand it to her. She cups it like a priceless treasure and hands me three of the scarves. I wrap one around my head, covering as much of my hair as possible, one around my shoulders, and I know exactly what I'm going to do with the third scarf.

A glance at Max brings a smile to my face. He towers over the villagers, but his smile is infectious. Everyone grins and laughs with him. They slap each other as if they're long-time friends, telling tall tales with a fantastic joke at the end. I simply look on at the man I've somehow managed to fall in love with over the past few days.

I'm not really sure when that happened, but I've been bit by the love bug, and dammit if it didn't strike hard. I'm desperately, achingly, head over heels in love with Max, and I don't even know his last name.

Mr. S.

Max S?

If S is really the first letter of his last name.

There is so much we don't know about each other, but I feel like it doesn't matter. Now, in addition to Max haggling with the villagers over the price of the pills, I wonder if someone around here might have a condom, or two, or three. With one look at the several women with swollen bellies, I figure that isn't something anyone around here would have.

Which sucks.

I'm ready for something more than a decadent, toe-curling kiss.

Max finishes up and returns with a bottle filled with six pills. Four are the size of horse pills. They're dull white in color. Two are smaller capsules, tinged blue.

"What's that?"

"I think it's penicillin. For all I know, it could be Viagra."

"I think that's a little blue pill, and I have a feeling that's not something you need."

He stretches his wounded arm and winces, drawing my attention to the cut under that shirt. I'm also concerned about his leg, but there's no good way to take a look at that here. We need a room, preferably one with running water, a bunch of bandages, and that bed I want.

It would be better to find a real doctor who spoke English and could help out, but we don't have that luxury.

"What do we do now?"

"It's siesta time. Everyone is closing down for a few hours."

"I don't get how they accomplish anything around here."

"Siesta makes sense when the middle of the day is sweltering hot. They save important business for the evening hours. Different place. Different culture."

"Different life."

"I'm sure it is."

"What about this bus?" He's stoked my curiosity about this pimped-out mode of transportation.

"The chicken bus?"

"Yes."

He smiles. "It hasn't come by yet. All we have to do is wait."

"Aren't you worried about..." I glance around and lower my voice. "Benefield and his men?"

"They're off in the jungle searching for us, headed North. Knox made sure to leave a trail they could follow that would take them away from the road."

"Wait a second. You knew about the road the whole time?"

"Of course."

"How does he know we'll head to the road?"

"We discussed it."

"When?"

Max loops his arm over my shoulder and pulls me into a hug. "We always have contingency plans."

"Oh." I'm amazed with how seamlessly the two of them operate together. The heat radiating off Max's arm reminds me I want to look at his wound. "You should probably take one of those pills." Hopefully, it really is some kind of antibiotic. "And I want to look at your arm."

He stretches it, wincing again. "It's just a bit stiff."

"Take the pill." I stare him down, not giving in.

"What if it's a blue one?" He lifts his brows suggestively.

"We'll deal with whatever comes up."

"Is that a promise?" His eyes smolder as he takes me in.

"Find some condoms, preferably unused, and yeah, that's a definite promise."

"That's a gross mental image."

"Did it take your mind off sex?"

"No, but kind of put a damper on it."

"Good, then it did the job." I point at a nearby boulder that's relatively flat on top. "Now sit down and let me look at that arm."

Max unscrews the pill bottle and swallows one of the larger pills down without water. That makes my throat hurt. Then he sits down and I do what I can with the angry red gash.

Definitely infected.

THIRTY-FIVE

Max
___

THE SKIN OF MY ARM STINGS. THE WOUND IN MY LEG THROBS. I DRY swallow two of the dull white pills and follow them up with a blue capsule.

This heat is giving me a headache and exhaustion pulls at my body, making it ache and respond sluggishly to my commands.

It's a mystery what I'm taking, although with the villagers help, lots of pantomiming, and showing them the wound on my arm, a consensus was reached among the women. I'm forty percent sure they gave me antibiotics.

I don't really know. Another one of my shiny buttons gets handed over in barter.

Who knew those damn buttons would come in handy like this? But a good button is like gold in a place like this.

I've got four left, along with the watch on my wrist. I'm saving that to secure a room for the night.

If we stop, that is.

The watch is nonfunctioning for what I need. The timepiece works, but all the fancy gadgets Mitzy embedded inside are defunct. Not that I'm terribly worried. There's a chip in me that will lead the Guardians right to me, with time.

And that's the kicker.

It takes time for all that fancy tech to kick in. We're in a race against who will find us first: Benefield or the Guardians. All I'm doing is keeping Eve and myself moving, making it harder for Benefield's men to track us.

I'm supposed to take two of the white pills, one of the blue, and do it again in the morning. God, I hope we're out of this place by then. I'm not going to feel good until Skye Summers, the Guardian's doc, takes a look at the red and angry wounds. It would be nice to get that bullet out too.

Each step becomes more difficult, but I've endured far worse. Like I told Eve, pain is but a state of being. I'll get through this like I've gotten through all the rest.

The good news is transport is on the way. The bus comes once a day as the sun goes down. I feared it would only come once a week. We aren't exactly in a populated region. But we're in luck.

After I sit down on the boulder, Eve gets to work on my arm. Using a brightly colored scarf, she somehow obtained while I was haggling over the pills, and a bottle of cloudy water, she gently cleans the wound.

My skin's angry red around the bullet wound, but there's no pus. The infection remains superficial at best.

But for how long?

I place my faith in the pharmacy skills of the villagers and swallow down the second white pill with a grimace.

"Come, sit beside me." I hold out my hand and love the way Eve settles in beside me. The gentle smile on her face is nothing short of beautiful, and the way her sea-green eyes sparkle with affection is heart-stopping.

God, I hope there's more than simple affection, or worse, gratitude, in those eyes.

I ache for her in the worst possible way. First chance we get, once I get her to a safe place, I'm laying claim to her.

Eve's mine.

No ifs, ands, or buts about it.

We shift over to a shaded spot, where I allow myself to fitfully doze. One of the things I've learned over the years is how to catch sleep where I can. Eve sits beside me, alert and watchful, as I let my body get some much-needed rest.

Sometime later, the deep roar of an oncoming vehicle pulls me to instant alertness. On my feet before Eve can react, I'm already stretching out a hand for her to get up. We jog the short distance to the road.

One of the things about riding a chicken bus is they don't always come to a full stop when taking on passengers. Sometimes, they don't stop at all.

American ideals of safety go out the window. This kind of public transportation is not like anything else in the world. It's dangerous, terrifying, and hair-raising, but surprisingly efficient.

A colorful pimped-out bus comes chugging down the lane. Bright yellows, reds, blues, and greens meld together in a garish display that's hard on the eyes but somehow seems to work perfectly.

We're remote enough that the bus doesn't look packed to the gills. Nobody appears to be getting off, which means the driver isn't slowing down. At least, not until I step out in front of it waving my arms over my head.

The bus slows, and I gesture for Eve to climb on board as the hydraulics hiss with the opening of the door. I run around to follow suit, and by the time I get to the door, the driver's already moving out.

We're lucky.

One bench seat in the middle of the bus is empty. Eve sits next to the window with wide eyes and white knuckles as the bus takes off.

These buses are built to last. There's no car, truck, or other bus it can't overtake with a roar of its engine, and the drivers push their vehicles to the limits on the rutted dirt roads, climbing steep mountains and navigating around hairpin curves.

There are no seatbelts. We bounce along, catching air with some of the bigger bumps. Each impact makes me cringe as the jarring jolt sends shooting pain through my injured leg.

Eve glances around, wide-eyed, a little bit terrified, but trusting enough of me to believe we haven't placed our lives in the hands of a madman.

She points to the driver. "Is that a monkey?"

Our driver is a happy man with a potbelly, a cigar protruding from between his lips, and a wide sombrero with red tassels hanging from the brim. But that's not what grabs Eve's attention. It's the tiny white-faced capuchin monkey sitting on the brim of the driver's hat.

It wears a studded red collar with a leash integrated into the hat. The monkey chitters to the driver, peeking over the brim of the hat, until the driver takes a nut out of a cup in front of him and hands it to the monkey. Its tiny hands grasp the nut and it scampers onto the top of the hat where it stares out the front of the bus, happily munching on its treat. All black, except for chest, throat, and face, he's cute, but obnoxious.

"Sure is." I take Eve's hand in mine and place it in my lap. "And that's not all."

"What do you mean?"

I point to the luggage rack across from us where a small wicker cage holds a red-feathered chicken.

"You don't say." Eve leans against me until the next bump in the road bounces her head off my shoulder.

Chicken buses are definitely unique. I'm not going to say anything to her about safety, accidents, or what the rest of this ride will turn into once people start cramming onboard. There is no such thing as a maximum capacity on these things.

I've ridden squashed in like a sardine and prefer it to an empty bus. Right now, every bump and jiggle is noticeable. When the bus is packed like sardines, all those bumps get absorbed as the bodies of others cushion you.

I lean forward and adjust the rifle on my back. I took Eve's sidearm from her. It's currently shoved in the front of my waistband, while mine is easy to reach at my back.

Two Americans traveling in these parts are certain to draw the attention of the locals. Add one who carries a rifle, and people take notice. Throw in a drop-dead gorgeous brunette, and the news will spread like wildfire.

This is good and bad. Good because it'll make it easier for my team to find us. Bad because it leads Benefield directly to us as well. I'm counting on Knox getting to Alpha team, and back, before Benefield tracks us down.

If Benefield finds us first, that's okay.

I'm ready for war.

I wipe at the beads of sweat on my brow and feel the heat radiating off my forehead. I've yet to look at the wound on my leg, but if it's anything like the one on my arm, our stint in the jungle did me no favors.

"How're you doing?" I take Eve's hand in mine.

The seats are small, made for the asses of children headed to school, not two grown adults, and most definitely not for a man of my size. Fortunately, I bracket Eve between me and the window, minimizing the bone-jarring bumps for her as we rattle down the road.

"Terrified." She pinches her eyes closed as another bump lifts us off the seat and slams us back down. "I haven't decided if it's better or worse with my eyes open or closed."

Knowing we're headed into the mountains with their narrow roads, steep drop-offs, and white-knuckled turns, I offer some advice.

"Keep your eyes closed." She gives me the eye, like I'm a lunatic, and I can't help but laugh. "Try to rest." I give her knee a squeeze and bracket her in, giving her as much support as I can.

As expected, the bus fills as we get closer and closer to civilization. As people pile in, the music, which was moderate when we boarded and only somewhat annoying, blasts at deafening levels. People wedge themselves three and four to a seat and crowd the aisle. The roar of the engine only adds to the pervasive noise. And, of course, there are the clucks of many a chicken sprinkled in for effect.

One of the feathered creatures stares out at me from the luggage rack overhead. Stuffed into a backpack, its head sticks out with beady eyes taking everything in. There's another bag that moves more than a piece of luggage should. I'm guessing a chicken, or two, is in there as well. One youth hops on board with a shoebox full of chicks. He's got over a dozen of them crammed into the small space. An old man with a bleating goat joins us at the next stop.

Somehow, through all that chaos, the driver displays a magical ability to hear passengers call out for a stop.

Like he did at the village where we got on, most stops are more of a slow roll. Passengers jump on and off with ease as the bus keeps moving. As for speed, there may be speed limits, not that they apply to us. Our driver takes the road as fast as possible, barely slowing for the curves. We careen wildly back and forth as the miles pass behind us and the sun slowly sinks below the horizon.

I tilt my head up to the ceiling and blow out my breath. It's going to be another long night.

THIRTY-SIX

Eve
___

HOURS PASS AS WE BOUNCE AROUND IN THE CRAZY BUS OVERFLOWING with people, chickens, two monkeys, and one bleating goat. My head throbs from the loud music and the constant roar of the engine as the driver works through the gears.

Once we hit the mountains, steep roads, winding curves, and cliffs dropping off into the darkness, make me grab a hold of Max. It's terrifying and a miracle we survive.

Max finally calls out to the driver as we pull into what I can properly call a real town.

We jump off the bus as it barely comes to a stop in the middle of a town square. At the north end, a beautiful church stands watch over the village. There's a pub, or do we call it a tavern in this part of the world? Who knows, and I don't care.

"What now?" My grip on Max's hand tightens. This place terrifies me, but with Max by my side, I feel marginally safe.

"We find a place to spend the night." Max's shoulders slump from exhaustion, reminding me he's going on two days without anything more than a brief nap.

"How do we do that?"

He points toward the church. "We pay our respects and ask the priest." Max takes off toward the church as I keep up with his long stride.

The door swings open and we enter the hushed quiet of a chapel. Max moves over to rows and rows of flickering candles. He lights a taper, then one of the candles. As he blows out the taper, a priest wanders out.

"Buenas noches. ¿Son ustedes visitantes? ¿Puedo ayudarles?" The priest eyes the rifle on Max's back with interest, but it doesn't seem to faze him.

"¿Habla inglés?" Max speaks to the priest while I watch the candles' flames flicker, casting ethereal shadows on the walls.

I'm not a religious person. Wasn't raised that way, but I always feel an overwhelming sense of peace when I step inside a church. That feeling overcomes me now, a sense of the outside world fading away.

"Yes, welcome. How may I help you?"

"Thank you, father. We are weary travelers seeking rooms for the night." Max's formality is strange but respectful. "Is there somewhere you might recommend?"

The two men talk for a time while I wander down toward the front and sit in one of the pews. Not sure what really overcomes me, but I bow my head and say a short prayer.

I pray for Max, hoping the infection will recede. I pray for the girls his team of Guardians hopefully rescued.

Max seems to think everything went well, but how can he know? He hasn't been in contact with anyone from the Guardians. I wish I had the degree of faith in myself that he does in his team.

I even say a prayer for my father.

I don't understand what I saw on that ledger. He and Benefield are connected. There's no way to deny it, but, despite my personal issues with my father, I really believe he's an honest man. Something had to have happened. At least that's what I hope, and I say a little prayer hoping it helps.

"You ready?" Max walks up behind me, laying a hand on my shoulder.

I place my hand over his and take a deep breath in and blow it out slowly. When I look up at him, all I see is devotion shining in his eyes. It makes my heart skip a beat. Whatever this is between us, it feels right.

We click.

"Where are we going?"

"There's a small inn a block away." Max pulls out a small stack of bills from his front pocket. He counts off two of them, then shoves the rest back deep in his pocket.

"Where did you get money?"

"Made a donation to the church."

"You did?" My brows tug together. "What did you donate?"

"My watch. I don't need it and he can get far more for it than I ever could."

"And he gave you cash?"

"Much less than the watch is worth and far more than we need to get a room. You want to stay for a bit?" He glances toward the alter.

I suddenly realize he must've been waiting for me while I prayed.

"Um, I'm good." Suddenly, I feel self-conscious.

Max and I thank the priest, who eyes his shiny new watch more than he pays attention to us. We take off to find the small inn, walking hand in hand the whole way.

After a short conversation in broken Spanish, Max has an honest to goodness, old-fashioned key in his hand. We wander up to the second-floor balcony. Our room is #1, but Max takes us all the way to the last room, #6.

"But…" I tug on his arm, thinking he's made a mistake.

Max shakes his head and presses a finger over his lips. He goes to the last room, does something to the lock, and we walk in. After he closes the door behind us I can't help but ask.

"Why are we in the wrong room? And how did you do that?"

"We're in this room because, if Benefield's men find us, which they'll do eventually, they're going to break into the other room first. This gives us a chance to hear them before they start looking in the other rooms."

Wow, that never would've occurred to me.

"How did you know this room was empty?"

"All the keys were hanging on the wall." He looks at me like that's something I should've noticed.

But I didn't. I totally suck at this Guardian thing.

The room isn't much, but it has two things I need. Three actually. There's a full-sized bed and a bathroom with a shower/tub combination. Feels like I'm at the Ritz after spending last night in the jungle.

Max checks out the room, then closes the door behind us. Instead of locking the door, he shoves the back of a chair beneath the doorknob, then shows me how to get it free in case I need to leave the room.

"But don't leave unless you're with me."

"What if I…"

"Uh-uh. You don't walk around anywhere without me."

"But…"

He gives me a look. "Pretty American woman, pretty *young* American woman, do I need to spell it out?"

"No." That's how I wound up here in the first place, partying down in Cancun without a care in the world.

Yes, I figured my father would put a security detail on me. It gave the illusion of sneaking away and giving him the proverbial finger. I thought I was safe, until I wasn't.

Then came that terrible house in Cancun, the shipping container which followed, and the harrowing ride in the back of a truck covered in a thick tarp. The heat alone almost took me out, but I survived. I survived and became the very special guest of Tomas Benefield.

"He's going to find us, isn't he?"

"He will." Max sits on the end of the bed and pats the mattress. "Come here."

He pulls the rifle from over his shoulder and lays it on the bed behind him, then he draws out the two pistols.

"Let me show you how these work."

"How about we take a look at your leg?" We have privacy now, and while I wouldn't call this place clean, it's cleaner than anywhere else we've been in the past twenty-four hours.

"After I know you're comfortable with your gun."

My gun?

"I've never had a gun before."

"I thought you said you've shot before."

"It was a really long time ago."

"Ok, listen up."

Despite his fatigue, Max gives a very thorough introduction on gun safety and shows me how to use the pistol until he's confident I won't shoot myself, or him, accidentally.

A deep yawn escapes him, and I realize how long it's been since he's had any real sleep.

"We need to get you in bed."

"Music to my ears."

"I didn't mean that!"

"You didn't?" The wounded look on his face makes me laugh.

"I mean I do, but you're in no condition..."

"Let me be the judge of what condition I'm in." He pulls me into his lap, then winces in pain as he places my bottom directly on his injured thigh.

I scoot off immediately. "How about this? We strip you down..."

"I like the sound of that..." The way he winks at me shouldn't be legal. I'm surprised I don't melt into a puddle of goo right then and there.

"We clean your wound. When do you have to take the rest of those pills?"

"In the morning."

"Okay, strip you down, clean your wound." I back away when he tries to grab me. "We each take a shower."

"Together."

"Don't think there's enough room in there for the two of us."

"You'd be surprised."

"Let's focus on cleaning your wound. You take a shower while I scrub your clothes. Then I'll..."

"You'll get naked while I watch…"

"You're incorrigible. You know that, don't you."

"I've been hard for you going on a week now. My balls are bluer than those pills I need to take."

"I think we can fix that."

"Liking the sound of this." He gives a cheeky grin. "Go on."

"We may not be able to 'do the deed,' but I'm pretty sure I can help you relieve some of that tension."

"Sounds perfect." Max yanks his shirt over his head and stands. He grabs at his belt buckle.

"You might want to kick off those boots before you get much further." I don't know where this sudden well of confidence comes from, but I'm loving this little back and forth.

We're going to have sex. No doubt about that. Not the in and out variety, but there is so much we can do. I'm especially interested in getting him in my hands and my mouth, and I'm pretty sure he'll be fine with that. The rest of it can wait.

I'm also keenly interested in finding out if his tongue is as talented down there as it is on my lips and when nipping on my earlobe.

My breath catches at the smooth expanse of his chest. Rock-hard abs, sculpted pecs, he looks like he belongs on the cover of a men's fitness magazine. I bet there's not an ounce of body fat anywhere on him.

Max sits back down, unlaces his boots, and kicks them off. "You going to just stand there and stare?"

I cross my arms over my chest and laugh. "You sure bet I am. I've been fantasizing about this since the first day I saw you."

"The day you saw me? You hated me on sight."

"I hated what I thought you were, but you're pretty damn easy on the eye. Any girl would want of piece of that."

"That?"

"You."

"And do you?"

"What?"

"Want a piece of me?"

I lick my lips as he stands and hooks his thumbs on the waistband of his pants. That bulge is back, and it's bigger than before—as if that's possible.

"I want all of you."

Max takes a step toward me. He cups my cheeks and leans down to place a feather-light kiss on my lips.

"I want all of you too." Max releases my cheeks.

Taking one step back, his gaze never leaves me as he strips out of his pants. Impossible to miss, the hard length of him tents his boxer briefs. With smoldering eyes, he kicks free of his pants and looks down at the angry red skin over his thigh.

"Oh my God!" I rush to him. It's worse than I thought. "Sit down and let me clean that."

The towels in the bathroom are barely clean. Turning on the water, I let it run until it steams. Then I head back where he waits for me on the bed.

Max bends over, examining the entrance wound. I go to my knees and start dabbing at the skin.

"I think I should take that shower." His hoarse voice draws my attention.

"No, we need to get this cleaned up. Scrub it as much as possible."

He lifts my chin with the pad of his thumb. "You on your knees right now is more than I can handle. I'm more than capable of taking a shower and cleaning this up."

"But…"

"No buts. Give me a minute. Okay?"

I glance at the hard length of him, suddenly understanding what he's saying. If I were bolder, I'd help him take the edge off, right then and there, but I'm kind of a chicken and scoot back.

"Um, okay."

"You should rest."

"If I lie down on that bed, I'll be out." I head over to the nightstand where he left my pistol. Following exactly what he taught me, I check the chamber and make sure the safety is on. "I'll keep watch while you shower."

"You don't have to do that."

"Someone has to. You can't do it all."

"Damn, but I love your fight. I'll be quick."

I swallow thickly, knowing pretty much that he's not just going to be cleaning out that wound. "You don't have to hurry if you don't want to."

"Normally, I'd take you up on that offer, but who knows how much hot water there is. You deserve to get some of the road grime and jungle slime off your body. We'll sleep in clean sheets tonight."

This is true, only there's one thing we won't have.

Clothing.

I plan on scrubbing our clothes until they're as clean as I can get them. If it wasn't so late, I'd duck out and find a pharmacist. There has to be some kind of store around here that sells antibacterial ointment and bandages. Until then, that third scarf will have to do the job.

While Max showers, I fidget on the bed. Every sound outside makes me jump. True to his word, Max takes a short shower. It's my turn.

Unlike him, I'm not bold enough to strip in front of him. I gather all his clothes and toss them in the shower with me to soak. My clothes go in there as well. My shower takes longer than his, but then I have a lot more hair than he does.

There's only bar soap, but I make due. Then I get to scrubbing our clothes. By the time I emerge from the bathroom, Max is already in bed, dead asleep.

He looks so peaceful in sleep. I crawl into the small bed beside him, acutely aware of my nakedness, and wonder if maybe I shouldn't stay awake and keep watch. Before I can decide, sleep finds me.

I wake with Max curled around me. His breathing is slow, even, and at peace. My smaller frame fits perfectly within his. My back presses against his front, which means his erection pokes the small of my back.

My bare back.

Our clothes hang in the bathroom, drying after our jungle and chicken bus ordeal. At some point, he threw his arm around me, locking me in place. It's heavy. Safe.

Wonderfully safe.

This, this is what I've been wanting since the day we met. Sexual chemistry, and the ensuing tension aside, a quiet moment like this is worth ten-thousand kisses.

His chest rises and falls, calm, gentle, soothing, while my heart speeds up. I could lift his arm and ease out of his embrace, but I don't want to ruin the moment.

With his hard body holding me, I feel soft, feminine, fragile, yet also tough, resilient, and most importantly, loved.

I survived months at The Retreat, the prisoner of a madman, then I found Max.

Or rather, he found me.

Breathing in his dark, masculine scent, I doze contentedly in his arms. Then I realize something important. His skin is warm.

Not hot.

Max's fever broke sometime during the night. With that thought, I doze contentedly, safe in the arms of the man I love. At least until he presses his hard length against me. Then I'm wide awake and thinking of only one thing.

THIRTY-SEVEN

Max

By NECESSITY, WE WENT TO BED WITHOUT CLOTHING. EVE STAYED IN the bathroom long after I was done, cleaning and scraping two days' worth of hard travel off our clothes.

Which means, my body wakes eager and hungry.

For her.

My arm drapes over the curve of her hips. My hand rests flat against her belly. I can't help my fingers as they trace out tiny circles across the expanse of her belly.

Eve wakes and her entire body tenses.

"Shh, go back to sleep." The desire to hold her in my arms wars with my need to fuck. Passion burns in my veins, penetrating all my senses, until my entire being demands release.

There's one huge problem with that.

No protection.

Not that there aren't other things we can try. I can't wait to kiss her creamy thighs and lick her clit until she screams. If I must wait to take her the way I like, I have no problem doing other things.

"How can I sleep when you're…"

"When I'm, what?"

"You know."

"Yeah, but I want to hear you say it."

Eve rolls over, and I almost complain until her tiny hand wraps around my extremely engorged cock.

"I can't sleep with this poking me in the back."

A low groan of desire stirs in the back of my throat. The feel of her hand on my shaft is enough to make me go insane. My balls tighten, and my cock feels like it's going to explode as blood surges into it with a vengeance.

I barely hold onto my restraint as the need to take her rips through me, violently, aggressively, and with the entirety of my being.

"Don't tease me." My teeth grate together as I struggle not to turn her over and fuck her like a dog. I'm barely holding on to the most base desire a man can have.

"Or what?" Her hand slides down my shaft, twisting and squeezing.

"Turn about is fair play." I clamp my hand on her wrist, keeping her from stimulating me more.

With the way I'm amped up, I'm more likely to be a one-pump-and-done kind of guy. That is not how our first time is going to be.

I'll have her screaming my name, multiple times, before I take my pleasure. My grip tightens until I force her fingers to release me. Once that's accomplished, I roll her to her back and move until I'm on top of her.

My very naked, uncovered, and unprotected cock stabs at her opening. It would only take one thrust. I could fuck her with all the passion swirling within me, heat her blood until she begged for release, and penetrate her body until our bodies meld as one, but where would the fun be in that?

Not when I have all the time in the world to savor the delights her body will yield. And I have no doubt Eve will yield to me. Already, the heady scent of her arousal floods my senses. Her wide eyes stare at me with passion and desire.

"Do you have any idea what you mean to me?" I stare down at her, dumbstruck this is happening. That this is going to happen.

Eve loops her arms over my shoulders. Her legs spread as I

wedge myself between them. No doubt in my mind, she won't stop me if I angle just a little and slide on home. It's where I belong, deep inside of her, joined as one, but I'm not so far gone to ignore the consequences such a decision would bring.

I stare at her for the longest time, losing myself in her sea-green gaze as I debate my next move.

"You're killing me," she says.

"I am?" I arch a brow, knowing exactly what she means.

What's wrong with a little tease? Eve doesn't know it, or maybe she does, but I'm going to do everything I can to blow her mind. This isn't going to be an in and out, rut and fuck until you're done, kind of thing.

I'm taking my own sweet time.

"Just kiss me already."

"Just a kiss?" I bend my head and brush my lips across her mouth. "Or do you want more?"

Eve grabs the back of my neck and forces my head down. "I want it all."

"All?" I arch my brow again. "I need something more specific."

With that, I shift my hand from the mattress to her side. My fingertips graze the swell of her breast, and I'm aching to finally get those in my hands.

With our gazes interlocked and simmering with the latent heat between us, I move my hand up, going as slow as I can stand, until I cup her breast. Her body arches, greedy and wanting, but I'm in no rush. The urge to shift my thumb just a bit and feel the puckering of her nipple is nearly overwhelming, but I force myself to take things slow. I never want to forget this moment.

"Do you like my hands on you?"

"Yes." Her breathy reply sings to my soul.

"What about my mouth?" I bend over her, moving to the corner of her ear, blowing softly and nipping as I go.

"Yes." Her body arches into my hand, filling it with the creamy smoothness of her breast.

That's all the invitation I need. Kissing from her earlobe, down the angle of her jaw, I continue the tortuous path down her neck, sweeping across her collarbone, with the intention of slowly, very slowly, moving down to her breast.

Eve's breaths alternate from low and deep to panting and fast as my lips take the meandering journey to her breasts.

This is fucking awesome for me because I'm learning what my girl likes, what she loves, and what she craves. I store all that information for later use.

When I have all the time in the world to drown her in pleasure.

I suck her neck, tasting her sweet essence, and imprinting it on my soul. My kisses deepen, turning fevered as I continue down.

Her breathing turns erratic, urgent, and fucking hot as hell. She tries to struggle, to take over, but in this, I am in charge. She will yield to my desires as I fulfill all of hers.

"Damn it, Max…"

"What?" I lift my head until her green gaze flickers at me, aroused, agitated, and totally turned on.

"You damn well know what?"

I do, which is what makes this so much fun.

But I don't deny her what she desires, only because I desire it as much as she. My body jostles hers as I shift down the bed until my head is even with the creamy expanse of her breast.

I could take my time and work my way in slowly, spiraling up toward the puckered nub of her breast. But why deny myself what I want?

I lave her tight nipple, flicking it softly with my tongue as her back arches beneath me. Her fingers stab into my hair, pulling and twisting at the roots, as I drive her insane, tormenting her breasts.

My tongue licks with sensual strokes, light then hard, a little nip of my teeth as she writhes beneath me. Damn, but she's hot as sin.

She's passionate, feminine, soft, and hard. Eve's my perfect counterpart. I plunder and claim moving from one breast to the other, unwilling to let one go without the worship she deserves.

Every touch, every kiss, and every nip is meant to entice and delight. I move from her breasts to the smooth expanse of her belly.

As her body heats, so does mine.

An answering fire simmers in my blood, banked for now, but not for long. We may not be able to have sex the way I want—at least not yet—but that doesn't mean I'm not going to destroy her for any other man and make her mine.

Eve's body shakes as my kisses skate across her belly. I use my body to spread her legs and make my way down to her core.

God, her essence floats on the air, an intoxicating scent that rocks my world. My hands move up. Each grasping a breast as my head lowers to kiss her core.

Her gasp as my lips lock against her clit is exactly what I need. Pleasure sparks in her body as her breaths catch and her hips grind on the mattress.

I can't handle it any longer, needing to taste her fully. My hands move from her breasts to grip her hips, then I lift her as I bury my face between her legs.

She cries out as I lick along her slit and nip her clit. When my tongue darts out to taste her essence, a strangled scream escapes her lips. I grip her tightly and begin a rhythm I know will drive her over the edge.

As my invasion continues, her legs tremble. Her body shakes. Eve comes apart in my hands.

Chest heaving, I bring her to an earth-shattering release.

Gently, I move back up her body.

I cup the back of her head as her glazed expression tries to focus on my face. I drink in her features, wanting to imprint this moment on my soul. Her sea-green gaze focuses, then her shy side returns.

"Uh-uh." I capture her gaze in mine. "You don't get to slip away like that." I lean down and meld my lips to hers, letting her know I'll always be there for her.

When we part, I slide a thumb along her jaw as I take her in. My exploration is unhurried. After all, I've got the rest of my life to stare at the woman I love.

Leaning closer, I kiss her again. Soft. Gentle. Full of love.

"You're fucking amazing. You know that, don't you?"

Her lids flutter and her cheeks heat.

"I've never…" She takes in a deep breath and covers her face with her hands. "That was—amazing." Her gaze returns to mine, and her hand moves to my shoulder. "Incredible."

"I like that. Keep it coming."

"Oh really?" Her feisty side returns as the last lingering vestiges of her release fades. "What are the chances a town like this has a place that sells condoms, because if that's what you can do with your mouth…"

I chuckle as her words trail off and roll to my side. "You're definitely stroking my ego here. Don't ever stop."

"I have no intention of stopping, and as for stroking…" She reaches down, between us, and takes my cock in hand. "I've got something in mind."

My entire body jerks. My hips practically levitate off the bed. Eve rises, sitting beside me. Her long, brunette hair tumbles over her shoulders and cascades down across her tits. She's a fucking goddess with the power to bring me to my knees.

THIRTY-EIGHT

Eve

MAX'S ENTIRE BODY TENSES THE MOMENT MY FINGERS WRAP AROUND his hard shaft. Velvet over steel, he's hard, long, and much larger than I thought.

His masculine scent fills the room. The heat of his body sinks into me. Strong hands glide along my shoulders and travel down my back. I've never felt this blissfully content.

This safe.

I feel him everywhere. Beside me. Beneath me. Over me. His fingers flutter through my hair, running through the tangles, straightening them out, as I hold him in my hand and lower my head down to kiss the tip of his cock.

I can't look away from the banked heat of his eyes as I slowly take him in. Max groans as I lick along the length of him. His hips jerk as I take him deep and swallow him whole. I lick and suck, jerk and squeeze until his balls draw up and his legs shake.

Max comes violently, shooting his essence down my throat as I lap and suck through his release. When his legs stop shaking, and I'm sure his orgasm has run through him, I slowly pull off.

Max smiles at me, then draws me up his body until we're once again lying side by side.

"That was exactly what I needed. Goddam, but you give great head."

I know what he means. Like him, I feel blissfully satisfied.

This thing between us feels right.

All I do is feel how perfect this moment is.

I feel the aching burn between my legs, which still lingers after he drove me up and over the edge. He cups the back of my head, fingers stroking through my hair as I lay my cheek against his chest. The beating of his heart soothes me.

Slow. Steady. Calm.

Strong.

His confidence is sexy. His ability to push through and past his pain shows a strength I can only hope to one day emulate.

"Do we have to get up?" I swirl my fingers over his chest, drawing lazy circles as I curl against his hard frame.

"We don't have to do anything at all." He shifts beneath me. "But I should probably head out and grab some food."

My stomach rumbles the moment he says that, reminding me the last food we had was on that chicken bus.

"I love the food down here, but I'd give a million bucks for a hamburger right about now."

"I don't think that's on the menu." Max shifts his body, separating us. He slides off the bed and strides over to the small bathroom while I watch his rock-hard ass.

Not an inch of fat on the man.

He shuts the door, then comes out a few moments later with his pants on. He tosses me my clothes then shrugs on his shirt. While he bends down to put on his boots, I dress in my somewhat clean but hard and scratchy clothes.

"Is there a place to shop around here?" I don't like how my clothes feel and fidget as they settle on my skin.

"Probably, but who knows when they open. We'll be out of here soon enough."

"How soon? How long will it take Knox to find us?" I lean down and grab my shoes.

Max watches with a hard stare. "Eve…"

"Yes?"

"I'm not taking you out of this room."

"Why not?"

"We arrived late at night. Nobody was up. The less we have people talking about us the better."

"But you're going out."

"There's a big difference between an American man alone and an American man with a gorgeous woman by his side. Especially with Benefield out there."

"So, what? I have to stay here?"

"You're safer here."

"I'm safer by your side. I don't like you leaving me alone."

"You won't be alone." Max wanders over to the bedside table and grabs my gun. "You've got this."

"And how long will you be gone? How long until I start getting worried?"

"You won't have to worry about me. I'm just headed out to get something to eat. Nothing fancy."

"You should stop and get some bandages for your leg."

"I will." Max tucks his gun under the waistband of his pants and pulls his shirt out over it. He reaches behind, testing the carry, then looks at the rifle leaning against the wall. "Let me show you how to use that."

"I'm good with my gun."

"Nevertheless..." Max doesn't take no for an answer and spends the next thirty minutes showing me how to handle the gun.

It's heavy. Smells like metal. And it's cold, intimidating, and something I never want to touch. Not that I'm anti-gun. It's just too big and awkward for me.

The next thing, before Max leaves, is another lecture about how to secure the door after he leaves. He shows me how to wedge the chair under the doorknob and how to kick it free.

"Now, when I come back, I'll give two fast raps on the door, followed by three slow ones. That way you'll know it's me." He demonstrates while I think it's all overkill.

"If it's this dangerous for me to be alone, maybe I should come with you?"

"Not happening." He gives me one long look. "I won't be long. Half hour tops. Probably a lot less than that."

"How's your leg?" It didn't seem to bother him when we were in bed, but now that he's up, he favors his good leg.

"Better." He pulls out the small bottle of pills we got at the tiny village, then pops the remaining pills in his mouth. With a grimace, he swallows them down without any water.

When I tried to take a drink out of the sink last night, he pulled me off, saying something about the safety of the water. The thought of mixing all this up with a bout of Montezuma's revenge— dysentery with diarrhea, cramps, nausea, and vomiting—kept me away despite my thirst.

On the chicken bus, he bartered for a bottle of soda with a pop-top. In the jungle, we found fresh water as it collected in the leaves of the trees.

Yet again, I can't wait to get home. First thing I want is a burger and an ice-cold glass of water. Then pizza. And a milkshake. I would die for some ice cream too.

"I'll be back before you know it." He draws me into a hug and kisses the top of my head.

"Promise?"

"I promise."

I take him at his word, but an unsettled feeling comes over me. Not superstitious by nature, I can't help the feeling something bad is about to happen.

THIRTY-NINE

Eve

Time creeps by while Max is gone. I pace the small room. My fingers clench. I wrap my arms around myself. Taking a shower comes to mind, but I can't shake this feeling that something's off.

How long has it been?

Not long enough.

I shake out my hands, then roll my neck, getting the kinks out from the lumpy bed we slept in last night. A goofy grin fills my face when I think about what we did in that bed, and what we'll do as soon as we get out of this place.

I lie back in the bed, staring at the water spots on the ceiling. One looks like the profile of a hunched-over old woman with a basket hanging on her arm. Another looks like a lopsided rabbit—one ear up, one ear down. There's a shape that looks like a baby's face, or maybe it's an old man?

Twiddling my thumbs, I close my eyes and count.

Still no Max.

A sudden puttering from outside makes me jump, but a quick peek out the cloudy glazing on the window only shows the signs of a small town coming to life. A moped zips by with a family of six magically balanced on the small machine. An old truck chugs along the road, belching black smoke into the air as it trundles by. A black SUV roars down the road, spitting gravel out from its back tires. Somewhere down below, a car door opens, then slams shut.

I return to pacing as it's the only thing that keeps my nerves under control.

Back and forth. Back and forth.

The stomping of boots up the stairs outside draws me to a halt. I cock my ear and hold my breath, listening hard.

There's a sudden crash and the splintering of wood. Several sets of boots make the floor tremble.

Then I hear my name being called out.

"Oh, Evie? Where are you? Come out, come out wherever you are."

No, no, no!

Benefield found me, and Max isn't here. I race around the bed to grab my gun. Max told me to keep the ratty curtains covering the windows closed, but they're moth-eaten with plenty of holes. If I can see out the blurry window, then he can see in.

Nothing happens for a moment. I breathe out and check my gun. Locked and loaded, I lean against the wall opposite the door and aim the gun at the door.

This lasts for only a few seconds as the gun is too heavy to hold like that. The stomping of boots sounds again. Closer this time.

I take in a shuddering breath.

Max, where are you?

There's another loud crash as another door gives way.

"Evie, don't play hide and seek. Come out and let's talk." Benefield cajoles from outside.

Never.

I'd rather die than go back to a living hell. I slide down to the floor, keeping my back to the wall. Drawing my legs to my chest, I prop the gun on my knees and point it at the door.

There's no place to hide, and there's no other way out of this room.

The stomping draws closer. Another door shatters. He's

methodically working his way down the row. Three more doors to go until he reaches me.

Reminding myself what Max said about the rifle, I glance over to the corner and debate my next move. If they come through the door, I'll only have one shot if I stay where I am.

But if I get up, take the rifle, I can shoot from the side of the room. I climb to my feet and tuck the gun at the small of my back. Moving as quietly as possible, I take Max's rifle and pray.

A chill works its way down my spine as Benefield's voice pierces the sudden stillness. It's far too close. I grip Max's rifle, check the chamber, thumb off the safety, and wait.

"Evie?" His voice sends chills down my spine. "Come out and all will be forgiven. Your daddy did this. He called in the cavalry to take you away from me. But you know who you belong to. You know who you love."

Love?

Is that what the sadistic prick of a man thought was going on?

"Don't make me come and find you."

Another loud crash makes the walls shudder. Adrenaline spikes. It floods my body, surging around and around. The urge to flee overwhelms me, but there's nowhere to go.

"Get out here, Evie. Don't make me punish you."

I lift the rifle and aim at the door. In the moth-eaten gaps in the curtains, shadows shift as men pass by. Impossible to know how many.

The door handle jiggles as someone tests the lock. My pulse hammers in my ears, roaring with fear.

A loud thump makes me jump. The door shudders. The chair shakes. My grip on the rifle tightens.

They're going to come in.

How long will that chair hold? How long will it keep the men out? Long enough for Max to return? But he only has a pistol against how many men?

"She's in there, boss."

My heart rate spikes. My breathing accelerates.

The door rattles. Something massive strikes it.

Once. Twice.

The wood groans. The chair shifts. I lift the rifle as the chair shatters and the door gives way.

A scream escapes me as a man barrels through. My pulse explodes with another surge of adrenaline. I squeeze and pull the trigger.

My ears ring with the concussive blast. The man crumples as he falls. More men barrel through. I squeeze off two more shots and miss. Benefield steps into the room. I lift the rifle and take aim.

The men charge as I shoot. One of them grunts as his body jerks and twists. He falls. But the other man closes the distance. He's on me before I take my next breath. The rifle is ripped from my hands as I let loose an ear-piercing scream.

Benefield crosses the distance. His brute tosses the gun and grabs both my arms. I kick and scream as a sinister smile fills Benefield's face.

"Ah, Evie." He shakes his head. "I'm so disappointed in you."

A sudden surge of strength flows through me. I kick the man holding me and free myself from his grip. I bolt toward the door, dodging Benefield as he reaches out to grab me. I make it around the bed before he yanks me off my feet.

I kick him. Benefield grunts as my heel slams into his groin. He releases me, and I'm off. Racing around the bed, I dodge the broken chair and whirl out of the room.

The way is open. No more men.

I sprint toward the stairs. Benefield pounds after me, breathing down my neck. He reaches out, catches strands of my hair.

He's too close.

All I can think about is that I can't let him grab hold of me again. I yank my head forward and wince as he rips out my hair. But I'm still free.

Still ahead of him.

I reach the end of the balcony. I twist around the corner and barrel down the stairs.

When I reach the bottom, Benefield is on me. His fingers snag the back of my shirt and he yanks me back.

I spin around, stomp on his foot, and drive my fist into his groin again. He grunts and releases me.

I scramble back, then spin again to run. I sprint out into the parking lot. He's right on me. His long arms reach out and he catches me again. I thrash in his grip, kicking and hitting, trying my best to get free.

I may be going down, but I won't go down without a fight.

This is my life, and I'm going to fight for it. I twist in his grip, sweep his legs out from under him. We go down in a pile of limbs, falling to the hard-baked ground.

My screams ring out as loud as my lungs can manage. But no one comes. Max isn't here.

I'm on my own, crushed beneath the weight of a monster with murder and retribution vibrating in his steely gaze.

Benefield punches me.

His fist connects with my jaw. Pain blossoms in my head and I see stars. Benefield's breath labors as he rears back to strike me again.

A shot rings out. Benefield's left shoulder jerks and a red stain blooms on his shirt. He glances up. Mouth open. Eyes hard. He reaches behind him and draws out a gun.

Benefield presses the barrel to my forehead and shouts. "I'll kill her. Swear to God, I'll put a bullet in her brain. Drop your weapon and show yourself."

I hold completely still as terror sweeps through me.

"Let her go." That voice. I know that voice.

It doesn't belong to Max.

"Let her go," Knox repeats himself.

If Knox is here... A fluttering in my belly fills me with hope. Max's team is also here.

FORTY

Max

BENEFIELD GRINS LIKE A MANIAC, LOOKING PLEASED WITH HIMSELF. He shouldn't look so smug, but then he doesn't know how many weapons currently aim at his head.

My weapon, courtesy of my team, points between Benefield's eyes and carries enough firepower to pulverize Benefield's corpse, but I can't take the shot.

None of us can; not while the barrel of his gun presses against Eve's forehead.

Sick to my stomach when I heard her screams, my team and I rushed back to the two-story motel.

As for how we met up, I ran into them on the street after I stopped a sweet, old lady to ask directions to the closest drug store. She answered with a smile and offered to show me the way. That was two blocks I could've jogged instead of walking calmly beside my new friend.

Like a good Boy Scout, I helped her cross the road and thanked her when we finally made it to the town's one and only convenience store.

With thanks made, I grabbed food, bottled water, and supplies to bandage my leg. It still aches like a motherfucker, but I'm not lost to fevered dreams. The infection isn't gone, but those antibiotics seem to have stalled its progression.

I limped out of the store as two trucks screeched to a halt in front of me. Knox jumped out, joined by Liam and Wolfe.

As I gave the briefest rundown of what happened, and where Eve was, her first scream pierced the air. We all piled into the trucks. Knox handed me a rifle and shoved a bulletproof vest at me.

We made it back to the motel only to see Eve racing down the decrepit stairs with Tomas Benefield on her heels. Another man runs behind them, chugging for breath, as blood drips down his arm.

Benefield grabs the back of Eve's shirt, and both of them tumble to the ground. She fights like a pro, but he's much larger and more powerful than she. He flips her to her back, clocks her in the jaw, as fire burns in my gut.

That's my girl. She's my life.

My entire gut twists with fear, but I tamp that shit down, locking it up where I'll deal with it later. Now is not the time for emotions. I focus in on the objective.

This is a hostage rescue operation now.

There's no need to speak to the team. We've worked together long enough that we each fall into our respective roles.

Axel, our lead sniper, sets up behind the cover of the truck. Griff stands with him, weapon held at the ready.

Liam and Wolfe spread out, running for opposite corners behind us. They'll make their way to the top of neighboring rooftops to provide overwatch.

Knox stands in the open, gun aimed between Benefield's eyes.

Griff flashes a laser pointer on the other man's chest until he gets the man's attention. Then the tiny red dot dances right over the man's heart. One step and he's dead. The fucker knows it too. Wolfe targets the same man.

Axel remains laser-focused on Benefield. He'll take the shot if he can. Right now, with Eve a hostage, Axel waits for my signal.

This kind of teamwork doesn't just happen. We move as a single entity, having rehearsed this scene hundreds of times, with thousands of variations.

We work as one. Breathe as one. We're a band of brothers and we fight as one.

Eve holds perfectly still. Her chest rises and falls with ragged breaths. Unlike my teammates, she's never experienced anything like this before. She doesn't know what I need her to do.

"Let her go, and we let you live," Knox calls out.

I let him take the lead because I need Eve to know my entire team is here. She's smart, fiercely intelligent, and I pray she trusts me enough to place her life not only in my hands, but the hands of my team.

"How about not." Benefield keeps his gun pressed to Eve's forehead.

He glances around, trying to identify my men. He'll see Knox, Griff, and Axel. Liam, Wolfe, and I stay hidden.

"Where's your boss?" Benefield casts about, knowing I'm here but unable to find me.

"Release the girl," Knox continues. His objective is simple.

Stall.

He keeps Benefield engaged, giving time for Liam and Wolfe to achieve their objectives. I'm hooked back into our internal communications, courtesy of a new earpiece Knox handed me as we sped over here.

"Not going to happen. I let her go, and you put a bullet in my head." Benefield's smart. He knows there's no way we're letting him go.

"Alpha-five in position." Liam's voice speaks in my ear, letting me know he's in position.

A few seconds later, Wolfe reports in.

"Alpha-six ready."

"Copy that." It's go time. I make my move, revealing myself to Benefield. "Drop your weapon and release the girl."

Eve's entire body relaxes the moment she sees me. It's like a punch to the gut seeing the amount of trust she has in me.

"Never." Benefield sneers at me. "She's mine. You hear me. Her father gave her to me." Benefield's voice rises in pitch with a whole lot of crazy layered on top.

He gives us a small piece of a puzzle. The link between Benefield and Deverough is something to sort out later, but now we know there's most definitely something going on.

"I don't think he sees it that way." I want to chime in and tell Benefield that Deverough hired us, but there's nothing to be gained by that.

Benefield jerks Eve to her feet. The gun moves from her forehead to her temple. All I see are the whites of her eyes. Her fear is palpable, and I don't know how to tell her what I need her to do, but then something comes to me.

I tap the side of my leg, knowing she watches my every move. I tap two times fast, then three times slow. It's the signal I told her I'd use when I got back to the room. I pray she understands what I mean. We've only got one shot at this.

Eve blinks. Her lashes flutter, twice. Then she blinks three times slow. She knows I'm trying to tell her something.

I keep my voice low, just enough for my team to hear through the comms. "We go on three."

"Copy that." As our sniper, Axel responds. The other guys understand as well. They'll be ready.

Benefield drags Eve back toward a waiting black SUV. The man who's with him holds his hands up and out, but he moves with Benefield.

If Eve gets in that car, it's game over.

"Hold." I tell my team to hold their shots.

Eve clutches Benefield's arm where he holds her tight against his chest. She releases one hand, lets it fall. Her eyes flutter again. Two times fast. Three times slow. Then her brows pinch together, seeing if I understand.

I give a very slight nod.

"Ready." I speak to my team.

I tap my leg, drawing everything out. Two times fast. Then as I tap out the last three signals, I count down for my team.

Tap. "One."

Tap. "Two."

Tap. "Three."

The moment I tap the third time, Eve twists in Benefield's grip. She ducks her head and reaches behind her back. She brings up her gun as a shot rings out overhead. It's followed by another, and a third coming so fast the two sounds merge together.

Benefield's head whips back. His entire body topples backward. Eve's gun is out, and she fired a shot at point-blank range. Benefield's entire midsection is blown apart.

Eve takes two steps back and drops the gun. I don't worry about Benefield—he's dead as a doornail. I race to my girl, catching her in my arms before she falls to the ground.

"I'm here. I've got you. I've got you." I repeat it over and over again, holding her tight to my chest as her body shakes and shudders.

Eve loops her arms around my neck and buries her face against my neck. Deep, soulful sobs rip from her throat as she cries.

My men take care of clean up. Benefield's man is secured. My team finds more bodies upstairs.

I take Eve to one of the trucks and sit with her in the back seat, holding her and telling her everything will be all right.

"You're safe. I'm going to take you home."

I have no intention of taking her home. Until Mitzy and the rest of the tech team figure out Deverough's role in all of this, Eve stays with me.

And I'll kill any man who says otherwise.

FORTY-ONE

Eve
―――――

Benefield's dead.

After months of enduring the unspeakable, I'm finally free. It feels surreal as Max and his team drive us away from that town. I barely process climbing out of the truck and onto a waiting helicopter.

Max never leaves my side, and it helps. My mind's not engaged in what's going on around me, but I feel Max.

His presence guides me, reassures me, and makes me feel safe.

The helicopter takes us to an airport. From there, we board a luxury airline. Not commercial. The entire inside is built with nothing but first-class accommodations on board.

"Welcome, Miss Deverough." A tall, mountain of a man with shock white hair greets me inside the plane.

"Forest, leave her alone." A diminutive brunette pushes the man to the side. "Can't you see she's in shock?"

"Just being friendly," he says.

"Be friendly later. Max, get your girl settled, then let me take a look at you." She turns toward me with a smile. "You're safe, Eve. You're with the Guardians now, and we're going to make sure nothing like this ever happens to you again." She makes a shooing motion and Max guides me all the way to the back of the plane.

Max gets me settled into a seat in the back. He tucks me in with a pillow and blanket. There's a click as he fastens a seat belt over my lap, then he settles in beside me and holds my hand.

The engines wind up and then we're moving. The large plane bumps over the pavement. There's a slow turn, then a roar as the jet engines engage. I'm pressed back into the seat as we take off.

It's only then that I relax and close my eyes.

It's over.

The nightmare is finally over.

FORTY-TWO

Max

A FEW WEEKS LATER

~

"What did Skye say?" Eve peeks over the couch as I wander in after a long day of getting poked and prodded. She puts the book down that she's reading and pops to her feet.

"Everything looks good."

I'm encouraged by my checkup with Doc Summers. I had immediate surgery once we got back to headquarters and spent the next few days in bed with a concoction of antibiotics flooding my system to fight off the infection.

I described the pills I took, and after a brief image search to identify them, Doc Summers concedes it wasn't a total boneheaded move to take pills some strange healer in a village doled out.

"Good enough to go back to work?"

"I've got a few weeks on Medical Hold. She wants a little more physical therapy before clearing me for duty." I drop my bags on the floor, toss my keys in the bowl sitting by the door, and go to greet my girl. "I understand why Griff was such a pain in the ass when he got sidelined."

I hate not operating.

I hate not being able to work out with my team even more. I go to the gym with them, do what I've been cleared for, but I miss our runs.

"You really are amazing, you know that?" Eve meets me halfway. Her arms wrap around my waist and she lifts on tiptoe to kiss me.

The light floral scent of her perfume, combined with her natural essence, is a heady intoxication that my dick can't ignore. I've gone from flaccid to fully erect in the span of a nanosecond.

But that's the way it is with Eve. My body aches for her all day, every day.

And she's all mine.

She's been in meetings with Sam and Mitzy, going over what she knows about her father's business. The ledgers we retrieved are great, but they're built on a cypher Mitzy's team has yet to decode.

On our return, I assumed Eve would stay at The Facility, where all our rescues go, if that's what they want. She lived through incredible trauma, and while she meets with the therapists at The Facility to talk that shit through, Eve decided on her own to stay at my place.

I didn't know that until Doc Summers finally gave me the go-ahead to leave the hospital. That's when I realized Eve moved in.

And I absolutely love it. I end each day holding her in my arms. I wake each morning with her beside me. I can't imagine living any other way.

"You taste like heaven." I claim her mouth with greed and hunger. Drawing her to me, the kiss deepens as I splay my hand across the small of her back, holding her possessively while devouring her with a kiss.

I need her in a soul-desperate way, craving to make her mine in a way that goes beyond the pleasures of sex.

Eve appears to need no encouragement from me. Her head tilts back. Her mouth parts. Her breathy sighs send me higher and higher, lifting me to breathtaking heights.

I swear the temperature in the room rises, but that's not the case. This is the heat between us growing into a firestorm of need. I rub my tongue along the seam of her lips as she grips my shoulders, holding me tight. I ache to take her. It's a powerful need, a thirst to make her mine that I'll never fully slake.

I'll never get enough of my girl.

My hands drift down over the roundness of her ass. Fingers digging, I cradle her in the warmth of my hands. She opens for me, gifting me with a toe-curling moan of desire.

My girl is hot for me; nuclear hot.

Unlike our time in Colombia, there's nothing stopping us from having sex, and we may be going at it hard and fast. Eve especially enjoys the hard and fast part of it.

My Eve is a hellion in bed.

After a few conversations, where Eve blushed a thousand shades of red, we decided nothing would stand between us. Doc Summers tested us both.

Eve talked about the possibility of children. She's not ready to take that step and neither am I. Doc Summers helped with that as well, arranging all the appropriate appointments.

I release the lock I have on Eve's lips and take a moment. I never want to forget the joy on her face.

"Hurry up and fuck me." Her impish smile warms my heart.

I can't help but chuckle. Some of her shyness, at least around me, is gone. She's bold, tells me what she likes, and isn't afraid to take what she wants.

That's all the encouragement I need. I toss her over my shoulder, caveman style, and take my woman to bed. Her tiny shriek, and the light tapping of her fists on my back, only make me walk faster.

Once in the bedroom, I toss her on the bed, loving the way she bounces lightly on the mattress.

"Clothes off, bubbles." It's a corny nickname, and I don't use it much anymore except during sex.

She shimmies out of her shorts while I kick off my boots and strip out of my pants. The creamy white skin of her tits demands a little extra attention and I indulge myself while she squirms beneath me.

"Get off, you oaf. I can't breathe." All her squirming only makes my dick ache.

"Then stop squirming." I lave her nipple with my tongue, then bite down until I pull another shriek from her mouth. My girl likes a tiny bit of pain with her pleasure.

For the next few minutes, all I do is play with her tits: squeezing and sucking, nipping and biting. One day, I plan on making her come from nipple stimulation alone.

Until then...

I move my kisses down the flat expanse of her belly, driving her insane with how slow I go. She squirms and twists. Her fingers dig into my hair and she tries to push me down, forcing me to "Get to the good stuff." Her words not mine.

Her arousal floods my senses and when I get between her thighs, I lap up her sweet essence as she greedily writhes and twists beneath me.

It doesn't take long to make her come. Her cries fill the room as her back arches and her pussy contracts. I send her flying a second time, enjoying her response to my touch.

But then, I can't stand it any longer. I've held onto my restraint long enough. My desire demands to be unleashed.

With the taste of her on my tongue, I move up her body, until we're eye to eye. Her sea-green eyes, half-hooded with lust and filled with desire, greet me and beg for more.

I notch the head of my dick at her opening. She bites her lower lip in anticipation.

"Hard and fast?"

She gives a little nod as I thrust, ramming all the way in.

Each time I pull out, I experience a terrifying emptiness, but that disappears as I ram back in and settle right where I belong. I take my girl hard and fast, just the way she likes it until the pressure in my balls grows heavy and my skin tingles.

My release coils at the base of my spine, then speeds along with each powerful thrust. Eve breaks beneath me, uttering a low, keening wail of pure bliss. I follow Eve right over that cliff, as a wave of pleasure rushes through me.

We come back to earth together, joined in the most intimate way, and that's when I tell her what's in my heart.

"You're mine. Always and forever." I reach over to the nightstand, where I hid the ring last night. "I need you to say yes."

"Yes, to what?" She doesn't understand, thinking I'm playing a game, but the moment I slip the diamond ring on her finger, tears well in her eyes. She stares at the diamond as it glitters, then throws her arms around my neck. "Yes. Yes. Yes! Forever, and ever, yes."

We spend the rest of the evening in bed, making love, forgetting to eat, and loving every minute of it. At some time, we doze off.

I wake later, in the middle of the night. Eve's curled against my side. Her hand rests on my arm, and that diamond manages to sparkle in the darkness.

It reminds me of something Doc Summers always says, *"There's always light in the darkness. Our job is to find it, and let it shine."*

Well, I found the light of my life and I'm never letting her go.

FORTY-THREE

Knox

THE STENCH OF PISS, BEER, AND PUKE BLENDS WITH THE ACRID SMELL of unwashed bodies creating a noxious assault on my senses. Half of Alpha team, the bachelors, Liam, Wolfe, and I, troll New Orleans, looking to blow off a little steam after yet another fruitless lead.

We spent the day at the docks in the sweltering summer heat. Now that the heat of the day is lifting, we're ready to grab drinks, find some chicks to bury ourselves in, and basically chill out.

As for the other half of Alpha team, Max is back in California, recovering from injuries he sustained when we rescued his woman, Eve Deverough. Axel and Griff work to shake down Carson Deverough, the shipping mogul who bartered his daughter's freedom, for what?

That's the all-important question, and one we don't have answers to as of yet.

Hopefully Axel and Griff will discover something of value. Meanwhile, Liam, Wolfe, and I look for a contact hinted at in the ledgers Max and I pulled out of Tomas Benefield's operation. That monster is dead. Killed in Colombia when he put a gun to Eve's head. His entire sex-trafficking operation was taken out during that mission and we obtained the ledgers of every transaction. Every girl whose life was stolen and every monster who paid to enslave them.

Those ledgers, something we all thought would be gold, are encoded in a cypher our technical genius, Mitzy, can't unravel. Though, she's hard at work trying to bust that code.

For now, all we have is one name, a date, and a time.

Lei'lani is the name. Tomorrow is the day. Three in the morning is the godforsaken time.

We're still working on the where.

Each nugget of information leads us further down the path of taking down another asshole intent on stealing lives and destroying dreams.

Since Deverough is a shipping mogul, our suspicion is this meeting will happen at one of the many docks. Mitzy's narrowed down the possibilities to a few commercial operations. No surprise, it has to do with shipping containers.

The question is, who is Lei'lani?

What is her role in all of this?

Is she a business partner of Deverough's?

A competitor?

Perhaps, we'll figure something out and solve a piece of the puzzle. Maybe Mitzy will come through, like she always does, saving the day in the tenth hour. Or maybe, our visit to New Orleans will leave us empty handed, like the last four times Alpha team descended on this town.

"Lots of potential action tonight." Liam watches the crowded street. Eyes alert, head on a swivel, he's not looking for enemies.

"Tone it down." I slug Liam in the arm. His libido is out of control.

"The night is young." He shoves me right back, grinning like a fool. "The possibilities are endless." He returns to checking out the chicks we pass.

The French Quarter, like every night before this one, pulses with vibrant activity. Half the people are stoned, drunk, or otherwise riding one high or another. Festive music pours out of jazz clubs and trickles out of dueling piano bars to mingle with the rhythm of the street and a city coming alive.

It's still early enough that families are out. Mom's and dad's, with eager teens, tweens, and kids with no business being out this late, clutch their children's hands as they drag their young ones to the safety of their hotels for the night.

Couples brave the later hours, seeking one thrill or the next. Boisterous groups of college kids vie for attention from the opposite sex. The bravado of the young men brings a smile to my face. The coy smiles of the girls make me shake my head.

It's barely after nine. This city is only just waking up. Which means the skirts get shorter, the dresses grow tighter, and the heels climb higher as chicks eager for a night of partying fill the street.

We pass by a gaggle of sorority co-eds with micro-mini skirts and skintight tops practically sprayed onto their bodies. My gaze naturally drifts to admire what they advertise. Two of the girls aren't wearing bras and from the look of their skirts, they're not wearing panties either.

It's tempting. Liam takes a long look at them as well, but I yank on his sleeve and pull him along.

"Aw, you're no fun." Liam grumps, but he doesn't resist.

"Those girls are a walking smorgasbord of STDs and bad decisions. Best keep your dick out of those waters." Before I finish talking, a group of guys move in on the girls, eager for an easy conquest.

"Let's get some chow." Wolfe prowls restlessly beside me.

He too, scans the crowd, only he's not checking out the chicks. His eyes are on the men, and boys with too much liquid courage, who are out looking for trouble. They're the ones whose intellect rapidly falls in direct correlation with the alcohol level in their blood.

"We just ate." Restless, and growing more agitated by the minute, my senses are on full alert.

"Still, it's better than walking the streets." Wolfe's tired of being on the prowl.

Honestly, I am too.

We're out here because I'm restless. Dinner was beyond amazing. All New Orleans food is fabulous, but my skin started itching halfway through the meal; a sense something is off. Not that I can put my finger on what's bugging me.

Not that there's any reason to be concerned. The three of us present a formidable force. We're taller than those around us. Broader and more muscled, it's obvious we're either military, ex-military, or bouncers headed to work for the night.

"Still hungry." Wolfe growls a little, showing his frustration. "Wings and beer? How's that sound?"

"Oysters. I want oysters." Liam pipes in and I give him another shove.

"The last thing you need is more oysters." Oysters are one of my favorite things, but feeding Liam's raging libido sounds all kinds of wrong.

As we stride down the packed street, the crowd parts seamlessly before us and closes behind us. We attract attention, both good and bad. People are wary of three large men walking around like they own the place.

"I can do wings." With Max on Medical Hold, due to his injuries, I'm acting commander of Alpha team. The whole team is in New Orleans, trying to dig up some kind of actionable information.

Wolfe rolls his eyes and groans. It's all for effect.

He's the strictest of the three of us when it comes to taking care of his body. Wolfe isn't one to mix business and pleasure. That little bit of fun falls to Liam, the party guy of the group.

"Wings and beer sound great." Liam struts beside me, showing off his physique to any woman who looks, and there are a lot of woman who take notice. "Add a little pussy into the mix and I'll call it a good night." He points to a seedy looking bar. "How about that?"

Three burly bouncers guard the entrance to a strip club. Two girls with dental floss thongs gyrate near the entrance, enticing anyone with a pulse to join them inside.

I consider it for half a second. A bit of a striptease, followed by a lap dance, would be enough to take the edge off, but this restlessness inside of me grows stronger as the evening wears on.

To be honest, I want more of a challenge. A vigorous lap dance simply doesn't cut it for me. Besides, the idea of spending the rest of the night with jizz in my pants is unappealing at best.

"We're not here for cheap hookers." I march right past the strippers and continue on as if I actually have a destination in mind.

I don't. I'm aimless and looking for—something.

Wish I knew what the fuck that was.

"Nothing wrong with a strip club," Liam pouts. He trails behind us, rubbernecking the strip club, but then catches up when it's clear I won't be stopping. "We could stop for an hour…"

Liam is a looker. He's got the Hollywood thing down pat; blond hair, blue-eyes, a smirk a mile wide. He's the charmer of the group and never fails to fill his bed.

I'm his complete opposite, dark hair, dark eyes, more of a scowl instead of a smile. I'd like to think I'm easy on the eye, but girls flock to me because I've got the bad boy vibe down pat.

"You can deal with not getting laid one night." I scan the way ahead, looking for something that will satisfy each of us.

"Says who?" Liam joins me in lockstep as we prowl down the crowded street.

"Says me." I jab at him with my elbow, but Liam reads me before I can connect. He dances out of reach, avoiding me, while taking a look at the crowd.

We're a triple threat, working as a team until we each have a girl draped over our arms.

A den of sin and loose women, this city is ripe for the plucking, and there are more than enough women intent on riding a stallion for the night to go around.

Too many.

Liam's eager for pussy. In stark contrast, Wolfe's steadfast beside me. More of a stalker, he scans the crowd for something suitable for his tastes. He likes his women wide-eyed and innocent, says it makes it that much more fun when he defiles them, ruining them for any man who comes after him.

I'd say it was all bravado, but I've seen the string of broken hearts Wolfe leaves behind. The man has a magic dick.

As for me, New Orleans suits my tastes just fine. I like my sex nameless and guilt free. Two consenting adults scratching a mutual itch, with no strings, no connections, and no bother once the sun comes up.

No names exchanged.

No mess to deal with later.

Fuck then walk away.

Relationships are messy and I don't need that kind of complicated shit in my life.

The problem with Liam is there's no time to take a woman back to the house we've rented for the duration. After a quick romp in the sheets, most chicks turn bitchy when they get the heave ho' at two in the morning. Liam never lets his women spend the whole night. As soon as he's done, he sets them free.

I get it, but it's not safe for a woman to be walking on the streets at two in the morning. It's also not safe going to a stranger's house either.

Double standards much?

With Max out of action, I've had to step up and take on the lead. The guys look to me to adhere to the rules and keep everyone in line.

They're testing me too, looking to see what they can get away with in Max's absence. I don't like Alpha team being a man down, but for this kind of reconnaissance work, we don't need the whole team.

We pass by a crowded bar. The balcony overflows with a boisterous crowd. Young women eye us.

The girls call out and we stop for a moment to admire the goods. Wolfe sniffs the air while Liam raises his hand. Dangling from his fingers are over a dozen strands of beads.

The girls need no more prompting than that. Liam doesn't even need to ask. Before I know it, half a dozen or so girls flash their tits at us while they shout into the air.

"Come up here!"

"Party!"

"I'll show you a good time."

No doubt they would at that, but Wolfe's not interested. He moves on and I follow. Liam lingers for a moment to toss beads into the air, rewarding the girls for their little show.

I kind of regret walking away. The only good thing about this assignment are the easy lays. There hasn't been a single night we haven't scored it big. Whether it's hot and sweaty sex in the bathroom of a bar, or hot and sweaty sex twisting the sheets in our rental, none of us lack for female companionship.

Honestly, it's too easy. Boring comes to mind.

Not that I mind getting blown in the back of a bar, or fucking some nameless chick in a sketchy bathroom. I do draw the line at doing it in an alley. In New Orleans, that's just asking for trouble.

I have to say it gets tiresome and feels like cheating when women drop their panties with a suggestive crook of my finger, or one flagrant wink.

What I wouldn't give for a bit of a challenge.

Music pours into the streets as local bars fill with eager patrons. Beads crunch underfoot, discarded after being tossed from the balconies overhead. The stifling heat of the day recedes as cooler, nighttime temperatures roll in, but that does nothing to quench the smell of stale beer filling the air.

Liam calls out to more chicks partying on the balconies, urging them to flash their tits. It surprises me how many take him up on the offer, especially when he's out of beads.

But that's Liam.

Women turn stupid around him.

We stop to watch street performers, enjoying their amazing acrobatics. I drop cash in the till and we move on.

An itching between my shoulder blades draws me up short. Liam and Wolfe take a step before coming to a stop. Second time this night my spidy-senses have gone off.

"What's up?" Wolfe scans the crowd, looking for the threat.

"Not sure." I glance around, wondering why it feels like I've got eyes on me.

There's no way three men of our stature, walking together, don't draw nearly every eye. But there's curiosity and then there's *attention.*

Somebody watches us and I want to know why.

"Hey, how about that?" Wolfe stops in his tracks and points to a bar hopping with activity.

The sign overhead says *Callie's Bar.* Advertisements outside promise cheap shots, rowdy music, and girls dancing on the bar. It sounds just about right.

"You good with that?" I turn to Liam. No need to ask. The devilish grin on his face is answer enough.

"Let's do this." Liam claps his hands together.

People spill out onto the streets. Music pours out of the bar as patrons yell, shout, and grind. The three of us walk in, pushing past the press of people while we head for the bar.

"What's up handsome?" A pretty woman with golden skin and coffee eyes, takes our order. I hand her a fifty up front.

"Tequila shots for me and my friends."

"Sure thing." Her mischievous eyes twinkle. "Body shots?"

"Perhaps in a bit." I peel off another fifty and boldly tuck it in her cleavage, letting my fingertips linger half a second too long.

Her eyes round and her pupils dilate. Give it another few seconds and I bet I can get her to take me to the back for a quick one-and-done fuck.

"You got it, handsome." She plucks the fifty from her cleavage and shoves it deep in the back pocket of her denim shorts.

While I consider pushing for that trip to the back room, that tickling sensation returns. I glance around the room, but see nothing out of the ordinary, until a flash of white catches my eye.

A crackle of energy whips through the air. A beautiful woman with white-blonde hair and golden eyes stares at me from the back of the room. Like a punch in the gut, I stagger as a bolt of lightning shoots through me.

I turn away to catch my breath and focus on the here and now. Plenty of women have stared at me in my life, but none with ferocity and hunger like that.

The bartender slides over a shot of tequila and I slam it down before turning around for a double-take. Sure as shit, the woman's still staring.

I blink, and convince myself this weird pulsation isn't real, but the captivating woman continues to stare. It's not a come-hither stare of attraction. It's angry and full of the same shock coursing through my veins. As if, she likes what she sees when looking at me, yet hates herself for it as well.

Odd.

And not the usual vibe I get from women. For the most part, they're hungry and eager, not pissed off with full, kissable lips pressed into an angry line.

Why the hell would she be pissed at me?

Once she realizes I return her stare, she quickly schools her features, turning that anger into an expressionless mask. She turns to a pretty Latino chick standing beside her and whispers in her ear. The Latino turns toward me, takes me in, then gives a curt nod.

They're talking about me.

I look over at Liam, but he's already talking up some chick. Wolfe scores a seat at the bar. He watches a girl dancing over him on the bar, and shamelessly looks up her skirt. With that wolfish grin fixed on his face, no doubt the two of them will be hooking up tonight. He waves over the bartender, points to something on a bar menu, then grins at the chick shaking her ass with all she's got.

With my team suitably entertained, I turn my attention back to my white-haired beauty. Only she's no longer there.

What an odd exchange.

Younger than me, but not by much, she's older than the college co-eds packed shoulder-to-shoulder inside this bar. Curious, I head over to see if I can track her down. A woman like that is hard to lose sight of in a bar.

Then I spy her near the jukebox. Nifty little trick there, getting the patrons to pay for the music blaring over the speakers. Slowly, I wind my way between gyrating bodies, picking my path with determination through the crowded bar.

She turns her back to me, but from the set of her shoulders, she knows I'm coming. Nice way to lure me in, but she doesn't know I'm a master at this game.

I take my time, pause to do a little bump and grind on the dance floor with an eager college chick whose eyes turn to saucers when I move in. It's short-lived, however, as I don't stay there long, not when my attention spikes on the woman with the snow-white hair.

My relentless approach doesn't go unnoticed. While my quarry acts like she's unaware of me closing in, her body telegraphs everything as I read her like a book.

Well, I did say I was bored. This is definitely spicing things up. To say I'm intrigued is an understatement. As for my quarry, her skin-tight dress hugs all her curves while leaving the smooth expanse of her back bare. No bra. I like that.

And from the way that red dress hugs her tight ass, I'm pretty sure she's wearing absolutely nothing underneath. I eat up every sensual detail of her bare skin, eager to feel the heat of her body beneath my hands.

She leans against the jukebox, perusing the songs, keeping her back to me. I walk up behind her, lean in close, and sweep the hair off her shoulder until the pearly-white skin of her neck beckons.

"Pick something slow, pumpkin."

A tiny shiver ripples down her spine as my hot breath rushes over her skin, but her spine stiffens and her shoulders roll back. Very slowly, she pivots in her five-inch fuck-me heels. Her head barely reaches my shoulder, which means the broad expanse of my chest is all she sees.

Slowly, her head tips back. Her graceful neck arches. My breath hitches while waiting for her to drag her gaze up my body. The urge to bend down and lick the delicate arch of her neck overwhelms me.

I reach, intent on grabbing her by the waist, when her golden gaze finally reaches my eyes. My hand stops less than an inch from her skin.

Mesmerizing.

I expect her golden eyes to swim with desire and simmer with lust, but those pretty eyes are hard, cold, and brittle. It's a shock to my system, but then her gaze softens as she takes in my face.

"Now why would I want to pick something slow? Especially when I like it hard and fast." Low and sultry, she issues an invitation laced in a challenge

I lean in and dip down until my lips are at her ear. "So I can hold you close, of course. Lick that elegant neck of yours. Suck on your ear. And kiss you until you forget how to breathe." When I pull back, a smile spreads across my face. "If you like it hard and fast, I can do that too."

Her golden eyes swim with lust and spark with desire. It takes a moment before she realizes it, but then she blinks and takes a step back.

"Does that work on all the girls? I'm surprised you haven't asked me out back for a quick fuck while we're at it."

"I'm not opposed to that." Actually, I'm more and more interested as the seconds pass.

~

Rescuing Lily is waiting for you!
To see what happens between Knox and Lily, get your copy today!
Get my Copy of Rescuing Lily

Please consider leaving a review

I HOPE YOU ENJOYED THIS BOOK AS MUCH AS I ENJOYED WRITING IT. If you like this book, please leave a review. I love reviews. I love reading your reviews, and they help other readers decide if this book is worth their time and money. I hope you think it is and decide to share this story with others. A sentence is all it takes. Thank you in advance!

CLICK ON THE LINK BELOW TO LEAVE YOUR REVIEW
Goodreads
Amazon
Bookbub

Ellie Masters The EDGE

If you are interested in joining Ellie's Facebook reader group, THE EDGE, we'd love to have you.

The Edge Facebook Reader Group
elliemasters.com/TheEdge

Join Ellie's ELLZ BELLZ.
Sign up for Ellie's Newsletter.
Elliemasters.com/newslettersignup

Also by Ellie Masters

The LIGHTER SIDE

Ellie Masters is the lighter side of the Jet & Ellie Masters writing duo! You will find Contemporary Romance, Military Romance, Romantic Suspense, Billionaire Romance, and Rock Star Romance in Ellie's Works.

YOU CAN FIND ELLIE'S BOOKS HERE:

ELLIEMASTERS.COM/BOOKS

Military Romance

Guardian Hostage Rescue Specialists

Rescuing Melissa

(Get a FREE copy of Rescuing Melissa

when you join Ellie's Newsletter)

Alpha Team

Rescuing Zoe

Rescuing Moira

Rescuing Eve

Rescuing Lily

Rescuing Jinx

Rescuing Maria

Bravo Team

Rescuing Angie

Rescuing Isabelle

Rescuing Carmen

Rescuing Rosalie

Military Romance

Guardian Personal Protection Specialists

Sybil's Protector

Lyra's Protector

The One I Want Series

(Small Town, Military Heroes)

By Jet & Ellie Masters

EACH BOOK IN THIS SERIES CAN BE READ AS A STANDALONE AND IS ABOUT A DIFFERENT COUPLE WITH AN HEA.

Saving Abby

Saving Ariel

Saving Brie

Saving Cate

Saving Dani

Saving Jen

Rockstar Romance

The Angel Fire Rock Romance Series

EACH BOOK IN THIS SERIES CAN BE READ AS A STANDALONE AND IS ABOUT A DIFFERENT COUPLE WITH AN HEA. IT IS RECOMMENDED THEY ARE READ IN ORDER.

Ashes to New (prequel)

Heart's Insanity (book 1)

Heart's Desire (book 2)

Heart's Collide (book 3)

Hearts Divided (book 4)

Hearts Entwined (book5)

Forest's FALL (book 6)

Hearts The Last Beat (book7)

Contemporary Romance

Firestorm

(KRISTY BROMBERG'S EVERYDAY HEROES WORLD)

Billionaire Romance

Billionaire Boys Club

Hawke

Richard

Brody

Contemporary Romance

Cocky Captain

(VI KEELAND & PENELOPE WARD'S COCKY HERO WORLD)

Romantic Suspense

EACH BOOK IS A STANDALONE NOVEL.

The Starling

~AND~

Science Fiction

Ellie Masters writing as L.A. Warren

Vendel Rising: a Science Fiction Serialized Novel

About the Author

ELLIE MASTERS is a multi-genre and best-selling author, writing the stories she loves to read. These are dark erotic tales. Or maybe, sweet contemporary stories. How about a romantic thriller to whet your appetite? Ellie writes it all. Want to read passionate poems and sensual secrets? She does that, too. Dip into the eclectic mind of Ellie Masters, spend time exploring the sensual realm where she breathes life into her characters and brings them from her mind to the page and into the heart of her readers every day.

Ellie Masters has been exploring the worlds of romance, dark erotica, science fiction, and fantasy by writing the stories she wants to read. When not writing, Ellie can be found outside, where her passion for all things outdoor reigns supreme: off-roading, riding ATVs, scuba diving, hiking, and breathing fresh air are top on her list.

She has lived all over the United States—east, west, north, south and central—but grew up under the Hawaiian sun. She's also been privileged to have lived overseas, experiencing other cultures and making lifelong friends. Now, Ellie is proud to call herself a Southern transplant, learning to say y'all and "bless her heart" with the best of them. She lives with her beloved husband, two children who refuse to flee the nest, and four fur-babies; three cats who rule the household, and a dog who wants nothing other than for the cats to be his best friends. The cats have a different opinion regarding this matter.

Ellie's favorite way to spend an evening is curled up on a couch, laptop in place, watching a fire, drinking a good wine, and bringing forth all the characters from her mind to the page and hopefully into the hearts of her readers.

FOR MORE INFORMATION
elliemasters.com

f facebook.com/elliemastersromance

twitter.com/Ellie__Masters

instagram.com/ellie_masters

BB bookbub.com/authors/ellie-masters

g goodreads.com/Ellie_Masters

Connect with Ellie Masters

Website:
elliemasters.com
Amazon Author Page:
elliemasters.com/amazon
Facebook:
elliemasters.com/Facebook
Goodreads:
elliemasters.com/Goodreads
Instagram:
elliemasters.com/Instagram

Final Thoughts

I hope you enjoyed this book as much as I enjoyed writing it. If you enjoyed reading this story, please consider leaving a review on Amazon and Goodreads, and please let other people know. A sentence is all it takes. Friend recommendations are the strongest catalyst for readers' purchase decisions! And I'd love to be able to continue bringing the characters and stories from My-Mind-to-the-Page.

Second, call or e-mail a friend and tell them about this book. If you really want them to read it, gift it to them. If you prefer digital friends, please use the "Recommend" feature of Goodreads to spread the word.

Or visit my blog https://elliemasters.com, where you can find out more about my writing process and personal life.

Come visit The EDGE: Dark Discussions where we'll have a chance to talk about my works, their creation, and maybe what the future has in store for my writing.

Facebook Reader Group: The EDGE

Thank you so much for your support!

Love,

Ellie

Dedication

This book is dedicated to you, my reader. Thank you for spending a few hours of your time with me. I wouldn't be able to write without you to cheer me on. Your wonderful words, your support, and your willingness to join me on this journey is a gift beyond measure.

Whether this is the first book of mine you've read, or if you've been with me since the very beginning, thank you for believing in me as I bring these characters 'from my mind to the page and into your hearts.'

Love,
Ellie

THE END

Made in the USA
Las Vegas, NV
14 July 2023